The Other Lane: A Modern Fairy Tale

Marla Holt

Published by Marla Holt, 2018.

Chapter One

Cristo's Coffee House was a trap—a horrible stinking tar pit of a job that threatened to smother Lane beneath its bubbling surface. It was the worst coffee shop in Topeka, and today, it was competing with itself for its own prize in awfulness. Not only had she stayed up too late, then had to skip her shower because she'd missed her alarm, but also Sarah had called in sick for her shift. Lane had to balance the phone on her shoulder while steaming milk because she'd had a line out the door all morning. As the cherry on top of her misery sundae, her most obnoxious customer sat on the sofa just opposite the bar, staring at Lane, passing judgment from her ugly thrift store sofa-throne while also ignoring her daughter.

It was bad enough that Lane had to serve the pathetic line of middle-aged men who perched at the bar to flirt with her. She didn't need an audience who had everything but liked to spread rumors about which of the suitors was Lane's sugar daddy this week.

Lane shot a glare at the petite, staring woman as she finished the last of the late morning lattes. This one for the heavyset lawyer said goodbye and threw a purposeful dollar bill in the tip jar. The crowd switched from the morning loafers to the lunchtime regulars. A retired couple between rounds of golf looked over their menus. Talia sat with her mom on the sofa, waiting for Talia's dad to join them. When she wasn't looking, Abe sneaked onto the stool the lawyer had just vacated and was already hiding behind his newspaper.

Abe was the kind of man who knew he was attractive. Tall and lean, he had slick black hair he wore swept back like he had stepped out of the 1940s, with a short black beard. Two silver streaks started at his temples and wrapped around like tiger stripes. He wore tailored suits and Lane made a game out of guessing what color his tie would be. Today it was a dark blue twill.

Close.

She'd guessed navy.

The only blemish she'd ever seen on his attire had been the first day he'd visited Cristo's last January. Abe had forgotten to remove the ugly, red Kansas-shaped name tag that identified him as a lobbyist. He had also been wearing a woven silk tie the blue-green color of the ocean that Lane was certain came from an Italian tie-maker she'd studied in school.

She warmed up a mug for his black coffee, then tugged the newspaper down along the center fold just far enough to meet his eyes. He wore a fond, questioning expression that, had she not been used to his beauty by now, might have made her blush and stutter.

"You gonna order something, or you gonna loiter at my counter all day?" she asked.

"Coffee?"

Lane held out the mug. He brushed his fingers against hers for the second day in a row. When Lane narrowed her eyes at him, he winked at her and flashed a cheeky grin. She pretended not to notice, but read his newspaper while he

Talia's mom gave Lane an appraising look as she walked them to the door. "You know, if you didn't encourage those guys, this kind of thing wouldn't happen so often."

Lane smiled and held the door open for them. "Thanks for coming. I'll see you tomorrow," she said.

She finished her cleaning quickly, and the familiar process calmed her. Exhaustion settled in as she hauled the trash out to the dumpster, and she hoped the pain in her feet would dull enough to let her get some sleep.

Lane stopped in the bathroom to check her reflection in the mirror before she left. Her hair was frizzy, so she brushed her fingers through it and redid the braid. The tiny stud in her nose winked in the artificial light, but Lane only saw the dark circles under her eyes and the contrasting paleness of her complexion.

Javier wasn't the only one who gave her a nickname that implied she was pretty. Her sharp jaw and high cheek bones were softened by subtle dimples in her cheeks, and her blue eyes were large and bright. She was curvy and soft. While she found her contours pleasing, most of the time, she tried to camouflage them with too-big thrifted men's shirts. But Lane wanted to be noticed. She opened an extra button on her shirt and dug in her bag for a tube of lip gloss. She rolled down her sleeves to cover the fading hand print, hoping it wouldn't bruise.

There were no customers in the liquor store when Lane limped in. A football game droned from the TV over the beer case. Shawn was typing so intently at his computer he didn't notice her at first.

" Hey," she said, and he looked up, adjusting his faded blue ball cap. Too preoccupied with whatever story he was currently writing to spend much time on his appearance, Shawn's overgrown, honey blonde hair curled around his hat. His button down shirt and holey jeans were shabby, but his skin still glowed golden from his summer tan.

"Hey, Gorgeous," he said, "What are you still doing here?"

Lane leaned on the counter, trying to take some of the pressure off her sore feet. "Sarah called in sick."

"That's bullshit."

"And so were the tips," Lane said into the countertop. "So I need a bottle of wine that costs less than twelve dollars."

"Red or white?" Shawn asked.

"Now, you know I'm not a white wine kind of girl." She was so tired, it was the only joke she could muster.

"Right. We got a new brand of cab. It has a hedgehog on the label, so it'll be around for about five minutes."

"How much?"

"Nine bucks."

"Sold," Lane said, but did not move.

"You want me to get that for you?" He asked.

"If you don't mind." Lane slid down the front of the counter until she was a heap on the floor. "Is it okay if I sit here for a few minutes?"

Shawn retrieved the wine and joined her. She lay her head on his shoulder and he rested a hand on her thigh. The heat of his palm melted through her jeans.

"Stay as long as you like. It's been dead all evening."

She closed her eyes and listened to the football game. "How do you write with this garbage going?"

"I don't even notice it anymore."

"It would drive me crazy."

"I can write through almost anything."

"It's your superpower."

"I like to think I have a couple of superpowers." Shawn squeezed her leg.

Lane knew what he meant. "Want to come over?" she asked.

"I suppose I could let you feed me soon."

"Is that all I'm good for?"

Shawn took her hand. "You know I think you're amazing. It's our damn schedules that get in the way."

"Are you free tonight?"

"I've got papers and homework," he said. "I could come over after my shift next Friday."

"So long?"

"It's all I've got. Take it or leave it."

"You know I'll take it," Lane said.

Chapter Two

Lane set the timer on her phone and collapsed backward over the arm of the sofa, her feet dangling. She would give herself ten minutes of counting to six for each inhalation and each exhalation. She'd found it was the most efficient way of transitioning herself from a bad day into a night's worth of work in her studio.

Celia usually came over on Wednesday nights. Her friend would drink wine and lavish attention on Pilot, Lane's fluffy black cat, while Lane wove or knit. Because she'd been at the coffee shop so late, Lane had called and canceled, but she missed Celia's company.

Her friend was sensible in a way that Lane couldn't wrangle for herself. Celia was chic, slight and petite with wavy blonde hair the color of post rock. A proper hairdresser trimmed her hair so she didn't have to use fabric sheers every few weeks like Lane did. Celia never had mascara rings under her eyes. She wasn't bowed by debt like Lane was. Celia didn't even have any student loans. She owned her own house *and* had a savings account. Because she hated the job she'd had since college, a pharmaceutical sales rep, she dabbled in real estate on the side. Dabbled. With hundreds of thousands of dollars. While Lane was hoping the fall weather would stay mild so she didn't have to turn the furnace on.

If Celia were here, she would have told Lane to call the cops on Javier. She would have told Talia's mom to mind her own damn business, and she would have told Lane to stop pretending with Abe and take his fancy wool pants off already.

The memory of Abe's fingers on the back of her hand zipped through her, and she sucked a breath in through her teeth.

It had hurt Abe that she'd kept her divorce from him. When she'd been upset, he'd reached for her hand.

That shouldn't make Lane smile, but it did. She held her hands to her cheeks to feel the flushed skin that wouldn't stop being rounded by her grin, even after she told it to.

Abe Fujikawa had a thing for her.

She'd suspected that maybe he wasn't like all the others, but they never talked about anything that mattered. Lane always kept the tone light and teasing on purpose, because the one or two times she hadn't, like this morning, a feeling stronger than polite amusement crept up on her.

For two inhalations, Lane let that tingling pleasure of that sensation cascade over her, but on the third breath, she swallowed it and exhaled it through her nose.

If he couldn't see how ridiculous they would look together, she would have to be the practical one. Him, tall and handsome, in his bespoke suit. Her, short, rounded, and dressed in threadbare plaid. She would look like a gold digger. Like an ornament for him to dress up and wear on his arm for all the fancy to-dos he got up to with his fellow Republicans at the Statehouse.

He was a fucking Republican. But somehow, despite the sick feeling Lane got in the pit of her stomach when she remembered the latest letter she'd received from her Senator, detailing why he wouldn't be voting the way she'd asked him too, Lane couldn't hold Abe's politics against him. Like a seasoned professional, he never came down one way or another on the drastic tax cuts the governor had pushed through. And he had once told her he thought expanding healthcare coverage was a good thing, which went against the party line.

Their differing opinions, rather than a point of contention, gave them an excuse to linger together over her bar. Telling him he was wrong was her favorite part of the day, and with the election coming up in November, there was plenty of opportunity to tease him. From the way he flashed his white teeth between his perfect lips, she suspected he enjoyed her needling.

That made Abe dangerous.

There was a reason Lane didn't have any friends but Celia—Shawn didn't count. She had too much to do if she didn't want to be stuck in the worst coffee shop in town forever. Her ill-fated first marriage had knocked her so far down, she'd spent the last four years of late nights and hard work clawing her way to the precarious position she was in now. If she wanted to maintain it, try to improve it, it would take all her concentration.

Lane wasn't dissatisfied with her life. She had her job for stability. She had pride in her degrees, one in textiles, one in ceramics, because she had never chosen one over the other. Lane had Celia and Pilot for company. She had Shawn for sex. She had her house for comfort. Why would she gamble her equilibrium on Abe when she knew he would lose interest in a few weeks?

She wouldn't. It was all too important.

Lane loved her house like it was a person. She fantasized about buying it when she had the means. It was small and square, painted white with green shutters and a wide green porch. The windows ate half the wall on all four sides so the soft beige carpet never looked drab. Though the only bedroom was small and the bathroom smaller, the main living area was open and airy. The only separation between the living room and kitchen a breakfast bar she'd outfitted with hanging hand blown glass lights she'd traded a set of her mugs for.

Lane had painted everything white except the kitchen cabinets, which were a cheery yellow. She had shoved a small round table in the corner by the back door where her sewing machine lived. All the thrift store furniture was fitted with crisp white slipcovers Lane had sewn herself. She'd made brightly colored pillows from tie-dye experiments she'd done in school. Her walls were decorated with her school projects, silk paintings, woven tapestries, ceramic masks. Vases and pots peppered every surface.

The house was hers, even if she didn't own it. It was just hers. She couldn't have designed a better studio if she'd built the house herself. She did her textile work in the living room, where she'd stationed her spinning wheel and her little table-top loom. Her ceramics studio was in her garage, the wheel in one corner, the kiln in the other. She'd lined the walls with cinder block shelves to hold her works in progress before they sold.

While Lane dabbled in knitwear design and sold a few scarves every winter, the only money she made was from her pottery. She sold in a few shops around town, and had a trendy, if only mildly successful Etsy shop. She made just enough money to keep going. While her oversized coffee mugs were her most popular product, her favorite thing to make was the Japanese style handleless teacup. Her professor had always called them *yunomi*.

When she threw *yunomi*, Lane didn't worry about money. She didn't think about how she rarely spoke to her father and to her siblings even less. She didn't worry who else Shawn was sleeping with or that it might be a hard winter, and she'd finally have to break down and trade her moped in for a car. When she threw *yunomi*, her lonesomeness mattered less.

Her timer went off. Lane rolled to her feet. The kiln needed to be unloaded and then filled again. There were pots to trim and finished work to inventory and price. If she was lucky, she'd sit down at her wheel to throw a few mugs for the art museum gift shop before midnight. She needed to warp her loom and finish her scarf series, but now that would have to wait.

The small snatches of income she made from selling her pieces was worth the work. Each sale was another small shuffle toward independence. She'd been moving at the same plodding pace since she'd left Brad. If only her personal and professional gains could keep pace with the sprinting she'd been doing to outrun her past.

Lane had met Brad the first semester of her freshman year at the University of Kansas. They had a class together and always went to the same coffee cart after, though never together. Sick of waiting for him to notice her, Lane had asked him a question about that day's reading assignment.

His sleepy brown eyes had sparked, and he'd asked her over to study. He'd made her feel brilliant and beautiful, so she'd stayed the night. That Thanksgiving, he'd taken her to his mom's, and the whole house was full of food, and family, and laughter. They were married by the end of her sophomore year, just after he graduated. Soon after, he moved them thirty minutes west to Topeka for his job, and that's when everything went wrong.

As a student, he'd been smart and impressive. He'd aced all his psychology courses. He'd scored an impressve internship that led to a fantastic job. He'd been disciplined, going to the gym every morning, never eating or drinking too much, and never overdrawing his checking account. But after they were married, Brad had convinced Lane to take time off school so they could save money for the down payment on a nice house. Then, after they'd moved in and Lane expressed frustration with the coffee shop she'd worked at, he'd encouraged her to quit. When she'd said she'd rather go back to school, he'd purchased her everything she needed to make her art at home. But Lane grew anxious at home all day by herself, and she was back in a coffee shop before she'd gotten her art business off the ground.

When she was home with him, Lane had felt like she was letting Brad down, forsaking the dishes for designing a new lace motif on her knitting needles or the laundry for perfecting a tall vase on her wheel. She lived for the weekends when he would take her out. He loved taking her anywhere, dinner and drinks, a movie, a play, a coworker's party. He would wear her on his arm and make her laugh and she would remember what things had been like when they had been in school, when Brad had been proud of her.

It had taken Lane a long time to figure out what Brad liked most was to show her off. One night he'd taken her to a play, and she'd made herself a dress for the occasion: black, low cut with a flared skirt. He hadn't been able to take his eyes off her all evening. When they'd returned home, and he'd traced the deep V of her neckline, he'd said, "Every man in that theater tonight was jealous that you were on my arm, not theirs."

It struck Lane as a strange compliment, but she'd been distracted by his hands and thought he'd been complimenting how she looked in her dress. Over the next few months, she came to suspect that his chief joy in being married to her was that she was pretty and she was his, and that he'd never seen her—the real her—at all, not even that first day in line at the coffee cart.

A few months later, the arguments had gotten worse. He claimed she was hiding money, and went through her purse, which prompted her to open a second bank account and save her tips, just in case. When he refused to let her go back to school, saying he wouldn't pay for it when he had already bought her everything she needed, Lane moved out.

She took the job at Cristo's because it was in a part of town he never visited. She met Celia there, and they'd been inseparable since. The day after Lane signed the lease on her house, Celia and Lane had backed a U-Haul up to Brad's garage. The two of them had loaded up all of Lane's dormant art equipment while Brad had stood against the doorway, his arms crossed, never moving to help. She hadn't seen him since.

That she was sitting down to throw after midmight and would have to skip warping her loom if she wanted to sleep at all was a small price to pay for maintaining everything she'd worked for since then. Little by little, she was getting where she wanted to be. As Lane switched from mugs to *yunomi*, she told herself that she was content.

• • • •

LANE ONLY SLEPT FOUR hours. It wasn't enough. She felt hung over even though she'd never opened that bottle of wine. She was on her third cup of coffee by eight, and Eric, her recently divorced IT guy morning regular still sat on the front stool. The disoriented air of dejection clung to him, and Lane pretended to listen while she watched for Abe's gray Mercedes out the front window.

It was ten-thirty before Abe slid onto the stool, nodding to Lane as she finished up a cappuccino.

She set a mug under the hot water jet to warm while she stretched the milk for the cappuccino. Her heart thudded. He was leaning forward onto the counter, his newspaper still folded by his elbow, waiting for her. Now would be her best chance to let him down gently.

"I'd almost given up on you," she said, sliding the warmed mug across the counter and into his hand.

"I had an early meeting."

Lane gave him an apologetic smile. "You should probably give up on me though."

Abe pursed his lips and folded his brow into a frown, but rose to fill his cup. He was silent as he watched Lane help a string of customers. She could feel his eyes on her back the whole time.

"Tell me why," he said as she rinsed the milk pitchers in the sink hidden under the bar.

Not meeting his eyes as she said, "I don't date."

"You don't date who?" he asked. "Republicans?"

"For starters."

His lips curled into a smile, and she couldn't help but giggle, which made him smiled wider.

"Really though," she said, "I don't date anyone."

"That's too bad. I've been drumming up the courage to ask you to dinner for weeks."

"Now you don't have to."

"I think I'll still give it a shot."

"The answer's no."

"I know the chef at this little locally owned place. I'll take you there if you're free tonight."

"Still a no," Lane said.

"What are you doing instead?"

Lane wanted to tell him it was none of his business, but she enjoyed the banter, so she told him the truth. "I didn't get my loom warped last night because I was here, and I have a scarf series I needed to finish about three weeks ago." She'd been working on a series of bulky, vibrant houndstooth scarves for the holiday season, claiming the fuchsia and sapphire blue for herself.

"I can bring the food to you."

"How many times are you going to make me turn you down?"

"I'm an optimistic guy, so a few more."

"So long as we have an understanding," Lane said, then waved at him as she escaped into the kitchen.

Allison made a show of looking put out as she switched places with her. Over the sound of chopping cucumber, Lane heard Abe ask Allison, "She's not coming back out, is she?"

Allison said, "Dude, I know you think she's hot, but she's at work. She's got shit to do."

Later, as Lane was handing off the shift to Sarah a delivery guy from the flower shop down the road arrived with a heavy glass vase full of tall pink roses addressed to Lane Benjamin.

As she reached for the card at the center, she tried to remember if she's ever told Abe her last name.

The card read:

You're not just a barista.

—AF

Chapter Three

Celia stumbled through Lane's door, arm's full. Lane scooped the roses up so her friend could catch the bags of takeout threatening to spill their dinner onto the floor.

"Next time you charm a man into sending you presents, can you make sure it's something lighter?" Celia asked. "You know, like diamonds?"

"I'll try not to make it a habit," Lane said.

"I don't know, this Mr. Fujikawa strikes me as the kinda guy who likes giving gifts. I'd hold out for diamonds."

Lane plunked the flowers down on her coffee table, placing them at the center of the living room. Celia seated herself on one of the stools at the breakfast bar and uncovered the meal she'd brought.

"Too bad I'm not the kind of girl who likes getting them." Lane joined Celia.

"What's going on there?"

"He's trying to get in my pants."

Celia grabbed two forks out of the drawer. "I knew that. What else?"

"Nothing," Lane said. "You want wine?"

"Please," Celia sank onto her stool and buried her head in her arms. Her voice came out muffled as she said, "I'm so bored at work I'm thinking about becoming a drunk just for something interesting to do."

"Attractive." Lane popped the cork on the hedgehog wine and poured one glass. She'd heard how much Celia hated her job a million times over the last year, but Celia never did anything about her situation. Lane suspected she mostly liked to complain.

"I'm serious. If I don't get out of there soon I'm going to explode."

"So, get out."

"And do what?"

"Sell houses."

"Boring."

Lane handed of the glass of wine to Celia, then opened the foam box in front of her. Inside was a spicy pasta dish topped with shrimp. "Stalk the sexy bartender full time?"

"I'm not stalking Michael"

Lane pointed at her food with her fork and raised an eyebrow. "This isn't from Lustrio?"

"Of course it is."

"Any luck yet?"

Celia ordered takeout from the swanky Latin-Fusion restaurant so she could sip a martini at the bar and flirt with him while the food was prepared. Lane was familiar with the maneuver.

"Did I mention I was considering becoming a drunk?"

"Not well, huh?"

"He was dealing with some computer problem, and I didn't even get to talk to him."

"Is that why you're so cranky?"

Celia scowled. "No, I'm cranky at you."

Lane, who had been moving all of the shrimp to the lid of her box, scowled right back at her friend. "What did I do?"

"A beautiful, successful man sent you flowers and you're acting like it's an insult."

"It kind of is," Lane said.

"Do you know what I would give to have a man like that send me flowers?"

"I do, actually," Lane said, and took her first taste of the pasta. It wasn't bad, but it would be better with sausage instead of shrimp. "But we're very different about these things."

Celia was eating all her shrimp first. "Right. Because you attract men, and I scare them away."

"Don't be ridiculous."

"I'm looking at the overwhelming evidence."

"What evidence? We're both single," Lane said.

Celia threw a shrimp at her. Lane deflected with the back of her hand and it fell onto the carpet. "You are the only person in the world besides Shawn who would say you were single."

"Then it's good we found each other."

Celia grew pensive, then after what must have been a fortifying glass of wine, she said, "You know I saw him out with the blonde again." When Celia was in Lawrence, courting doctors for her pharmaceutical company, she used catering from the same coffee shop Shawn frequented.

"I figured," Lane said. "I've haven't seen him since the semester started."

"You think she's this term's student girlfriend?"

"She must be." Lane shrugged.

"Does he ever say anything to you?"

Lane shook her head, her appetite vanishing.

"What a dick," Celia said. "I can't believe you prefer that over Mr. Fujikawa."

"Abe's not any different. He may even be worse."

"You can't tell me you don't like him," Celia said. "I've seen you two together, and it is disgusting."

Celia was referring to Labor Day. Lane's boss had insisted on being open at the regular time, even though Lane had told him it would be dead. So, Lane sat by herself for half an hour in the empty shop before Abe came in for breakfast.

He was her only customer for two hours. To pass the time, Lane showed off a set of her teacups. He'd asked to see her pottery the week before, and she was curious to see what he thought. He corrected the way she pronounced the Japanese terms she'd learned in school. When she accused him of pretending to know Japanese to impress her, he'd let loose a long monologue in the language he claimed was his first. Then he translated it for her in a single sentence: "You have a lot of nerve calling me a fraud when you're a white woman selling Japanese pottery."

While the words were accusatory, his tone had remained light and conversational. But where they had been leaning in toward each other over the counter, Lane stepped back. "You're right," she said. "I've struggled with that a lot."

"Damn, I was hoping to get a rise out of you."

"Why? Because hurt feelings at being called a racist are more important to most white people than admitting it could be the truth?"

"Mostly because you're breathtaking when you're angry."

"Don't flirt with me," she said. "Let's talk about it this."

It was reckless to talk to Abe like that. They spent the next two hours discussing imperialism and its historic relationship to art. He told her about how his daughter, Gretchen, was learning that having a white mother wasn't enough to spare her prejudice. And that even though he had Japanese parents and grew up speaking Japanese, when he was in Japan, he was an American.

When Celia came in, they were talking about WWII and the US bombing Japan. She took one look at them, heads together over the counter, Lane playing with the clasp of the watch still on Abe's wrist and pretended to get a phone call.

"That still makes me sick," Lane said. "That we did it all was abominable, that we did it twice is unforgivable."

"I'm only here because of that second bomb," he said. Then he told her that both his grandfather and great grandfather had done their medical studies in Nagasaki, which was also where most of the Catholics in Japan lived. His family had moved east by the time the war had started, but his grandfather had been serving in a field hospital with one of his old colleagues, who had been trying to convert him to Catholicism for the duration of the war. His grandfather had resisted until the bomb fell on Nagasaki. The family had been Catholic ever since.

"You're Catholic?" Lane asked.

"I was raised Catholic," he said. "Very different."

"How did your family wind up here?"

Abe explained that his father grew up to be a nuclear physicist instead of a doctor, and his parents moved to the states in the sixties for work. They started out in

Massachusetts, his dad working for a university there. Then they moved to Kansas in the eighties for research. Outside a brief stint in Tokyo before he had to give up his dual citizenship, Abe had been in Kansas ever since, but his dad was back at MIT.

She wanted to ask about his watch, as she fiddled with the end of the old leather strap that never quite stayed tucked in. Lane didn't doubt that eighty years prior, the watch had been the height of fashion, but the yellowed face and cracked leather band wasn't on par with the rest of Abe's impeccable wardrobe. Instead, she said, "Wow. My ancestors were just regular old hillbillies. I don't even think they were moonshiners."

Abe laughed, touching the fingers of his watch hand to the inside of Lane's forearm. "I've never told that whole story before."

"Horse shit."

"Seriously. No one's been interested."

Before Lane could reply, Celia hollered from the bulk bean display, "When do you get your new shipments of beans? All the ones you have now suck."

Abe sat up straight, pulling his hands back to the edge of the counter like he hadn't noticed Celia was there.

The Celia beside Lane in her living room was giving the same look she had on Labor Day. "If I hadn't said anything, you two would have been doing it on the counter in like, three minutes."

"It wasn't like that," Lane said.

"I'm surprised it took him another two weeks to ask you out."

"I wish he hadn't." Lane didn't know what she was going to do with a persistently amorous Abe. The flirting and the over tipping had been bad enough. Now he wanted to take her out. In public.

"You should go."

"And be the funny story he tells the next barista or waitress or whoever? No thanks."

"He doesn't think of you that way."

Lane scoffed. Her appetite thoroughly ruined. "How do you know?"

"Because we talked in the parking lot this morning after you shot him down. When I found him, he was leaning over his car giving himself a pep talk."

"Wait, what?" Lane could not picture Abe *needing* to give himself a pep talk. "What did he say?"

"He looked at me like I was nuts, because he had no idea who I was. Once we established my identity, he was all ears." Celia's Cheshire Cat grin caused dread to well in Lane's already churning stomach.

"Oh dear God, just please tell me you didn't say anything embarrassing."

"I told him that you're scared shitless because you like him too much, and that he shouldn't let you pretend otherwise."

Lane pushed her food away so hard it almost fell off the other side of the counter. "It's time to change the subject," she said.

"You don't have to get pissed off that I'm right," Celia said. "You could embrace it and get married instead."

"What would you really do if you quit your job?" Lane asked. It was a question that Lane knew would make Celia just an angry as Lane was.

Celia said, "I have no fucking clue. Why do you keep asking?"

"Because I want you to be my business manager." Only severe annoyance could have made Lane admit that secret aloud.

"You what?" Celia blinked her ire away.

"It's a day dream of mine. You take care of selling my work and I am free to make whatever I wanted all day long."

"Why have you never said anything?"

"I can't pay you," Lane said. "I don't have any money."

"That reminds me," Celia said. "Your stupid flowers made me forget." She reached into her back pocket and threw a stack of twenties on the table. "That's for you."

Lane counted the money. "You can't give me three hundred dollars."

"I'm not, that's your cut."

"Of what?"

"That blue scarf you gave me for my birthday last year. I sold it."

Lane's heart missed a beat. "Why would you do that?"

"Because Doc Jacoby asked where he could get one for his wife, and when I told him it was a one of a kind, he asked me how much. He handed me four hundred for it right then and there."

"You can't just sell a gift like that. Do you know how long it takes to weave with beads?"

"I know, I should have said five hundred. But at least now you can get that yarn you were drooling over the other day."

"I can't spend this on yarn," Lane said. "I should put it in my student loan fund."

"This is business money, you pay business bills with it, not personal ones."

"Except I don't make enough money on my textiles to justify buying that amount of supplies."

"And you won't until you invest a little more time and money into them."

"I don't have either of those."

"Hello." Celia tapped the money that Lane had left on the counter. "Buy your yarn."

Lane frowned at the bills. "What would I do with that much yarn?"

Celia threw her hands in the air. "Jesus, you getting in the way of your own brilliance drives me up the fucking wall."

"I don't have the time."

"I'll find the time for you." Celia said. "I just hired myself. Make me a list of everything you want to do by tomorrow."

Chapter Four

Lane had Fridays and Saturdays off, so she didn't see Abe until Sunday. He watched her work while his daughter fiddled on her phone. Then he waited an extra twenty minutes to fill his empty coffee mug until she was alone at the end of the bar refilling the air pots.

"Did you get my roses?" he asked.

She didn't meet his eyes. "Oh, those were from you?"

"You have more than one admirer with my initials?"

"They could have been from Allison, her last name is Finnegan."

He frowned. "You knew they were from me."

"I did," Lane said. "They don't change my answer though."

"That's all right," he said. "I'll ask again tomorrow."

"What makes you so sure I'll change my mind?"

As he emptied the light roast pot, his lips parted into a slow, sure grin. "Labor Day."

Lane blushed, so he pushed on. "That was fun. Let's do it again Thursday night."

"Why Thursday?"

"That's your Friday, right?" Lane nodded. "Best night for a first date."

"Why not actual Friday night?" she asked.

"We can go out then too if you like." He winked.

Lane rolled her eyes and peered around him. Abe followed her gaze. His daughter stared at them, frowning. "Times up, Dad," Lane said.

"Gretchen shouldn't mind a little harmless flirting. She was texting a boy when I left." Abe gave his daughter an unapologetic grin, and Gretchen rolled her eyes and crossed her arms.

"Not the same thing," Lane said and slipped away.

But during the week Abe didn't relent. On Monday, he asked her what she was doing Thursday night instead. She only answered because she knew he'd keep pestering her if she didn't.

"I have a tight schedule to keep if I'm going to make any money over the holiday season."

"Has anyone ever told you that you work too much?"

"Yeah," Lane said. "My ex. It's part of the reason we're not married anymore."

Abe bit his tongue, and she could tell he wasn't sure if she was serious. Lane let him wonder.

On Tuesday he tried again. "You know they're doing *Pirates of Penzance* at the Lied Center this weekend. I could get us tickets."

"You like Gilbert and Sullivan?"

"I played Frederic one summer in college."

"Bullshit," Lane said

"Really, I did." He leaned toward her over the counter. "I have a degree in performance. I worked as an actor for two years after college."

"How the hell did you get from there to lobbyist?"

"By way of law school."

"You're a lawyer too?"

"I passed the bar. I keep up my license, but I hate courtrooms."

"Any other professions I don't know about?"

"I'll let you know at dinner on Thursday."

"I'm not having dinner with you on Thursday."

"I still have two whole days to change your mind."

"Good luck," Lane said, and left to help Allison.

On Wednesday, he was late, tennis running longer than usual, and read his newspaper while he ate lunch. Lane was too busy to talk, but he lingered until the lunch hour slowed. When she paused to count out tips, he loitered by the register to ask if she'd changed her mind yet.

She stopped counting so she could meet his eye. "I wasn't joking when I said I don't date."

"I didn't think you were, but I like you, Lane."

"You like a lot of women, I think."

"I've dated a lot of women," he said. "And been bored senseless by most of them."

"That's not very nice."

"They weren't all that interested in me either."

"But you still slept with them?"

He pushed back a lock of new hair that hung over his right eye. "That's not what I'm after, if it makes any difference."

"And what are you after?"

"Honestly?"

"Pretend you're in court."

He grinned. "Well, Your Honor, I'm looking for a wife, and I'm having a terrible time of it."

All the color left her face, and her eyes bulged in shock.

He laughed, "Just so we're clear, that wasn't a proposal."

Lane nodded, her eyes still wide.

"But I do think we have potential," he said. He reached up and smoothed her bangs out of her eyes again while she stared at him. "Just think about it."

Lane had no choice but to think about Abe's line. It had to be a line, right? He couldn't be serious. He didn't want to get married again, did he? And neither did she, right?

Lane didn't notice when Celia bounded in grinning like an idiot. It took her a second to register what Celia was saying, and she had to ask her to repeat it.

"I just walked out on my job," she said. "And if everything works out, in a couple of weeks, you're quitting too."

Lane shook her head to clear it, then asked, "Have you gone insane?"

"I figured out how we're going to go into business together," Celia said. "And we both have to quit our jobs."

"You can afford to quit your job. If I quit, I'm done for."

Celia walked around the bar and helped herself to a mug. "I have a plan," she said. Then, as she poured her coffee, she outlined an idea to Lane about how she would invest some of her savings and sell the last couple of houses she had still on the market so she and Lane could go into business together.

"And I've already started a business plan using the list you gave me—but I need way more input from you to get going."

"When did all this happen?"

"A couple nights ago at Lustrio," she said as pulled a stool up to the bar.

"You started planning our business while you were bar stalking Michael?"

Celia nodded so hard that her coffee spilled over her fingers. "And the only spot left open was next to this totally nerdy looking guy. He was clean cut, glasses, polo and khakis, the whole thing, but he was sitting there, drinking a whiskey and balancing the books."

"Their accountant was working at the bar?"

"One of the perks of the job, I guess." Celia shrugged, but her grin still shone too bright.

"Have you been drinking?"

"Not since then, why?"

"Because you're being weird."

Celia frowned. "And you're being a downer."

Lane rolled her eyes. "So, what did this nerdy accountant have to say?"

"I told him about you and asked him if he had any experience with investing in small scale businesses and if he had any advice, and we talked about it all night, and he made it sound so simple that I decided to just do it."

"You have lost your mind," Lane said.

"I talked to my actual accountant. She thinks it's sound."

"How does quitting our jobs figure into this?"

"We need the time to work."

"And how do we pay our bills in the meantime?"

"We'll have enough money to pay ourselves for a little while."

"Right," Lane said. "Sounds risky."

Celia obviously wasn't concerned because her grin turned wicked. "Speaking of risky, I ran into Mr. Fujikawa in the parking lot, and he was wearing a smile. Were you two talking dirty?"

"I have a mountain of dishes I'd rather do than talk about him," Lane said. She'd tallied how many women he'd dated in the time she'd known him, and how many times he must have used that marriage line. He was an actor. He was good at delivering lines; it was supposed to be believable.

"Fine," Celia said, crossing her arms on the countertop, "I'll wait until you're off, because I don't have anywhere else to be." Then she did an awkward little shimmy Lane took for a celebratory seated dance.

• • • •

LANE'S MIND WAS STILL reeling so much from Abe's not-a-proposal when he arrived the next morning that her stomach swooped into her knees when she saw him. When she offered him a mug, he thanked her. As she turned away he said, "Can I ask your opinion on something?"

"You can ask," Lane said.

He sighed. "There's this woman, and I—"

Lane raised an eyebrow, and his grin turned sheepish. At least he knew he was ridiculous.

He started again, "So there's this woman, and I see her almost every day. I'm crazy about her. I think she's perfect, smart, pretty, gorgeous eyes. She curses like a sailor, and she's too young for me, but she has big dreams. Her ambition is my favorite thing about her."

"And?" Lane asked.

"And I know she likes me, but I'm pretty sure someone broke her heart, and she's afraid to take a chance on me, so she keeps turning me down."

"Is that your theory?" Lane asked, her eyebrow still high.

"And then, right when I think I've made a pretty good case for myself, her best friend corners me in the parking lot and shoves this into my hands." He pulled a folded deli napkin out of his shirt pocket, the kind that Celia kept in her glove compartment. "And it's tempting, because it could work, but it could also backfire right when she almost trusts me."

He handed her the napkin. It read, "Try Thursday night, 6:30." Then it listed Lane's address. Underneath that, Celia had written, "Bring Sunflowers."

"If you were me, what would you do?" he asked.

Lane gave him back the napkin. "How young is she?"

"Mid to late twenties, I think."

"And how old are you?"

"Forty-two."

Lane pretended to think. She'd estimated he was forty-five. "Fifteen years isn't too bad," Lane said. "Not ideal, but not creepy."

"Good to know," he said.

"What makes you think she likes you?"

"She always *looks* happy to see me, and when we talk, she's interested, even though we tend to disagree."

"Is that all?"

He shook his head. "Sometimes while we're talking," he reached out a finger and brushed her wrist, "She'll play with my watch."

Lane bit her lip, and nodded. She never touched his watch on purpose. Her fingers did it on their own, like they were seeking the solace of cool water after being singed by flame.

"Any advice?" he asked.

Lane took a deep breath, and tried to keep her voice disinterested as she said, "I'd give it a shot. What do you have to lose?"

Abe smiled. "Maybe I will," he said. "See you later, Lane."

"See you."

Chapter Five

Lane finished her shift in a kind of haze, not able to believe she'd just given Abe permission to show up at her house. The spot on her wrist where he'd touched her still hummed with satisfaction. She replayed the scene in her mind over and over until Shawn came in near the end of her shift. She hadn't talked to him for more than a week, and the sight of him dispersed the fog Abe had caused in her mind. Abe unnerved her. He excited her, made her hope. Shawn, on the other hand, was simple. He needed companionship, food, and sex, and Lane was good at all of those things.

She poured herself a cup of coffee and joined him at his table, placing a hand on his shoulder as she walked behind him. He covered her hand with his own, giving it a quick squeeze before releasing it and pulling off his headphones.

"Good afternoon, gorgeous."

"How are the papers?"

"It's like they don't teach writing in high school anymore," he said. It was one of his favorite rants, but Lane could tell he had a lot to do, because he went straight back to grading instead of giving her an example of a mixed metaphor. Lane took the hint and moved to stand, but Shawn put his hand on her knee to stay her.

"Sorry, I'm grumpy about these," he finished the sentence he was reading. "I'm rewarding myself for finishing these today by having dinner with you tomorrow. We're still on for that?"

"Of course. Someone has to make sure you're taking care of yourself." She could tell he'd been busy, because he hadn't shaved for at least a week, and had the beginnings of a patchy beard growing in. His hand fell away from her leg as she stood. She tugged on the bill of his hat. "Get back to work. You have a deadline to meet."

He caught her hand and and pulled her back down toward him, kissing her on the lips. "See you tomorrow."

Lane forgot her coffee.

He had never just kissed her before.

Lane's relationship with Shawn had always been confusing. They never lacked for something to talk about, and they had physical chemistry, but he at once attracted and repulsed her. He was intelligent, with bright blue eyes and a tan that never quite seemed to fade. Her series of first encounters with him had taught her not to trust him, even as she had also been drawn to him.

The first time Lane had seen Shawn, he had been standing outside the liquor store door, smoking as Lane locked Cristo's up for the night.

"Hey," he nodded at her as he flicked his cigarette into the gutter. She'd said it back, like she recognized him.

He'd watched her start her moped and put on her helmet, then said "Have a good night," over the sound of her engine as she rode away.

The next day, Shawn had come in for coffee. He'd seated himself at the counter and they'd talked about books and school. Lane had still been working on her degrees then, and he had just started his MFA in Creative Writing, and he hadn't outright flirted, even though Lane could feel Shawn watching her work. He had been himself, and he'd listened to her. It had been nice after spending so much time alone.

He'd told her F. Scott Fitzgerald was his favorite writer and that she should read "Bernice Bob's Her Hair." When he'd offered to let her borrow the book it was in, and invited her to stop by pick it up after class sometime, Lane hadn't miss the glint in his eye.

Because she'd been lonely, Lane had agreed.

Two weeks later, Lane had followed Shawn home from campus. Expecting a sparse, dingy apartment with dirty socks in the corners, she had been surprised to find it clean and neat, furnished with candles and curtains.

Lane had stopped in the center of the living room and turned in a circle. "You don't live here by yourself."

"No. Stacey lives here too."

"And Stacey is?"

"My girlfriend."

"Oh." Lane had said.

"Is that a problem?"

"Not if I'm just going to borrow a book, but I thought this was supposed to be more than that."

Shawn had joined Lane in the middle of the living room and draped an arm over her shoulder. "It can be, if you like."

"Yeah." Lane had sighed and shrugged him off. "I've had enough drama in my life. I don't want to get involved in anyone else's."

"Bad breakup?"

"I guess a divorce qualifies as a breakup."

"Yikes." Shawn had backed up a step.

Lane had scanned the bookshelves by the window. "Do you have the book?"

"You're uncomfortable."

"Your girlfriend could walk in any minute."

"And you're just here to borrow a book."

"Sure, completely innocent," Lane had said.

"I didn't mean to offend you." He'd pulled *Flappers and Philosophers* off the shelf and held it out to her.

Lane had tucked the book in her bag and left.

A few days later, a girl in Lane's weaving class updated them on her English TA having an affair with the students in the class. When Lane asked, and the girl said, "Shawn something or other," Lane wasn't surprised.

After that, Lane had refused to see Shawn outside the coffee shop. He would sit at the counter so they could chat between customers, but that was all she'd allowed. It was there that Lane had asked him why he lived in Lawrence and worked part-time in Topeka. His answer, like everything he did, had been to help his writing. He'd needed more diverse characters.

Lane had asked if he was finding them. He'd answered, "In spades."

Then, one day about a year ago, Shawn had skipped the counter and chosen a table in the back. When she'd finished her shift, Lane had sat down across from him. Making herself comfortable, she'd propped her feet up in the empty chair and checked her phone to see if she'd made any Etsy sales. There'd been none, and she'd dropped her phone on the table with a clatter.

"Stacey's moving out," Shawn had said, closing his computer. "She got a job in St. Joseph."

"I'm sorry." Lane had straightened her spine and met Shawn's dejected eyes. "Are you OK?"

"No." He'd shrugged, looking miserable. "We've been together for three years."

"Is it just because of the job that she's moving?"

"She says I'm more committed to my writing than I am to her."

Lane'd had to stifle a snort. Shawn wasn't committed to anything *but* his writing. If he'd just been writing all the time, Stacey wouldn't be leaving.

"Anything I can do?" Lane asked Shawn.

"Keep me company sometimes?"

"Sure."

Shawn had come over once every couple of weeks after that. At first, it had just been dinner and company, but one evening, he'd brushed her hair back over her shoulder and asked if he could kiss her. Lane had told him to take her to bed instead.

When she'd woken up, Shawn had been gone, but she'd found a note on her pillow. It read:

> *You are beautiful.*
> *You are phenomenal.*
> *I'm sorry I needed to leave.*
> *I want to share this sacred space again with you soon.*

"Are you fucking kidding me?" Celia had said, handing Lane back the note a couple of days later. "Please tell me you aren't naive enough to think this shit is sexy."

"No," Lane said, tucking the note in her pocket. "I don't. I want to know what you think."

"That you could do better."

"I'm not sorry."

"I'm not saying you should be sorry. But how many times you've told me that you know this guy can't be faithful to you."

"I haven't asked him to be."

Celia scrunched her nose in disgust. "So, you're what? Just sleeping with him?"

"It's nice to be touched."

"I get it, honey. Really, I do," Celia said, placing a comforting hand on my knee. "But I also know that's not what you want in the long run."

Lane hadn't argued. She hadn't known how to tell Celia that all she'd been looking for was balance.

Lane hadn't deluded herself into thinking of Shawn as a serious attachment. The first time he'd spent the night hadn't been out of any regard for Lane, but because he'd been drunk. Lane had cooked for him as usual, and he'd brought rum, and they'd both drank too much.

Afterward, he'd pulled his cap from the mess clothes at the foot of the bed and smashed it down over his fluffy hair. Then he'd pulled his pack of cigarettes and his zippo from his jeans. He'd offered one to Lane, who declined, and then lit a cigarette for himself.

Normally, Lane would have plucked the cigarette out of his mouth and drowned it in her water glass. She had always exiled him to the porch to smoke before, but she'd been feeling generous that night.

"Your place is the perfect artist's house," he'd said, blowing his smoke to the ceiling. "How'd you find it?"

"Celia."

Shawn had ashed his cigarette over the melted ice in his rum and coke glass. He'd still had the dregs of his last drink in his hand as he'd lead Lane into her own bedroom with his other hand on the small of her back.

"Celia hates me."

"Celia thinks you hold me back from looking for a proper relationship."

Lane had pulled the sheet up to her armpits. She'd sipped water from a green plastic cup, trying to wash her drunkenness down. Shawn had been naked except for his ball cap. He'd always been lean, and Lane could see his muscles as he moved. His skin had glowed golden in the yellow light from the lamp on her cinder block bedside table.

Shawn had chuckled deep in his throat. "Celia doesn't know you as well as she likes to think."

"You think you know me better than she does?"

"Of course I do," he'd grinned at her, his eyes unable to focus on her face. She'd wondered if he'd been sneaking shots, or if she held her liquor better than he did.

"Because you're sleeping with me?"

"Sure. And because I'm writing about you."

"No. You're writing about a girl who resembles me."

"I'll let you read it when I'm done. Then you can tell me which you think it is." Shawn had smiled at her like he knew all her dirty secrets, but he hadn't.

"Let me read it now."

"I can't do that."

"Why not?"

"You'll try to make yourself look better."

Lane had gestured up and down the length of her naked body. "Is there any reason I would want to look better?"

"Of course not. But it's like I'm drawing your portrait. If you look over my shoulder, only half your face is shaded in and you'll be asking my you only have half a face."

"What if I want to know what you think of me, only half shaded in?"

Shawn had dropped what his cigarette in the glass, the water smothering the smoldering tobacco. He kissed Lane's neck. "It doesn't work like that."

He'd kissed his way across her collarbone. Lane had flipped off his ball cap by the bill, annoyed that he had it on.

"How does it work?" Lane had asked, placing her cup on the side table next to his glass so she could wrap her arms around his neck.

"There are two types of story. Comedy and Tragedy."

"Which am I?"

"I only write comedies," Shawn had said, pulling the sheet down, revealing Lane down to her hips.

"Why?"

"I don't believe in tragedies." He'd kissed his way down the slope of her left breast, then rested his forehead just over her heart.

"But you said—"

"It's about perspective. Even the worst situation can be funny if you give it the right words." He'd trailed his lips back up to her chin, pushing her back into the pillows as he went.

"You don't think people hurt?" She asked.

"Yes, but that doesn't mean you can't take delight in that pain."

When he'd pushed the sheets off the bed and climbed back on top of her, she'd pulled him close and kissed him on the mouth, even though he tasted like nicotine.

"How do you find the right words to make something terrible, funny?"

"You find terrible things and funny things and then you try on all the words that might fit."

"Show me," she said.

"What's the saddest thing you can think of?" He'd propped himself up on his elbows, peeling the skin of his belly off of hers.

Lane didn't even have to think. "A child dying."

The smug smile he'd been wearing between kisses disappeared. "Fuck, Lane." He rolled so he was sitting beside her.

"You asked."

"That's not something I can do on the fly."

"Then put it in my story."

"That's not where your story is headed," he'd said, a grin playing at the corners of his mouth.

"Then put it in somebody else's story, but you have let me read it."

Lane had pulled him back down to her. "Show me what you can do with words," Lane had whispered and kissed him, wanting to believe even the worst of the worst might someday be less painful.

"Give me some time," he'd gasped as Lane snaked her fingers between them and grazed her fingernails along the inside of his thigh.

Lane had scratched hard enough to make Shawn curse, but this time, instead of rolling away, he'd thrust inside her, his pace matching the intensity of Lane's scratches.

"Shawn, no." But he hadn't heard her.

"Shawn. Stop," she'd said, as she'd caught him under the leg with one of her feet and pushed him off.

"What the fuck?" Shawn had scowled as he'd found himself on his side without her.

"Get a condom or get out."

"I forgot." He'd retreated to the dresser where she kept a box in the top drawer.

"It's my one rule."

"You can't give a guy a break when you're pulling moves like that?"

"I'm not throwing you out," Lane had said.

He'd hovered above her, condom in place, but Lane had kept her legs closed. She'd reached for his chest and taken out her annoyance by dragging her nails across the soft skin over his heart.

"God, you're hardcore," he'd breathed.

"I'm pissed." Lane had propped herself up to kiss where she'd just scratched.

"It won't happen again."

Lane had bit him then, so he would remember.

"Are you going to finish my story?"

"Yes," he'd said. "And it will be funny and sad, just like you like to read."

Lane had kissed his lips. "Okay."

As far as Lane knew, he'd never finished that story, but then again, she'd never expected him to. The whole point of it was to impress her into sleeping with him, and he already had that. After they'd been together a few times, he stopped talking about her story, and she basically let him come over whenever he wanted, which wasn't often anymore.

But then he had kissed her in public, and Lane didn't know what that meant, but decided it was safest to assume it meant nothing.

Chapter Six

A car door slammed, and Lane came back to herself. She'd spaced out again, which she'd been doing all afternoon instead of working.

After giving up on her weaving project Lane donned her best, trying/not trying clothes, a cropped black cardigan over a tight black t-shirt. Then, with a few minutes to burn she'd settled onto the porch steps with the sweater she was designing and tried to knit until Abe arrived. The car door wasn't his, but her neighbor's. Lane waved back at him and resumed her knitting.

After knitting a few rows, Lane suspected Abe was late. When she checked her phone, it was already almost seven. Almost thirty minutes late on the first date. Lane was not impressed.

Maybe he wasn't coming.

She knit a few more rows. Lane didn't design sweaters often, but she'd dreamed this one up over the summer, thinking she'd have it done to wear in the fall. She'd have it done just in time for spring at this rate.

When she checked her phone again, it was quarter past seven.

He wasn't coming. That made everything easier.

She could pretend this had never happened. They were better off as friends anyway.

Lane only had six more rows before she reached the end of the lace section, and if she went inside, she'd have to work on something that was less indulgent than self-publishing knitting patterns.

As she neared the end of the fifth row, she heard car tires crunch over fallen leaves. She raised her eyes without lifting her head to see Abe's gray Mercedes park right in front of her. Lane went back to her knitting, listening to the sharp tap of his oxfords on the concrete. She heard the crinkle of plastic and could see the thick stems of four or five giant sunflowers out of the corner of her eye when he stopped in front of her.

"You're late," she said.

"I would have called, but I don't have your number."

"You've never asked," Lane said. She turned her work and started the sixth row.

"Would you have given it to me if I did?" he asked, leaning in to look over her shoulder.

Lane shrugged. "Depends on what you wanted it for."

"To call and tell you I got held up at work." His voice came from close to her ear, almost a caress. Lane wasn't buying it.

"I imagine that happens a lot."

"I usually take on more than I can get done in eight hours." Lane felt more than saw him lean his elbows back against the porch steps, though she could make out his long legs in her peripheral vision. "What are you working on?"

"A sweater."

"Isn't it hard to see what you're doing out here with that black yarn?"

"I don't have to see," Lane said. "I have to count."

"Point taken." He was silent until she finished her row. When Lane spread the lace out in her lap to check for mistakes he leaned in close again, "That's pretty. Did you design it?"

Lane shook her head. "It's an old motif, I adapted it to fit onto the sweater in the way I wanted."

"It looks great."

Lane let go of the fabric and it snapped back into a jumble of yarn in her lap.

"So," she finally looked at him. He was wearing the same navy shirt and gray trousers he'd worn that morning. He'd rolled his sleeves up to his elbows and his navy and white checked tie hung loose around his neck. Abe was even more gorgeous this way, and she Lane had to avert her eyes.

"You were running late, but you took the time to stop for flowers?"

He handed her the bouquet. "I had the intern grab for me this afternoon."

"Is that an approved use of company time?" Lane asked.

"Maybe not," he grinned like he wasn't sorry, "but now Chester feels important because he's the only one who knows the flowers are for a woman, not a client."

"He won't tell anyone?"

"The whole place will know by morning, but he's the one who's got the dirt." Abe's leg brushed against hers as he leaned in closer to watch her knit.

"And what dirt did you give him on me?"

"All I said was that I was trying to convince the most baffling and beautiful woman I'd ever met to have dinner with me."

"Beautiful, huh?" Lane turned her attention the flowers, tracing the petals on the smallest head, trying hard not to remember how Brad had thought she was beautiful too.

"Yup." Abe reclined backward, his elbows on the top step, his legs stretched out in front of him. "And I'm not going to let you make me feel guilty for saying so, whatever your hang up is about your looks."

"Pretty confident for a guy who was an hour late."

"You wouldn't give me the time of day if that was the only reason you thought I was interested."

"Maybe." Lane stood. He followed, jumping to his feet with ease. "Wait here while I put these in some water. Then we can go."

When she returned Abe held out his hand. Lane hesitated, then wrapped her fingers around his. A thrill ran up her spin when he smiled.

"Thanks for giving this a shot." His voice was softer now, his brow less sure of himself.

Lane pretended not to see the vulnerability in him. She wasn't sure she was ready for it. "Tonight must be an awful lot of pressure. You've got to impress the hell out of me and convince me you're not a sleazy show off all in one night."

Abe squeezed her hand. "I'm good under pressure." He led her down the walk to his car. "You think I'm sleazy?"

Lane nodded. "And vain, but you have good taste, so I can forgive the vanity." She tugged on his tie with her free hand.

He caught her fingers and brought them to his lips, kissing her knuckles. A line of fire shot straight up Lane's arm, burning even after he'd withdrawn.

"You getting in?" he asked.

Lane studied the stitching on the passenger seat. With everything else she'd been feeling, she'd forgotten that going out with him meant getting in his car. "I haven't been in a car since last winter when the snow was bad."

His eyes shot to where her moped was chained to the porch, as if he was afraid she would insist on taking that instead.

"My mom died in an accident when I was a kid."

"That's awful. I'm sorry."

Lane nodded and ducked into the vehicle, trying hard not to clench her fists and grind her teeth.

Nervous violins sang from the speakers, and Lane commiserated, but the song ended as they pulled away from the curb. The DJ started in on the pledge drive.

Abe grumbled and switched to CD. The sticky sweet beat of a boy band assaulted them. Lane covered her ears and he switched the stereo off. "Sorry," he said. "Gretchen's."

"Surely you can hook your phone up to this thing," Lane said, spying a dock.

"I always forget about that."

At the next stop sign, he dug his phone out of pocket and handed it to her. "Have at."

She found his music app and scrolled through the selection. "All you have on here is Mozart and David Bowie."

"I use my phone for work."

Lane chose *Ziggy Stardust*, because it was from the year Abe was born.

"You know we have the same birthday?" he said.

"Your birthday is on Valentine's Day too?"

"No. Me and Bowie. January eighth."

"That's cool. Sharing your birthday with a legend."

"Not as cool as Valentine's Day. That's one of my favorite holidays."

"I hate it." She curled her lip, and he laughed before turning serious again.

"Tell me more about you and your family. I just realized I know nothing."

Lane explained that her mother had been a teacher, killed when Lane was twelve. Her dad still lived in a small town in western Missouri that Kansas City was eating away at. He was a carpenter and worked all the time. They got along, but he was too distracted by his new girlfriend to call often. She had two older siblings, Pete who was four years older than Lane, and Meredith, who was six years older. Both lived out of state with their families, but they all came back to her dad's for Thanksgiving and Christmas. Without their mom there to hold them together, they'd all sort of drifted into separate lives.

"Sounds like you're pretty much on your own."

"I have Celia," Lane said with a shrug.

"That's not enough."

"What about you?" she asked. "You have Gretchen, who's what, sixteen?"

"She turns fifteen next week."

"You two seem close."

He explained that Gretchen lived with her mother, but she spent Sundays with him, so he did what he could to make them count. Gretchen was a freshman at the Catholic high school, and was a good student, but lazy in math. She kept a blog he pretended not to know about, and she wanted to be a lawyer when she grew up, but not because her parents met in law school.

"Then why?" Lane asked.

"I asked her that once," Abe said. "She said she thinks it's the best way to help people, but I didn't press her for what she meant by that."

"Sounds like an ambitious kid."

"That she does get from her parents."

Abe pulled up in front of the burger place near the local university, the one with the ping pong bar. The interior was hardly more than concrete and bar stools with loud music. It was the last place she'd expected him to take her.

"Is this okay?" he asked when she stared at him instead of getting out of the car.

"It's great," Lane said. "I didn't think you would like it."

"Good food, good beer. What's not to like?" It was the awful slogan the bar used in their radio commercials. Abe mimicked the voice over work perfectly, and Lane couldn't help her laugh.

The line to order was long, and while they waited, he told her about his dad, who'd moved back to the east coast after his mom had died. They'd lost her to cancer five years ago. "That was one of the hardest years of my life," he said, "and I was thirty-seven. I can't imagine what it was like to grow up without a mother."

"You get used to it. It's harder losing a child."

She hadn't meant to say that. The words had spilled past her lips without her permission. Lane winced at herself. Partially because she never talked about it, not even with

Celia, and partially because it was the worst thing she could bring up on a first date.

Abe stared down at her, his parted lips unmoving. She'd startled him into speechlessness, likely a first for him.

Wrapping her arms around her stomach, Lane said, "So now you know that happened."

Abe's knuckles grazed her arm before falling away. "Tell me."

"After we sit," Lane said. Then, to ease the intensity she could feel from his eyes as he reevaluated her, Lane stood straighter and forced her arms down by her sides. She tried for a breezy, unaffected tone when she asked, "What kind of beer do you drink? Something expensive and pretentious?"

"I like to support our local breweries," he gave her a little grin as he followed her lead. "Is that pretentious?"

"In an insufferably hipster way."

Before he could protest, it was their turn to order. Abe ordered an expensive sour—sixteen dollars a glass expensive—to go with his cheeseless bacon burger. Lane stuck with her trusty wheat beer and a cheeseburger she wasn't sure she would have the appetite to start.

Abe led her to a booth. He took an experimental sip of his beer then asked, "When did you lose your child?"

Lane shifted her feet against the cement floor. "Five years ago. He was stillborn."

"You were so young."

"I was twenty-two." Lane sat on her hands to keep from picking at her fingernails, and made herself meet the sympathetic look in Abe's eyes head on.

"When I was twenty-two, I was skipping auditions in Tokyo to go hiking outside the city."

"Might explain the discrepancy in our maturity." Lane knocked him on the shin with her toe.

He grinned at her, just for a second before settling back down into sincerity and concern as he feet settled between hers beneath the table. "Someone so young shouldn't have to carry so much."

Lane shrugged.

"You had to do it all by yourself."

"I was married."

"But it wasn't a good marriage, I don't think."

Lane spun her beer on its coaster. "No. Losing Silas was the beginning of the end."

"And you've been on your own ever since." Abe hooked one of her fingers from around the glass and pulled her hand into his. His coffee colored eyes reflected her sorrow back on her. His hand was rougher than she expected, and she traced a callous on his palm with her thumb.

"I keep busy," Lane said. "I feel better that way."

"Tell me," he said again.

Lane told him that she missed Silas every day, that she hadn't been trying to get pregnant, but that she'd hoped having the baby would make things better. When she'd lost the baby during labor, an unforeseen complication they said, and didn't want to try again right away, she lost whatever was left of the connection she'd had with Brad. The more she drifted, the more he tried to control her, so she left.

It wasn't until Abe squeezed her hand and made a shushing noise that Lane realized she'd been trembling. "And then you put yourself through school," he kissed her knuckles, but whatever other words were on his lips stalled when the kitchen called their order.

"Don't forget the extra pickles," she said, and he flashed her another grin as he stood.

Lane fortified herself with a sip of her beer as Abe returned with their food and a to go box full of pickle spears.

"What did you do, bribe the cooks?"

"Never be surprised at what a generous tip will get you."

"Damn, and here I thought I was special."

"You are," he smiled and offered the pickles. "I tip you most."

"Then it is a strategy to get in my pants?"

A slow smile spread over Abe's lips, but he kept his eyes on his burger as he added mustard to the bun. "I'll admit to wanting to make sure you remembered me. How's that?"

"Honest enough," Lane said. She let him take a few bites of his burger while she pushed her fries around her basket with the end of her pickle. Then, when he paused for another gulp of beer, Lane asked. "So, what happened?"

His mouth still full, he raised his eyebrows in question.

"With your ex-wife. I told you about my divorce. It's your turn."

"Ah, that." He took another long drink. "She had an affair with a colleague."

"Tell me." Lane echoed the simple way he'd inquired about Silas.

Between bites, he told her the story of coming home one night to find Roxanne in bed a guy she worked with. He explained that the divorce had been messy and long, and how she'd won custody of Gretchen and their house. She still lived there, married to the guy she'd been sleeping with. They had two boys together now. He told Lane it took him two years to feel like himself again. When he decided it was time to start over, he did so from scratch. He bought a dilapidated farmhouse west of town and had been renovating it himself for the last ten years. Abe's eyes lit up as he told her he'd only lived with subflooring in the kitchen for two years because he hadn't been able to make his mind up on tile and had eventually gone with hardwood. Or how he'd slept on a futon in his living room while he'd built his bedroom, and he was still getting used to his new mattress.

"How far west of the city?" Lane asked when he paused.

"Dover." It was a small town that hugged I-70.

"You drive across the county just for coffee?" Lane asked. Cristo's was on the southeast edge of the city.

"To get coffee from you," he said.

"You must really like me."

Lane had been teasing, but Abe reached across the table to smooth her bangs out of her eyes. "Glad you're getting the picture."

When he tried to cup her chin, she leaned back, out of his reach. "Aren't you afraid we'll argue all the time?"

"Isn't that part of the fun?"

"I'm serious. We have nothing in common."

"Because you want to raise taxes?" It was an old joke from when they'd first met, and he'd discovered she was liberal. She'd never taken the bait before, but tonight, she would bite.

"I don't want to raise taxes. I do think it's bad policy to force women to have babies then shame them for applying for help when they can't afford to feed and clothe their kids on crap wages, and to cut funding to education every year, so that by the time these kids get to school, there's nothing there for them either."

"But without tax incentives to attract large businesses to the state, they won't have the revenue to pay for any of that so-called aid."

"Tax incentives and no taxes are two different things," Lane said. "No taxes from the large corporations means Kansas doesn't have the money to pay for anything, and next thing you know, the Republicans will be wanting to raise liquor taxes again, and you'll have every grocery and liquor store in the state pounding on your door wanting to know what you're going to do about it."

Abe smiled. "They already are."

Abe worked for the liquor lobby, coordinating with grocery stores that wanted to expand liquor laws in the state so they could carry more than 3.2% beer. His work had brought him out to Cristo's for the first time. Because Lane's boss also owned the liquor store next door, the law prevented him from serving alcohol in the coffee shop. Randy was in the unique position of being a small business owner who might benefit from changing the laws, while most liquor store owners were afraid the huge chains would put them out of business.

"What are you going to do about it?" Lane asked.

"Same thing I tell my clients to do, wait and see how the election comes out."

"Please, let's not talk about the election."

"I think we've been doing pretty well so far."

"Our politics wasn't what I meant when I said we had nothing in common," Lane said.

"The race thing?"

"You really think that would be a problem after Labor Day?"

"The age difference then."

"I don't think you're that much older than me."

"I know several people who would disagree."

"Are you one of them?"

"Some days." He leaned against the back of the booth, dropping the last bite of his burger into the basket. "Whatever you think of me, I've never dated anyone so much younger."

"And whatever rumors you've heard at Cristo's, I've never dated an older man, but it doesn't mean I think it's a big deal."

"Then what are you worried about?"

"The money thing."

"What money thing?"

"You can't tell me you haven't noticed that we're from two different social classes."

"Is this where you tell me we can't be in a relationship because you're just my barista?"

"No," Lane said, wiping the salt from the fries off her fingers. "It's where I remind you that you have money and I really, really don't."

"I already know you won't tolerate me buying you much more than dinner."

"Good," Lane said. "As long as you know I don't want your money and you don't try to give me any, we're good."

Abe laughed. "Darling, I think we're going to be just fine."

"Darling?"

"You don't like it?"

He didn't pronounce the word like the men Lane had grown up with. They had always said it in a condescending way, leaving off the "g" like they were cowboys and she, their darlin', was the little woman. When Abe said it, she could hear the hint of New England in his voice.

"I feel like you've had a crush on me a lot longer than I realized."

Abe smiled and drained his beer. "You want to play ping pong?"

"Only if you don't mind a girl kicking your ass," Lane said. And her ruse lasted until she was standing at the table, paddle in hand, Abe waiting for her to serve.

"Okay," she said. "You got me. I have no idea how to play this game."

Abe tried to teach Lane how to play, but after an hour of her embarrassed giggles and him chasing after her bad shots, she'd had enough. They gave the table up to some college kids and retired to the bar. Lane leaned with her back against the bar, sipping her club soda. She watched the fluid game the new guys played, wondering if she'd ever be able to follow the ball and wield a paddle at the same time. Abe chatted with the bartender about the brewery in the western part of the state as he tried their new beer.

A red-haired guy broke away from the pool table and hovered nearby. Lane was aware of his presence but pretended she didn't see him. When he hadn't moved after a full minute, Lane chanced a glance to her right. Sure enough, his eyes were roving over the curve of her hips. She scowled when he noticed her attention was on him, and he gave her a wink and a grin she took to mean *in a minute, sweetheart.*

Then he stepped up and clapped a hand over Abe's shoulder and said, "Hey, Mr. Fujikawa, sorry things didn't work out with your waitress."

Abe turned around, a smile on his face. "Hey, Chester." He shook his hand. "What are you doing here?"

Chester gestured toward the pool table. "The guys and I play pool on Thursdays. What about you? Drowning your sorrows?"

Abe's smile never faltered. "Just playing ping pong." He draped his arm around Lane's waist, pulling her into his side. "Chester, this is Lane." Chester suppressed a splutter. "Lane, Chester. He's the intern who picked up the sunflowers for me."

Lane wrapped her arm around Abe so she wouldn't have to shake Chester's hand. Abe's grip tightened like he was claiming her, and while the warmth of him made her stomach flutter, she pinched his side all the same. He didn't even have the decency to flinch.

"Thanks," she said to Chester. "It's nice to meet you."

Chester's eyes lingered over Lane's chest before he muttered a reluctant, "You too."

"Can we get you a drink?" Abe asked, and Chester's face turned to Abe before his eyes did. "No thanks. I should get back to my game, but it's good to see you," he said.

"Stop by my office tomorrow and we'll set a time to play tennis."

Chester's eyes bulged. "Sure. Thanks, Mr. Fujikawa."

"See you tomorrow," Abe said, and turned his attention back to Lane. He clasped his fingers around the swell of her hip and buried his nose in her hair, inhaling before kissing the top of her head as Chester backed away.

She scowled at him. "Wow, you're like, his sleazy lobbyist hero."

"The way he was staring at you was inappropriate."

"One could say the same about you trying to out-macho your intern."

"Didn't want the poor guy to embarrass himself."

"I can handle my own unwanted suitors, thanks."

A dimple appeared between Abe's eyebrows. "I wanted it to be clear that we're together."

"So you could blow him off without him noticing?" Lane would tease him about how sexist he was later.

"If I was blowing him off, I wouldn't have invited him to play tennis."

"You'd really play with him?"

"Sure," Abe smiled over at her. "But I wouldn't go easy on him."

"So, it would be a short game," Lane said.

"Probably."

"Did I smell good at least?"

"Like coffee," Abe said. "And flowers."

When he dropped her off a little while later, he opened the car door for her again, and held her hand on the way up the walk.

"Did you have a good time?" he asked.

"I did," she squeezed his elbow. "Ping pong, who knew?"

It was a beautiful night, crisp and clear and not too chilly for the end of September. The smell of the neighbor's spent charcoal hung in the air. A dog barked at them from a few houses away, and the wind blew fallen leaves across the sidewalk.

Lane could see Abe's smile illuminated by the porch light as he stopped in front of her door. A lock of hair hung over his right eye.

"We should do it again," he said. "Soon."

Lane turned to face him. "Use that phone number I gave you."

He released her hand and took hold of her hips, pulling her up against him. "I will." Abe stooped so he could reach her lips. It was a sweet kiss, soft, a little lingering, but not too long.

"Do you want to come in for coffee?" Lane asked.

A new grin broke over Abe's face, smug and wolfish. He kissed her again, more boldly than before, his thumb tracing the line of her hip through her clothes until Lane had to pull back to catch her breath.

"Not tonight," he said. "I'm trying to convince you I'm not as sleazy as you think."

Abe smoothed her bangs out of her eyes, kissed her a final time, then left her standing on her porch, clutching a box full of pickles.

Chapter Seven

Desire interrupted Lane's sleep that night. She kept feeling the pressure of Abe's hands on her hips, the softness of his lips against hers, the sturdiness of his body as he held her. She dreamed he'd come in, that he'd undressed her laid her back on her bed. That he'd covered her in kisses while he grasped her hips and drove deep inside of her. The fantasy lingered for a few minutes after she woke up. Lane rolled over in bed, clenching her thighs together, hoping to minimize the ache she hadn't expected to feel.

All day Lane flitted from one project to the next, unable to concentrate on one thing at a time. She trimmed her *yunomi* and glazed the bowls that sold well in her Etsy shop. She wove, she spun, she sketched out a lace shawl design, but didn't spend more than an hour on one thing, alternating between smiling to herself as she remembered Abe's kisses and fretting about what to do when Shawn arrived.

• • • •

DINNER WAS READY AT midnight. Lane heard Shawn's car, and met him on the front porch, pleased to see he'd brought wine with him from work. He was clean shaven again, but his blonde hair still curled out against the edges of his cap.

Lane wrapped her arms around him and greeted him with a kiss, to see if he still heated her in the same way after kissing Abe. Shawn was warm and familiar, and his heat was just contagious enough that Lane was glad the night she'd been looking forward to for two weeks had come.

"Hey, gorgeous," he said, and continued to kiss her until they were both breathing heavy in the chill midnight breeze. "It's good to see you too," he said.

"Come inside."

He followed her into the kitchen. "It smells amazing in here."

"That's because I am a phenomenal cook," Lane said, even though pasta and garlic bread were easy. Lane pulled a plate of cheese and olives out of the fridge set it on the counter next to the sunflowers.

"You wanna do the honors?" Lane held out the corkscrew for Shawn, who already had a handful of olives.

"The flowers are nice." Shawn's mouth was full as he spoke. "You didn't have to go to so much trouble."

"I didn't. Those were a gift."

"From whom?" She resented the fact that he wanted to know, but she'd promised herself she wouldn't lie to Shawn about this, not like he did to her.

"Abe Fujikawa," Lane said. "You've seen him before, at Cristo's."

Shawn thought for a moment, then his eyes narrowed with recognition. "That Asian guy with the suits?"

"Yeah."

"Isn't he like fifty?"

"Does it matter how old he is?"

Shawn shrugged in response, still popping olives into his mouth. "So, why's this guy sending you flowers? He think he have a chance or something?"

"Would it bother you if he did?"

"It might if I thought you were interested."

"I might be," Lane watched for his reaction. "He took me to dinner last night."

Shawn bristled and crossed his arms. "Do you like him?"

"Yeah," Lane said. "He took me to the Pong Bar, if you can imagine that."

"He wants you to think he's cool. Distract you from how old he is."

"Abe is cool," Lane said. "I had a good time."

"What, so you're fucking this guy now too?"

"Sha-awn!" Lane snapped at kitchen towel at him.

"What the hell else am I supposed to think?"

"Not that!"

"Then why are you telling me?"

"I'm trying to be honest."

Shawn's shoulders relaxed. "I thought you didn't date."

"I didn't, but Abe's been asking, and I thought why not?"

"What about me?" He asked.

"We're not dating," Lane said.

"That's been established." A hard edge had crept into Shawn's voice, because they'd had this conversation before.

"Then, what's your question?"

"You know what, nevermind. Go out with whoever you want."

"I don't need your permission."

Shawn uncrossed and crossed his arms. "You know he buys like hundred-dollar bottles of wine to impress women with,"

"Is that a bad thing?"

"It's a thing sleazy guys do to get girls into bed."

"How much did you spend on this?" Lane asked, picking up her glass and took a sip.

Shawn snorted. "Not a hundred bucks."

"I'm guessing the only difference is your budget," Lane said, unable to stifle a laugh.

He smiled and reached for her. "I don't trust that guy. He'll hurt you."

Shawn had wrapped his arms all the way around Lane's waist, pulling her close. His nose was in the crook of her neck, and he pressed his lips to the exposed skin next to her collar. He lifted her chin with a gentle finger and kissed her like he had at the coffee shop, short and sweet.

"Lane," he ran his fingers through her hair, brushing her loose locks away from her neck. Shawn never called her by her name and hearing him say it while he was holding her sent a shock through her like lightning.

She could feel the words she had wanted once upon a time building on his lips. But he never said them—just stood there holding her too long until the moment had passed. She wouldn't have accepted them anyway. She'd learned her lesson there a long time ago.

"I can take care of myself." She patted his side and pulled back.

He sighed and gave her some space.

Shawn refilled his glass and moved the wine to the table while Lane plated the food, working in silence because there wasn't anything else to say.

When the sound of their eating was too much for her, Lane asked, "So, how was work?"

Shawn talked about his shift most of the way through the meal, and by the time they were opening a second bottle of wine, it was like the tense moments in the kitchen had never occurred. When they'd finished it, Shawn led Lane to the sofa and pulled her into his lap. He ran his finger over the waistband of her jeans.

"Does this guy change anything between us?"

"I think he does."

"You're seeing him again?"

"I'd like to."

"Don't spare my feelings or anything." She tilted her head to the side, not sure which feelings she wasn't sparing.

"Is that why you don't tell me about any of the girls you sleep with?"

Lane felt Shawn tense beneath her. "How do you know that?"

"I'm not stupid."

"You've never said anything."

Lane sat back. "You were the one fucking around and I'm supposed to bring it up?"

"How was I fucking around?"

Lane slid off his lap. "You just admitted you've been having sex with other women."

"It can't be cheating if we're not together."

"Then why get all defensive when another man takes me out to dinner?"

"I never said I didn't *want* to be together," Shawn said. "This whole arrangement was your idea."

"That's not the way I remember it," Lane said.

"Then tell me."

"You were lonely after Stacey left, and you knew I didn't have anything going for me, so you took pity on me."

"Or maybe I was smart enough not to let you slip away."

"Then why aren't I the only person you're sleeping with?"

"You never asked me to be monogamous."

Lane threw her hands into the air. "That's because I know you can't be."

"Bullshit."

"Do you have a good example of when you have been?"

Shawn's lips formed a narrow line.

"I didn't think so."

"What about you?" he asked.

"I haven't been with anyone but you."

"You know there are rumors about you and your counter guys." Shawn stood too close, his hard gaze accusing.

"Rumors."

"Not just rumors anymore, though, are they? You're seeing one of them now."

"One date with Abe is not the same as juggling six or seven men."

"Why do you want to go out with any of them? Am I not good enough for you?" His question would have sounded more sympathetic if her if he didn't look like he wanted to punch something.

"I want to have a real relationship someday."

"Gaa!" Shawn roared shook his balled fists at the ceiling. "God, you so fucking infuriating!"

"You think after all I've been through that I don't deserve that?"

"Here it goes, Lane's sob story," Shawn said. "My husband was an ass hole, boo hoo."

Lane wanted to slap him. "That is the worst thing you have ever said to me."

"You act like you're the only person who's ever been in a bad relationship."

"You have no fucking clue who I am."

Shawn shook his head. "Gorgeous, I know you better than anyone."

"Bullshit," Lane said. She shoved past him into her bedroom, rifling through the bottom drawer of her dresser where she kept a photo album she never looked at, but couldn't bring herself to throw away.

"Here," Lane said when she returned to the living room, thrusting the photo album into Shawn's hands.

"What is this?" Though it was obvious enough. It was a pastel blue binder with a rocking horse and a rattle on the front could only be a baby album.

"Look at it," she said. "Every page and then tell me how well you know me."

He sat down and she circled behind him so she wouldn't have to see his face.

The photo album had been a shower gift from her former mother-in-law. It was filled with snapshots of Lane during her pregnancy with plenty of blank pages for once the baby had arrived. The second to last photo was Lane at thirty-six weeks, sitting in the rocking chair in the nursery, folding baby clothes. The blanket she had woven lay folded over the crib railing to her left, the teddy bear they had picked out on the changing table to her right. She smiled at

Brad behind the camera. That other Lane looked happy. She wasn't, but she could have been.

There was only one photo after that. It was a black and white picture of a newborn the hospital had given them. Printed underneath was his name and birth stats. Lane had them memorized.

Silas Benjamin Schultz, July 14th, 3:48 pm, 7lbs 14 oz. 21 inches. Born Sleeping

Those words still infuriated Lane. Her son was dead. He was born dead.

Shawn stared at the photo for a long time.

"Your baby was stillborn?" He asked.

"Yeah."

"Why would you keep that from me?"

"I don't talk about it much."

Shawn faced her. "You could have told me."

"I couldn't," Lane avoided his eyes. He embraced her anyway.

"Why?"

Tears pinged in the corners of her eyes. Lane wasn't sad anymore. She was angry at herself for telling him, furious at him for being kind now.

"Because giving you that much of me was like admitting I thought we had a future together."

"But we could have a future." He held her so tight she couldn't breathe. "I don't want to lose you. Lose this." He pushed her shirt up, his hot hand searing the skin on her back.

"This is it, Shawn. No more," she said against his lips as her fingers unfastened his belt.

• • • •

THE SUN WOKE LANE. She was still on the living room floor with Shawn's arm draped over her bare waist. His fingers danced over the skin on her tummy. She rolled into him, his skin molten even in the chilly morning air. He reached back and pulled the throw off the sofa, covering her with it.

"You're awake."

"Mostly." Lane kept her eyes closed. Her head pounded from too much wine.

"I have to go soon," he said. "I have work to do at home, and I have to be back at the liquor store at three."

"Sure, I've got work too."

"You're not awake." He kissed her forehead.

"Sure, I am," she said.

Shawn smoothed her hair out of her face and ran his fingers from her jaw, down her neck to the tip of her shoulder and back again. She shrugged her shoulder to shake him off.

"I think we should make it official," he said.

"Make what official?"

"Us. You and me."

"Don't be stupid." Lane opened her eyes and rolled away from him.

"Why is it stupid?"

He sat up and Lane followed, covering herself in the blanket.

"Do you not remember the huge fight we had last night?"

"I remember it ending pretty well." The corner of his mouth pulling up.

"Everything is not magically better because we fucked." Lane spied her jeans and her bra around the corner of the sofa and reached for them.

"You finally opened up to me."

"I only showed you that photo album so you'd know how much of a dick you were being."

"I was trying to tell you how I feel about you, but you wouldn't listen."

"So you insult me? Do you know how much work it took to just function after my marriage ended?"

"No, I didn't know, because you never told me the whole story." Shawn fumbled getting his t-shirt over his head in his frustration. "I'm sorry," he said. "I'm sorry your baby died, and I'm sorry your ex was a douche, but I still don't see why that means we can't be together." He crushed his hat down over his hair and stopped in front of her. "What else aren't you telling me?" He reached for her face, but Lane leaned away, and he dropped his hand.

"Nothing."

"You belong with me."

"You're only saying this because you think you have competition," she said.

"I do have competition," Shawn said. "that fucking yakuza thinks he can steal you away from me."

"I'm not a thing," Lane said. "I can't be stolen."

Shawn rolled his eyes. "All I'm hearing is that you want to see this guy again, and you want me to be okay with it."

"You see other people all the time!"

"I can stop."

Lane collapsed onto the sofa, covering her eyes. Her head was pounding. She wanted to go back to bed. "No, no, no, no, no, no, no," she said.

"No?" He was on his knees in front of her.

"Stop promising me things," she said. "You don't even know what you want right now."

"And you do?"

"I know I'm not going to say I'll be in a relationship with you when I think you're acting out of jealousy."

"What can I say to make you believe me?"

"Nothing," Lane said. "It's over. I'm done."

Shawn sighed and checked his watch. "I have to go."

"Okay," Lane shrugged.

"Will you please just think about it?" he said.

"You too," Lane said. "Think about that yakuza comment and tell me in a few days you aren't jealous."

"Lane..." He reached out for her, but she dodged him again.

"Fine. I'll see you later." He let himself out.

Lane rubbed her eyes, poured herself a glass of water, and retreated to her room. She swatted the box of condoms off her dresser annd oto the floor before crawling back in bed.

Chapter Eight

L ane awoke to a voicemail from Abe.

"*I was hoping to catch you early enough to convince you to have breakfast with me, but you're probably already busy making more tea cups. So, even if we don't have a chance to talk tomorrow, I'm looking forward to seeing you then. Oh, and keep next Saturday night open. There's somewhere I want to take you.*"

What a cocky-ass bastard. Not once had he asked her if she wanted to go out with him, just told her when and where if she was free. She texted him as much. He responded by asking if she would like to go out to lunch.

> **LANE:** *Not today, Handsome. But I won't make you wait too much longer.*

Again, he responded immediately.

> **ABE:** *I'll remind you of that Monday when you tell me you're too busy.*

Lane laughed.

> **LANE:** *You mean you'll badger me until I feel sorry for you again?*
> **ABE:** *That's not why you went.*

A wicked grin split over her face as she typed.

> **LANE:** *Nope. It was because of your ties.*

ABE: *That's only marginally better.*
LANE: *Know anyone else who would recognize your sea blue grenadine tie?*

His last message filled her with warmth.

ABE: *See, we have plenty in common.*

The rest of the day, she expected her phone to light up again with Abe not taking no for an answer, but he didn't. The next text was from Celia, asking what she was working on, and if she wanted some company. Lane declined with the excuse that she was headed to the library.

At least once a month, Lane spent her Saturday afternoon at the library flipping through all the popular magazines. She looked for repeated colors and textures and fabric patterns in the ads to get a sense of what coming trends would be.

The new magazines were full of chunky scarves like the one Celia had sold. Except the one she'd made Celia was made from bamboo and silk and with crystal beads. It had been on her loom for weeks. Lane was still annoyed that Celia had sold her gift, but her big yarn order had shipped that morning. She'd ordered enough yarn to make Celia's scarf in eight different colors.

Inspired by Abe's messages that morning, she'd warped her loom with a thick white yarn she had spun out of alpaca and silk, planning to turn the intricate pattern from his tie into a woman's stole. The weaving would be laborious, but the finished piece would be worthy of the bridal magazine Lane was thumbing through.

Lane sketched out a few more ideas for scarves, mostly the triangular knitted kind she favored, but thinking into the looming winter, she sketched out some hat and mittens sets too. Celia wanted her to design knitting patterns to sell online, but Celia didn't understand that each pattern had to have a sample knit and photographed, as well as the pattern written and formatted to brand, then advertised. To Lane's mind, it was a lot of work up front for little pay off.

Celia had pulled up a graph and spouted some figures based on passive revenue streams, and Lane had tuned her out. While her friend was still working daily on their business plan and shooting Lane texts about storefronts and coffee and how to use Ravelry, Lane remained skeptical. Any business that rested solely on her creative ability was doomed. Too many early mornings and long days consumed with grief and worry had left Lane feeling old and tired.

Her two-hour mid-morning nap had helped after the late night. Though the headache from the wine still lingered behind her left ear, and the emotional exhaustion of sharing her grief two days in a row made Lane want to hide.

Shawn had behaved exactly as she'd expected him to, which was why she hadn't told him about Silas sooner. He still thought he could fix every problem with a good fuck. The emptiness, the fear, the grief that followed Lane daily were a mystery to him. He couldn't understand how often she re-lived that awful moment in the hospital when, instead of laying her baby on her chest, they rushed him to a table and gathered around him without a word to her. He wouldn't understand why she marked his birthday each year with a long walk. How she thought about what they would have done together that year had he lived. That she couldn't ride past the neighborhood elementary school without her heart breaking.

Before she'd told Shawn about Silas, that she was almost two years older than him had never mattered. She knew he'd had an easy life, his break up with Stacey his one difficulty, but she'd been attracted to his confidence and his dedication to his dreams. He'd allowed her to mother him, taking him shopping for clothes to wear when he taught and cooking him dinner. In return, he'd given her the physical tether she'd needed to survive.

The problem was, Lane woke up feeling like she'd aged fifteen years, and Shawn's renewed offer of monogamy wasn't what she wanted anymore. He'd told her what she wanted to hear, and maybe for a while he would do as he said, but in the end, she'd go back to being just one of the many. And he'd never noticed the urn on her dresser.

Chapter Nine

Lane had just closed the oven door on the day's first batch of cinnamon rolls when Celia knocked on Cristo's front door. She hopped from one foot to the other, holding her pink pea coat closed, as she waited for Lane to let her in.

"Oh my god, it's cold out there!" Celia's blonde ponytail swung as she danced through the coffee shop.

"You'd be warmer if you still had a scarf," Lane said.

"Next time I come over, I'll pick one out of your collection." Celia grabbed a mug from on top of the espresso machine and helped herself to a cup of coffee. It had become routine not long after they'd met for Celia to keep Lane company while she baked before Cristo's opened for brunch at ten. If Lane had found any of the other girls with a friend in when the shop wasn't open, she would have had a fit, but since Lane ran the shop by herself most Sundays, she allowed herself the indulgence. Otherwise, she might not see Celia until their usual Wednesday night dinner.

"You think I'm giving you another after you sold the last one?"

"Call it advertising." Celia grinned at Lane. "And I won't apologize."

"You could at least pretend you're sorry you don't have your scarf anymore."

"I loved it, you know that. But I'd been looking for an opportunity to help you out. When I saw it, I took it."

"Speaking of which, I read what you sent me. I'm not comfortable with you putting up all that money."

"You'll pay me back," Celia brushed her off. "How serious are you about the roasterie idea on your list?"

"You don't think it would be fun?"

"I think it would be blast, but what about your art?"

"Sell it in the front window."

"You wouldn't have as much time to devote to it as if we worked out of your house."

Relying on only her art to support them both terrified Lane, so she'd thrown something onto the list she *knew* she could make work. "I like working with people," Lane said. "I don't want to be cooped up by myself all the time."

Celia nodded, a too knowing set to her eyes, but said. "You make me a list of everything we'd need. I'll look into properties."

"I'll work on it tonight."

Lane worked in silence for a few minutes, listening to the rustle of the newspaper as Celia read and drank her coffee. Celia's phone pinged and she giggled. It was strange for Celia to be so cheerful on a Sunday morning. Usually she came in grumpy and frustrated after drinking too much at Lustrio as she tried to get Michael to notice her. This morning she didn't look hungover at all.

"Why are you in such a good mood?" Lane asked. "You've missed three opportunities to tell me I'm not living up to my potential."

Celia broke into a grin. "I got lucky last night."

Lane spun around from beating eggs, clapping her hands around the whisk. "You got Michael into bed?"

"Oh God no."

"Then who?" Lane frowned.

Celia turned the page of her newspaper and wouldn't meet Lane's eye. "Andrew."

"Who the hell is Andrew?"

"You remember the accountant I told you about? The one I met at Lustrio?"

Lane nodded.

"He was there again last night, and I sat next to him again to pick his brain and he bought me a couple drinks, and he has a fantastic apartment downtown, and oh my God," Celia giggled. "It was good."

"You slept with your accountant?"

"Not my accountant, just an accountant."

"Not the type of guy you usually go for," Lane said, imagining a delicate-looking pale man in a purple polo and khaki pants next to Michael with his unruly hair and tattoos.

"Nope," Celia said, "but I don't even care."

"Are you going to see him again?"

Celia's smile melted as fast as ice in hot coffee. "I don't want to talk about it."

Lane shrugged and turned back to her scones. She wouldn't press it. Celia hadn't had a long-term relationship since her sophomore year of college, and even that had only been six months long.

After a few minutes of silence Celia said, "A little birdy told me you've been quite the busy bee this weekend."

"I've been weaving," Lane said. The white stole was just as complicated as she'd expected it to be, and it had kept her from thinking too much.

"Shawn said you went out with both him and Mr. Fujikawa."

"When did you talk to Shawn?"

"When I stopped by the liquor store yesterday. He went on and on about how you were using Mr. Fujikawa to make him jealous."

"He would say that," Lane said.

"Does that mean Mr. Fujikawa showed up on your doorstep and swept you off your feet?"

"Not quite." Lane told Celia about how Abe had interpreted her instructions.

"Whoa," Celia said. "How long before you had his pants off after that?"

"I haven't slept with him," Lane said.

"Pity. How was the date?"

"He took me out for burgers and rolled up his fancy silk sleeves to teach me how to play ping pong. We had a good talk. He has no idea how casually he throws money around, but he was sweet. He walked me to the door and kissed me goodnight and everything."

"Are you going to see him again?" Celia asked, turning Lane's question around on her.

"He told me to keep Saturday free, so I guess I will then."

"But you slept with Shawn Friday night?"

Lane felt her cheeks turn bright red. "Not my proudest moment, but yeah."

"Why?"

"I don't know," Lane said. "Shawn and I had it planned before Abe even sent the roses."

"You could have canceled."

No matter how she put it, Lane looked bad, even though she felt innocent. "I still didn't know how I felt. Abe has been a pleasant surprise the past few weeks, and Shawn is so separate from any other part of my life."

"That's not how Shawn sees it," Celia said. "And I bet if you asked Mr. Fujikawa, he wouldn't see that way either."

Abe was one thing, but if Shawn saw them as more than what they were, he'd never said anything to Lane before she'd gone out with Abe. Since late last night Shawn had sent her three text messages, which was three more than she'd had from him in the six weeks since the semester started. He'd told her she was the most beautiful woman he'd ever met, and the strongest. He'd told her the other women had only been him biding his time until Lane was ready for something more. He'd told her that he missed her, that he couldn't stop thinking about her, that he was still working on her story. Lane hadn't responded, and she didn't mention them to Celia either.

"What did he say?"

"That he'd wanted you two to move in together, but now he has to wait for you to get Mr. Fujikawa out of your system—though the name he used wasn't half so respectful."

Lane scrunched her nose in distaste. "We have never talked about living together. We've never talked about anything."

"I never thought he was very bright," Celia said.

"He didn't listen to a word I said."

"Except when you spilled the beans about Silas."

Lane punched the scone dough into a disc. "I didn't want to tell him, but he was being such an ass."

"Does Mr. Fujikawa know?"

Lane nodded. "We were talking about our families and it just sort of came out."

"I think it's clear how you feel" Celia hopped off the counter to refill her mug. "And you should tell Shawn before he does something stupid."

Lane didn't bother telling Celia she was right, turning the conversation back to business planning instead. They discussed the best locations in town for a new coffee shop until the doors opened. Then, Celia slipped over to her favorite table in the back where she would spend the day drinking coffee and reading her newspaper.

Abe and Gretchen arrived at eleven and sat at the table in the front window. Abe winked at Lane when he filled his coffee mug, but every time she looked up, he was either joking with his daughter or hidden behind his newspaper.

By quarter to two, the shop was almost empty. Lane gathered her cleaning supplies as Abe approached the end of the counter.

"I didn't expect to see you up here today," she said, flipping an air pot around so she could fill her mug.

"Gretchen said it was all right if I talked to you about the symphony."

Lane peaked around Abe to see if Gretchen was watching, but the teenager was reading something on her phone.

"The symphony? Is that what's going on next Saturday?"

"It's the season opener," Abe pulled an envelope out of his jacket pocket. He was wearing a stone gray shirt under a black leather jacket, and Lane quelled the urge to stroke her hand down the buttery soft sleeve. "There's dinner before and a gala after. All the information you need to know is in here." He handed her the envelope.

"Sounds fancy," Lane said.

"A little bit. It's my favorite night of the year."

"That's a lot of pressure for a second date."

"Who says it has to be the second?" he asked with a grin. "There's plenty of time to make it our third or fourth date. If we try, we might even be able to make it our fifth."

Peaking around Abe again, Lane caught Gretchen staring at them. She'd expected Gretchen to frown and roll her eyes like usual, but she gave Lane a small smile instead.

"I'll give you Saturday night. We can talk about the rest of the week after I've looked this over." Lane tapped the envelope.

He stood back, pouting. "I'll see you tomorrow?"

Lane nodded. She'd always looked forward to Abe's visits, but she had also feared them. Keeping a barrier up against his charm sometimes left her with tight shoulders and a headache. Giving herself permission to feel again was liberating.

Inside the envelope was a schedule of events on symphony letterhead, including a note that the dress for the evening was black tie.

"A love letter?" Celia asked as Lane joined her at the little round table in the back. "What's it say?"

Lane handed it over. "It says I need an expensive dress by Saturday."

Celia read the invitation. "You do need a dress, but it doesn't have to be expensive."

"Black tie means floor length gown," Lane said. "Unless you have one I can borrow, I'm screwed." Celia was about as big around as Lane's thigh, so it was unlikely that Lane would be able to alter anything of Celia's. Maybe she could sew two of Celia's dresses together. That would be a look.

"You can sew yourself a better than any gown you'd find around here anyway."

"In a month, maybe. Not in a week." Though Lane was already planning what she could do with the supplies she had on hand. There was the black silk fabric she'd been saving since Brad, but she knew there wasn't enough of it. Gowns meant lining, and tulle, and maybe boning. While Lane could sew, it was more of a hobby than an expertise.

"It'll be great. You'll make a gorgeous dress, you'll look stunning on that beautiful man's arm, and you'll meet a bunch of people who will drop five hundred dollars without blinking an eye for a handmade stole like the one you'll be wearing."

Lane knew the stole Celia meant. She'd spent the last year knitting it in her spare time.

"So now this just isn't a high-pressure date, it's also work?"

"In our kind of business," Celia said, "we're always working."

"I'm not going to get anything done if I spend the whole week sewing a dress."

Celia tipped her champagne flute up and drained the last few drops of her virgin mimosa. "Yes, you will. You will have a dress you designed to show off at a fancy event full of fancy people with enough money to commission one."

"I don't want to be a dressmaker," Lane said. "But it wouldn't hurt to have a good dress or two in my portfolio."

"Now you're getting it. Never turn down honest money."

"Didn't you turn down an offer on that last house you're trying to sell?" Lane asked.

"That's because it was so low it was insulting," Celia said. "But we'll work on your undervaluing problem. Perhaps Mr. Fujikawa can help."

• • • •

PILOT PURRED ON HER lap as Lane sketched out a few ideas for her dress at her table later that evening. She'd pulled her bin of fabric out of the basement as soon as she'd returned home and found about as much of the black silk as she'd expected. She'd been thinner in that life. There was a huge amount of a silky black gauze that she'd purchased with the ambitious intention of designing a line of lingerie back when Brad was pushing her into starting her own business instead of going to school. The idea was absurd to her now, but she was grateful she had any materials to work with at all.

Two more texts had come in from Shawn as she worked. The first one had asked if he could come over. Lane told him not to. A second had come a few minutes later asking if he could call. Lane had asked him to accept that whatever they had been was done, and to please respect that. Just as Lane stretched and deposited Pilot on the floor, a third message pinged on her phone.

SHAWN: *I'll give you a few days.*

Lane tamped down her trepidation and outrage. Brad had never listened to her either, and she'd gotten out of that mess. She'd get out of this one too.

Chapter Ten

"**H**ave dinner with me."

Lane had been grinding beans and hadn't heard Abe approach, but when she checked over her shoulder, there he stood, leaning against the counter.

"I don't even get a good morning?" she asked.

"Good morning, darling. Have dinner with me tonight."

"You're one note today."

"I'd like to spend time with you someplace more private." As the door opened again he added, "And where I have your undivided attention."

Lane tsked as she handed over a mug and turned her back on him to serve the new customers.

When she had a moment, she said, "I can't go out to dinner because I have to work on my dress."

"You're making a dress?"

"Well, I didn't think flannel would be appropriate." She plucked at her shirt collar. His brow furrowed and his lips tightened as he realized *why* she was making a dress. Before he could say anything, she added, "Besides, it's what I do. Gotta put that degree to work somehow."

"It sounds selfish now to ask you to take a break for dinner, but I'm asking anyway."

There was a beat of silence as Lane waited for him to ask, and he waited for her response. Was he was making a point of not asking now?

"I've been to dinner with you, and it took four hours for burgers and beer."

"I'll set a timer for two hours," he said.

Lane shook her head. "I don't think you understand what a feat it is I'm undertaking. It'll be a miracle if I get it done in time, even if I eat cereal for every meal."

He sighed, his eyes on the counter. "I didn't mean to be a burden."

Lane patted his elbow and let him pout.

. . . .

ABE CAME IN EARLY EVERY morning that week, but it wasn't until Thursday that it was slow enough to exchange more than a few words.

"How's the dress coming?"

"Don't even talk to me about the dress." Lane fanned her face with both hands. "It's like I'm back in school, and it's time to turn in your final project, and you know it's shit, but it's all you have, so you make it work."

"That bad, huh?"

"It's not the design." Lane warmed his mug. "The design is solid. It's that I have to sew on a million little beads to make it work. I hate beads."

The lock of hair that sometimes fell into his eye was already escaping. "So, leave them off. No one will know."

"It needs them," Lane said. "It's what turns the dress into a gown."

"I've never understood women's fashion," Abe said as he sat down.

"It's okay," Lane reached out and tugged on his green striped tie, "Most men don't understand men's fashion either."

Abe caught up her fingers and brought them to his lips. "I always suspected you enjoy the way I dress."

"Your style is impeccable," Lane said. "But I've got a question for your lawyer brain."

"What about?"

She explained the business plan she and Celia were building, and her questions about the funding.

His grin faded as his expression turned thoughtful. "Have you talked to an accountant?"

"She's talked to two."

"I'm assuming she has this written out somewhere if you're applying for a loan."

"I can send you what I have," Lane said. "If you don't mind looking it over."

"Of course. How far are you guys into this?"

"We're looking at a spaces in the North Topeka Arts District Saturday morning."

Abe's smile was back. "You are exactly what NOTO needs."

"Don't get too excited before you read the plan," Lane said.

"Fine, but I'm glad you're looking into it." He stood to leave. "Don't stress out too much about the beads. It's supposed to be fun, remember?"

"I'll try," Lane said, but there wasn't any feeling in it.

• • • •

WHEN CELIA PICKED LANE up Saturday morning, Lane was so nervous her hands shook. She'd finished the dress around midnight. She would have had it done sooner, but she kept pausing to read Abe's email response to their business plan. He'd told her to go for it, that Celia's plan looked solid, and if they followed it, she shouldn't have any trouble making up her side of the money. He told her not to let the fear of not being able to pay Celia back keep her from pursuing her dreams.

It had only been a few sentences, but she had read them in his voice, and she had believed them. It had been a long time since someone other than Celia had believed in her.

In the cold morning sun, Lane was not as confident. What if they couldn't make it work? What if they opened a shop and then had to close it within months. There was no way Lane could pay back her part of the money. She'd have to sell her kiln and her loom, and all her other art supplies. Then where would she be?

Worse off than she was now for sure.

Celia, calm and cheerful, offered Lane coffee and a bagel, while they talked about espresso machines. By the time they met the realtor, Lane's panic had returned to its usual low level of constant anxiety, and the trembling had stopped.

The first two properties they looked at did nothing to allay Lane's fears. They were little more than husks that would take months of work and a larger budget than she and Celia had to rehabilitate.

The third building was nestled in between some of the more popular shops in the redeveloped district. Lane had to admit that it was promising. The outside had a worn facade with chipped yellow paint and white trim. There were two big front windows flanking the door, one blocked by a giant hand-lettered for lease sign.

The inside had hardwood floors that needed refinished but seemed sound. There was a nook in the front, right next to the window which was the perfect place to display Lane's work. A long counter already bisected the front of the shop, but they would have to extend it to make room for the roaster. There might even be space for a small oven. Turning in a circle, Lane could see the place coming together already.

"Some of the plumbing might need updated if you were wanting to open a coffee shop," the leasing agent said.

"What about storage?"

"There's a closet and an office, and there's a basement, just through here." The leasing agent lead them to the back of the shop where a set of rickety looking wooden stairs led to a cold, cobweb ridden basement.

"The basement would have to be finished," Celia said. "Is that up for negotiation?"

"I'll ask the owner," she said, and led Lane and Celia back up the stairs.

• • • •

AFTER FOOD TRUCK TACOS, Celia drove them back to Lane's where Celia painted Lane's nails and helped her get ready for the symphony.

"When do you think we could open, assuming everything goes smoothly?" Lane asked.

Since they'd left the third building, they had talked about it as if they'd already leased it, even though they'd looked at two more buildings, and had an appointment to look at a couple outside NOTO later in the week. Lane already knew what the space she wanted.

"As early as six to eight weeks. The basement work will take longer, but we could have our grand opening the First Friday Art Walk in December if we hustle."

"It will take me at least that long to make sure we're stocked." On top of selling Lane's work, part of the plan was to serve coffee in her handmade mugs.

"Get started on it, keep track of your receipts, and I'll come by to help while we fine tune things. And it would help if you quit your job."

"Quitting my job is scary. Wasn't it scary for you?" Lane asked.

Celia shrugged. "Not really. I'm more nervous about my date tonight."

"Andrew again?"

She nodded. "I don't want to talk about it."

Chapter Eleven

L ane was so excited about her storefront that she forgot to be nervous about her date. So when she opened the door at five o'clock, Lane pushed up on her toes and kissed Abe square on the lips. He hesitated before he leaned into her, his hands moving to her hips. There was whiskey on his breath, like he'd had a drink before he left home. Was the whiskey for his nerves? Or was that just the way he did things?

"Hey," Lane said, then stood back to let him in.

"Hello." Abe raised his eyebrows as stepped past her and into the living room. By the time she'd shut the door behind him, his attention had shifted from her to her home. She took a moment to admire him as he turned in a loose circle in her living room, his hands in his tux pockets. He was tall and his tuxedo made his shoulders look broader than normal, even if he still stood in his usual casual slouch.

Lane watched Abe realize she'd made each decoration—every painting, every pot, every pillow—herself. Pilot lounged on the back of the sofa, and Abe reached out a hand to scratch the cat behind the ears as if they were old friends. He smiled at Lane when he caught her staring.

"That was some greeting," he said.

Lane tried not to blush as she tossed her stole over her shoulders. "I can't be glad to see you?"

"You've barely tolerated me so far. I wasn't expecting a kiss."

Lane double checked her appearance in the hall mirror. She had her hair pulled into a sleek braided bun, pinned low. The sparkle of her nose ring echoed the flash of the beads in her stole and on her dress.

"I'm having a good enough day to admit I enjoyed kissing you last week."

Abe appeared in the mirror behind her, the light dancing in his coffee-colored eyes. He played connect the dots with the beads on her shoulder and asked about her day. Lane told him about the storefront she wanted while they drove. They were still discussing it when Abe pulled Lane's chair out for her at their table.

There were already two couples and a middle-aged gentlemen seated there. Glasses of water and goblets of white wine sat at each place setting. Lane was the youngest person in the group, though Abe was running a close second. One of the silver-haired men was staring at Lane's nose ring in disapproval.

"I'll bring all my clients in once you're open," Abe said.

"I'll give you a commission if you can sell one of my cashmere scarves."

Abe sipped his wine. "I'll trade you coffee for comm—"

"Abraham," a woman's voice came from behind them. "I thought I might see you here."

Abe wore a wide, beaming smile as he stood and faced the newcomer. "Nicole. How are you?"

Lane examined the stranger from her seat. She was both taller and thinner than Lane. She was about Abe's age. Her hair was elaborately done with auburn-dyed curls escaping to frame her face. She looked elegant as she smiled at Abe, but that smile faltered when he offered her his hand instead of leaning in for a peck on the cheek.

"I'm doing well. Keeping busy with the election," she said. "You?"

"I've got a few events coming up. How's Scottie doing?"

Her son, Lane guessed, or maybe her dog. She looked away from them, pretending not to eavesdrop. She gazed around the room, taking in the many bouquets of dark roses along the wall. The centerpieces were arranged of sunflowers and wildflowers, the same on every table. Most of the heads she saw seated around the tables were silver, interspersed with brown or blonde. Very few were true black, like Abe's hair, though one or two were close, with hair about the same color as hers. A soft classical piano played in the background.

"It's just Scott now. He's old enough to play football, so he couldn't be happier."

"Did he make running back like he hoped?" Abe asked.

Abe hadn't taken his eyes off Nicole's since she arrived. Only she held his attention as they spoke. His smile was large, his eyes bright, his charm in high gear as he inclined his head toward her. Nicole kept edging in closer to him, as if she expected to be embraced. As if she was used to having his arms around her.

They had dated then.

"He did, but he's not starting this year. Next year." Nicole captured Abe's elbow. "How's Gretchen? Do you still see her often?"

"Every Sunday. She turns fifteen this week and she's been begging me to teach her how to drive." Abe bumped into Lane's chair, and she almost slopped water down her dress.

"I hope she doesn't aim to learn in your car. It would be such a shame if she wrecked it."

Abe stood so close Lane felt him shrug. "Actually, I'd prefer her to do it in a safe car."

"Why would you want to risk that beautiful vehicle?"

Lane had to hold in a snort. Abe had just answered that question. Even though this woman was clearly an idiot, Abe still gave her his full attention.

"How else am I supposed to teach her how to drive?"

"What about that old truck you were always hauling tools around in?"

"That truck is filthy. Gretchen won't go anywhere near it."

"The house project is still ongoing then?"

Abe nodded as Nicole stepped forward, so that her nose almost met Abe's chin. "Speaking of, do you know what this fall weather keeps reminding me of?"

"It always makes me crave apple pie," Abe said, the soul of innocence in the face of her sultry tone.

"Silly." She giggled. "I keep thinking about that fireplace of yours." Nicole straightened Abe's white pocket square. "I've missed those nice, hot fires." The breathless way Nicole spoke left Lane in little doubt what had gone on in front of Abe's fireplace.

That was it. Done being ignored, Lane pushed back her chair and ducked under Abe's arm. He rested his hand on her waist and grinned down at her, delighted surprise in his eyes.

"Introduce me to your friend?" Lane asked.

"Nicole, this is Lane Benjamin. Lane, this is Nicole Meadows. She's the head of the governor's press office." Lane nodded at Nicole, doing her best to look impressed. "Lane's an artist," Abe finished.

Nicole's eyes flicked to Lane's nose ring. "Oh," she said, offering her hand. "What do you paint?"

Lane took Nicole's hand, determined to give it a good, hearty shake, but the other woman barely touched Lane's fingers before she withdrew.

"Silk," Lane said. "Sometimes wool. Sometimes porcelain. Mostly I make coffee for this guy," and nudged Abe with her elbow. He laughed, but Nicole's expression turned sour.

"You make him coffee?"

Lane nodded, "Every morning."

"Abraham always has been an avid coffee drinker."

Abe looked down into Lane's eyes, and she recognized him again. "Don't forget about breakfast."

"You're right," Lane said, even though he only rarely ordered one of the breakfast sandwiches Cristo's had on the menu. "How could I forget about breakfast?"

"What a lovely arrangement you two have." She pretended to notice something behind them. "If you'll excuse me."

Abe helped Lane back into her chair, chuckling to himself. He rested his hand on Lane's shoulder. "I'm sorry about that," his thumb grazed the neckline of her dress. Lane felt eyes on the back of her head and turned to look over her shoulder to find Nicole glaring at her from a few tables away.

"Don't pay any attention to Nicole, she's not very nice," Abe said.

"Are we going to be running into a lot of your ex-girlfriends tonight?" Lane asked.

Abe scrutinized Lane's frown, evaluating how much trouble he was in. "Can I thank you for saving me from her?"

"I would have done it sooner, but you didn't look like you needed it."

Abe was not apologetic. "I was being nice."

"You were being charismatic," Lane said. "And charming, even though you can't stand her."

"You don't think that degree in acting doesn't come in handy?" He lowered his hand to her knee, and Lane looked at his fingers. His constant encouraging touches were easier to endure than his ever-smiling eyes.

"I'm not impressed with Stage Abe. I can't tell whether he's sincere. Or how often he tries to pull that shit on me."

His tone was serious, his voice soft as he said, "I tried the first day we met. You saw right through it."

Lane remembered little about their conversation the first day he'd shown up at Cristo's. The expensive charcoal suit and red name tag had taken too much of her attention. She remembered not taking his flirtation seriously. He'd been trying way too hard to impress her dressed the way he was, which told Lane he was used to being around people in suits and not around younger women in red flannel.

"Too bad no one else can tell how full of shit you are," Lane said. Abe failed to stifle his laughter as the silver-haired men glared at them.

During dinner, Lane spoke to the middle-aged woman next to her about her recent trip to Germany to visit her son. The wife of the disapproving older man asked Lane where she had found her stole and Abe had encouraged her to pass her business card out to the table.

"That's not tacky?" Lane whispered in his ear.

"No. That's what events like these are for," he whispered back.

After dessert, Abe escorted Lane across the street to the concert hall and up the stairs to the mezzanine. They were greeted with glasses of sparkling white wine. Before Lane had a chance to even sample the wine, someone had called to Abe.

She met three staff members who worked for the same state senator, the director of the historical society, and the governor's campaign manager before Abe suggested they take their seats just to have a moment to themselves.

She was surprised when he led her to the balcony, but when Lane asked if they were good seats, he said, "You keep talking about elected officials like that, you're going to get me in trouble."

Lane shrugged and took her seat. It wasn't her fault the governor's campaign manager had asked her opinion on his candidate. She'd only been honest. "If he hadn't asked for my vote, I would have been perfectly polite. Did I embarrass you?"

Abe clasped her hand over the armrest and leaned in close. "I think you're brave," he said, and kissed her. She expected a gentle peck since the balcony was filling with people, but the kiss was hard, and a little too urgent for being in public, even if it was brief.

Lane didn't tell him that what he took for bravery was outrage. She liked that one of them thought her courageous.

The concert was better than Lane had ever expected it to be. Then again, the only thing she had to compare it to were her brother's highs school band concerts. Those had been full of ill-timed squawks and too flat horns. Here, Lane could feel the drums in her chest, and the vibration of the strings hugged her, the mellow woodwinds held her in their thrall.

Abe was rapt, closing his eyes sometimes to allow the music to wash over him.

When the show was over, the seats around emptied. Lane and Abe stayed seated until the balcony was empty. They didn't speak until they were at the car when Lane said, "Thank you for bringing me."

Abe kissed her again. This kiss was tender and slow, as if he was savoring it, like maybe he thought he might never have the chance to kiss her again.

"The party isn't over yet," Abe said. "This next bit is most people's favorite part."

The crowd at the party was thick by the time they arrived. A swing band played. A few couples danced, but most chatted with drinks in their hands. The networking that had started at dinner had picked up again here.

"Would you like a drink?" Abe asked.

"Gin martini?"

Celia had come by the night before and played bartender while Lane finished her dress. Lane had been most nervous about this part. She didn't drink often, and though she was sure Abe wouldn't have cared if she ordered a club soda with lime, she'd wanted to give cocktails a try. After sampling a few drinks, she decided she didn't like whiskey or vodka, and they settled on a gin martini.

Abe linked his arm through Lane's and led her toward the set of tall tables near the dance floor. Between the bar and the table, they were stopped six times. Lane met two legislators, an architect, a real estate developer and two fellow lobbyists and their spouses. Most of the encounters were short, claiming they only wanted to say hello, but after the fourth introduction, Lane realized that she was the attraction. Not that there was anything special about her, other than that she was Abe's date. It seemed Abe had a reputation of never bringing the same woman to the symphony twice. Speculating on who it would be each year had become an elite-set past-time.

The way each couple they met stared at her, had Lane guessing there must have been a pool, and all of them had lost. A chubby, unknown twenty-something in draped black silk was not who they had expected him to bring. Always happy to subvert expectations, Lane chose to find the confounded expressions amusing rather than annoying.

"I'm sorry about the interruptions," Abe said. "It's something of a joke I'm not married."

"Always happy to entertain," she said, unable to keep the sarcasm out of her tone.

He ran a hand down the length of her arm. "You look beautiful," he said.

Lane looked down at her dress. She'd made a sleeveless, short, form-fitting dress of the opaque black silk, then draped the gauze over it in a Grecian style, with sprays of beads at one shoulder and cascading down through the gathered fabric at her hip. It was the best thing she'd ever made, even if she'd almost gone blind sewing on all the beads.

"I like how the dress came out."

He leaned in closer, the ice in his whiskey clinking. "You are talented."

"And way too cool for all these people here."

"Too cool for me too. I confess, I've been hiding most of my nerdiness from you."

"I'm sure you've always been cool. I'll bet you were homecoming king."

"Remind me to hide my yearbooks from you."

Lane cocked her head, running her eyes from the top of his well-coiffed head to the tips of his shiny shoes. "What were you then?"

"An awkwardly tall, skinny Asian kid with thick glasses and shaggy hair."

Lane didn't hide the way her eyes roamed over him, trying to find the younger version of him. "When did you become you?"

"In my senior year of high school. I took my first acting class, and the teacher encouraged me to audition for the spring musical. I was Curly in *Oklahoma!*" Abe sipped his whiskey, a self-satisfied grin curling his lips.

Lane rolled her lips under her teeth to keep from laughing. "That is the nerdiest story I have ever heard."

"It was a life-altering experience."

Lane couldn't hold back her giggles. "Did you perm your hair?"

"Nah, I wore a cowboy hat."

"I'm sorry I missed that."

"Don't be, I wasn't that good."

"You're good at playing yourself anyway."

Abe laughed and drained his drink. "Dance with me."

"Okay, but I've never had a dance lesson in my life."

Abe ignored her and pulled her close. Lane did her best to follow his lead. After she stopped thinking about what she looked like and responded to the pressure of Abe's hand on her waist, she had fun. At some point, she forgot about everything but the way he held her, the subtle spicy scent of him, the smile on his lips, the whiskey on his breath.

When the band took a break, Lane sneaked out to the powder room while Abe braved the bar to get them something to drink. He was saying goodbye to another colleague when Lane returned. His eyes went soft as he held out a bottle of water. She prepared herself for him to say something sappy when a booming voice said "Abraham!" behind her.

Lane turned around to see a short, robust man with an auburn beard and wide blue cummerbund stride up to Abe with his hand out.

"Brian! How's it going? How's the campaign?"

"Fantastic, fantastic." Brian clapped Abe on the shoulder. "Would be even better if you decided to work on the side of small business come this January. You might be able to get some things done, you know."

"So you always tell me."

"I know, I know, you like where you're at." Brian spied Lane. "Are you going to introduce me to your lovely friend here?"

Abe stepped backwards to put his arm over Lane's shoulder and nudge her forward. "Brian, this is Lane Benjamin. Lane, this Brian Benton, Kansas House Rep for the 50th district."

"It's nice to meet you," she said, offering her hand.

He shook Lane's hand so hard she nearly bounced. "What do you do, Lane?"

"I'm an artist," she said.

"Ah, so you're a small business owner!" Brian said.

Lane didn't know how to answer, but before she fumbled all over herself like she had at dinner, Abe said, "She's getting ready to open a little shop up out North." Abe turned to Lane. "Representative Benton fancies himself the champion of the small businessman, which is why he opposes most of the work I do."

"Oh, Abraham, let's not bore her with talk about our work." He looked at Lane. "My wife has been admiring your wrap all night. Now, she's just stepped out to the ladies room, and I thought I might sneak over and see if you can tell me where I might get one for her for Christmas."

As Lane said, "It's one of my original pieces," Abe reached behind them for her bag, grabbed a business card from inside and handed it to his friend.

The representative slid the card into his wallet. "Fantastic. I'll call you next week. Now I better hop along before the missus comes back and catches on." He scooted off before Lane could say another word.

Abe was still grinning and laughing to himself as he turned back to the table and picked up his whiskey. "You should charge him double—triple what you would charge anybody else. Make him put his money where his mouth is and really support small business." Abe noticed Lane scowling at him. "Don't worry, he's good for it."

"You went through my handbag."

His face fell. "Getting in good with someone like him could earn you enough money to launch your own business without Celia's help."

"It took me a whole year to make the one I have, I can't get him one by Christmas and open my store at the same time."

"So he'll give it to her for her birthday."

Lane said nothing and looked at the floor. It wasn't that easy.

She felt Abe step nearer, he wrapped his left arm around her waist and pulled her to him, placing his right index finger under her chin and tilted her face up to his. His nose hovering over hers. "I didn't mean to offend you."

Despite her annoyance, she liked the way he held her, coaxing her out of her shell, the way he had on the dance floor. Abe couldn't have known the old hang-up from Brad, so Lane explained how he'd gone through her things, looking for hidden money.

"I'm sorry," he said. "It won't happen again."

Lane straightened his tie. "Remind me later, and I'll give you your own stack of business cards to give out to all your friends with deep pockets."

"That's my girl."

He'd referred to her as "His girl" when they'd spoken to one of his colleagues earlier, and Lane had told him she didn't find possessiveness attractive. This time, he had a wide, knowing smile on his face, so Lane pretended to be annoyed, and said, "There you go being possessive again."

"Aren't you though?" he asked.

"No," Lane said. Then to wipe the cheeky smile off his face, Lane pulled down on his lapels and brought his lips to hers. What she had meant to be a soft, short kiss heated as his tongue licked the seam of her lips, and she opened for him. His beard tickled her chin as he leaned into her. Lane grazed his lip with her teeth as heat pooled low in her belly.

"Whoa there, darling," he said, stepping back. "We're in public."

"Pooh."

"Do you want to get out of here?"

"What time is it?" she asked.

Abe checked his watch. "Almost midnight. You have to be up early?

Lane leaned her flushed forehead against his chest. "Not as early as normal, but too early."

"Then let me take you home," he said.

· · · ·

ABE HELD HER ARM ALL the way up the walk to her front door. They stood gazing at one another for a long time. The breeze rustled the fallen leaves. Lane shivered and the wind picked up the hem of her skirt, blowing it out behind her and waking them both from their trance.

She stood up on her toes and kissed him like she had at the gala, teasing him with her lips and tongue and teeth. She pressed her breasts into his chest, cursing the layers of fabric between them. Lane had been fantasizing about this moment for a week, but she hadn't been sure if she wanted to take this step until he moaned and dug his fingers into her hips. Then he exhaled as he pushed her away.

"I should go," he said.

Lane latched onto his shoulders, tugging him back. "You should come inside and help me out of my dress."

Chapter Twelve

Lane pulled Abe into her bedroom. She turned on the lamp, grabbed a condom from the drawer, and shooed the cat away. Abe sat on her double bed, slipped off his shoes and socks and tucked them out of sight. Lane kicked off her heels and stepped into his arms.

They took turns disrobing one another between fevered kisses: her shawl, his tie, her sash, his jacket, her overdress, his studs and links. Lane slid Abe's shirt down his arms and reached for his belt. Abe traced the back of her dress in search of the zipper. He placed kisses down her neck and across her collarbone until he found it, then pushed her dress to the floor. Underneath, she wore only a pair of black lace panties.

He ran his hands down her sides and up to tease her breasts. Lane moaned, her hands still on the heated skin of his flat stomach as he explored one breast with his hand while his tongue explored the other. Abe seemed content to play there all night, but Lane couldn't wait. The gentle tugs of his tongue against her nipple made her core pulse with need.

To coax him along, she slid her hands down his sides and worked his fly. Abe's breath hitched in his throat when she dipped her hand behind his waistband. He was smooth and soft and hot in her hand. Her insides jolted, as if they could fling themselves upon him. She wanted this man, and she wanted him now.

As if Abe keyed into her urgency, he stood and shucked his trousers to the floor, then laid Lane down across the bed and stripped off her lace. He kissed his way back up her body while she stroked his back. When he reached her lips, he gave her one final hot, brutal kiss before he sat back. Lane heard the crinkle of foil, and the next second he was filling her. The weight and heat of him was ecstasy as Lane met his first thrust with her hips.

But then he slowed down again, shifting his position every time she writhed against him, urging to him to move faster.

After the fourth time he shied away she whined. "Why are you teasing me?" Because she had expected more.

He chuckled against her neck. "Trust me."

"I'm getting impatient."

"What do you want me to do?"

Lane nipped his shoulder. "Just pound me."

"Not my style, darling." He shifted again, back and a little to the left, and Lane gasped and bucked against him. "There we go." He kissed her and rocked his hips faster as her breath grew heavy. "Better?"

"You are . . . an arrogant . . . bastard."

His lips twisted into a smile against her shoulder, but neither one spoke again until Lane clamped her legs down around his hips and let out a string of curses as she dug her nails into his back.

"Fuck, Lane," he said, and drove deep once, twice more before collapsing on top of her. "Holy shit."

She laughed and smoothed his hair out of his eyes. "I've been wondering what it takes to make you curse."

"You," his breath came in quick pants. "You are like fire."

They lay under the covers, their limbs entwined for a long while, her head on his chest, his fingers tracing designs over her middle.

"And you wanted to go home," Lane said.

"I didn't want to keep you up."

"Worth it," she said, snuggling into him.

"Your bed is soft," he said, "Like a cloud."

"It's ancient. The bed that gets passed around to whoever needs one. I'm burning it as soon as I can afford it."

"I like it," he said.

"Then you can have it."

"It's a little small." He stretched out one leg and his foot hung off the end of the mattress.

Lane giggled into his shoulder. "Guess I better keep it for now."

He was quiet for a minute, then said "I like your house."

"I love it here," she said, then told him how she and Celia had rescued her equipment from Brad's house and set up the ceramics studio in her garage.

"Can I watch you make your tea cups?"

"Some other time. It's cold out there, and the sooner we get up, the sooner you'll go home."

"I can't stay?"

Lane ignored the hurt in his voice. She longed to sleep curled up next to him like this. But she could already feel fear and uncertainty licking at her body like tongues of flame. She needed time to remember where he ended and she began. Even if was just a few hours. "I get up early, but that doesn't mean you have to."

He outlined her lips with his finger as if memorizing their shape. "You have worn me out."

"You should sleep."

"When can I see you again?"

"Celia and I are working on business stuff every night this week."

Tightening his arms around her middle, Abe said, "Do not make me wait another week."

"How about you come over after you drop Gretchen off tomorrow?" That crush of fear curled around her toes like embers igniting a virgin log, but she smothered it. "I have to work in the garage, but I could order takeout."

"I'll be there."

Lane yawned.

"I should let you get some sleep," he said.

They kissed goodnight on the front porch. She waited until his car was out of sight before going in to bed. When she turned her phone on to set her alarm, she ignored the voicemail from Shawn.

• • • •

CELIA KNOCKED ON CRISTO'S front door the next morning, and Lane scowled. Her friend beamed and bounced, while Lane grumbled good morning trudged back to her work, already behind.

"So, how did the big date go?" Celia asked as she poured herself a cup of coffee.

Lane groaned.

"That bad, huh?"

"No, the date was perfect. Fairy Tale. It was Cinderella, except I had to make my own damn dress."

"Then why so grumpy?"

"It went late, and there was dancing, and I'm tired and sore, and you are too chipper."

"You haven't read the paper?"

Lane hunched over her batter, her arms dangling at her sides. "No."

Celia opened the newspaper to an article about the gala. It was sprinkled with photos of important looking people but at the bottom was a photo of Abe and Lane kissing. His face was mostly obscured by hers, the light flashing in her nose ring. The caption read, "One amorous couple embraces after a dance."

Lane stared at the photo. "Can they even print something like that?"

"It's cute!" Celia said. "You guys are adorable."

"It's an invasion of privacy."

"You were the ones making out in public."

Lane grunted and returned to her cinnamon rolls.

Celia didn't speak for a while. Lane took sips of coffee and felt herself burn off the fog clouding her mind.

Out of nowhere Celia asked, "So, how was the sex?"

"It was only our second date."

Celia barked a laugh. "You are no prude, honey. Fess up."

Lane sighed. Celia was right, getting busy on the first date was Lane's M.O. "Fine. We left the gala after eleven, but he didn't leave my house until two. Happy?"

Celia clapped. "Yes! Tell me everything."

"Only if you help me catch up," Lane said. "It's your fault I'm so tired."

"How is it my fault?"

"You were the one commanding me to go out with Abe."

"I didn't tell you to stay up until two in the morning fornicating."

"If you want to hear about it, you have to bake."

"Fine," Celia grabbed an apron. "But I want every detail."

After reliving the symphony, Lane was back on schedule, and in a better mood. Celia loped away to refill her coffee mug and conveniently forgot to come back.

"How was your night?" Lane asked. "You had plans with Andrew, right?"

"He made me dinner."

"How's that going? And more importantly, when do I get to meet him?"

"I don't want to talk about it," Celia said.

"You guy have been out what, four—"

"Five."

"Five times in the last two weeks. That sounds serious."

"Still don't want to talk about it."

"I just told you about Abe's secret tattoo—" something in Japanese on the inside of his right bicep—"and I don't even get to know what Andrew made you for dinner?"

"He made pasta. Now, how are you coming on our logo design? I want to get business cards printed the second we sign the lease."

"You really aren't going to tell me about him?"

"No."

"Besides moonlighting for Lustrio, I don't even know what he does. He could be a secret agent or an assassin."

"Do you have a draft with you?" Celia asked.

Lane snorted and pointed with her spatula. "In my bag - the little sketch book."

Celia rummaged through Lane's messenger bag until she found the right notebook, and they never got back around to subject of Celia's new boyfriend.

When Abe and Gretchen arrived, Lane had trouble keeping a straight face. Each time she met his eyes across the shop, he would smile wide and Lane would blush as she remembered what he looked like from below.

It didn't take Gretchen long to catch on, and when she spotted Abe and Lane exchanging glances one too many times, she socked her Dad in the arm. He flinched and rubbed his bicep, the one with the tattoo.

At five til two, Lane was packing up, when she heard Abe's voice behind her. "You're not leaving already?"

Lane tied her scarf tight. "I'm beat."

"I'd apologize, but I'm not sorry."

"I wasn't complaining," Lane said. "Where's Gretchen?"

"She's outside trying out the cellphone lenses I got her for her birthday."

"Those things are so cool," Lane said. "I want some too."

"Perhaps Gretchen will share."

Lane grinned. "It didn't look like she appreciated sharing you with me."

"She was giving me a hard time, but she's fine with us."

"Good." She reached for his hand across the counter. "I'll see you later?"

"Definitely."

Outside, Gretchen stood next to Lane's moped, photographing the last leaf on the young tree Lane locked her bike to. Up close, Gretchen resembled her father.

"Hey," Lane said.

"Oh. Hi." Gretchen backed away from the moped. "This is yours?"

"Yep. Had it since I was eighteen." Lane started the engine. It would take a few minutes to warm up.

"Is it fun?"

"I like it. Most people think I'm crazy, but I hate cars."

"I can't wait to learn how to drive," Gretchen said. "Dad's going to teach me as soon as my mom takes me to get my permit."

Abe's Mercedes was two spaces over. "That's a nice car," Lane said. "I learned to drive in an ancient Buick with a stolen stereo and no air conditioning."

Gretchen made a face. "That sounds awful."

"It was a boyfriend's car," Lane said. "It got used for a lot more than driving lessons—but I probably shouldn't tell you about that."

Gretchen snickered. "Have you had a lot of boyfriends?"

"I went through them pretty quick in high school, but I've been a bit more serious since then."

"My dad goes through women like water." Gretchen crossed her arms in disapproval.

"I'd noticed. He used to tell me about all about it."

"And you went out with him anyway?"

Lane shrugged and tried to hide her smile. "I made him work for it."

"You really like him then?"

"I do. Does that bother you?"

It was Gretchen's turn to shrug. "He's been in love with you for ages. My mom thinks he's lost his mind."

"Because of how young I am?"

Gretchen nodded. "She saw the picture in the paper this morning and freaked out about what a bad example it is for a man his age to be sleeping with a twenty-year-old."

Lane cringed. Had her mom said those words to her daughter, or had Gretchen been eavesdropping. "I'm twenty-seven, if that helps any."

"That's how old my parents were when I was born."

"I know."

"My dad's never dated anyone younger before."

"And I've never dated anyone older, so it's new territory for both of us."

Gretchen looked skeptical and asked, "What do you want from him?"

"Nothing, really." Lane shook her head, admiring her moxy. "Well, maybe for him to let me pay for dinner some time, but I know he won't."

A small grin twitched at Gretchen's lips. "He's old fashioned that way."

Lane was about to make her excuses to leave when Gretchen asked, "Do you know what happened between him and my mom?"

Not sure how much of the story Gretchen knew, Lane opted for bare facts. "He told me she had an affair."

"She broke his heart," Gretchen said. "And he broke the windows out of Greg's truck."

"Oh." Lane's eyes bulged as panic ignited inside her.

"He didn't tell you that part, I guess."

"No," Lane sighed. "He sure didn't. Why are you?"

Gretchen ran her hands through her long hair. In the sun, the black strands had a hint of red in them. "Daddy likes to leave that part of the story out and pretend he doesn't have a temper." When Lane's eyes widened further, Gretchen said, as if she could see Lane's stomach twisting itself into knots, "Don't worry, that's not normally how he handles things."

"Oh," Lane wasn't sure if that was meant to be a reassurance or a warning.

"It's been a long time since he's been this happy." And Lane had the impression she'd passed some sort of test.

"I think he's lonely."

"He's not very good at hiding it."

"I see that too," Lane said. She adjusted her bag on her shoulders and held out her hand. "It's nice to officially meet you, Gretchen."

"You too, Lane." Gretchen gave Lane's hand one solid shake.

Chapter Thirteen

Abe arrived shortly after eight, arms laden with food and drink.

Frowning, Lane blocked his entrance. "I was going to order takeout."

"This is takeout." He lifted the bags for emphasis, then handed her one of the bottles.

"Sparkling apple juice?"

Abe ducked down, touching his lips to hers. "You're too polite to tell me you don't drink."

"Because I'm busy. I'm not a teetotaler or anything."

He pushed past her and unloaded his bags on the bar. "I also brought sake."

"Does that mean you brought Japanese food?" She hopped on her toes trying to see over his shoulder.

"It does. An off-the-menu special from a place where they can cook like my mom did." He turned around and scooped her into his arms.

"Sounds fancy."

"It is, but my mind's not on food."

"What then?" she ran a finger over soft hairs at the corner of his mouth.

Abe snagged that finger between his teeth, and heat blossomed in Lane's core.

"I have been thinking about you all day," he said.

"About me or about me naked?"

Abe feigned thoughtfulness, "Both. More the latter."

Lane giggled and wrapped her arms over his shoulders. "Last night was fantastic."

"You wanna do it again?" he asked, his hand already sneaking its way up her shirt.

"Fuck, yes."

• • • •

THEY LAY ENTWINED AGAIN afterward, Lane tracing the lines of his stomach as he inhaled the scent of her hair. Abe had retained what he'd learned about her body the night before, and there had been none of the awkward start and stop that had driven Lane crazy. This time, after exploring her with his tongue, he rolled her on top of him. After she'd sunk onto him, he'd positioned her hips so he hit that spot that made her breath come heavy. And then he hit it over and over again as she moved on him until she was screaming for him, and he cursed as he chased her over the edge.

It had taken them a few minutes to catch their breath, and they had been laying together in silence ever since.

"Did you work all afternoon?" he asked. His voice was soft, a whisper that nearly blended into the white noise of heater kicking on.

"I slept some," Lane said, "But not for long. You?"

"Gretchen had homework."

"Did she tell you we talked?"

Lane felt him nod. "She said she liked you and asked if I'd get her a moped."

"Would you?"

"No. Those things are death traps."

"Never going to convince me of that."

"Doesn't mean I'm not going to try to get you to give it up."

"Save it," Lane said, "I'll never own a car."

"What about the car you told Gretchen you learned to drive in? The one with no stereo?"

"Oh God, that wasn't mine. That was Derek's."

"Who's Derek?"

"One of my high school boyfriends. She didn't tell you?" Lane said.

"Tell me what?"

"My joke about how I didn't mind learning to drive in such a heap because we didn't just use it for driving lessons."

Abe remained quiet.

"It was funny," Lane said. "Girl talk. She laughed."

He sat up and pushed Lane away. "You told my daughter, who's turning fifteen on Tuesday, that instead of learning to drive, you had sex in the back of your boyfriend's car?"

"I didn't say we had sex," Lane said, but she knew that didn't matter.

"But you did."

"Of course I did. I was sixteen."

"Jesus, Lane." He moved to the edge of the bed.

"I wouldn't tell Gretchen that."

"But it's okay to hint at it?"

"It's not like it's a secret that teenagers have sex."

"Yeah, but there are ways to approach it that don't make it look like you encourage it."

"I never apologized for having sex then, I won't do it now."

"You think it's fine then? No problem?"

"I'm not saying it was responsible, or smart, but it was my choice."

Abe shook his head. "And if Gretchen came to you and told you she was having sex, what would you do?"

"I'd make sure she was on birth control and answer her questions, and then tell her to talk to you about it."

Lane couldn't see Abe's eyes in the dark room, but she could tell he'd rolled him all the same. "Wrong answer."

"That's all I wanted when I was that age," Lane said.

"You could have benefited from having a parent who cared about where you were and what you were doing."

"Do not judge my dad by my actions."

"And don't tell my daughter it's no big deal if she has sex."

"I wouldn't do that."

"You may as well have already."

"It was a joke, Abe. She knew it was a joke."

"It was inappropriate."

"So now I'm in trouble for wanting your daughter to like me?"

"If your method is suspect. Yes."

Lane curled in on herself at the edge of the bed. "When I was her age, I didn't listen to anyone, especially not my parents. I would have loved having someone like me to talk to."

"Gretchen isn't like you."

"And thank God for that," Lane said.

Abe scowled at her sarcasm, like he didn't understand his own double standard, but she kept herself on topic. "I'm just saying it's possible you can't give her everything she needs."

"That's my job," he said. His voice was clipped.

"You're delusional if you think you can give her everything."

"You wouldn't say that if you had kids."

Lane swallowed her breath like she'd been slapped.

She watched Abe's back go rigid as he realized he'd forgotten about Silas. He hadn't realized his words would cut so much deeper than he meant them to. It didn't stop tears from welling in Lane's eyes. She wiped them away before he could face her.

But he remained where he was, his back to her, his words still hanging in the air between them.

Abe broke the spell after a few heavy moments and reached for her, an apology forming on his lips. "Lane, I—"

Lane dodged him. "Fuck you, Abe." She was out of bed and dressing before he even turned around.

"Lane," he said, but his voice was weak.

"Like you're some shining example of chastity. Like your daughter doesn't know you've slept with ten women this year alone."

Standing to face her, he said, "It's not been ten." He pulled on his jeans slowly, like he'd had the wind knocked out of him. "Did she say ten?"

"Ten's my count, including me." Lane yanked her camisole down by the hem. "*She* said you go through women like water."

"Apparently you treat men the same way."

"I was an unhappy kid. It took me awhile to figure out that sleeping with boys wouldn't make them like me, but that doesn't give you the right to judge me for it."

"And you weren't judging me just now? You haven't been judging me for months based on the number of women you guess I've slept with since I've known you."

"The number has nothing to do with it," Lane said. "It's your attitude. You talked about those women like they were nothing because they didn't fit some magic criteria. I didn't—don't want to be that."

Still only half dressed, he fussed with his undershirt, searching for the neck. Abe said, "I don't think of women that way. I don't think of you that way at all."

"But finding out I was the school slut pisses you off?"

"Well, yeah. A little bit."

"Wrong answer."

She wanted to bolt. She wanted to race out of the house and ride her moped too fast until dawn. When she returned, Abe would be gone, but he was between her and the door. If she tried to push past him, he would take hold of her and try to calm her down.

"What's the right one?"

"Not calling a woman sleeping with someone who isn't you a slut for starters."

"Now you're putting words in my mouth."

"It's what you think," Lane crossed her arms.

Long, silent moments passed as they glared at each other in the dim streetlight filtering between the blinds. When Abe finally spoke, his voice was quiet, and his words were deliberate.

"I think you are a talented, intelligent woman, and that maybe you're picking a fight because something else is bothering you."

Lane stared at the wall over his shoulder, not wanting to admit that he was right. She wanted to tell him she couldn't date a misogynist and kick him out, but she caught her reflection in her dresser mirror. Her hair was a wild tangle. Her eyes blazed like a fire, and she wondered if Abe looked the same when his temper got the best of him. She didn't want to admit that what Gretchen had said to her had festered all afternoon, especially after their romantic night at the symphony. She hadn't signed up for another relationship based on fear and manipulation, and those flames of fear had been burning brighter all day.

"Why'd you beat up what's his face's car?" When Abe jerked back in shock, Lane added, "After you found him in bed with your ex-wife," in case he didn't know what she was talking about.

"Where did you hear that?"

"Gretchen told me." Lane's voice was smaller than she wanted it to be.

He swiped one hand through his hair. "You two had quite the talk, didn't you?"

"You left that part of the story out the other day."

"How I got arrested and lost custody of my daughter isn't a first date story."

"Why'd you do it?" Lane asked.

Abe's dark expression turned stormy, and Lane saw the lightning flash in his brown eyes. "Because I had just found him screwing my wife."

"Why not beat up her car?"

"Wouldn't have sent the same message."

"What? You mess with my property, I'll mess with yours?"

Lane thought maybe she'd crossed the line, that his temper would snap, and she'd see what he'd been hiding from her. She wanted to cross that line, to see what he was capable of before she got in too deep, but he let out a humorless laugh and shook his head.

"If you'd ever met Roxanne, you'd know how ridiculous it is to suggest that I could even pretend to possess her. You two have that in common."

"Then why?"

He sighed. "I don't remember deciding to do it." Abe gave up on his shirt, dropping it to the floor as he sat on the edge of the bed. "I went out on the porch to give them a chance to get dressed. To calm myself down, and that truck was parked right in front of the house. It was brand new. Immaculate. One of those giant, spotless trucks that only men who work in offices drive. I got so angry at that damn truck."

"You really got arrested?" Lane sat down beside him.

He nodded. "Roxanne's ruthless."

"That doesn't seem fair," Lane said.

Abe shrugged. "It's not."

"I'm sorry."

Abe cupped her chin, "Darling, it's not your fault."

"Still 'darling?'"

He looped his hand back into her knotted hair and kissed her like he was surfacing from a deep dive, and she was clean, bright air. "You're not going to scare me off with one little fight."

"These are the things I'm afraid we'll always fight about."

"I don't mind," he said.

"You don't think we're doomed?"

He brushed her bangs out of her eyes. "Are you going to be faithful to me?"

"Of course. Will you?"

"I will never lie to you, Lane."

"I'm a fan of honesty."

Abe kissed her forehead. "Good. Then we can work everything else out."

Chapter Fourteen

When Lane got off work on Monday, her euphoria at giving her boss her two weeks' notice was dampened by another missed phone call from Shawn. Before Lane could listen to his voicemail, a new text from Abe pinged, and she tapped that instead.

She and Abe had been texting all day. He'd started it by sending a photo of himself dressed for work, because she'd teased him the night before for wearing jeans.

"I wear jeans all the time," he'd said.

It had been almost midnight before they'd made it out to the garage. They had taken their time making up from their argument. Then, Abe had brought the sake out with them, keeping Lane's tiny cup filled, even though she'd only taken a sip or two between mugs.

"I've barely seen you without a tie."

Abe had cracked a joke about how she'd seen him without a lot more than that.

"You know what I mean." Lane had described how in her mind, he was always dressed like he had been the first day they talked: charcoal gray suit, sea blue artisan tie, and a cocky grin as he'd hit on her.

"I didn't hit on you," he'd said.

Lane had concentrated on shaping her mug while she'd tried to pull his exact words from her memory. "I asked if you'd come to talk to Randy about business and you gave me this lurid grin and said that I was the reason you were there, like you expected me to fall all over myself at the compliment."

Abe had shrugged. "Sometimes that works."

Lane had believed him. She'd had a hard time meeting his eye at first, thinking him far too handsome to look at straight on.

"I remember you calling me a cockroach."

"I didn't call you a cockroach. I called lobbyists cockroaches."

"But I am a lobbyist."

Lane has cut her mug from the wheel and prepped for the next without comment. Just because she was sleeping with him didn't mean she approved of his career.

"I said that before you tried to hit on me," Lane had said. "Didn't discourage you one bit."

Abe had refilled his sake cup, examining the server as he did so. It was stoneware with a blue and green glaze. Lane had made it in school. If Abe was surprised that she'd had the proper accessories for his sake, he never let on.

"You were gorgeous and a captive audience. You can't blame a guy for trying."

Again Lane had said nothing. All her counter guys shared that sentiment.

"I left you alone after you shot me down."

Lane had snorted at that. "If by left alone, you mean you pestered me five days a week for the next nine months."

It had been Abe's turn to sit silent. He woudn't to apologize for something he wasn't sorry about. When she's glanced up, he'd worn a contented smile as he'd watched her.

He'd worn the same grin in the selfie he'd sent her that morning. He'd dressed in a light gray suit and his sea blue tie. The caption read, *Better?*

Lane had responded in the affirmative, then reciprocated with a photo of herself smiling in front of the espresso machine.

Lane deleted Shawn's voicemail without listening to it, hoping he would get the picture and give up.

• • • •

AT THE END OF HER SHIFT on Tuesday, Lane was sweeping the floor when Shawn sat down at the bar. He was dressed in his teaching clothes, a tan checked button down shirt paired with brown khakis. The colors made his fading summer tan glow and matched his burnished hair.

"What are you doing here?" she asked. "I thought you had class."

"You aren't returning my phone calls."

"I've been busy."

"What have you been up to?"

Lane looked around the shop. They were coming up on the two o'clock lull, and the place was deserted. The only other people were Talia and her mom, plus their friends. They'd met a friend for a late lunch and both women were chatting on the sofa in the back while their children dozed on their laps.

Lane handed Shawn some coffee and filled him in on her latest developments with Celia.

"Were you working with Celia when I called you at eleven on Saturday night?" He asked.

"No," Lane said, "I was out with Abe."

Shawn nodded, as if it was what he expected. "I was hoping to come by yours then, so we could talk about us like we said we would."

"There's not much to talk about," Lane said. "We haven't seen each other in more than a week. And when I'm done here next week, we won't see one another at all."

"You're quitting?"

"My last day is next Thursday."

"How are you going to pay your bills while this new business gets off the ground?"

"That's part of what Celia and I are working on."

Shawn looked thoughtful for a minute and was about to say something when Lane had to help a customer. When she returned, she found him fidgeting on his stool, fists clenched on the counter in front of him.

"What's wrong?" Lane asked, but she knew. Lane hadn't been able to hear the conversation over the noise of the espresso machine, but she hadn't missed the way Talia's mom kept glancing from Lane to Shawn and back again. Of course she'd noticed there was something between them. And of course she'd let Shawn overhear one of her rumors. And of course she had to fucking be here now to witness this.

"You're sleeping with him, aren't you?" Shawn said.

Lane didn't answer.

"It's fine if you are," Shawn said. "We haven't made any commitments to one another yet."

"And we're not going to."

Shawn spun his mug in a circle on the counter. "He's not why you want to end things?"

"No," Lane said. "I can think of a million reasons why before I even get to Abe."

"Like?"

"Like how we never made being together a priority."

"We could move in together. Then we'd see each other every day."

"You want to move six months before you finish your MFA?"

"Why not? I meant to bring it up the night those damn sunflowers ruined everything."

Lane gaped. "Because you're applying for teaching positions all over the country, and I'm opening a business here."

"I can get a job within an hour of here."

"You know it's not that simple."

"You don't want me to move in?"

"No."

"Why not? We could be good together, Lane."

"I want monogamy, and that's something you can't give me."

"And you think this guy can?"

"This isn't about him," Lane said again.

"I can be monogamous," Shawn said.

Lane needed to leave soon. She was supposed to meet Celia downtown to fill out paperwork with a notary. Lane worked on tidying the bar, neatly folding the newspapers as she and Shawn spoke.

'I'm not sure you can."

"If I have the right motivation, sure I can."

"What motivation?"

"To make you happy."

"I don't think that's enough."

"And I don't think our story's over," he said.

Lane couldn't help the skeptical look that came over her face. Everything was a story to him. He was looking for symmetry and meaning when there wasn't any.

"I'm done," Lane said. "It's over."

"I would be a fantastic boyfriend."

"It's too late, Shawn."

"How can I prove to you it isn't?"

"You can't," Lane said.

"I can," Shawn pounded his fist on the counter, and Lane's eyes darted to Talia's mom.

"Whatever happened to that story about the girl with the nose ring who rides a moped?" Lane asked, more curious than anything else.

"Stalled at the climax," Shawn said.

"Is it a comedy or a tragedy?"

"You know I don't write tragedies."

"Maybe that's your problem," Lane said.

He reached for Lane's hand, keeping her stationary in front of him. "Are you being metaphorical?"

"The story is about me, right?"

"Of course."

"Then I'm taking myself out of it, and you can put whatever ending you want on it."

He let go of her hand. Lane gathered her things.

"You're leaving?"

"Yes," Lane said, taking off her apron as Allison walked through the front door. "Celia and I have an appointment downtown in twenty minutes." Lane tucked her scarf behind the zipper of her leather jacket, wishing that the weather was nice enough she didn't have to warm up her moped for so long.

Shawn followed her outside. "You're just going to blow me off?" Shawn's voice was composed, but Lane could see the stiff fury in his gait, the annoyance in his eyes.

"I don't know what else you want me to say" she said as she started her bike.

"Say you'll give us a chance."

"I've been doing that for the last year."

"So that's it? You're just going to be with that sleazy lobbyist now?"

"I've seen him more in the last two weeks than I've seen you in the last month," Lane said.

Shawn stood too close to her, grasping the zipper on her jacket sleeve. "I'll finish your story." His voice was hoarse and pleading. "I'll finish your story. And it will be sad and funny and beautiful, just like you like to read."

"That doesn't prove anything, Shawn."

"Just give me time to write it. Give me until your last day here, and I'll bring the story to you. Just," he pulled her closer, "don't make a decision until then, okay?"

"I have to go," Lane said, and pulled out of his reach, before hopping on her moped, and zipping out of the parking lot.

Chapter Fifteen

Thursday morning dawned cold and blustery. A chill wind bit into Lane's cheeks on her way to work, but the bitter weather didn't touch her mood. She and Celia put the finishing touches on their plan of action the previous night and were going on Friday to sign the lease agreement.

Now that she and Celia were done planning, Lane could spend her evenings as she wished. She intended to spend them all with Abe.

"How late are you working tonight?" she asked him as soon as he arrived at Cristo's.

"Eight or nine. Why?" He collapsed onto the stool with a grunt and remained hunched over the counter instead of sitting up straight.

"I thought you might like to buy me dinner," Lane said with a smile.

"You're free?" He raised his head.

"Yup. You interested?"

"Of course," he said, and tried at a smile.

"You feeling okay?" she asked.

He sighed and nodded, grabbing hold of her hand. "It's been a long week, and missing you is exhausting."

"You are so full of shit," she said, but he neither chimed in on the joke nor elaborated on what was bothering him.

"What do you want to do?" he asked. "More mugs to make?"

"I can get all that done this afternoon," Lane said. "What I want is to see your house."

They might not have spent as much time together as they would have liked since their first date, but every time they had, there had been two or three stories about his house.

"My house?" The subject didn't light up his eyes like it normally did.

"You know, the one you've spent the last ten years building? I want to know what that looks like."

He took a deep breath and sounded less than enthused. "If that's what you want, I'll pick you up when I get off."

"You gonna talk about what's on your mind then?"

"It's nothing. But I'm glad to have something to look forward to."

When he arrived on Lane's porch at nine, the sky was spitting icy rain. The wind was so strong, Abe's trench coat billowed around his legs. Lane had traded her jeans and threadbare western shirt for a dress and leggings with her tall boots with a flowy cardigan. A bag of overnight things was slung over her shoulder.

"My God, you are a sight for sore eyes," he said, and pulled her into his arms. His nose buried in her neck, his hands went straight to her hips. His lips found hers and Lane could feel him relaxing into her—a dammed river cleared to flow.

When he backed Lane into the side of her house, scrabbling with the fabric on her dress, Lane pressed her palms into his chest to ease him back. He groaned in protest.

"Wait til we get to your place," she said.

"Four days is too long."

"You've seen me every morning at Cristo's."

"Not the same."

Lane had been so busy, she hadn't realized how much she'd missed his voice, his smell, his touch, until his hands had landed on her hips. She tugged on his tie, "Maybe I can make that up to you."

His first real grin of the day spread over his lips. "How?"

"I'll show you later."

"We could go inside, and you could show me now."

"Why don't you want to bring me to your house?" Lane asked.

"I do," he said. "But I'm tired and I'm hungry and I'm impatient, and I miss you."

Lane tugged his hand, pulling him down the walk toward his car. His words sent a shiver down her spine, but she wouldn't let him stall any longer. "I haven't eaten either," she said. "what do you want for dinner?"

"This late, I figured we would order a pizza."

"Someone delivers out there in the sticks?"

"I'm not that far out," he said, and held the car door open for her. He was right. The drive to his house from hers was fifteen minutes on the highway, then a few minutes of winding country road before they turned down his maple-lined drive. They were close enough to the city she could see the orange glow in the distance.

The house was huge, long and wide, two stories tall, and blue. It had a large wrap around porch and a full balcony on the second floor. The remnants of rose bushes and ivy clung to the porch rails. The garage was a separate building hidden behind the house. Abe parked his Mercedes next to a beat up, mud-splattered Toyota truck. Leading her by the hand, he brought her around to the back, onto a large patio furnished with a grill and potted plants, and through the unlocked back door into the kitchen.

He paused to hang his keys and coat on a hook and slip off his shoes. Following his lead, Lane peeled off her boots.

"You don't have to take your shoes off," he said, and flipped on the lights.

Lane meant to reply, but the room around her took all her attention. His kitchen was massive. The room had high ceilings and a long island in the middle. Stools lined one side, a sink and gas stove top built in on the other. The rest of the kitchen was long, clean lines of stainless steel and white tile. Professional grade pans hung from a rack on the ceiling.

Abe grabbed a rocks glass from one of the shelves. "Would you like something to drink?" he asked.

"What do you have?"

"Whiskey, wine, gin, sake, soda, water."

"Soda's fine," Lane said.

He reached for a taller glass and filled both with ice. "Feel free to explore," he said. "What would you like on your pizza?"

"Pepperoni's fine," Lane disappeared into the butler's pantry. Abe followed close behind. He handed her the glass of soda before opening a cabinet and pouring himself some expensive looking bourbon.

"The laundry's behind that door," he motioned behind him with his glass before he took a sip. "And you're welcome to any of the wine you like," he pointed to the rows lining the wall opposite the cabinets. "And the rest of the house is through there," gesturing to a door behind Lane.

She pushed through the door into the dining room, furnished only with a long farm table, then wandered into the living room, which, no surprise by now, was sparsely decorated. There was a long, low brown leather sectional positioned in front of a large fireplace. A huge television hung on one wall, opposite a sweeping staircase. The room was painted a calming blue, but no art hung on the walls.

Each room showed signs of not quite being finished. The trim was missing around the floorboards in the dining room. There were no outlet or light switch covers in the living room. A can of paint and a level sat on a shelf in the kitchen next to his water glasses.

She was investigating the alcove under the staircase, filled with books, mystery novels, scripts, and law texts, when Abe met up with her. "Would you like to see the upstairs?" he asked.

She nodded and held out her hand. He led her up the stairs and down a long hallway to the last door. It opened to a bedroom with white walls and a handmade quilt on the queen bed. "This is where my dad stays when he visits," he said. The next room had mint green walls with white accents. It was the only room that was fully furnished and decorated so far. "Gretchen's room."

"She has good taste," Lane recognized two prints from a well-known blog on the wall above the desk.

"We redecorated last year when she decided she'd outgrown pink."

He led her past two closed doors, naming them bathroom and linen closet as they went. Opening a third door, he said, "This is the last room under construction."

It was small, and three walls were partially painted yellow. Tools were piled on saw horses in one corner. The makings of a bookcase leaned against the far wall.

"What's it supposed to be?" Lane asked.

"I had always planned it for a nursery," Abe said, "But I've been thinking an office is more realistic."

"You want more kids?" Lane asked.

Abe ran a finger over the grain on the bookcase, the ice in his glass clinking. "I always wanted a big family, but I've been trying to resign myself to that part of my life being over."

"It doesn't have to be," Lane wasn't prepared to promise herself for the role, not yet, so she said nothing more.

He took her by the hand, kissed her fingers, and brought her through the last door in the hall. "This," he said, "is my room. I finished it over the summer."

Lane stood in the middle and spun in a circle. His bedroom was bigger than her entire house. There was a king-sized bed, a set of plush armchairs, a second fireplace, a desk, a large walk-in closet, and a private bath. The walls were the same cool blue as the living room, but the bathroom showcased terracotta tiles and warm coral paint. The shower was separate from the bath and had two shower heads with a built in bench. The tub was wide and deep and large enough for two. The toilet had its own stall near the door. While Lane stared into the mirror over the double sink, Abe flipped a switch by the doorway. The tile beneath her feet hummed and warmed.

"Heated floors?" she asked.

"Just in here," he said, but he wore a satisfied smile.

"Your bathroom is more for sex than getting clean," she said.

"Care to test it out?" he asked. "I only finished it in August, and it's been woefully underused."

"We might miss the pizza."

"Later then." Abe guided her down the servant stairs and grabbed a heavy blanket from a closet in the living room. Lane followed him out the front door to the porch. He spread the blanket over them on the porch swing. "This is my favorite place."

Coyotes howled in the distance. Livestock guardian dogs barked in response. She could hear the spit of sleet against the porch roof, and a bitter wind reached them on the swing. Lane burrowed into Abe's side. He tucked the blanket in closer around her, mumbling that he should start a fire.

"Not yet." Lane rested her head on his shoulder and tucked her feet under the blanket.

Abe kept the swing in motion, his bare feet on the cold wood. "It's a pity it's so dark. In the morning I'll show you how beautiful it is out here."

"I'd like that.". They swung in silence for a few minutes. Abe ran his fingers over her thigh until he found the hem of her dress, which he traced. An unfamiliar sensation swept over Lane, so foreign that at first, she could only identify it as an absence of restlessness. She was so used to needing to move, to getting the next thing done, but in that moment, Lane was content to spend her entire life with Abe on his porch.

"Do you like the house?" he asked.

Lane wasn't sure how to answer. It wasn't that she didn't like it. The house was beautiful, but its emptiness made it feel hollow and cold. "It's so big."

His laugh had no humor in it. "You hate it. I knew you would."

"No," Lane said. "But the idea of you living here by yourself makes me sad. It must be so lonely."

"I never meant to live here alone for long. I meant to get remarried, have five or six more kids, maybe a dog or two."

"Five or six kids, huh?"

"That's up for negotiation obviously."

"I'm not even confidant in my ability to have one."

A long sigh deflated his chest, and he ducked his head to capture her lips. Lane wasn't sure why, but even though she'd decided she didn't like whiskey, it tasted good on him. His kiss was slow and sweet and sad. "Here I am, feeling sorry for myself," he said, "and you've had it so much worse."

"Is that what's been bothering you all day? Self-pity?"

He shook his head. "I don't always like my job very much in the fall, especially during election years."

"What's wrong?" she asked.

"The politics of it wears me out."

"But you work in politics."

"I can handle a certain amount of insincerity, but when session's out, and during election years, it's like everyone is playing a part all the time, and I want someone to say what they mean instead of trying to spin it. When I compare trekking that terrain to being with you, I wonder why I put up with it."

"You're thinking of quitting?"

He shook his head. "I've done this long enough to know if I can make it to January, I'll love it again."

"You're a strange man," Lane said, burying her frozen nose in folds of his shirt.

"And you're cold," he said. "Come inside, and I'll get a fire going."

The pizza arrived as soon as Abe had the fire lit, and Lane hadn't realized how hungry she was.

"I took a custom order from your representative friend," she said.

"Brian called?"

"I quoted him twice what I normally charge. He didn't even hesitate, just said he'd put the deposit in the mail."

"I told you," Abe said, tossing the crust from his third slice back in the box, and collapsed against Lane. "You should be charging double that."

She flicked the new hairs out of his face. "Maybe in a couple years."

A lazy smile played at his lips as he snaked a hand under the hem of her skirt. "You'll be out earning me well before then," he said.

"I'd have no idea what to do with that kind of money."

"Run away with me," he said.

As he covered her body with his, Lane was tempted.

Chapter Sixteen

At dawn, Abe slid under the covers on Lane's side of the bed. His skin radiated heat and smelled like soap. He entwined his legs with hers rained kisses down on her neck as he pushed the shirt she wore, an old one of his she'd pilfered from the closet, up over her hips.

"Time to get up, darling."

Lane curled into him. "Too early."

"It's almost seven." His hands roved higher, brushing the underside of her breasts.

"Are you trying to wake me up or get fresh?" Her voice was hardly more than a murmur.

"I was thinking of using one to accomplish the other. Who knows when I'll get you back in my bed." He rolled so he was on top of her, working the buttons on her shirt.

"Hmmm," Lane said. Her eyes were still closed when she said, "I was thinking tonight, unless that's too soon."

Abe's fingers stilled. He maneuvered sideways so he was sitting next to her. Afraid she'd said something wrong, Lane sat up too, but his expression was tender, his eyes bright. "I'd like to spend every night with you," he said. "So no, not too soon."

"We'll have to see if we can work that out," Lane said.

He kissed the top of her head and disappeared into his closet. "I've got coffee brewing," he said. "And there's a towel for you in the bathroom if you'd like to shower."

"That would be nice," Lane said, stretching as she looked for her clothes. She'd expected them to be strung across the room from the vehemence with which Abe had disrobed her the night before, but they were all neatly folded on the seat of an armchair, her overnight bag on the floor next to it.

She was rummaging through her bag for her hairbrush when Abe emerged from the closet, still doing up the buttons on his blue shirt, a gray tie draped over his shoulder. Lane was unprepared for the wave of affection that washed over her as she watched him dress. A heavy, not unpleasant feeling settled in her chest she wasn't ready to name.

After her shower, Lane took another trip through his closet and chose a navy v-neck sweater, the kind he would wear under a sportcoat in the winter. It was too long for her, and she had to roll the sleeves. He was so lean, the sweater fit across her chest, and was just baggy enough everywhere else to look intentional when paired with her jeans and boots.

She found him reading his newspaper in the kitchen, sipping coffee. "That sweater looks better on you," he said, as he poured her a cup of coffee. "Come on, I want to show you outside."

Lane rolled the coffee over her tongue before she followed him out the door. She nodded and smiled. He'd just passed one of her most important tests. A mental check mark got ticked off next to "can make good coffee" in her mind.

Shivering on the back patio, Lane saw the barn she'd failed to notice the night before. The wood was weathered, with chunks of red paint missing from the siding. The husks from the summer's sunflowers swaying against its outer walls.

"Restoring that should probably be my next project," he said. "But I know nothing about barns."

He led her out into the frosty grass. He kept the lawn near the house well-groomed, but further back, there was a long swath of tall grass that grew above Lane's eyeline, but Abe had cut a footpath through it. "It's not original," he said. "This was farmland for about one hundred years before I bought it, but I replanted it with native grasses. I think of it as my own little prairie preserve."

The trail wound and twisted through the grass until Lane was sweating and thought they must be miles from his house. But when it let out into a line of cedar trees, they were at the eastern edge of his property. She turned around and there was his driveway only a few hundred feet away.

They sat together on the porch swing, watching the low sun peak through the clouds as they finished their coffee, long gone cold. "I run through the trails most mornings," he said. "Three laps are just about two miles. You're welcome to join me."

"I already get up at four-thirty for work."

"And you sleep until noon on weekends to make up for it."

Lane scowled at him. "Where do you get that idea?"

"When I asked you to breakfast two weeks ago, you were still in bed."

"How do you figure?"

"Because it's the only time you haven't responded within five minutes. I called at nine, you didn't text back until noon."

She blushed. "I don't usually, but I drank too much the night before."

Abe raised his eyebrows. "*You* drank too much?"

Lane cringed, hoping he wouldn't ask her anymore about it. "You know, friends talking, wine flowing, no knitting in my hands to keep me busy."

The smile never left his face, and he ran his fingers through her hair. "I did the same thing that night," Abe said. "Except Jeff and I were watching football. No knitting allowed."

Lane scrunched her nose. "You watch football?"

"It's a trade. Jeff plays tennis with me, I watch football with him. You don't approve?"

"As long as I don't have to, I'm fine with it."

Abe beamed, crinkles appearing in the corners of his eyes. He planted a kiss on the top of her head. "My dad will be pleased I've found a woman who understands traditional gender roles. He's always said that's been my main problem."

Lane hopped off the swing, leaving her empty mug on the porch floor. "I was going to offer to make you dinner tonight, but just for that, now you're on your own."

Jumping up after her, Abe said, "That sounds nice. What are we having?"

"I'm having roast chicken," she said as she disappeared inside. "Enjoy your fast food burger."

"That's not fair," he said, following her through to the kitchen. "I didn't even know you cooked."

Lane stared into his open refrigerator. "It's a good thing one of us does," she said. All that was inside was an assortment of outdated condiments, an empty jar of pickles, and the box of leftover pizza. She pulled the box out of the fridge and plopped it on the counter. "This is pathetic. Do you eat out for every meal?"

"Not every meal."

"Who doesn't at least have bread? Or eggs?"

"Someone who wasn't expecting company."

Rolling her eyes, Lane flicked open the box and wrestled a slice free. "You didn't think we were going to hang out my place forever, did you?"

"Really?" Abe asked. "Cold pizza for breakfast?"

"Well if you had anything else. . ."

He grabbed a slice for himself. "I'll do better next time."

"You don't bring women here, do you?" Lane asked. "Well, except that Nicole woman. She seemed familiar with your living room."

Abe shook his head. "That Nicole woman and I were together for nine months."

"Oh." Lane frowned at herself. "I'm sorry. I didn't realize-"

"That I'd had any serious relationships since Roxanne?" he said. "I've had a couple."

"I'm sorry," she said again.

"It's fine," he said. "How would you know?"

"I figured if you were serious about someone, you would have married them by now."

Abe tossed his crust back into the box. "I'm serious about you."

"That much I knew," she said, and kissed him.

Chapter Seventeen

Lane arrived in front of the space that would soon be Benjamin & Cris Roasterie early Saturday morning. She parked on the street next to Celia's Jeep, and took the gas station coffee Celia handed her.

"What is this?"

"Our only competition for a mile, and all the other places that serve coffee within two miles aren't any better."

"There's a McDonald's." Lane said, taking the cup.

"Yeah, but we'd never get those customers anyway."

Lane shrugged in agreement and sniffed the coffee. It smelled scorched and fishy. "I think we've got this." She set it down on the sidewalk with no intention of drinking it, though something warm would have been nice in the chilly wind.

"How's Mr. Fujikawa?" Celia asked.

Lane told Celia how she'd made Abe help her cook dinner the night before, forcing him to handle the chicken from start to finish, because he was such a baby about touching raw meat. Then she showed off the necklace he'd given her: a little green, tarnished copper heart on a silver chain. He'd seen it at the Statehouse gift shop and thought of her. Lane had taken a class with the local artist who made it.

Celia suggested they contact her about selling with them and then asked, "Have you heard from Shawn?"

Lane groaned and filled her in on what he'd said when he stopped by on Tuesday.

"He's writing you a story to win you back?"

"I don't know, he spouted so many things, like the story and moving in together that are just so ludicrous I lost track. I thought by not calling and not stopping by, he'd gotten the picture, but there have been times over the last year where we didn't talk for two weeks, and then when we got together things were just as electric as ever, so maybe he's holding out for that?"

"Even though you've told him it's over like a million times?"

"Listening isn't his strongest suit."

"You think he'll have a story for you on Thursday?"

"He's not good at follow through either."

"Good," Celia said. "Fuck him."

Lane nodded but frowned. It seemed wrong to be so unsympathetic toward him. They had been something to each other, even if Lane still wasn't sure how to define it. "What did you do last night?" she asked to change the subject.

"Andrew and I coded the new websites."

"He knows how to do that?"

Celia nodded. "He didn't have much of a social life in his early twenties."

"How old is he now?"

"Thirty."

"You going to tell me about him?"

Celia looked to the sky and sighed. "I'm afraid to."

"Why? Things seems to be going well."

"Everything is great when I'm with him. We talk and we flirt, and everything feels natural. It's like I'm you."

"What's that supposed to mean?"

"It means you have the easiest time with men of anyone I've ever seen."

"Yeah, but my track record stinks."

"Right, that's why you're having to fight off two men who are so different that the only thing in the entire world they agree on is that you're a catch."

"That's just what it looks like from the outside. I made a complete fool of myself yesterday at breakfast." Lane colored just thinking about the comment she'd made about Nicole.

"In your case, it just made Mr. Fujikawa fall even more in love with you, because you are adorable. If I screw up, Andrew's gone."

"I think you are the definition of adorable," Lane said.

"That's sweet of you."

Lane rolled her eyes. "Why are you so afraid of screwing up?"

"Because I always do."

"I'd blame the lame exes more than I'd blame yourself."

"That doesn't mean I'm not going to scare him off."

"If he's making you dinner and helping you code our websites, he's gonna be around for a while."

Celia gave Lane a weak smile, "If you jinxed us, I will kill you."

"So," Lane nudged Celia with the shoulder, "tell me about him."

Andrew's last name was Reynolds and he worked as an accountant for a 501(c)3. He'd never been married. He had come close once before, but they hadn't been able to agree on fundamental things like kids, he wanted them, she didn't, so they broke up.

"But you don't want kids," Lane said.

"I'm not trying to marry him. We just started going out."

"Alright then. When I do get to meet him?"

Celia pulled her phone out of her jacket. "The leasing agent is late."

"Come on, if he's helping out with the business I should meet him."

"Only if you promise not to flirt with him," Celia said.

"I wouldn't flirt with him."

"You wouldn't mean to, but you would."

Lane didn't think she would, but she didn't know how to tell Celia that what she called flirting, was just being friendly. "I can invite Abe along, make a night of it."

"So he can laugh while you flirt with my boyfriend?"

"He won't. When he feels threatened he gets possessive then pretends he's not a misogynist when I call him out on it. It's hilarious."

"Maybe," Celia bounced from one foot to another.

"I'll check with Abe tonight and find out which night coming up he's not planning on working until ten."

The leasing agent arrived, and Celia put on the smile she used when she spoke with doctors she didn't like. It took them almost an hour to go over the lease terms and sign all the papers, by which time, the contractor, who was on time for his appointment, waited outside.

They spent two hours with him, going over plans for the space. He thought they could get the shop floor up and running in five weeks. The basement, as predicted, would take longer.

After lunch, they headed back to their new shop and taped leaves of old newspapers in the windows. In the waning afternoon sun, Lane climbed the ladder they had found in the basement and painted their new logo on the window, a B&C surrounded by a circle like a cattle brand. The words "roasterie and boutique" ringed the outside of the circle. Below that, she painted "coming in December," followed by their web address.

That evening, Lane rode out to Abe's covered in paint. She was lighter than she'd been in years—more confident. There was no way the roasterie wouldn't work, she and Celia were brimming with too many ideas and too much enthusiasm. Then there was Abe. He had told her he was hers if she wanted him, hadn't he?

The warm reception he gave her implied he was. Abe sat on the porch swing sipping a beer when Lane parked behind his truck. He met her on the lawn and swung her in a circle before kissing her.

He was just as dirty as she was, covered in paint and sawdust. He'd spent his day finishing the bookcase in the nursery, which he showed her before they got cleaned up.

They showered together in his fancy two-person shower, taking advantage of the space to pass the time until their dinner reservation. Lane clung to Abe's wet skin so hard she left eight half-moon shaped welts on his shoulders.

He took her out to his Japanese restaurant for dinner, where he spoke to the staff in Japanese and ordered them something off menu. They were seated in front of the sushi chef, Akihiro, who was about Lane's age and spoke English with a thick accent. They watched him prepare appetizers for the diners while they drank sake and waited on their entree. He gave them samples of the different rolls he made as he teased Abe for showing off to the pretty American girl.

"You mean by bringing me here?" Lane asked.

"Bringing you here so he can pretend he speaks Japanese."

"Is that why he won't teach me?" Lane asked. "He said it was because he didn't want to emphasize the age difference."

"That's a valid concern," Abe said. "And Japanese is my first language," he said to Akihiro, the chef.

The chef cringed playfully. "Sorry to say, but your Japanese is not so good."

"I lived in Tokyo!" Abe said. "I never spoke a word of English."

The chef nodded. "You lived in Japan when I was this high," he held his hand below the lip of his work table. "And I spoke Japanese better then than you do now." Then he turned to Lane and winked. "Why you wanna go out with this old, fake Japanese man?"

"I have no idea," Lane said. She finished the last sip of sake in her cup. "What are you doing later?" she asked him as Abe refilled her glass.

Akihiro blushed. Abe said something to him that could have been a threat or an apology, Lane couldn't be sure. Then Abe wrapped an arm around her shoulders. "I don't know why I keep refilling your drink," he said. "You've clearly had too much."

Sunday, Lane left Abe sleeping to work her last brunch shift at Cristo's.

Abe brought Gretchen in early for breakfast, and Lane caught him staring at her more than once. Gretchen watched her father watch Lane. She kept up the pretense of being disgusted with him, but she smiled and chatted with Lane about music and how she was liking her camera lenses.

Sunday night, Abe came to Lane's after he dropped Gretchen off so Lane could work in the garage. She showed him the sake set she had made him, which had just come out of its bisque firing. Abe thanked her by taking her back to his house, showing her out to the balcony on a second unseasonably warm night to look at the stars. They stayed there until after midnight, sandwiched between two blankets, ignoring the stars.

On Monday, Lane was at Cristo's until almost four o'clock, teaching her replacement how to order and schedule. At home too tired to work on the commissioned shawl, she fell asleep on her sofa and didn't awaken until seven when Abe almost knocked down her door to make sure she was all right.

Tuesday was an easy day for Lane, but Abe had to work late. He came to her house when he was off. She made him dinner, trying her hand at cooking something Japanese. Lane apologized for her novice dish, but he assured her her noodles tasted good and her miso was superb. She didn't believe him even after he swept her knitting notes off her dining room table and laid her back on it.

Wednesday night, Abe promised to be home by six. Lane, who didn't believe him told him to text her when he was leaving the office, promising to meet him at his place. At Cristo's that morning, he'd worn the same downcast scowl he had the week before. So instead of waiting for Abe to leave work, she rode over to his house at five and let herself in the back door he never locked. She brought with her everything she needed to make her favorite pasta dish, a garlic butter sauce with capers and artichokes and sun-dried tomatoes served with chicken.

Lane prepared the food in Abe's kitchen, listening to the violin music he already had in his stereo. It was cute he still listened to CDs. She chose a bottle of wine from his collection and set it on the counter next to two glasses. When Abe texted that he was on his way home an hour later than he'd said he would be, Lane put the angel hair on to boil and poured him a glass of his whiskey. She'd changed into one of his work shirts, too long for her, but too snug to button over her chest. With the sleeves rolled up, the front open over her camisole and the ends tied around her waist, she was confident she looked as cute as she felt. She hoped it would all be enough to cheer him up.

Abe would know she was there before he opened the door. She'd parked her moped next to the garage as she'd become accustomed to doing, and all the lights in the kitchen were on and visible from the outside in the descending dusk. That didn't stop her satisfaction with her surprise as the headlights from Abe's car illuminated the Western bank of windows. She had to stop herself from bouncing on her toes when he stepped through the back door.

"How did you—" but his question died on his lips as the aroma of the food hit him.

Lane took his laptop case and his coat, hanging them on the hooks by the door as he slid off his shoes. "When did you get here?" he asked instead.

"A couple hours ago," she said as she handed him the whiskey.

Abe took the drink but didn't seem to notice it.

"I hope that's okay." It hadn't occurred to Lane that it might be an invasion of privacy. "All I did was cook. And turn on the stereo and borrow a shirt..." Lane took a deep breath when he didn't speak. She couldn't read his expression. "Shit."

Abe huffed a laugh. "You broke into my house to make me dinner?"

"It's not breaking in if the door's unlocked," she said. "But I'll never—"

The rest of her words were drowned out as Abe cut her off with a hot and greedy kiss. His hands squeezed her hips and a low, growl-like moan rumbled in his chest. "Darling, you are welcome here anytime."

"This is okay, then?"

He traced the curve of her hip up, burying his cold fingers under the fabric at the dip of her waist. "This is perfect. Ideal even."

Lane squirmed and giggled as he hit the ticklish spot below her ribs. "Don't get used to it. I'm not going to cook for you all the time just because you can barely feed yourself."

"I don't expect you to." Abe kissed her neck, nipping his way to her ear where he whispered, "But coming home to you? That I could get used to."

Lane shivered. The idea of living with him flooded her with warmth. She liked the suggestion, but she didn't think she could live in his house. "You need something to help fill up this place," she said. "The emptiness is so heavy. Doesn't it weigh on you?"

"Sometimes," he said, and released her as the oven timer sounded.

"You should get a dog."

"I'm not home enough." The soft clink of ice against glass followed his words.

"You might come home earlier if you had a reason to," Lane said.

The soft swish of Abe's socked feet against the hardwood neared, and his hands wrapped around her waist from behind while she stood at the stove top. He pressed his warm body into hers and buried his nose in her hair. "I'd rather that reason be you," he said. "If I had known you were already here—"

"You still would have been an hour late," Lane said. "But I'll think about it."

With a kiss to her neck, he released her to light a fire in the living room. They ate in front of the fireplace, drinking the wine as they made their plans for the weekend. Lane teased Abe about bringing work home. They did the dishes together, and Lane thought maybe she could get used to sharing a home with him after all.

When the kitchen was clean, Lane knit on Abe's sofa while he finished up work on his laptop. She fell asleep to the violin music she'd put on the stereo. Abe woke her and took her up to bed where he made love to her as slow and sweet as the music they'd been listening to.

"I hope every week can be as good as this one," Lane said afterward, cuddling up to Abe's side.

"Me too, darling." He kissed her hair and draped an arm over her hip. "Me too."

Chapter Eighteen

Preferring Abe's closet to her own, Lane continued pilfering his clothes. She never wore anything too expensive and chose pieces she rarely saw him wear. He still greeted her with a smile and a kiss no matter what she was wearing, so she didn't think he minded. She'd started her last day at Cristo's in one of his house-building shirts, a threadbare blue and yellow plaid that had gone out of style in the 90s. As she stood in front of her open closet, considering their plans for the evening, a round of ping pong and drinks after his dinner meeting, Lane wanted to trash everything inside.

Lane was on the brink of a new life. There would be no more frigid early morning rides past Lake Shawnee. No more counter guys staring at her boobs. No more Talia's mom making snide comments and spreading rumors. No more working her ass off for minimum wage and being afraid to turn her furnace on in January. No, this new life would be full of new people, new friends, and new love, and it was going to be so much richer than what she'd been living. She could feel it.

A new life called for new clothes. Lane had always wanted to design her own wardrobe and craft it herself by hand. Since it was the day she was going to start making her living as a designer, she might as well start designing for herself. The afternoon slipped away as she sewed herself a black top with a swath of fabric gathered at her hip that flattered her chest and clung to her waist. When Lane was satisfied with the fit, she made herself a sandwich and ate as she sketched out what other essentials she would need.

The night before, Abe had mentioned the holiday parties he attended each year, one given by his firm, another by a former senator, and another given by a contractor friend of his. Lane was absorbed in sketching out a little black dress to wear to these, wondering if one was enough, or if these were the kind of people who expected a new dress for each event when she heard the creak of a step on her porch, followed by a frantic rap on her door.

Lane popped up with a smile, fluffing out her flirty skirt and adjusting the fitted top before she unlocked the door. "I thought you were going to text when you—Shawn?"

Lane hadn't heard from him since the previous Tuesday afternoon when she'd tried again to tell him that they were over. She'd thought he'd finally given up, but here Shawn stood with red eyes and rumpled clothes. He held a stack of printed pages covered in red marks fanned and crumpled in his balled fist.

"I can't do it," he said, shaking the pages at her. "I can't make it funny."

Lane didn't unlatch the screen door. "You can't make what funny?"

"Your story. I can't make anything about a child dying funny."

"It's not funny," Lane said. "It's a tragedy."

"I don't accept that." He shook the papers again and paced the short length of Lane's green porch. "There has to be some way. I've tried and tried, and nothing comes out right—everybody comes out warped and cruel."

"Stop trying to make it funny then. Make something else funny."

He stopped moving and peered at her through the screen door. "I'm not giving up."

"What are you doing here?" Lane asked. She heard her phone chirp behind her: the text from Abe she had been waiting for.

Shawn's face fell. "Last week, I promised you I'd write your story—by today." He held out the papers to her, but she only stared. She remembered the story part, but she didn't remember anything about a deadline. "It's not done, but I haven't slept, and I haven't eaten. I've worked nonstop to prove to you that you're wrong about me."

"It's too late, Shawn. It's over. I've told you that."

"It's not over," he stomped his foot. "You don't get to just say it's over—not after more than a year."

"It is over," Lane stepped out onto the porch and closed the door behind her.

Shawn's eyes drank in her clothes, lingering on her accentuated curves. The top Lane had been so comfortable in a few minutes before now made her feel exposed.

"My God, you are gorgeous," he said as if the air had been knocked out of him.

"Abe's going to be here any minute, so I would appreciate it if you could leave," Lane said, pulling at the hem of her shirt and doing her best not to panic as Shawn's face turned red.

"Shit, Lane. This was my day. Couldn't you just give me one day?"

"I've given you a year and you didn't give a damn about me until Abe came along. Now go."

A rueful grin spread over Shawn's lips. "Does he know about us? He doesn't, does he?" He let out a dry chuckle. "Jesus, Lane, don't you think he deserves to know he's not the only guy you're fucking?"

Lane couldn't help the derisive laugh that burst from her throat. "Because you've always been so straightforward about the multitude of women in your bed."

"Ah, gorgeous, don't be like that." Shawn stepped forward to cup her chin, but Lane dodged him.

"You're too late," Lane said. "You blew your shot."

"I'm not letting this other guy take you from me," he said.

"I can't be taken. It's my choice who I'm with," Lane said. "I choose him. I love him."

"No, Lane," Shawn said. He reached for her hand, but she slapped his fingers away. He stepped forward and wrapped his arms around her, squashing her arms to her sides. "No," he said as she tried to squirm away. "I love you."

Shawn kissed her, crushing her lips into her teeth.

Lane was so shocked that for one heartbeat, she let him. On the second, she squeezed out of his arms and headed down the steps. Lane halted when her foot hit the first stair. "No."

Abe was stood frozen halfway up the walk. A bouquet of wild sunflowers wrapped in newspaper dangled from his left hand. His frigid expression wasn't angled at her. His eyes were on the spot where she had just been. Where Shawn still was.

"Abe," Lane collected herself and descended the stairs. "It's not what it looks like."

"It looks like I walked in on something I wasn't meant to see." His voice held no emotion.

"It's nothing. It's over."

"Didn't look over," he said, shifting his glance to her. Lane felt her heart seize and go cold at the barren, icy expression on his face.

"I can explain it," she said.

"I don't need an explanation." His eyes flicked back up to Shawn. Abe clenched his jaw and narrowed his eyes. He pulled himself up to his full height from his usual easy slouch. His whole body turned taut. His right fist opened and closed.

Lane took a step back and glanced over her shoulder. Shawn was leaning against one of the columns that flanked the porch steps, his arms crossed, his face neutral.

"Were you going to tell me about him?" Abe asked.

"There's nothing to tell," Lane said.

Abe took a deep breath and barely moved his mouth when he spoke. "There's another man standing on your porch, looking at me like I'm the one in the wrong, and I'd like to know why."

Panic roared in her stomach like flame as Shawn brushed past her, holding his hand out to Abe.

"Shawn McAllistor," he said.

Abe shook his hand but said nothing.

"It seems we had a miscommunication about whose turn it is to take out our girl here." Shawn tried to wrap his arm around Lane, but she ducked around him to stand beside Abe.

Abe's cold eyes followed her, and she took a quick step away from his side, finding nothing by disdain there.

"We did not have plans," she said to Abe. "Shawn's angry that I broke things off with him and he's throwing a fit about it."

"We never broke up, gorgeous," Shawn said. "You just stopped answering my calls."

Lane wanted to smack the stupid grin off his face.

"Is that true?" Abe asked her.

"I didn't return his calls because I told him it was over, and he wasn't taking no for an answer."

"He's been harassing you?"

"Not until tonight," Lane said, but Shawn spoke over her.

"To tell you the truth, Abe. It is Abe, right?" Abe nodded. "I've been giving her a little space so she could get you out her system. We were negotiating the terms of our relationship before you came along. I've been trying to convince her to let me move in, but she doesn't think that's a good idea this close to me getting my masters in case we have to move away for work."

"Move in?" Abe looked at Lane, but she could only shake her head as tears that she was afraid to shed welled behind her eyes. Abe turned his attention back to Shawn, but asked her, "What's the truth?"

"That we'd been sleeping together," Lane said. "But that's it. It was never more than sex."

"Lane," Shawn said, feigning hurt.

"Don't you talk to me," Lane said, her chest so tight she could barely breathe.

"Don't diminish what we have."

Lane had never been a fan of swimming, and now she knew why. This must be what it felt like to drown, to be able to see the surface, but have no way to break through and fill her lungs with air. She was going to suffocate on the inefficacy of her words.

"Leave." She said to Shawn, desperate for the pressure to stop. "I don't want you here."

Shawn reached for her, but Lane danced behind Abe, who took a step forward to block Shawn's pursuit. His right fist was curled and twitching at his side. As she watched Abe grow more agitated, the tears Lane she didn't want to shed erupted into a choked sob. She didn't want this to happen, to expose Abe to this.

"She asked you to leave," Abe said.

"No offense man," Shawn said, either unaware of Abe's rising temper or unconcerned with it. "But you interrupted us."

"I was invited," Abe said. "You weren't."

"He wasn't," Lane said, but neither man heard her. Her voice had never mattered less than in this moment when two men were fighting over her as if she were property that could be disputed. And neither one cared what she wanted, only what he wanted to see.

"Look," Shawn said, taking one step nearer, "I get that you want to look macho in front of Lane, but your posturing is scaring her, and I'd like to comfort her."

Shawn's words were meant to manipulate Abe. Lane wasn't afraid, she was frustrated with the both of them, and devastated for Abe, for what she knew he was feeling, for his hurt and betrayal.

Abe, who hadn't noticed Lane crying, looked quickly over his shoulder. So she didn't have to see his contempt for her on his face, Lane kept her eyes on Shawn as she said, "You're only making things worse."

"Lane," he said, holding out his hand. "Please."

"Go home, Shawn."

Shawn tried to skirt around Abe, but the older man seemed to grow in both height and breadth as he blocked the way. "That's four times she's told you to leave. I won't give you so many chances."

Shawn smirked and tried again, but Abe squared his feet and raised his fist level with his shoulder, ready to strike should Shawn come any closer.

Confronted with the threat of violence, Shawn backpedaled with his hands in the air. "Whoa, there. Nobody here is looking for a fight."

Abe advanced, his fist still raised. "Then I'd keep backing up if I were you."

They traversed the yard that way, Shawn not even glancing back at Lane before he left. Abe didn't drop his fist until Shawn's car was out of sight.

Lane was frozen in place, her hands over her mouth until Abe faced her. None of the fury had diminished from his expression now that Shawn was gone. He stalked up the walk, looking as if he'd like to lay into her, and Lane steeled herself to fight for him.

Chapter Nineteen

Abe stomped past Lane so fast she didn't think he heard her mumbled thanks. At the porch stairs, he dropped the bouquet of wild sunflowers and kicked it into the bushes. Unsatisfied, he reared back and plunged his fist into the tin mailbox nailed to the railing. The crunch of metal was almost loud enough to drown out his strangled curse.

Lane was next to him before she knew what she was doing, reaching for his hand. "Are you okay?"

"No," he said stepping out of her reach, "I am not okay. What the fuck has been going on?"

"Just what I said was going on." Lane chanced moving a step closer to him. "Can I look at your hand?"

"No."

Lane rested her fingertips on his forearm. "But you're bleeding."

Wincing, Abe jerked away from her. "Don't touch me right now."

He looked down at his bloody knuckles. He flexed his hand a few times and huffed in shallow panting breaths.

"Are you okay?" she asked again.

"I don't think it's broken," he said.

"Do you want to go inside? I can—"

"I'm not staying," he said, still looking at his hand.

Lane shied away. Her throat felt as though it was closing in on itself as she watched the blood drip from a cut between his knuckles. It ran in a red rivulet down his hand and spotted the sidewalk. "Can we talk about this?" she asked, with little hope of him listening to her, but willing to try anyway.

Abe flexed his fingers. "Fine. How long have you been screwing the kid from the liquor store?"

"About a year."

"When was the last time?" he huffed great heaving breaths, and Lane's voice came out a timid and soft.

"Three weeks ago."

Abe's face turned red. "Before or after we went to dinner?"

"It was the next night." Tears pooled in her eyes again.

"The night after you invited me in?"

She nodded.

"Is he why you told me you didn't date—because clearly that was a lie."

"We weren't dating," Lane said. "I saw him maybe two or three times a month."

"Answer the question." His voice was so sharp, so unfeeling that Lane collapsed onto the porch steps.

"No. I didn't want to go out with you or see Shawn any more than I did already because I didn't want to date anyone."

Abe gave an angry grunt. She'd known he wouldn't believe her.

"Why didn't you tell me about him?"

"Because there wasn't anything to tell," Lane said. She wanted to touch him, to hold him. She wanted Abe to trail kisses up her neck and promise her this was just a fight, that they'd work everything out in the end. That maybe not tonight, but maybe tomorrow he would *hear* her.

"He told you he loved you." Abe joined her on the stairs.

"How long were you standing there?"

"Long enough to get a good idea of what's been going on."

"Did you hear me tell him I love you?"

"Yes." Abe angled toward her at last. She hoped to find fondness in his expression. She hoped hearing she loved him would soften the hard edges of his rage, would melt his anger, but he was still ice.

"That's the truth," Lane said. "I was confused at first. That night with Shawn was a mistake, but after our first date, I didn't expect to want a second, or a third, or a lifetime with you, but I do."

He shook his head. "I could have taken it," Abe said. "If you had just told me from the beginning that all you wanted was something casual, I would have been fine with it. I would have preferred that instead of making me think—" he pounded the porch with the flat of his left hand and Lane she jumped. "God, Lane, instead of making me think it was fine to fall for you. That was cruel."

"I didn't want something casual. You showed me I wanted something serious with you—only you." The tears made her voice thick, and it hurt her throat to talk.

"You already had someone."

"Shawn has slept with half of the women under thirty between here and Kansas City. You can't have someone like that."

"You're exaggerating."

"Celia will back me up."

"Of course she will. She'll always be on your side."

Lane took a deep, shaky breath, wiping her still falling tears from her eyes. "I'm trying to tell you how what we have is so much more important than anything that ever happened with Shawn."

"You were with him for a year. That's not nothing. And you let me think you were available. You made me think—" he cut himself off and looked away from her, out toward the yard. Lane thought he might have had tears welling up in his eyes and she attempted to rest her hand on his arm, but he shook her off again. "I asked you not to touch me."

"Then what can I do to make this better?"

Abe shook his head and flexed his hand like it still hurt. "I should go."

"Let me get you some ice." Lane rose to go inside.

"No."

"Then let me take you to the ER and make sure you didn't break anything."

"I told you it's fine."

"Let me do something."

"No." He stood. "I'm leaving."

"But if you go," Lane choked on her tears and had to start over. "If you go now, I'm never going to see you again." Tears she was powerless to stop dribbled off her chin.

"No, I don't expect you will." He looked at her for the first time since he had arrived. His eyes roamed over her body, taking in the tears and the new clothes and the necklace he'd given her. He was still angry, but all the rage and violence had left him.

"Do you really love me?" He asked, his voice hoarse, almost tender again.

"Yes, I love you." She loved his easy charm, his caring heart, the passion with which he felt everything. She could even forgive his casual sexism because at least he didn't argue when she called him out on it, but there was none of that in his eyes as nodded

"I wasn't completely wrong."

"Of course not."

A grim grin alighted across his lips for just a second and he ran his uninjured hand through his hair. "You know what Roxanne said that night?"

Lane held her breath and shook her head.

As he spoke, his voice rose with each word until he was yelling. "She told me she loved me—that she really loved only me. But it was all bull shit because she's married to someone else now. Not only did that bastard get my wife, he got my house and my daughter, and all I get is another woman to make a fool out of me."

"You didn't deserve that."

"Do you know what I did today to get you those flowers?" he motioned to the bouquet, trampled and half hidden in the overgrown evergreen bush, his voice still raised. "I stopped my car on the side of the highway with clients inside. I climbed a fence and cut them down for you while three married men made fun of me the entire time. I told them you were worth it, that these would make you happy, and they teased me some more."

"That's such a romantic story."

"I am a fool," he said.

"No, you're not."

"I was going to ask you to marry me," he said, and Lane gasped, surprised.

"You still can," she said too fast.

"I was going to do it at Christmas and give you some time to get your shop open. I talked the artist who made your necklace about a ring today."

Lane touched the charm that hung around her neck. "I practiced writing my name, Lane Fujikawa," she said.

Abe gave a mirthless laugh "Maybe I'm not a complete fool."

"If you ask me to marry you," Lane said, drumming up all of her courage, "I'll say yes."

Abe ran his left hand through his hair again, blood still dripping from his right hand. He sighed through his nose. "I don't want to get married anymore."

Abe closed his eyes and turned away from her.

He descended the three stairs.

Lane reached out after him, just missing his shoulder. "Abe, please don't go. It's not the same. Me and Roxanne."

He stopped. "It never would have worked anyway. You were always too young for me."

"It still can work," she said. "It's all just a misunderstanding."

"I'm done," he said. "I have to learn some time."

She wanted to ask him what he needed to learn, but she knew. He thought women would always lie to him, that they would always want him for the wrong reasons. But Lane didn't. She hadn't.

"Abe, please."

He took a deep breath and stepped back up on the bottom step. With Lane standing above him, they were the same height. He leaned forward and kissed her on the lips, pulling back before she had a chance to react.

"Goodbye, Lane."

And then he was gone.

Chapter Twenty

L ane didn't remember calling Celia after Abe left, but her friend arrived within minutes. She held Lane on the porch steps until Lane had no tears left to cry, then helped Lane into bed. She brought her food and water and tried to coax her to eat when Lane only picked at her food.

"I hate seeing you like this," Celia said on the second day. Lane only nodded.

In her mind, Lane kept replaying the last time she and Abe had shared her bed. Tuesday. It had only been Tuesday night, but it was like a dream to her now. How had they gone from sharing something so intimate to breaking up?

It wasn't their love making she remembered, but after, when they lay together before sleep settled in. She had rested her head on Abe's chest. He was propped against the pillows, one arm clasped around her torso, the other playing with her long hair.

"Tell me the whole story," he said.

"What story?"

"What happened with Silas. You gave me the essentials. I want the details."

Lane snuggled further into him but said nothing as she contemplated where the story started. Did it begin with the surprise positive? Or with the miserable pregnancy where Lane was queasy the entire time? Or did it start with the ill-fated labor?

Abe kissed the top of her head and buried his nose in her hair. She didn't understand why he liked her hair so much, but she enjoyed that he did. She took a deep breath and started. "We talked about why I don't use birth control, right?"

"Every kind you tried you reacted to negatively, so you gave up and always, always use a condom," he said, repeating back what she'd told him almost verbatim.

"Right," Lane nodded. "The only time I didn't resulted in Silas."

Abe kissed the top of her head again, and Lane went on. "I was scared from the moment I suspected, and I was sick the whole time. Neither of those things went away, and because fear and exhaustion are great excuses to read trashy novels," Abe interrupted with an amused snort, "I wasn't ready when my water broke three weeks early."

Lane felt Abe hold his breath beneath her.

"I was at work," she laughed softly. "I was working with this nineteen-year-old, oblivious philosophy major. He was restocking cups or something while I was putting together the bean order behind him. Out of nowhere I had this giant contraction and dropped my clipboard. He turned around to pick it up, and there was this loud pop and my water broke all over the place. Billy cursed and jumped back all wide-eyed and pale."

She paused as Abe tried to stifle a laugh. "It wasn't funny," she said, "I looked like I peed my pants!"

Abe guffawed, and Lane smiled.

"I hid in the bathroom, having continuous contractions until Brad picked me up forty-five minutes later."

"What took so long?"

"He was with a client."

"What's he do?"

"He's a counselor at one of the hospitals—or he was. I'm not sure what he's doing now."

All Abe said was "Mm."

"Anyway, the ride to the hospital was awful. It only took ten minutes, but I squeezed my knees together the whole way because I felt like the baby was going to come any second. And I was cursing my doctor for telling me first babies take their time, because that was a lie."

"But you made it."

"It was the hospital Brad worked at, and they were ready for us. They got me in and hooked up to all the machines and besides everybody poking and prodding me, everything seemed fine. I had to kick a nurse who kept trying to adjust a wire by my leg so they'd leave me alone."

"You didn't." There was a smile in his voice.

"Fuck yeah, I did. I knew what my body needed me to do, and she was too worried about a monitor wire falling on my leg to get out of my way and let me do it."

"And what happened after you kicked the nurse?"

"She backed off, they let me push unhindered, and a few minutes later Silas was born."

Abe hugged Lane closer. "When did you know something was wrong?"

Lane shrank into herself and whispered, "Almost immediately. The doctor had agreed to lay him on my chest, but she ran him to a table across the room instead."

All their mirth had evaporated. Lane's heart pulsed in her ears. Abe stroked her hair but remained silent.

"I couldn't see what they were doing, and no one said anything for ages. I kept asking Brad what was wrong, but he either didn't have the words or he was in shock. It wasn't until I was delivering the placenta on my own that anyone remembered me. Whatever went wrong had something to do with that, I think. They were all interested in it, and that's when I realized what had happened.

"The nice nurse though, the one I didn't kick, cleaned Silas up and brought him to me. I got to hold him for hours. I couldn't stop crying. I didn't stop crying for days, even after my dad and my brother and sister came and Brad filled the house with roses, I shut myself in the bedroom, not talking to anyone."

"Did you have a ceremony?"

"A small one," Lane said, knowing his eyes were on the urn on her dresser. "I don't remember much of it. I don't remember much of anything from that time. It was like the world went black and white, like I was walking around in this big gray cocoon. Nothing existed outside the grief."

Abe's finger caught her under the chin, tilting it up so he could see her face. He wanted to say something, she could tell, but he settled for letting her see the sorrow swimming in his eyes. Lane captured his lips with hers. He kissed her like he could take away the pain.

"You're good," she said when she broke the kiss and traced his bottom lip with her thumb.

He shook his head. "Keep going."

Lane sighed but complied. "My family left after a few days. Things have been a little awkward with them since then, even with my dad. It's like none of us know what to do with each other. All I had left was Brad, and he tried at first, but by the time I was ready, he'd given up."

"What did help?"

"Sunflowers."

"Sunflowers?"

Lane nodded. "A few weeks after the birth, Brad convinced me to go on a walk with him. It was sometime in August, and we walked to a park a few blocks from his house. I wasn't watching where I was going, and almost ran into a clump of wild sunflowers. There was this bunch right at my eye level, and I thought they were a pretty yellow color. I hadn't noticed color since the birth, so I stood there staring at them for the longest time. When I looked at the rest of the park, the grass was sun-parched and brown. The slide was red. There were a black dog chasing a blue Frisbee. Kids were playing on the swings, and some teenagers were playing basketball. Before I ran into the sunflowers, I hadn't noticed any of that. I brought the sunflowers home with me to help me remember that there were good things in the world."

"Did it work?"

"It helped. I still love sunflowers."

"I know. What else?"

"You know the rest, really."

Abe held her close. For a long while, they were silent, and just when Lane was about to give in to the sleep pulling at her eyes, he asked, "Would you ever want to try again?"

"Try what?"

"Having another baby."

"You know I do."

"You've never said, just never protested when I say I do."

"It's scary," Lane said.

Abe pulled the comforter up to her shoulders and adjusted the pillows so he was lying beside her. She thought she heard him say, "It doesn't have to be," before she drifted off.

• • • •

LANE COULDN'T RECONCILE the man who'd been so tender with the one who wouldn't listen to her or the one who'd caved in her mailbox. She couldn't accept he had gone that easily, and that it had been her fault.

She stared at the wall and tried to separate her grief over losing her son from the loss of Abe. And perhaps the magnitude was different, but the circumstances were the same. The building of hope, the growing of love, the expectation of joy to come, all to be blighted for her just now that other people described as the happiest moments of their lives. Instead Lane had failure, grief, longing, and deep gnawing emptiness she did her best to ignore before it consumed her whole.

The third day after she'd gone to bed, Celia brought Lane her phone. Lane had asked Celia to hide it away, claiming she didn't want to know if either Shawn or Abe tried to contact her.

"It's your dad." Celia held it out for her.

They didn't speak often, but when he heard Lane's hoarse, sullen voice, his casual tone shifted to protective. Lane hadn't taken the time to tell her dad about Abe when he was good news. When she finished her story, he offered to come take her out to dinner, but she told him she was fine, that she had too much work to do to get ready for her shop to dwell on it. It was a lie but telling the lie to her father motivated her to do something. Anything.

Later that night, she picked up her knitting.

When Celia sat at the foot of Lane's bed the next and asked what happened, Lane told her every excruciating detail.

After Lane relayed the part about Abe commissioning an engagement ring, Celia pursed her lips and frowned. "Hence all the 'he wanted to marry me' rambling?"

Lane nodded.

"Did you say anything when he dropped that bomb?"

"That I would say yes."

"And he walked away after that?"

"I asked him not to."

"Bastard." Celia patted Lane's knee.

"That's not fair."

"It is fair!" Celia smacked the bed. "He hears he can have the one thing he wants most, and he bolts?"

"He thinks I was cheating on him. He thinks I'm too young, and that I lied to him when I told him I love him."

"Then he's an idiot and a bastard."

"He has a right to be angry," Lane said. "I'd have gone nuts if some woman showed up and said she was still sleeping with him."

"Yeah, but you wouldn't have beat up his mailbox or thought up the most devastating thing you could to say before you walked away. You would have slapped him and kicked her out, and then you two would have stayed up all night fighting so you could spend the whole next day in bed making up."

"Right," Lane snorted, "I'm sure that's how it would go."

"Well you wouldn't have spouted bullshit about not marrying him because of something your ex did."

"That's not what happened."

"You said you would marry him, and he broke your heart. As far as I'm concerned, he's the bad guy, not you."

"But I started it by sleeping with Shawn," Tears pinged at the corners of Lane's eyes again. She wished she'd never met Shawn.

"Who cares how it started? You and I both know he's the one that's worse off without you, He's the one who chose to give you up."

"But I chose him." The tears welled and dripped down Lane's cheeks despite her efforts to hold them back.

"I know you did, honey." Celia rearranged herself on the bed so she could wrap her arms around Lane's shoulders.

"What am I going to do without him?"

Celia let Lane cry on her shoulder for a few minutes, patting her back and shushing her. When Lane's tears had tapered, Celia said, "Do what you were going to do anyway. Keep doing what you love to do."

Lane picked up the gray yarn in her lap. "What if I don't know what I love right now?"

"It'll come back," Celia said.

Lane held up the needles. The lace that hung from it looked like a jumbled mess, but Lane knew it was an illusion. As soon as it was soaked and stretched and pinned down until it was dry, the design would stand out against the yarn.

"Show me what you've been working on," Celia said.

Lane spread the lace between her fingers so Celia could get an idea of the delicate floral pattern.

"It's beautiful. You're going to finish that soon at this rate."

"Good," Lane said. "That's something done at least."

Celia traced a lace blossom with her fingertip and raised her eyes to Lane's. "Can you do me a favor?"

Lane took a deep breath. "Maybe."

"When you're done with this, will you get out of bed?"

Lane bunched the project back up on her lap. "I guess I have to eventually."

Celia's voice was quiet, but Lane could see the anxiety in her eyes. "I don't want to push you, but I need your help. We're starting construction tomorrow, and the first order of green coffee is coming the day after that, and we are getting resumes for knitters and baristas. I don't know what makes a good candidate for either of those, but you do."

"I guess I am kind of falling apart."

"That's okay. You're allowed, but you're going to need food, sunshine, exercise."

Lane nodded. "When the shawl is cast off . . ."

"Good girl." Celia got up to leave but stopped at the doorway. "I think you're amazing," she said. "And I'm sorry things with Abe ended this way."

Chapter Twenty-One

"What do you think, dearie?" The stylist asked as she spun Lane around to face the mirror.

Lane stared at her reflection. She hadn't looked in the mirror for a week. Her skin was paler than usual and the purple rings under her eyes were darker. Her chin appeared sharper and her cheekbones higher, a product of having barely eaten.

"I don't look that different," Lane said, referring to her hair. It was six inches shorter. Her bangs were trimmed so they didn't fall in her eyes, but her hair was still straight and black and fell past her shoulders."

"We didn't change that much," Celia's stylist said. She'd been trying to convince Lane to do something dramatic since she'd arrived, but Lane had been reluctant. Celia had forced her here with the promise that the symbolic gesture would make her feel better.

"We can always do more," the stylist said.

Lane pursed her lips. For the past four days and nights, Lane had done nothing but knit. She'd finished the shawl for Representative Benton's wife in one marathon session. Her wrists burned with fatigue. The top of her right index finger, where she rested the tip of her left needle while she arranged her stitches, was numb.

She said, "I've always wanted to go blue," just to see what the stylist would say.

The woman with spiky purple-red hair flipped Lane's hair over her shoulders, experimenting with different parts as she chewed her lips in thought. "With your coloring, a full head of blue would make you look sickly, and black is a good color for you. But," the stylist grabbed a comb and sectioned off a lock of hair on the left side of her part that ran parallel to the angle of her bangs, "if we did just this much in say, a sapphire, it would make your eyes pop. And if you got a sapphire stud for your nose, next time you see that ex of yours, he'll think twice about why he gave you up."

"I don't think I'll be seeing him anytime soon," Lane said. She was annoyed that Celia had told the salon why she was coming, but she acquiesced to the blue streak.

• • • •

THE DAY BEFORE, CELIA had joined Lane on her bed, Lane's phone clasped in her hand. "Let's talk about Shawn," she said.

"I'd prefer not to." Lane didn't lift her eyes from her knitting.

"Sure, but the asshole has called you every day this week."

"That's ballsy."

"I don't think he's going to go away until you tell him to."

"I have nothing to say to him."

Celia fidgeted next to Lane, adjusting a pillow behind her back. "While I don't think you owe him anything, I also think you need to make it clear that it is over. For your sanity at least."

Lane nodded.

"I've been thinking, that since he's a writer, maybe he'll respond to a letter."

Dropping her needles, Lane met Celia's gaze. "That might work. Why didn't we think of that three weeks ago?"

Celia shrugged. "New boyfriends, new business. No time."

Lane felt a smile tug on her lips for the first time in a week.

• • • •

THERE WAS A MAN IN her house when Lane returned from the salon. He was sitting with Celia at the bar eating a sandwich. They were laughing, but they stopped when Lane came in the back door. Both of them stared at her with wide, cautious eyes.

"Surely I haven't been that bad," Lane said.

Celia hopped in her seat and squealed. "Oh my God! The blue is perfect! You look better. Do you feel better?"

Lane shrugged, then she faced the man. He was dressed in a green polo and khakis and was only a few inches taller than Lane. He wore his dark hair neatly cut, but not too short. He was clean shaven and wore rectangular glasses with gold frames. His pointed chin matched his intelligent brown eyes.

"You must be Andrew," she said, extending a hand. He gave a firm handshake.

"And you're Lane. Celia never stops talking about you." He observed her as if she might also not be what he expected.

Lane raised an eyebrow. "Sorry if I don't meet expectations. You're not meeting me at my best."

"I was warned," he said. "I'm sorry."

"Thanks." Lane shrugged. "But at least my wretchedness allays Celia's fears I will seduce you and claim you for my own."

Andrew chuckled. "I'd picked up on that one. Unfounded, I think." They both looked to Celia who was pretending to be absorbed in a cafe furniture catalog.

He offered the plate of sandwiches. "Hungry? There's plenty."

Lane waved them off. The thought of eating made her stomach clench. "Not that you're not welcome to come over and raid my fridge whenever, but why are you here?"

Celia flipped the catalog closed. "The coffee beans came. They're on the porch."

"I guess I know what I'm doing this afternoon." Lane rummaged in the cabinet for the little counter top roaster she and Celia had ordered for the Lane to practice with. It wasn't the same as the professional models she'd used in the past, but it would help her get acquainted with the beans until their good one was installed at the shop.

"You are going to eat today, aren't you?" Celia asked after she and Andrew had helped Lane pile the burlap sacks in the corner.

"I'll order a pizza later," Lane said.

"And you're not going to climb back in bed as soon as we leave?"

"I was up when you got here wasn't I?"

As promised, Lane had finished the shawl in the night and let it soak for a couple of hours while she dozed. When Celia arrived at eight with a box of donuts Lane hadn't touched, Lane had been stretching the gray shawl across the living room carpet and pinning it to dry.

"Honey, you've been in bed for a week."

"I've got a project. You know how I like to be busy."

Celia scrunched her nose. "Did you mail the letter at least?"

"On my way to the salon."

"Good." Celia wrapped Lane in a quick hug. "Call me if you need anything."

That afternoon, Lane roasted batch after batch of beans, cupping as she went until she found a profile that tasted perfect, and then she practiced duplicating it. Aside from the whir of the roaster, her house was quiet. She worked until sunset when her head ached from dehydration and she was jittery from too much coffee on an empty stomach.

Pilot perched himself atop the pile of burlap bags and watched her clean up while she waited for her pizza. She'd planned to work on the design for the second custom shawl order as she ate, but the radio had play Mozart, and she hadn't been able to concentrate. She had promised herself she would not avoid things she enjoyed just because Abe had introduced them to her, Mozart, Japanese food, the symphony, but she could only manage the one slice of pizza before her stomach rebelled.

Lane knew the physical effects would subside, but the new stillness around her felt permanent. All her senses worked on overdrive. Color was sharper, shape more defined. Her sense of smell was keener, her ears caught every little noise. It made the silence and the stillness of her little house matter like it never had before. In the past, Lane had always relished her time there. Yes, she was lonely sometimes, but then she would go to work or Celia would come over or Shawn would visit, and Lane would build up enough reserve to fuel herself for a little longer.

Before Shawn. Before Celia. That had been the worst time. She had been completely, utterly alone. She'd had no money. All the family in town had been Brad's. All their friends had been his friends. She'd been so alone, that when Pilot, just a drenched black mess of a kitten, had been crying in the street in front of her apartment during a rainstorm, she'd snapped him up, wrapped him in a towel, and given him her last can of tuna, because that's all she wanted someone to do for her.

It hadn't been a surprise to anyone when she divorced Brad, but even those last few months of living in the same house with him, when he had given up on her, and she could no longer forgive his possessive and controlling behavior, she had at least been in the same house as someone who had also lost their child.

Sometimes, Lane wondered if Brad ever thought about Silas. About what he'd be doing now if their son had lived. About how their lives might be different. She couldn't believe they would still be married. It might have taken losing her child to realize how awful their relationship was, but Lane liked to think she would have figured it out anyway.

The worst part had been Brad's indifference. As soon as he'd realized he couldn't manipulate her into staying, into having another baby, into being the wife he'd wanted, all affection for her fled. Lane was left trying to divorce a man as mute and immovable as a tombstone.

This time, Lane knew what she wanted, who she wanted. Only, he didn't want her, and it was her fault.

Chapter Twenty-Two

It wasn't until the doors at B&C's were open that Lane reclaimed some semblance of normalcy. Having somewhere to go every day and people to interact with helped her regain the equilibrium she had lost in previous six weeks. She had barely left her house during that time for the sake of guaranteeing they had enough product to make it through Christmas. Sleep was still elusive, and her appetite had never returned, but the sharp pain of being alone had faded into a throbbing ache.

Lane did everything she could think of to make the hurt disappear. She started running in the mornings when she couldn't sleep. She worked hard all day. She read novels. She forced herself to eat so she wouldn't lose any more weight. In just a few weeks, her appearance had changed dramatically. The combination of too little food and too much work and exercise had transformed her into the sort of thin angular creature usually admiringly described as delicate. *She* could hardly look at herself in the mirror without the fearing she might break.

In her mind, Lane told herself that the relationship she mourned was too short to be of any consequence, but her body reminded her that the duration had nothing to do with how deeply she'd fallen. It was as if the memory of him telling her his plans of proposing at Christmas, about commissioning a ring, were lodged somewhere under her diaphragm, and with each breath they reminded her of what she'd wanted so badly, but could not have.

But Lane could breathe easier when she was behind the counter. She trained their new employees, and finally taught Celia how to make coffee. She spent her days with the baristas, Annie and Jack, roasting beans while they got the hang of things, and her evenings with Anita, her knitting coordinator.

Lane stayed up in her garage until she couldn't hold her eyes open any longer. Then she would collapse into bed and sleep until her mind caught up with her.

Their first week of business had been outstanding. They'd held their grand opening during the First Friday Art Walk, and had been bombarded the rest of the weekend with enthusiastic Christmas shoppers and curious coffee connoisseurs.

It hadn't taken long for business to fall into a rhythm. The clerks from the shops and art galleries up and down Kansas Avenue stopped in for late breakfasts before they opened for the day. The retired folks from the condos a few blocks over came in for lunch and to play cards.

B&C's even developed its own set of counter guys. A man in his forties who reeked of hash and patchouli liked to tell anyone who would listen about how the Earth was flat. One of the artists who had a studio next door came in every afternoon to talk to Lane about art school. He was a sculptor and though his medium was metals, he had done some work with ceramics. Erik was tall and thin and wore his long hair in a bun on the top of his head to keep it out of his work. He invited Lane up to his studio about every other day, but Lane guessed he really wanted to show her the mouldy couch in the corner. Harrison, an English teacher at the local university who wore sweater vests and overlong hair, liked to quiz Lane's knowledge on literature like she was seeking his approval instead of the other way around.

She kept hoping Abe might come by, but he never did.

There was only one regular who caught Lane's attention, but he didn't sit at the counter. He came in mid-morning, and Lane couldn't shake the feeling that she knew him from somewhere. He was about thirty, the same height as Abe, but bigger. It was hard to tell how broad and well-muscled he was under his brown Carhart coat, but his posture boasted an impressive figure. He wore his auburn hair long on top, swept back with the sides buzzed close, and his auburn beard was neatly kept, but thick and long, and sculpted to follow the contours of his strong jaw.

On their seventh day of business, Lane helped Annie get the ten o'clock rush served before she started roasting. Celia checked how many pounds of beans they had gone through the day before, and Lane asked her if she recognized him as he joined the queue.

Celia waggled her eyebrows. "I don't know, but he's just your type."

"He doesn't look familiar to you?" Lane whispered as she steamed milk.

She shook her head.

Where he had previously taken up residence at a table in the back and kept his coat on, that day, he sat down directly in front of the roaster. Lane could feel his eyes on her as she worked. He didn't glance away when she looked over her shoulder.

It wasn't until he shook off his coat, revealing his thick arms and a black and gray full sleeve with a koi fish over his left wrist that Lane placed him. She had admired that wrist in photographs of him holding a hammer or a saw on his blog. He was a local woodworker that Lane had stumbled upon while looking for people to possibly team up with. She'd been too intimidated by his success to contact him at the time. He was successful enough on Etsy to be featured on their blog more than once and ran a blog of his own that taught woodworking and featured photos that always showcased his tattooed, well-muscled arms.

Intrigued, Lane brought him his coffee instead of calling out his name. "Back again, huh?"

"Yup," he said. "I like your roaster. It looks like a train."

"Appropriate," Lane said, "Since we're so close to the tracks." Lane stuck out her hand, "I'm Lane Benjamin," she said. "The 'B' in B&C's."

He shook her hand. "Reed Ross."

"I know you as Twin Cedars guy," Lane said. "I've followed your blog for a while."

"Oh, yeah? What's your favorite project?"

"No projects for me. I just admire the scenery."

He laughed. "I didn't take you for the type to do the tutorials." When he smiled his gray eyes sparkled. Oh yes. This man knew exactly who his demographic was.

Lane rested her elbows on the counter, leaning forward onto them so her eyes were level with his. "I like your work, though. I'm saving up for one of your iPad stands for our register."

Reed glanced over at the generic plastic one they were using. The way he wrinkled his nose indicating he thought she needed an upgrade. "I can do one with your logo burned onto the back," he offered. "I like the cattle brand. Who does your artwork?"

"That's me," Lane said. "I also did all the mugs and most of the stuff up in the window."

"You're the roaster, right?"

"Me again."

He held up his mug, "And you make good coffee. Impressive resume. "

"High compliments from Mr. Internet-Famous, himself."

"You're welcome."

"I'll let you drink your coffee in peace." She stood up to leave, patting the counter like a judge with a gavel, adjourning court.

"I don't mind," he said. "Need me to build you anything else? A pour over stand to match your register? Some better shelves?"

Lane gave him her best flirtatious smile and said. "Maybe after we've made sure business is going to keep up long enough to warrant it."

"I'll have to keep coming back then," Reed said. Then added as Lane started to walk away, "So who's the 'C'?" Keeping her with him again.

"That would be the blonde going through the cabinets trying to see how much money we lost over the weekend, Celia Cris."

"You both have dude's first names as your last names."

"We noticed. It's why we're friends. You wanna join the club, Ross?"

"Really?"

"No."

"You're not serious very often."

"It's part of the business plan," Lane batted her eyes at him.

"Along with fooling people into believing this place is owned by a couple of guys named Benjamin and Chris?"

"We thought it would be funny if people came in expecting a couple of burly dudes only to find two scrawny little girls."

"Is she a shameless flirt too?"

"Only when she's trying to negotiate a contract," Lane said. "You got a business card on you?"

"Sure. You're serious about the iPad stand though?" He pulled a card out of his black leather wallet and held it out to her between his first two fingers.

"Definitely. And if I can wave this," Lane plucked up the card, "under Celia's nose, I might be able to get it that much sooner."

"Don't forget about the pour over stand," he said.

Lane just winked at him and handed the card to Celia before hopping back on the espresso machine to help Annie with the orders that had come in while she was talking to Reed.

"You know him?" Annie asked, steaming milk while Lane pulled shots

"Just met him," Lane said.

"It looked like you were asking him out."

"Nah. Remind me sometime and I'll tell you why I'm not dating ever again."

"Hardcore," Annie said.

Lane smiled over her shoulder at Reed, who continued to watch her. She felt good about herself for the first time in weeks, like maybe she could make this place work. And maybe there was room in her life for a few more friends.

Reed smiled back, a sly full-tooth grin and held up his left hand, twirling his wedding band with his thumb to make sure she saw it.

Chapter Twenty-Three

Christmas shoppers had bought out most of the pottery Lane had hoped would see them through the first three months. Only a few pieces had been left on the shelves at the store, and Lane had put her knitting on hold to catch up on coffee mugs. They'd even sold a few off the top of the espresso machine just to keep their customers happy.

Lane still had trouble focusing. She was so used to the shape of the B&C's mugs by now that she could throw them automatically, but her mind was restless, and she didn't like to work that way. Even *yunomi* made her heart race, so Lane turned off her wheel, pulled her chair up next to the space heater and sat quietly, trying to count her breaths, but the day replayed through her mind anyway.

She had been meeting with Anita in the early afternoon when a group of high school kids wandered in, Gretchen among them. It had been the first time Lane had seen her since the breakup, but Gretchen had come right up to her and asked her to help her pick out a birthday present for Abe.

Lane had excused herself, and asked, "Are you sure you want to get him something from here?"

"Of course," Gretchen had said. "He used to go on and on about how great your stuff was."

"Sweetie," Lane unconsciously used the same endearment Abe did, "that was a long time ago."

"Only a couple months. I want to get him something nice, and I want to see you even if he's being stupid about it."

A sad laugh had escaped Lane's lips. "You're welcome anytime. And so is your dad if he wants to come."

"He doesn't, but I'll tell him."

"What are you thinking?" Lane had asked, leading Gretchen up to the front. "All of our scarves are on sale after Christmas, and I know I have a couple he'd like."

Gretchen had headed straight for the pottery display. "There was something I saw on your Instagram." She scanned the shelves, then grabbed a square black sake server, part of a set with two little cups and a rectangular tray "This." She'd held it out to Lane. "It looks like it belongs in his kitchen, don't you think?"

"It does." There was a reason for that.

"Do you think he'd like it?" Gretchen had asked.

"I was thinking of him when I made it," Lane had said, and Gretchen had given her a smile like she'd suspected as much.

"What happened between you guys?" she'd asked. "Because you two were great and he was really happy and then suddenly he picks me up one Sunday and he's in a foul mood and his hand is bandaged. And all he'll tell me is that you two decided not to be together anymore."

Lane had bitten her lip to keep from telling Gretchen that *she* hadn't decided anything. Instead, she had said, "We weren't together that long."

"Whatever. My dad goes through women, and most of them don't even leave a dent, not even the long-term relationships, but he's mopey, and I want to know why."

Lane had pulled out a chair from the nearest table and taken a seat. Gretchen joined her. "Have you talked to him about this?"

"He won't talk about it," she'd said. "I don't even know what he did to his hand."

"I don't know what to tell you." Lane had been at a loss. If Abe hadn't talked to Gretchen about it, she hadn't been sure if she should either.

Gretchen had nodded and narrowed her eyes. "I need to know if you cheated on him like my mom did."

Indignation had replaced indecision, and Lane had levelled Gretchen with an annoyed look. "I was kind of seeing someone else when your dad first asked me out. It wasn't serious enough to turn your dad down, and after our first date I broke it off with the other guy. Things got complicated from there, but no, I didn't cheat on him. I'm not sure he thinks so though."

Gretchen had thought about it for a minute, then asked, "Did my dad hit this other guy?"

"No, he didn't hit anybody."

"Why would he think you cheated on him if you didn't?"

"Because the first guy showed up and wanted your dad to think that so he would break up with me."

"It worked," Gretchen had said. "Are you back with this other guy?"

Lane had shaken her head. "No."

Gretchen had chewed her lips as she thought it all over, then looked relived. "Good. I'm glad I don't have to hate you."

"Me too. I always hoped we could be friends."

"I'd like that."

A couple of hours later, Lane had still been recovering from the encounter, trying not to think about how sad Gretchen had made Abe out to be. She'd concentrated instead on roasting the beans they needed to mail out as samples in January. There had been only a few people left in the shop, and since it had been New Year's Eve. Lane had been about to tell Jack to close down early when Reed had stomped through the door. She hadn't seen him since the day they met, and she'd wanted to talk to him again.

Lane had waved as he passed her after he ordered. Reed hadn't reciprocate, but collapsed onto the sofa in the back, somehow filling the whole thing himself. When Lane had delivered his coffee, there had been dark circles under his eyes and his beard had been bushy. He'd taken his mug without looking at her and sipped immediately, either not burning his tongue, or too distracted by whatever was in his head to notice.

Lane had seated herself across from him, her feet on the coffee table. "Busy holiday season?" she'd asked.

"You could say that." Reed had frowned at her.

"Thanks for all the retweets. It's really helped drive traffic to our website."

Reed had grunted, still not looking at her.

"You okay?"

"I've not been sleeping much."

"That's how I started running," Lane had said. "I wasn't sleeping in the mornings, so I figured I might as well do something."

"I'm not much for cardio."

"Sure." Lane had leaned toward him, trying to get a gauge what exactly was the matter with him. "Because then you wouldn't have time for raking in all the money and going to the gym." They'd been the only two things Lane had ever imagined Reed doing: growing his business and growing his muscles—not necessarily in that order.

"You found time for it," Reed had said.

"I don't go to the gym. I sew."

"Right, sew and run and still get all your work done?"

"I have Celia to do all the boring business stuff. I just make."

"I have a guy for that too. I'm too busy with orders."

"Is that why you're not sleeping? Too much to do?"

"No."

"You wanna talk about it?"

"I'm not sure I know you well enough to have that conversation."

"Just trying to be friendly."

"I'm not really in a friendly mood. I needed to get out of the house is all."

"So now wouldn't be a good time to talk to you about your soap?"

Reed had whipped his head around to face her, his face twisted into a sneer. "My soap?"

"Yeah, your secret Etsy shop where you sell soap and beard balm and all that. I want it."

"How'd you find that?"

"I was looking for local shops. You used your own beard in one of the photos for the beard comb. I've got a great memory for beards."

"No."

Lane had been trying to tease his foul mood away, but his face had turned the same dark red as his hair. She couldn't figure out if he'd been embarrassed or angry? She'd tried again. "No? But I do, and yours, my friend, is worth remembering."

"I'm not selling you my soap."

"I'll ask you another time when you're feeling better." Lane had turned to leave.

"Hey, Benjamin."

His voice hadn't sounded so harsh when he'd said her name, and Lane had turned back around with a smile. "Yeah?"

"I'm not your friend, and I don't want to be your boyfriend, so go flirt with somebody else."

Lane had taken a deep breath, so she didn't curse, but then had changed her mind. No one talked to her like that in her own shop. "Fuck you, Reed."

She'd stalked away, leaving him to brood over his coffee by himself.

On his way out the door twenty minutes later, he'd set his empty mug and one of his business cards down in front of where Lane had stood, given her a curt nod, and left. Under his name he had scribbled, *I'm not always such a bastard.*

Sitting in her studio now, trying to reign in her heart rate, Lane acknowledged that the day had been too much, and that was okay. It was okay to be rattled by Gretchen's visit, and nervous that an unpleasant one by Abe might follow. At the same time, it was okay to enjoy Gretchen's company, just like it was okay to be pissed at Reed and concerned about him, even if she didn't know him. And it was okay if she wanted to know him.

With another round of deep breaths, Lane was ready to try another teacup. A book she'd read in school had said that to throw a truly masterful piece, the potter should be just as centered as the clay on the wheel. Lane knew that centered was the last thing she was, but the idea helped her keep her balance when she felt desolate. This time, when her mind wondered to Gretchen, to Reed, to Silas, to Abe, she was able to pull her thoughts back to the feel of the clay on the wheel and not let them linger on loss.

Chapter Twenty-Four

L ane stumbled through her front door, wobbly on her high-heeled boots after her night out with Celia. Tipsy, and more exhausted than usual, Lane peeled off her clothes and collapsed into bed. She turned on her phone for the first time all day so she could set her alarm. The last thing she wanted was to be late for brunch in the morning. The twenty-four-year-old barista who flirted with Lane every week at The Monkey had promised to make her carrot cake for her birthday. No one had made Lane carrot cake since her mom had passed, and she didn't want to miss it, even if she suspected he was angling for a job.

Three months into running B&C's, Lane had settled into a comfortable routine. On Sundays, B&C's was closed, and she had brunch with Celia and Andrew at The Monkey, a rival coffee shop, then an easy afternoon usually knitting or weaving on her sofa. Mondays, she opened the shop so that Annie could have two days off in a row. The rest of the week, she ran first thing, worked on personal projects in the morning, sewing or knitting just for herself for a couple of hours before heading in to B&C's. She would alternate between roasting and helping with customers until the afternoon lull when she would meet with Anita. Then, she would claim a table and work on designing or blog posts until the shop closed at seven. Sometimes Reed, who no longer wore the wedding ring he'd made such a show of, would join her for an hour or two in the evenings. He would set up his laptop next to hers and edit photographs or write blog posts. After helping Jack close the shop, Lane would ride home and work until midnight or sometimes later on whatever product the shop needed most, splitting her time between her loom and her ceramics studio. Celia joined her once every couple of weeks, providing conversation and a bed for Pilot to sleep on.

This was the first night Lane had truly taken off since her last date with Abe. Even on Christmas, when her sister had absconded with a bottle of wine and pulled Lane into the bedroom in the basement and demanded the details of the break-up, Lane had been knitting a new pattern sample.

For her birthday, Celia had taken Lane to dinner at their favorite local Italian restaurant, and then to the symphony. Afterward, they'd gone for drinks at Lustrio, toasting one another and their success with martinis and laughter. Despite being anxious about the possibility of running into Abe at the symphony, Lane had enjoyed her evening.

As her phone came back to life, Lane pulled up the only photo she still had of Abe, the one he'd sent her of him in his gray suit. She was used to living without him now, but she still missed him. She missed his conversation, their petty disagreements about politics, and especially his maddening self-assurance.

But the night wasn't about focusing on what she'd lost. Lane had spent the last four months mourning all of that. The night off, the symphony, the toasts with Celia were all about living in the present instead of focusing on what could have been. She was twenty-eight. She owned her own business. She had friends, a house, faithful customers. She wanted desperately for that to be enough. There had even been times lately where she had been nearly happy. Over dinner with Celia, Lane had almost been able to pretend.

"Did I tell you about the idea I had for baby vests?" Lane had asked as she nibbled on a breadstick.

"What about baby vests?"

"Little colorwork baby vests. We can make a million of them before next fall, and I know they'll sell out immediately, especially if you can get orders from those shops that bought all my scarves after Christmas."

"Have you ever thought about pitching something like this to a line? Selling them mass-produced?"

"I don't want to design machine knits."

"No, no, keep them handmade. Sell them on the idea that they're earning someone's mother a living wage."

"Maybe," Lane said. "I'll sketch out the designs and have Anita knit up a couple so you can see what you think."

"I can think of a million things we can do with your designs without even seeing a sketch. Tell me what you want to do with it."

"I'll start with designing a collection of five," Lane said. "I'd like to sell them here, but there's so much to do in that template, I could come up with fifteen designs and we could do three separate lines."

Celia reached for a second breadstick, "This is why I can't wait until the basement remodel is finished. You should be spending less time roasting and more time working on things like this."

"I like being up in the shop with the customers though."

"I know." Celia gestured with her fork. "And I appreciate the good having a home base has done us but selling your knitting patterns online has kept the heat on this winter."

"We've sold that many?"

"Someday we're going to have to face that your future in this business isn't going to be in the coffee shop."

Lane shook her head. "I'm not ready to even talk about it."

"Then let's talk about something else," Celia said.

"Can we talk about how you and Andrew were totally doing it in your office the other day?"

Celia narrowed her eyes at Lane. "What in the world gave you that idea?"

"Come on," Lane said, "Tuesday night? When you two went in there and shut the door?"

"He was giving me some advice on how to deal with some numbers."

"That's the best you can do?" Lane raised her eyebrows. "You needed advice with numbers?"

"But we were so quiet." Celia turned as pink as her dress. "How did you know?"

Lane laughed. She had suspected it of Celia for a while, but she hadn't really known until the previous Tuesday when the two of them walked straight into Celia's office without greeting anyone and walked out again half an hour later, looking slightly more rumpled than they did going in.

"It was the way you two left, shifty glances and frizzy haired. You barely even waved to me."

"Did anyone else notice?"

Lane shook her head. "Just Reed and me."

"Oh Lord," Celia dropped her fork. "I can't imagine what that guy would have to say."

Lane couldn't help but giggle. "He said, 'Did those two just have sex?' And when I said I was pretty sure you had, he said he thought it was the best thing he'd seen all year."

"Thank God it's only six weeks into the year and that comment isn't as sad as it sounds."

"I think he meant since his divorce." Lane pushed her food around her plate with her half-eaten breadstick. "It's the first time I've really seen him laugh."

"Glad my sex life is amusing to him."

"It was more like he had forgotten that people could like each other that much, and you guys reminded him of it. It was sweet."

Celia didn't say anything about how Lane hadn't taken one bite of her entree, and she didn't let that stop her from eating hers. She did look at Lane like she wanted to give her an out, like she understood that Lane couldn't eat because she was nervous, but she asked about Reed instead. "He hasn't said anything about the divorce?"

"Not a word."

"What gives?" Celia asked.

"I think he likes things the way they are. If he told me he wasn't married anymore, it might make it seem like he's interested in me, when he really just wants to talk to someone who recognizes his sad."

"That's crazy," Celia said.

"Divorce makes you crazy." Lane gave up pretending to eat and dropped her breadstick into her sauce.

"No, you're crazy if you think he's only interested in talking to you." Celia paused for a sip of wine. "That man looks at you like you are a ten course meal and he's been lost in the wilderness living off berries."

"What? You want us to have sex in your office?"

"Sure. There's a box of condoms hidden in the back of the bottom left drawer."

Lane, who had always admitted she thought Reed was good looking, reminded Celia that finding someone attractive and wanting to date them wasn't the same thing. When Celia told her it didn't have to be, Lane changed the subject. She wasn't interested in repeating her mistakes with Shawn.

"Are you going with Andrew to visit his mother next month?"

Andrew's mother lived in New York, in an old family building. Andrew had moved to Kansas for school because he was trying to get from under his family legacy of going to business school, then law school, and then running for office. While he was a faithful and active member of the Democratic party, he had no interest in running for office or pursuing a cabinet position like most of the men in his family. Andrew's mother, Rosemary, maintained that he was biding his time until he thought he had enough work experience to run for office in Kansas, no matter how many times he told her differently. Despite Celia's Junior League years, Rosemary thought dating a woman who owned a coffee shop was beneath her son's dignity.

"He wants me to, but it's right when the remodel is supposed to be finished and the new roaster installed."

"Why do you need to be here for that?"

"Someone's got to pay the contractor."

"I can do that."

"And what about payroll?"

"I can do that too."

"You have no idea how to do payroll."

"So, show me. You should be able to take a trip if you want."

"You don't take time off."

"That's because I don't have any fussy future mothers-in-law to meet."

"Andrew and I aren't getting married," Celia said.

"Whatever you say," Lane said, smiling at her friend. "But taking you to New York on a special trip to meet his mom says marriage to me."

"She is going to hate me." Celia hid her face in her hands.

"You might surprise her."

"I'm sure I will, just not in a good way."

"Maybe she'll like you so much, she'll try to convince you to run for office instead."

"Right. I'm sure that's exactly how it will go."

"So, you're going then?"

Celia drained her wine. "I guess I'm going."

"Good."

Lane was happy for Celia. She and Andrew suited one another, and Andrew was becoming a good friend of Lane's too. They had spent many a Sunday morning discussing activism and how to show B&C's support for sustainability and equality without losing too much business.

When Lane navigated away from the photo of Abe, she smiled when she saw a happy birthday message from Andrew. There were dozens of Facebook birthday wishes from her siblings and her customers, old and new alike. There was even one from Gretchen. Abe had not texted her—not that she expected him to. She hadn't said anything on his birthday, though she'd thought about it, before deciding that he didn't want to hear from her. And maybe it was the second martini, but Lane fantasized for a long while about what she would say if he did contact her.

She would yell at him first, probably. She would tell him off for not listening to her. For letting his ego and his pain be more important that her words when he used his own to devastate her so effectively. But she also wanted to listen to what he had to say. Lane was desperate to hear what he had to say to her after all these months.

Maybe that he hadn't stopped thinking about her. Maybe that he'd been wrong. That his pride wasn't worth what they'd been building. That he wanted to start over and try again with more honesty on both their parts.

But that was too much to hope for, and Lane wasn't even sure if that's what she wanted at this point. But maybe, if she could just see him again, she could tell him to go to hell for making her miserable.

All she wanted, really, was to be able to move on when everything else in her life was going so well.

Chapter Twenty-Five

The Monday after her birthday, Reed came in to install the iPad stand. He brought with him a single cup pour-over stand. Lane used it to prepare his coffee while he fiddled with the hardware. She had to keep squeezing in beside him to help customers while teasing him about how slow he worked.

"You know, I usually ship my stands and make my customers install it their own damn selves," he said after she had interrupted him for the third time. "I should charge you extra."

"Call it a birthday present."

"It's your birthday?"

"It was on Saturday."

"Your birthday is on Valentine's Day?"

"Every year."

"That must suck."

"Why?"

"Because you only get one celebration when you should get two."

"Or, it's great, because when you're pathetically single, your best friend takes you out to dinner and drinks and you completely forget it's also Valentine's Day, so you don't feel so pathetically single after all." Lane pouted out her bottom lip, hoping he'd feel sorry for her.

"All right," his shoulders dropped in an exaggerated show of defeat. "I'll call it a birthday present."

"How much do I owe you for the pour-over stand?"

"Nothing." Reed wasn't looking at her but concentrating on mounting the base of his stand where the plastic one had been.

"I have to pay you for it," Lane said.

"It's a prototype." He had a screw in the corner of his mouth that made him lisp. "Use it for a couple weeks and tell me how to make it better."

"Do I get a cut of the profits when you start mass producing them?"

He took the screw out of his mouth and smirked at her. "Only if we're married."

Lane swatted him with the towel she had been using to mop up spills all morning. "What an inappropriate way to propose. Shame on you."

Reed jumped, dropping his screwdriver with a crash on the tiled floor that drew eyes to them from all around the shop. "Watch it, little lady, you're going to hurt somebody with that thing."

"Little lady?"

Reed picked up his tool and returned to his project, "What? You're little."

"And a lady, I get it," Lane said, but couldn't hold back a derisive laugh.

"I'm going to stop talking to you now."

Lane tossed her towel into the sink and leaned against the counter next to where Reed was working so she could see his face. "Seriously though, how much do I owe you for the pour-over stand?"

"Nothing until I make one that's exactly what you need."

"In that case, I need one that's got at least three stations on it, maybe five, with built in scales."

"That will up the price considerably."

"Then I'll take three more free ones, please."

"And then I'll take that one back so I can make good coffee at home for a change."

"You can't start making your coffee at home, I need your four dollars a day."

Reed looked around the full coffee shop. "I think you'll be okay."

"That's a fluke," Lane said. "We're never busy on Mondays."

"You're always busy on Monday, because everyone comes by to see you."

"That's ridiculous. I'm always here."

"You know what I mean."

"Do I?" She cocked an eyebrow at him.

"I'm not complimenting you outright," he poked her in the shoulder with his forefinger. "You can't trick me into it."

"Why ever not?"

"Because you think enough of yourself as it is."

"I don't know what you're talking about. I am as modest as they come."

"And completely full of shit." Reed popped the iPad into the wooden frame and stepped back. "Okay, tell me how you like it."

Lane tilted the screen back and forth a few times, testing the action and rang up a few fake orders to make sure the height was good. Then she flipped it over so she could see the logo he'd burned onto the back, left of center. "My work does look good in cedar," Lane said.

"I'm sorry, your work?"

"Yeah. *My* logo. The one you traced."

Reed had opened his mouth to protest, but the sound of someone clearing their throat behind them made them both turn around.

Celia glared at them with her arms crossed. "No customers behind the counter."

"You're the boss," Reed collected his tools and coffee cup and escaped to a table at the back of the store.

"Remember, the condoms are in the bottom left drawer," Celia whispered to Lane.

Lane rolled her eyes and went to work sweeping the floor.

• • • •

THE WINTER HAD BEEN unusually mild, and even though it was mid-March, the weather had been sunny and warm for weeks. The tulips were up a month early and the redbud trees were in bloom. Foot traffic had increased so much that after watching passersby stop and peer in through the glass after close three nights in a row, Lane decided to keep B&C's open an extra couple of hours. Maybe it would help the local beers they'd just tapped sell.

So far Lane had served coffee and cake to a few older couples, and some of the girls who worked in the gallery down the road had stopped in for beers on their way home. One of the college kids who had been in drinking coffee and studying switched to beer after he'd seen the others order.

Lane was tempted to text Celia the good news but decided it could wait until she got back. She didn't want to interrupt Celia's time with Andrew.

Before she'd departed, Celia made Lane promise that she would spend a night out with someone—anyone, as long as Lane got out of the house. Lane still hadn't been anywhere special. The highlight of her week had been when Gretchen had asked Lane to teach her how to knit. They'd settled on Wednesday afternoons for their lessons, but somehow, Lane didn't think a knitting date with her ex-boyfriend's daughter would meet Celia's criteria, even if the idea of deliberately going somewhere and trying to meet someone made Lane's stomach turn. She had been compiling a list of everything she thought was more important than dating when a big black motorcycle pulled up in front of the shop. A tall rider in jeans and a black leather jacket dismounted.

"You're open late," Reed said, sitting down at the bar right in front of Lane. He straightened his helmet-mussed hair and fluffed his beard with his fingertips.

"You ride a motorcycle," she said.

"Only way to get around when the weather's good. You like it?"

"What was that? Yup, that was the sound of my panties sliding to the floor."

Reed laughed. "John Irving, *A Widow for One Year*."

Lane applauded with a slow clap. "And that was my one of my best obscure, inappropriate references. What'll you have?"

"Whatever you've got on pour-over."

Lane prepared his drink, watching him as he pulled his phone out and scrolled through his notifications.

"Make some more sales?" Lane asked, setting his mug down in front of him a few minutes later.

"A few. Enough."

"Anytime you want to sell with me, just let me know." Lane hadn't given up on getting his soap in her store, though he still resisted. He didn't say why, but Lane thought maybe he didn't want to be known around town as the men's skin care guy.

"It's not happening," he said, then took a sip of his coffee. "But I do have a question about something."

"Shoot."

"What's the best way to ask a girl out when she spends all day in a coffee shop and you'd normally start by asking her out for coffee."

"I'd probably ask her out for a drink."

"Even if she serves booze too?"

"Sure, just take her someplace different from where she works. Someplace fancy. There aren't a lot of excuses for wearing a little black dress in the coffee biz."

"Do you have a little black dress?" he asked.

"I have a couple," Lane pretended he wasn't trying to ask her out.

"I'll bet you look good in them." He grinned.

"That's the idea anyway."

"You probably look better out of them." His grin turned dark and wild, and Lane felt the first pull of attraction she'd known since Abe had broken her heart.

Lane blinked once, trying not to gape. "Good to know your intentions are honorable there, Ross."

"Hey, you didn't shoot me down outright, that's something."

Lane pretended to clean the counter. "Were you actually wanting to take me somewhere, or just undress me?"

"I'm mostly trying to gauge if you're interested in either one."

"Why?"

"Because I'd like to see you more," he said. "A lot more."

Lane stared at him. He was leaning forward with his arms crossed on the counter, his back straight. It was a posture Lane had come to think of as his pose, because he only did it to show off the muscles in his arms and to make his black t-shirt stretch tight across his chest.

"How about Saturday?" she asked. It would get Celia off her back at least.

"This Saturday?" Reed put a finger down on the counter top like the date was written on the wood in front of him.

Lane nodded. "Pick me up out back at eight. Bring the motorcycle."

Reed raised his eyebrows. "You like the bike that much?"

Lane winked. "No motorcycle, no date."

A smile slowly parted Reed's beard.

Chapter Twenty-Six

After two long days of being covered in dust and dirt from moving her studio, Lane was glad she had scheduled herself a little time off. While the roaster had been moved in and installed by professionals, Lane had driven back and forth over the river, filling Celia's Jeep with boxes until all of her textiles supplies, everything from buttons to wool to her sewing machine, loom and spinning wheel, were now in her new studio at B&C's. She could feel the fatigue in her arms and back. If she hadn't planned this night with Reed, she would still be down there, cursing and tired as she unpacked.

Despite their jokes about little black dresses, Lane had put in effort to look like she wasn't going on a date. She wore her usual B&Cs uniform of black tank top and cardigan with boots and jeans. She'd pinned her blue and pink houndstooth scarf under her leather jacket. Her hair was braided over her right shoulder, her messenger bag slung over her left.

When Reed pulled up she was leaning against the back door with her helmet in her hand. He parked, his gaze alternating between her and her moped.

"You drive a scooter?" his voice interrupted by the chuckles he was trying to suppress.

"Don't laugh at me. We can't all be big burly motorcycle riding men."

"Thank God for that," Reed said. "Where do you wanna go?"

"Your choice. As long it's not too loud."

"I like your place."

"I'm only in this for the motorcycle ride," Lane said.

Reed reached up with one gloved hand and lightly brushed the underside of her chin upward. It was the kind of gesture usually followed by a kiss, but Reed stayed at arm's length. "I remember. Hop on, little lady."

Lane touched her fingers to his wrist, and he looked at her like she might kiss him instead. "My heart got broken a few months ago," Lane said.

Reed raised his eyebrows at her.

"I'm still not completely over it."

He took her hand, squeezing her fingers. "There's no pressure, Benjamin."

Lane nodded followed Reed onto the bike, securing herself against him, wrapping her arms around his waist, and grounding the heel of her boots over the foot rests. Reed tapped the back of her hand to signal that he was about to move, and she tightened her grip. He was solid, like tree trunk. Lane enjoyed being pressed against something warm and breathing and responsive as much as she had expected. It had been too long.

She watched over his shoulder as he crossed the river and steered onto the highway, headed from the northeast to the southwest side of town, the longest ride he could take her on without leaving the city. The wind whipped around them, loud against her helmet, but Lane could see the stars as the sky turned to black.

Reed pulled into a space right in front of a local piano lounge.

"Swanky," Lane said, pulling off her helmet.

"You approve?"

"Why wouldn't I?"

"Because you're a hard woman to impress." Reed held the door open for her. His stride was long and swift, and Lane had to add a bit of a jog to her step to keep up with him.

"What gives you that idea?"

"Until I showed up on my bike the other day, I haven't seen you impressed with anything but yourself." He offered Lane a stool at the bar and sat down to her left.

"I'm not that bad."

But before Reed could reply, the bartender asked for their order. Reed handed over his credit card and ordered a Jack and coke. Lane ordered a martini, and Reed scoffed at her.

"You hafta order the most uppity drink in the place."

"I'm sorry; did you ask me out because you like me, or because you wanted to put me down all night?"

"I thought we were still teasing," he scowled.

"You haven't been teasing since we got here."

"I'm trying, but you're hard to read."

The bartender sat their drinks down in front of them. "I'm hard to read? I told you exactly where I stood. You are impenetrable, like a stone wall with a beard."

Reed smirked into his drink. "Now see, I thought you at least liked the beard."

"I do," and to prove her point, Lane reached up and buried her hand in it until she found his jaw underneath. Then, because she was annoyed with him, she raked her fingernails across his skin.

He winced and held his cheek, "Damn, you are confusing."

"How's that?" She took a long sip from her drink. Perhaps this wasn't a good idea after all.

"At B&C's you're all smiles and sass, but tonight you can't decide if you'd rather shut me down or arouse me."

"At work, I'm a flirt," Lane said. "The rest of the time, I don't sleep, I don't eat, and I work around the clock. I'm not a very happy person, actually."

"Wow, this guy who broke your heart really did a number on you didn't he?" Reed asked with a half-smile.

Lane glared. Thinking about Abe was the last thing she wanted out of this night. "Yeah, he did."

"Wanna talk about it?"

"There's not much to say. He wanted to marry me, and then he didn't."

Reed whistled one long, low note.

"What about you?" Lane asked.

"What about me?"

Lane grabbed his left hand, heavy and rough in her smaller, coffee stained fingers. "The first time I met you, you wore a band here." She touched his ring finger. For the first time, Lane looked into Reed's eyes, and recognized sadness and apprehension there. He pulled his hand back and used it to pick up his glass. Reed was left handed. Lane hadn't noticed that before.

"My wife got a job in California, and while I was working on selling our house, she met someone else and decided she didn't want to be my wife anymore."

"Did this happen sometime around the time you bit my head off?"

"Something like that."

"Were you ever going to tell me that you got divorced, or were you just going to let me think I was being courted by a married man forever."

Reed wrinkled his nose like it itched. "You knew I wasn't married anymore."

"No thanks to you. I only found out because Annie told me she saw it in the paper way after the fact."

"I didn't want to talk about it. Still don't, in fact."

Lane laid her hand over his wrist, and he looked down at her like he was surprised she was touching him. "I've been there too."

"You're divorced?"

"Almost five years ago."

"Your husband cheated on you?"

"No. Our baby died, and I didn't take it so well."

"Shit."

"Pretty much."

"How old are you?"

"Twenty-Eight."

"That's a lot of life you've crammed into your twenties. Divorced, jilted, and lost a kid."

"I don't like to do things halfway," Lane said, and Reed let out a dry, humorless laugh.

He raised his nearly empty glass, "Here's to being a couple of sad bastards." Lane raised hers, and they both drank.

"Is this your first date since?" Lane asked.

Reed finished his drink and signaled for another, nodding at Lane.

"Me too. Sorry about the rocky start."

Then, to Lane's surprise, Reed leaned over and kissed her. It was short, but firm, and he had to steady her on her stool so she didn't fall over backward. Lane squinted at him as he leaned over his new drink.

"At least you aren't hitting me," he laughed.

"Yet," Lane said, and he laughed harder.

"So long as you're laughing at me," Lane pulled her phone out of her bag.

"Are you taking a picture of your drink?" he asked.

"I need proof that I got out of the house."

"Why?"

"Because I promised Celia I wouldn't sit at home alone the whole time she was gone." Lane sent the photo. "Now I need one of you."

"I don't do silly cell phone photos."

"So do a serious one. Be broody. Or, flex, that would make her day."

"You're not sending Celia a picture of me."

Just then, Lane's phone buzzed with a text from Celia, asking who she was with. She showed it to Reed.

"See, I have to. Just be your usual smoldering self and we'll be done."

Reed glared at her, but it only made him look more attractive. She snapped it and sent it to Celia.

"That," Lane said, "is a keeper." She handed him her phone so he could see.

"Not bad." He flipped through her phone photos, which were mostly snapshots of her pottery in progress or knitting charts.

"What are all the colored squares about?" He showed her a photo of a color chart she'd sent to Anita.

Lane dug in her bag and pulled out her sketchbook. "That goes with this," she said, opening to the page where she had sketched out a little pale blue sweater with a pea green and white fair isle band across the chest. "Each little square is a knit stitch. It's shows you how to make this part," she traced the X's O's with her fingernail.

"It's a knitting pattern?"

"It's part of one," Lane said.

"Where do you go from here?"

"I write the directions and Anita and I work out the kinks. Usually we'd either go into production ourselves or publish the pattern online. This is a set I designed so Celia can shop the series around to department stores. That's part of what she's doing while she's on the east coast." Lane tucked her sketchbook back in her bag.

"I didn't realize you were doing business on this level."

"I just have the ideas. Celia's the one who has all the follow through. I was going to sell the sweaters in the shop next fall, but Celia's always thinking bigger."

"She should offer consultation services."

"It's on her list," Lane shrugged. "But she wants to be in business at least a year before she tells other people how they should run theirs."

"I might be interested. I've been wanting to scale up for a while. I have a guy who helps me out in the shop, but I need help with more than sanding and cutting."

"Start selling with me and I can get you something a little sooner."

Reed set his tumbler down hard on the counter. "Nah, that might be a conflict of interest."

"With what?"

"With this," he said, and leaned forward to kiss her again. She was prepared this time, and he didn't have to keep her from falling off her stool.

"Oh," she said. His kisses were like a kick in the gut, desire and heartache mingling there.

"What's next?" he asked.

"For what?"

"After you clothe all of the country's wealthiest babies, what's next?"

"I'm probably going to teach Annie to roast. I don't want to, but in another year's time, I'm not going to have time to do it."

"Isn't your passion really with the textiles anyway?"

"Of course, but the whole point of the roasterie was to help develop a community."

"You two are going to outgrow it in no time."

"Without it, I'm just a sad chick at home, working by myself all the time."

"Thus the promise to your friend to get out."

"Exactly." Lane's phone buzzed again.

"What's she think about me as a prospect then?" Reed asked.

"Pleased. She's been after me to ask you out for ages."

"Why haven't you?"

Lane shrugged. "Because I am an emotional mess, and I figured you might be too."

"That's practical of you."

"Last time I wasn't practical it didn't work out so well."

They were both quiet for a moment. Lane was trying to leave behind the acidic feeling in her stomach that was telling her it was too soon to be here. She enjoyed Reed's company, despite his inability to talk about himself. Her body responded to his proximity and all his little touches. Lane wanted him to touch her everywhere. She wanted to feel loved, even if it was only for tonight, but she wasn't sure was ready to actually be loved.

"What about you, Mr. Woodshop?"

"My coffee accessories line is taking off."

"How are the pour-over stands doing?"

"Catching on."

Lane drained her drink and slid her olive off the toothpick with her teeth. "You know what goes together even better than coffee and woodworking?"

He raised his eyebrows in question.

"Fiber arts."

Reed smiled. "Here I was hoping that maybe you'd be interested in me for sex, but all you want to do is employ me."

"Maybe not all," Lane said, and she didn't miss the way his eyes darkened as they swept down her body.

"Would you like a refill?"

"No thanks. I'm kind of a lightweight."

The mood had turned strained with sexual tension, and Lane held Reed's eye, waiting.

"You wanna get out of here?" he asked a minute later.

"Where do you wanna go?"

He reached one big burly arm out, the one covered in tattoos, and clasped her hand. Lane followed the black and gray waves up his arm, watching the Koi on his wrist turn into the dragon that was mostly hidden by the cap of his sleeve.

"I'm dying to see what all that construction at your place has been about recently."

"You want to hang out in my closed coffee shop?"

"Well, yes," he brushed his fingers up the length of her arm and cleared his throat. "But downstairs. Where there's some privacy."

Lane allowed the words to hang between them for a few minutes, even though there was no way she was going to turn him down.

"All right. Let's go there."

Reed asked for the bill, and Lane tried not to talk herself out of what they'd just decided to do. She pinned her scarf and stood to put on her jacket. He threw his jacket over his shoulders and slid his arms through both sleeves, eyeing Lane like he was afraid she might bolt.

"You okay, Benjamin?" Reed asked as the emerged from the restaurant.

"I'm fine," Lane said, even though she wasn't so sure.

Chapter Twenty-Seven

L ane flicked on the stairwell light just inside the back door of B&C's. Reed followed her in, then pressed her palm to his chest where she could feel his heart pounding.

"It won't settle down."

"I'm nervous too." Lane placed his hand over her heart, which beat just as hard as his.

Reed traced upward with his fingers, running his index finger over the length of her collarbone. "You're so delicate, like you've been carved from willow."

"You feel like you're made of stone." Lane poked at his chest.

He laughed and pulled her closer so that he could kiss her. His hands were eager, and he smelled like cedar and spice, the sharp flavor of the cola clung to his lips. "I haven't been touched since December," he whispered.

"October." Lane slipped her hand inside his jacket and balled his t-shirt in her fists. This would be different than with Shawn. This wasn't just sex. It was the start of something. Maybe even something good.

"Give me a second." Lane stepped back. Reed's hands lingered on her waist as she pulled but dropped to his sides as she disappeared around the corner.

"What—?" He asked when she returned, but when Lane held up the little foil pack, he said, "Oh."

Lane stood up on her toes and pressed her lips to his, sweeping over his teeth with her tongue. Reed held her tighter, almost picking her up off the ground. She liked the pressure on her back and concentrated on turning his breath ragged with her tongue and teeth.

When she led him down the stairs a few minutes later, she didn't bother turning the lights on. They could see everything they needed to with the lights from the staircase.

The tattoo on his left arm extended from his wrist up his shoulder and ended with the dragon's head on his chest, clouds of smoke pluming over his shoulder onto his back. He had a swallow on his right shoulder. Lane could just make out the name Susan over the wing, but it was hazy, as though he were in the process of having it removed. He had a blanket of hair across his chest that traveled in a line downward, hiding some of the muscle definition Lane knew was there by feel.

Reed traced the stretch marks on her tummy with reverence, his touch gentle, as if he was afraid he would break her. But when he laid her back on the big sofa and covered her body with his, he was just as intense as Lane hoped he would be. Lane clung to him, digging her nails into the back of his shoulders while his beard tickled her neck. He panted in her ear as she moved against him. Her groans were much louder than she meant them to be as his powerful thrusts ricocheted through her.

He nipped at her neck with his teeth and sent her over the edge. Lane had to dig in her nails just to hang on until he finished too.

Reed buried his face in her braid, propping himself over her on his elbows and toes in some form of plank position. He swore in her ear, but then sighed contentedly as the tension in his body eased. Lane ran her fingers through his hair and let out a wanton laugh.

"What's so funny?" he asked.

"Nothing, lately I've been thinking I might never have sex again, and then this happens."

Reed kissed her neck. "Glad I could help you out with that."

"Likewise," Lane said, reaching back to switch on the lamp on the table behind them.

Reed's eyes traveled over her naked chest and down. Lane should have taken the opportunity to admire his naked chest as well, but she liked watching him appreciate her. When he noticed her watching him, he kissed her as if he might be ready for more, but then pulled back and sat up. "You are like fire." He pulled his boxers from the pile of clothes and slipped them on.

Abe had said that also.

"Why do you say that?" she plucked her own clothes from the floor and dressed.

He shook his head, as if trying to clear it. "I mean I don't want this to be a one-time thing."

"I didn't think it would be," she said, but he hadn't heard her.

"I want you to know that I heard you when you said weren't over the asshole that bailed on you, and fuck knows it's probably too soon for me too, but I'm not stupid enough to let you—"

"Reed, stop." He was babbling, pacing her studio, barefoot and topless with his jeans barely buttoned. Lane, who had dressed more swiftly had all but her boots back on.

She traced the dragon down his arm. "Let's not decide what all this means tonight."

He grabbed her hand. "That gives you too much time to think of a reason why this was a bad idea."

"I think this was good for both of us." Lane grasped both his arms and staring up into his stormy gray eyes. "And if I have any reservations it's because I don't want to hurt you."

He put his finger under her chin again, his gray eyes searching hers, likely for regret or apprehension, but Lane only gave him understanding. Finally, he said, "I don't want to hurt you either."

Lane didn't believe Reed had it in him to hurt her, so she kissed him. She wrapped her arms around his neck, pulling him down to her, rolling her tongue over his lips.

Reed put his hand on her hips to slow her, then took a deep breath and stepped back. "Let's not hurry," he said, as he disentangled himself. "Show me around." He motioned to the room and almost tripped over her spinning wheel.

Intrigued, he knelt to examine the construction. "How much did you pay for this?"

Lane cringed. "Maybe six hundred, ten years ago?"

"Really?"

"Why, thinking about breaking into the biz?"

"Maybe. It might be fun to make one."

"We could do it together. You can talk about the process of building one on your blog, and on my blog I can talk about customizing a spinning wheel for a specific purpose."

"There you go trying to employ me again."

"You're talented."

"I should read your blog."

"You come here every day and you don't read our blog?"

"What do you write about?"

He stood up and walked around the studio as Lane spoke from the sofa. He still didn't have a shirt on, and Lane could see the scratches on his back, the three below his right shoulder blade still glistened just a little bit. "I'm doing a series of tutorials about making slipcovers for these sofas, and we run knit-a-longs. I did that series about roasting coffee. Celia does social media tips and business posts, specials that we're running. Right now, I'm planning a series about sewing myself a new wardrobe."

"Do people really want to read about you making yourself twelve tiny black tank tops?"

"Believe it or not, they do."

Reed was inspecting her floating bookshelves. "Did your contractor do these?"

She wet a hand towel in water from the sink. "You'll have to ask Celia." Lane approached him from behind, placing a hand on his shoulder so he would know she was there. "Your back is covered in scratches. You look like you've been wrestling with a tiger."

Reed went still when Lane touched him, then she felt his silent chuckle. "I guess I won then, because this is the best I've felt in months."

"I didn't have to tear you up so bad."

"You didn't do it on purpose."

"I owe you a free coffee or something."

"That's quite the discount. Men are going to be lining up to get scratched, just you wait."

"You're not supposed to say why I owe you a coffee," and she swatted him with the towel.

Reed picked Lane up around the waist and carried her over to the sofa she had just arranged, and dropped her on it, limbs flailing. He followed her down, tickling her sides, laughing with her.

They were still laughing when he said, "I should go," and grabbed his t-shirt off the floor.

"Sure, I need to get home too." Lane tried to sound cool, but she was disappointed. Instead of saying anything, they both donned their jackets and climbed the stairs.

"I had fun tonight."

"Yeah," Lane said. "Me too. We should do it again."

As Lane tied her scarf around her neck, Reed reached out with a gloved hand and played with the fringe that hit near her waist. Then he used it to pull her into his arms. "Thanks for coming out with me tonight."

"Thanks for telling me you wanted to see me naked."

"Is it too soon to make plans for next weekend?"

"I'll plan on seeing you then," Lane said.

"Good." He leaned down and kissed her like he really didn't want to go. "I'll see you later."

"Later." Lane said.

Reed waited until Lane was on her moped and riding away before he took off, following her part of the way home before branching off to go his own way. It didn't surprise her that he probably only lived a few blocks away from her.

Chapter Twenty-Eight

The roaster in the newly remodeled basement at B&C's held three times as much coffee as the old one, meaning that even while they added new wholesale customers, Lane was spending half as much time roasting. With more time and fewer interruptions from customers, she was catching up with her knitwear designs.

Lane's new studio looked like an updated version of her house. The room was open, with the roaster near the stairwell. All her textile supplies were stored in the white cabinets along the far wall. Hidden around the corner from the stairs was the sofa she and Reed had utilized their first night together. Across from it was a second sofa, a coffee table in between with armchairs capping the ends, all covered in white covers Lane had sewn. Her spinning wheel stood by one armchair, her loom on its stand next to the other. Her old duct-tape dressmaker's dummy stood behind the far sofa, wearing the dress she'd made for the symphony gala. That dress was too big for her now.

Her new dressmaker's dummy, a professional model ordered in her current measurements stood next to a long narrow work table with her sewing machine pushed to one corner. A pink and white striped scarf was draped over its shoulders so it didn't stand naked, but Lane wasn't working on any new garments. The project that she was devoting to every spare minute to was still on her loom. She was weaving a wide fabric out of a thin, roughly spun natural linen yarn. When it was finished, she planned to print flowers on it and sew it into infinity scarves. She hadn't told Celia about the idea yet, waiting until she had a prototype to show her, but Lane had the feeling that once she did, Celia would be on the phone with one of the contacts she'd made in New York to find out who would pay the highest price to contract the design.

The trip to the east coast had been successful, which Celia claimed helped to make up the horrendous effort of being nice to Andrew's mother, who Celia described to Lane as a tiny, pinched, hateful shrew.

They talked about the trip and their new business prospects for hours upon Celia's return. Lane had stayed to help Celia close while they'd gone over ideas for keeping their new prospective buyers engaged. Reed had showed up just before they'd locked the doors. He'd carried a full paper grocery bag and kissed Lane in greeting. The news from Celia's trip had been so exciting, Lane hadn't given Celia any details about her date.

"I thought I'd bring you dinner," Reed had said.

"Thanks. Celia and I are about done here."

"Mind if I head downstairs and set up?"

"Go ahead." Lane had given him a warm smile. She hadn't seen or heard from him since their date two days before. While that usually would have made Lane nervous, she found herself unconcerned. She was grateful for the time to work out her feelings. She liked him. She couldn't shake the memory of how good he'd felt between her legs, and wasn't sure if she should want him there again, but she did nonetheless.

When he'd gone, Celia raised her eyebrows at Lane, "I take it your date ended well?"

"We had sex," Lane said.

Celia had clapped and bounced on her toes. "Ah, I knew it! Are you dating now? You two could be so good together."

Lane had shrugged. "I think he's setting up date number two right now." She motioned toward the stairs.

"Then you should go find for sure," Celia said, waggling her eyebrows. "I can finish up here."

If Reed had wanted anything more than dinner and a repeat of Saturday night, they hadn't gotten to it. They'd talked about their respective works-in-progress while they'd eaten roasted chicken and a spring salad. But as soon as they'd heard the back door close behind Celia, Reed had pulled Lane into his lap, murmuring something about how he wasn't just interested in her for the sex, even as he'd slipped a hand beneath her bra.

During the ensuing weeks, Reed proved his words as he doted on her. He brought her meals in the evenings and rubbed her shoulders and wrists when they got sore from overwork. He broke up Lane's routine, coaxing her to lounge with him after trysts in her studio and kidnapping her for long motorcycle rides on the weekends.

When they were together, she found it so easy to rely on him. When she was on her own, Lane wondered why. Despite making her body available and continuing their flirtatious banter, she hadn't given him anything. Reed knew nothing about her past or her family outside what she'd told him on their first date. She still didn't know the details behind his divorce, if he had siblings, or if his parents were still living, but he left her languid and relaxed, and she slept better on the days they were together. That was something, at least.

Five weeks into her knitting lessons with Gretchen, Reed still called Gretchen her "Knitting Student" even though he'd interrupted their lessons more than once. That Gretchen had any other relationship with Lane had never occurred to Reed, even though he knew Lane had been approached by customers multiple times and she'd directed them toward other teachers instead.

When Reed had tramped down the stairs during their second lesson. Lane had been working on her newest sample, a white and gray striped shawl with lace flowers on the border while Gretchen knit a rectangle. Gretchen showed a natural aptitude for knitting, and they had settled into chatting when Reed came in search of his sketchbook.

What Reed called his sketchbook, was a worn leather file folder held shut with a cracked leather strap wrapped around an ivory button. It was so old the button was made of real ivory. Inside, he kept sketches for new woodworking ideas, but they were scribbled on the backs of napkins, receipts, printer paper, whatever he could get his hands on when inspiration struck. Lane retrieved it for him, and he gave her repeated small pecks on the lips as he confirmed their plans for the next day, the epitome of a man smitten.

Lane tried not to look embarrassed at Reed's open tenderness.

"There have been rumors upstairs about you two," Gretchen said after Reed clomped back up the stairs. "When did you start going out?"

"A couple weeks ago," Lane said.

Gretchen concentrated on her stitches, counting and recounting the row she'd just knit, then said, "Daddy's seeing someone now too. I don't know her name, just that she's a professor, and he's taken her out to dinner a couple of times."

"Gretchen," Lane said, but she didn't heed Lane's warning tone.

"He's not excited about her like he was you. He says he's trying to play it safe, but I think he still misses you."

"Gretchen, please," Lane said. "Let's leave the history between me and your dad in the past."

"If it's so in the past," Gretchen said, dropping her needles in her lap, "How come my dad keeps a ring engraved with your initials on it on top of his dresser?"

"What?" Lane couldn't breathe, like someone large had taken a quick, nonchalant step onto her chest.

"He keeps your engagement ring right out in the open." While Lane mulled over the implications, Gretchen smiled and kept talking. "I mean, it's really pretty. Mostly sapphires with a couple of diamonds. I think the band is silver, and it sits right on the corner of his dresser like he looks at it every day. And I feel like that's got to mean something, right?"

Lane gaped.

Gretchen's face lit up as she asked, "Have you guys been talking?" as if she'd just stumbled upon a secret.

Lane shook her head, her tongue dry. "No. I have no idea why he has a ring with my initials on it."

"Well, not quite your initials." Gretchen's smiled turned mischievous. "It says *To LBF, with love ASF*, but 'LBF' obviously stands for Lane Benjamin Fujikawa."

That rat bastard had just assumed she would change her name. The nerve of him should have made her angry, but Lane almost laughed as she remembered how he never had asked. Lane didn't want to find it endearing, but she missed even that about him. As she realized that was exactly the name she would have gone with, a deep ache for him bloomed in her chest. He didn't have to ask, because he knew her that well.

Lane swallowed the emotion, because he had rejected her. He had chosen not to hear her, and now she was moving on.

"That could be anyone. Now tell me about the symphony." Lane redirected the conversation back to the story Gretchen had been sharing before Reed interrupted them.

No more was said about the ring that week, but the next week, Gretchen recounted how Abe agreed Lane was an ideal knitting teacher. She babbled on about Abe's polite interest in his daughter's new hobby, how it didn't bother him if Gretchen and Lane were friends. She was recounting Abe's recollection of how much Gretchen and Lane had in common when Lane interrupted, asking if Gretchen really wanted to learn how to knit, or if she was just on a mission to reunite Lane with her dad.

"Both," Gretchen said with an unapologetic smile.

"I only signed on for the knitting," Lane said. When Gretchen pressed the point, Lane reminded her about Reed and that her dad had a new girlfriend too.

"Actually, they broke up," Gretchen said, triumphant. "I told you it wouldn't last—just like you and that Reed guy are temporary because you don't want to be lonely."

Lane forced a change of subject, and when she met up with Reed later that evening, Gretchen's words reverberated with her. *Temporary...* Was that how Lane thought of Reed? She didn't think that was how he thought of her.

Over dinner, Reed shared his newest idea, which was, of all things, mailboxes. It seemed silly not to let him practice with her when her mailbox was still caved in on one side. Reed wanted to make her a new one as soon as he examined the damage for himself. He was perhaps, too enthusiastic about.

Lane thought he was trying too hard to prove he could be a good partner. But they weren't partners. They could be with some effort. In private he was sweet and trusting, but when he'd asked her what happened to her mailbox, she'd lured him inside by whispering salacious suggestions in his ear rather than answer the question.

To Lane's relief the fourth knitting lesson passed with zero mention of Gretchen's father. Lane was unprepared when, a few minutes after showing Gretchen how to knit in the round, Gretchen said, "My dad told me something I didn't know about you the other day."

Lane frowned, "Sweetie, I thought we were done with all that."

"Here me out," she said. "I'm going somewhere."

"All right then. What did he say?"

"He told me that you were kind of a Buddhist."

"What?" Lane was nothing of the sort.

Gretchen explained that when he'd picked her up on Sunday, she and her mother were arguing because Gretchen had brought home a book about Zen. Roxanne had insisted that Gretchen was Catholic and would remain Catholic, while Gretchen had said she could be whatever she wanted.

"She tried to ground me, but Dad showed up then, and she has to let me go with him. And I think he must have called and talked to her later, because I never did get grounded, but Mom's still pissed."

Lane tried to imagine how that conversation would go. Abe had given up on his Catholicism in college, explaining to Lane that he never really had believed, though he'd gone to mass with Roxanne while they'd been married. From what Lane had gathered, Roxanne and her family were devout, and Lane was curious to know what he'd said in defense of his daughter.

"I'm not Buddhist," Lane said. "I'm not anything."

"Don't you want to know why he thinks so?" Gretchen asked.

Lane stared at the dress from the symphony and contemplated putting it away for the hundredth time. It was like a sparkling black ghost, mocking her for remembering that night with fondness—for innocently believing that she and Abe forged an unbreakable connection then.

"Because of my teacups," she said. "But that's not the same thing at all."

"Daddy said that making them is your meditation."

Lane couldn't argue. It was true, but she'd always considered it more a meditation on throwing technique than anything else. She was anything but Zen. She wasn't even calm. But Abe had seen her throw. He'd witnessed her working just enough to notice the difference between how she approached her tea cups, and how she approached everything else. But he was over reaching with his assessment of her apparent Buddhist-ness. Except, was he trying to forge a stronger bond between Gretchen and herself?

Before Lane could suggest it, Gretchen said, "I wish I were an adult. It must be nice not to have anyone telling you who you are or what religion to be."

"I've never had the religious pressure," Lane said, "But there are always going to be people trying to make you be who they think you are."

"It's not just parents?" Gretchen wrinkled her nose.

"Everyone does it a little bit, I think" Lane said. "Every man I've ever dated has wanted me to be something I'm not."

"Even my dad?"

"Especially your dad."

"How?"

Lane chewed her lip, trying to phrase it properly. "Your dad has a lot of double standards when it comes to women."

Gretchen nodded. "Is that why you don't want to get back together."

"No, I can handle misogyny. I don't want to get back together because it turned out we wanted different things."

Lane hadn't meant to say it. It was the kind of things adults said when they didn't want to explain complicated situations to their children. Lane didn't like to think that was how she would parent, but she didn't want to talk about how she couldn't handle losing something dear to her again, and she hoped Gretchen would get the hint.

When Lane brought her eyes back to her knitting, she saw that she'd knit across a whole row where she should have purled.

As she tinked back, Gretchen said in a quiet, somber voice. "I think you're wrong." And when Lane didn't say anything, she added, "Daddy told me about your baby."

"Does he tell you everything?" Lane asked but regretted the sarcasm in her voice immediately.

Gretchen shook her head. "He said that's why you need to make the tea cups. That you still carry loss with you everywhere and that all you ever wanted in the world was a family of your own. For a while, he thought he could give that to you." She paused, meeting Lane's eyes, which had grown watery against her will. "Then he got really quiet for a long time and stared out the window like he expected you to ride up on your moped any second. When you didn't, he sighed and said he still misses you every day."

Lane allowed the dramatic silence following Gretchen's revelation to permeate the air for a count of sixty, then said, "You're good. Maybe you should get into theatre."

"Thanks," Gretchen preened. "I've been practicing."

"Did any of that really happen?"

Gretchen nodded.

Lane bit her lip and said the one thing she'd promised herself she'd never tell Gretchen. "Tell him I miss him too."

Chapter Twenty-Nine

L ane had been thinking about her conversation with Gretchen for the past ten days. Part of her was ashamed of herself for using Gretchen as a messenger, and part of her was disappointed in herself for admitting that she missed Abe at all. More than either of those feelings, Lane harbored the secret hope that message delivered, Abe might turn up unexpectedly at B&C's. Maybe they could talk. Maybe he would listen to her this time. When she was upstairs, she found herself glancing up every time the door opened. When working in her studio, she would make excuses to wander upstairs, just in case.

Reed hadn't noticed.

She was finally on her way to his house for dinner. She'd never been, even though he lived close enough to walk. That she would stay the night had been an unspoken part of the invitation, and though they'd been sleeping together for six weeks, they had not yet spent the night together. Reed had asked her more than once. While she was still hesitant to take that step, she felt she owed it to Reed to give the relationship a fighting chance. It wasn't fair, especially with as much effort as he'd been putting in, to continue to hold him at arm's length. Gretchen had been right. Lane did want a family, and it was foolish to keep waiting for Abe to show up.

Both Lane and Reed had been so busy with work, they'd barely seen one another in the past week. Lane had missed him, had craved his heavy body on top of hers, itched to make him smile. Reed's smiles were so rare, that she congratulated herself every time she wrested one from him.

Lane arrived just as the sun was going down on Saturday night. He had the door open, because the weather was warm and breezy, but the screen door was locked. A red Irish Setter barked at her from inside the house. Lane had known about the dog, but she'd thought it would be smaller, never having seen one in person before. This dog's head was level with her hip.

Reed appeared from the depths of the house before she had a chance to knock. "Samson!" he spoke firmly to the dog, who stopped barking, but wiggled with excitement and blocked the door.

"Hey," he said, holding Samson back with his foot so Lane could come in. "Benjamin, meet Samson."

Lane offered her hand to the dog, who was already sniffing her knees. Reed continued speaking to his dog. "Samson, this is Benjamin, she's a friend." Then Reed pulled her into a lingering kiss.

"Is that how you introduce all of your visitors to your dog?"

"I like to treat him like he has feelings. He's my roommate."

"You are lonely," Lane teased. "Using your dog as an excuse to kiss people."

Samson settled down enough to let Lane pet him, and she scratched him behind his floppy ears. Reed scratched the dog between his shoulders and laughed. "The introduction was for him. The kiss was for me."

"Did you notice that you and your dog have the same hair color?" Lane asked, looking around the living room. His house was small and cluttered. The living room had a small, old sofa in one corner. The rest of the room was populated with wooden chairs and end tables, all in Reed's favorite cedar stain. There was an old TV set in the corner, hooked up to a nice speaker system. Everything was a little dusty, including the candles spread across the room that had never been lit. The well-worn hardwood floors were bare, and piles of books and bills were scattered in precipitous stacks around the room.

"Uncanny right?" Reed grinned down at her.

"Has it always been that way, or is that a recent development?" Lane returned his smile. Reed was standing so close she could feel the tension jumping between them like lightning between storm clouds.

"He was brighter red when he was a puppy, but he's darkened as he's aged." Reed leaned forward and kissed Lane again, holding her as he dragged his teeth over her bottom lip. She had come to recognize this as his signal that he'd like to undress her.

Even though she was impatient for more, Lane laid a hand on his chest and gently eased him back to arm's length. "Don't get sidetracked, now," she said. "I'm starving."

"But you never eat anything," Reed said.

"I will tonight. I've never had a man cook for me before."

"I cook for you all the time," he said, his hands still at her waist, his fingers skimming the hem of her shirt. "Otherwise you'd never eat."

"I can feed myself just fine, thank you."

"But you don't," his fingers slipped under her shirt, tracing upward toward the bottom edge of her bra. Lane had never seen him this impatient before.

"Just because you don't approve of what I would choose to eat," Lane said, stepping back and adjusting her shirt.

Reed took her hint and reached for her hand instead. "Without me you would live on coffee and cereal."

"Don't forget peanut butter," she said, letting him lead her down the hallway toward the kitchen. "I love peanut butter."

"None of your old boyfriends cooked?"

"Not a single one," she said.

"Now I feel like I should have made you something fancy, but I was just planning to grill." He stopped at the fridge and pulled out a plate covered in foil, never dropping her hand. With the variety and volume of food he brought her, Lane expected his refrigerator to be stuffed full. Inside though, was a foil covered pyrex, a carton of eggs, a stack of steaks, and various condiments in glass jars. For all his talk about how she needed to eat more vegetables, he didn't seem to have any.

"I'm not about to be picky."

"You're not picky?" He raised an eyebrow.

"Not about this," Lane said.

"Right." His was voice disbelieving but his smile sincere as he led her through the back door onto the wooden patio.

She'd seen the photos of his backyard on his blog when he'd built the patio the summer before. She was pleased to see he still had strings of lights in the trees. There was a grill he'd built out of cinder blocks in one corner and a small wrought iron table with two chairs in the other. He'd lit tiki torches to keep the bugs away, and the coals inside the grill were already glowing.

"You want something to drink?" He asked. "I bought a bottle of gin."

"You don't like gin."

"But you do."

"If I drink gin, what are you going to drink?"

"I also bought a bottle of wine."

"Wine's perfect."

Reed retrieved a bottle and two glasses, Samson following the whole way. He poured a glass for Lane, and one for himself, then loaded the grill with kabobs.

Lane followed him, trying to figure out what he was cooking. "You're not making me something weird, are you?" Even though she liked the food he brought her, she still hadn't been able to figure out why anyone would voluntarily not each cheese.

"My food's not weird," he said. "It's just food."

"What are we having then?"

"There's steak, onions, mushrooms, and cauliflower on the kabobs. That's bacon wrapped asparagus in the foil, and I've got a beet and apple salad in the fridge."

"You call that not fancy?"

"It's not stove top steak and salad I have most nights, but it's not gourmet."

Lane stifled a laugh. Where did he keep the greens for his salad? "Sounds delicious to me."

Lane watched him cook and let him keep her wine glass full as they ate on the patio, Samson under Reed's feet the whole time. Lane slipped the dog a piece of her steak when she thought Reed wasn't looking, but the dog smacked his chops so loudly he gave her away.

"I'm not going to cook for you anymore if you're not going to eat it."

Lane kicked his calf with the side of her foot. "I ate more tonight than I have in months. You just give me you-sized portions when I'm about a quarter your size."

"Save what you can't eat," he said. "I'll scramble it into eggs for our breakfast."

"I'm spending the night?"

"Aren't you?"

"I don't know," she shrugged. "It seems like a big step. We've been keeping it kind of low key up until now."

Reed had taken a bite off Lane's plate, and took his time chewing while he thought about how to answer her. "I'm not asking anything more of you than I have up until now." He stroked Lane's wrist with his forefinger as she tapped her fork against her plate, as if trying to coax her out of her nerves.

"You're asking me to share your bed."

"I'm asking you to not walk home through my neighborhood at midnight."

"It does get a little sketchy over here doesn't it?" Lane said, thinking about the steep decline in quality of houses that happened in the few blocks between her place and his.

"Cops in full riot gear tackled a guy on my lawn a few days ago," he said.

Lane grimaced. "That's a little scary."

"Not as scary as when they raided the house next door for drugs."

"You're not doing a very good job at selling me on staying the night." She pulled her hand away and crossed her arms. "In fact, I think you should move."

Reed stood and picked up their plates. "I've done way too much work on the garage to move." He disappeared into the kitchen.

Lane followed, bouncing on the balls of her feet. "Is that where your shop is?"

He grunted as he dumped the leftovers in a pyrex dish and covered it with the foil he'd grilled the asparagus in.

"I wanna see. I wanna see."

"You get so excited about work."

"Don't you know me at all?"

"Come on then." He grabbed his keys off the counter and led the way through the back yard to the garage. From the outside, the garage looked like every other garage on that alleyway, peeling paint on crooked walls, and a roof with a few shingles missing. But inside the walls were lined with stacks of fresh lumber and tools hanging from pegboard. It smelled of cedar and stain. The floor had such a thick layer of sawdust on it that a whole horde of hamsters could have lived in it comfortably. There were projects in all states of being. Pieces for a bench cut out by the door, a stack of phone cases carved and waiting to be customized on a workbench, three pour-over stands drying by the window.

Reed showed her the system of clipboards he used to keep his orders organized, planning each week based on the orders he'd received by Sunday morning.

"I'm impressed," Lane said. "How do you do all this with only one employee?"

"I don't think I've impressed you so much since I rode up on my motorcycle," Reed said, "And I have pulled some pretty remarkable moves since then."

"I'm serious." Lane slapped his arm as he waggled his eyebrows at her. "Celia and I have had this idea for a while about promoting other artists and small business by setting up a Kansas based online marketplace—an extension of what we offer in the shop. But we hadn't gotten anywhere on it because we didn't have the time to coordinate it. You would be perfect at it."

Reed wrapped his arms around Lane as she spoke, pressing his hips into her suggestively. "All right, little lady, let's not get carried away."

"Do you think you'd have the time over the summer?"

"You're not going to be happy until I'm on your payroll, are you?"

Lane stood up on her tiptoes and ran her fingers through his hair. "No, I'm not."

Reed tightened his hold on her waist. "Why don't we talk about it more over breakfast?" he whispered and pressed his lips to hers.

Chapter Thirty

Reed's bedroom, like the rest of his house, was small. His bed took up most of the floor space, but he had painted the entire room white, including the floors, and with the windows open and the morning sun filtering in through his white curtains, the room felt big and airy.

Lane had been awake for a few minutes but had been playing possum. She was curled around Reed, who lay on his back, his left arm around her shoulders. He scrolled through his phone with his other hand. Lane adjusted her head on his chest so she could see, but he felt her move and turned off the screen.

"Good morning." He kissed her forehead. "Sleep okay?"

"Yes." Lane stretched against him. "Who's the blonde?"

Lane felt his heartbeat tick up. "That was Susan."

"She's pretty," Lane said.

"She sent me an email last night after we went to bed," Reed said. "She's coming to town next week to pick up some of her stuff, and I was just..." he trailed off, looking at the wall.

"You were missing her," Lane finished for him.

"Yeah, I guess."

Lane disentangled herself and leaned over the side of the bed to fish her phone of her jeans. She pulled up the photo of Abe and shoved it into Reed's hands.

"That's Abe," Lane said. "I still look at it at least once a day."

He stared at the phone in silence for more than a minute. "That is not who I pictured."

"Because he's older or because he's not white?"

"Both, I think." Reed handed her phone back to her. "And because you never said how pretty he was."

Lane snorted.

"What? You can call my ex pretty, but I can't say the same thing about yours?"

"Usually, when a man calls another man pretty, it's not a compliment." Lane laid her head back on his shoulder, but Reed didn't relax.

"Handsome, then. Dapper. Your Abe Whatshisface is a regular prince charming."

"Fujikawa," Lane said. "And don't be petty, Susan and I don't exactly have a lot in common looks wise either."

Reed unlocked his phone and the photo of Susan he'd been looking at popped up. Susan was blonde and tall and buxom. She wore red lipstick with hair elaborately styled in some vintage curls. She had tattoos and wore a vintage-inspired dress with heels and sweet pink cardigan. She looked like a pin up girl. Seeing the other woman's curves made Lane aware of the hollowness of her own cheeks, the thinness in her limbs. It had been six months now, and she wished for her curves back more than ever. Would Abe even recognize her if he saw?

"I guess not," Reed said.

"What happened there?" Lane pulled the sheet up between them.

"I told you, she got a job in California."

"I meant the whole story."

"You going to tell me why Dapper Dan left you at the alter?"

"It wasn't that dramatic, but sure."

Susan had been looking for a new job for years. She'd said there was only so much call for tattoo artists in Topeka, Kansas. The market was saturated, and she wanted to move someplace where she could grow. Reed, who had always lived in Topeka, didn't want to move because he thought he and Susan should build their own community up around them. It was one of the things he'd found so attractive about Lane. Their differing opinions on the matter had been a rift in their marriage for years. When Susan had landed a position in an up and coming shop in the Bay Area, he had refused to move at first, not realizing that Susan had been at her end. She'd had the divorce papers drawn up before she'd left, but she hadn't delivered them until she'd met someone else because she'd hoped Reed would come around. By the time he had, it had been too late.

He'd read about Lane in the paper, and he'd come in to B&C's for the express purpose of meeting her—of seeking out someone who he could give to Susan as an example of making it work—and of maybe implying that Lane was interested in him so Susan would be jealous and come home. He had planned to tell Susan all about his first exchange with Lane, how she had stood so he could see down her shirt, how she had flirted—but then the divorce papers had been delivered, filed by a lawyer friend of theirs with a court date set just after the New Year.

"I didn't realize that you might have been able to see down my shirt until later," Lane said. "But I do remember thinking that you were pretty persistent for a married guy."

"It wasn't a nice thing to do," he said, and Lane told him not to worry about it.

"What about you?" he asked. "Why didn't this Fujikawa guy marry you?"

Lane explained her past, starting with losing Silas and ending with Abe leaving her a sobbing mess on her porch steps.

"That's what happened to your mailbox?" he asked, disgusted.

"That's what happened to my mailbox."

"He normally violent?" Reed asked.

"No." Lane shook her head. "Never."

Reed looked like he didn't believe her. "And that's it?"

"Should there be more?"

"You let him beat up your mailbox, tell you you weren't worth marrying, and then you just let him walk away?"

"What else was I supposed to do?"

"Give him a couple of days to cool off then show up on his doorstep and tell him what an irrational douche he is."

"That's what you would do," Lane said.

"No. That's what the Lane I know would do." Reed wrapped his arm around her and pulled back up against him. He kissed her temple.

"You never call me that."

"Seemed appropriate," he said. "Why have you never gone and slapped some sense into him?"

"Because I've never forgiven him."

"For the marriage thing?"

"That and other things."

"But you still love him?"

"Yes."

Reed picked up her hand, closing his fingers over hers. "So, if he showed up, out of the blue, would you hear him out?"

"I would."

"I see."

"He won't."

"Right."

"What about you?"

"What about me?"

"When Susan gets here next week, where's she going to stay?"

Reed's hand stiffened in hers. "Here I guess."

"And you're sleeping on the sofa, are you?" Lane asked. The sofa was tiny, and his spare bedroom was where he hid his soap making operation.

Reed didn't say anything.

"It's okay," Lane said. "You don't have to explain anything to me."

She sat up again, and Reed rolled onto his side so he could see her face. "That's very understanding of you."

Lane shrugged, "That's because I'm trying to drum up the courage to tell you that I don't think we should do this anymore."

Reed pursed his lips and wrinkled his nose like he smelled something rotten. "Because Susan might sleep over?

Because I can send her to her parents' house. They only live an hour away. I—"

Lane placed a finger over his lips. "No, because I think we missed each other."

"How?"

"If I had met you before Abe, I would have loved you so hard," Lane said, her voice breaking as tears pinged at her eyes.

"But before Abe, I would have been married to Susan," Reed said, wiping the tears as the leaked through her lashes.

"Exactly."

"But we have each other now. Things are going so well."

"They are. Which is what scares me."

"Because you're still in love with the guy who totaled your mailbox."

Lane nodded.

Reed sighed and pulled her back into his arms. "Say we stop all of this, then what?"

"Then you come work for me."

He laughed, his body shaking against hers. "Is it that simple?"

"I think it can be, if we both agree."

He held her tighter. "What if I agreed to come work with you, and we kept seeing each other?"

"We'd end up getting married."

Reed's gray eyes brightened, and a smile played at his lips. "I could handle that," he said.

Lane smiled at him for just a moment, and she could see it. It would be easy to live with him, to let him take care of her, and cook for her. They would work themselves silly and have artsy, edgy children with auburn hair and gray eyes. On weekends, Lane would lay with him in bed like this, and they would make love as the sun rose. It would be a nice life. She closed her eyes to try to hang on to the potential of it, but all she saw was Abe staring at her in awe as he told her he wanted to come home to her every day.

"Except, you'd rather be married to Susan," Lane said as she opened her eyes.

"No," Reed said. "I was married to her for six years and sometimes I miss her but—"

"And I'd rather be married to Abe," Lane said, cutting off his excuses.

Reed's lips disappeared into his beard, and for the first time, he spoke to Lane with coldness in his voice. "That's it then, isn't it? You prefer the man who abandoned you to the one that's asking you to stay."

"I told you at the beginning I didn't want to hurt you. I've been careful not to."

Reed sat up and positioned himself so he wasn't touching her. "Guess what, Lane?" He splayed his palm over his heart. "This hurts."

"I know." More tears spilled down her cheeks. "I wanted this to work. I wanted to be as good to you as you were to me, but as amazing as you are, I can't shake him."

Reed's expression softened and he reached for her and pulled her into his arms. Lane had never felt so pathetic in her entire life. She was breaking up with him, and he was comforting her. Still, she clung to him as he stroked her back and kissed her neck. He was a good man, and she didn't want to give him up.

She brushed her lips against his and when he responded, she ran her tongue over his teeth. Like lightning he flipped her onto her back. Covering her body with his own, Reed said, "Tell me what I can do to fix this." Then he kissed her, grinding his hips into hers so Lane could feel how much he wanted her. Lane opened her legs for him, even though they didn't have a condom.

"It's not your fault," Lane said, rocking into him. "I'm the one that's broken."

Reed panted. "Don't say that. You just need more time."

Afterward, they lie together, limbs still entwined. There was no laughter at their climax, no smiles and happy kisses at the end. They held tight to one another for a long time, and Lane could feel the wetness of Reed's tears gathering on the pillow, though she would never let on that she knew he was crying.

"I'm sorry," she whispered, and he shushed her.

"I'm not going to force you to stay if it hurts you," he said. "I tried that with Susan and it only pushed her further away."

"Will you still come over for coffee?"

"I'll still bring you dinner even." His strong, callused fingers stroked her hair.

"You're very mature, Ross."

Reed shook his head, and continued to stroke her hair, tracing the blue stripe behind her bangs. After a few minutes, he asked. "Are you ever going to tell Fujikawa how you feel?"

"Probably not."

"What are you afraid of?"

"You mean aside from soul-crushing rejection?"

"Yes."

"That he's moved on. He could have even found someone else to marry by now."

"He wants to get married that bad?"

Lane nodded into his chest.

"That's ridiculous," Reed said. "Believe me, he knows what he's lost."

"Why are you being so nice to me?" Lane asked.

Reed rested his chin on the top of her head. "I'm trying to be your friend, Benjamin," he said. "I think I'm off to a pretty good start."

"You mean aside from the fact that we're still naked in bed together?"

"Aside from that, purely innocent." The flat tone of his voice didn't match the flippancy of his words.

"You're okay with this?"

Reed didn't answer for a long time. "I will be."

"Then we should probably get up." Lane sat up and Reed followed her this time, each reaching for their clothes.

"Hey, Benjamin."

"Yeah?" She turned around and he pulled her into one last kiss.

"Dude is an idiot."

Lane reached up and scratched his beard. "Thanks."

Chapter Thirty-One

L ane hadn't seen much of Reed in the past two weeks. He'd come in for a meeting with Celia and dropped by a box of soap but had failed to keep good on his promise of bringing Lane dinner or taking coffee breaks with her. So when he turned up on her doorstep on Sunday afternoon, it was a surprise. She had been out in the ceramics studio when she heard his motorcycle rumble to a stop out front.

"Hey," she said, as she circled the garage. He nodded at her without saying anything as he dug tools out of his saddle bags. "What's the special occasion?" she asked.

"It's Mother's Day," he said.

Technically, he was right, but she couldn't fathom why that would bring him over. Unless getting her pregnant had been part of his plan that last morning they'd been together. For the last two weeks, Lane had been terrified it might be the case, but all the tell-tale symptoms that her period was going to start in a few days were there, and she had ceased to worry.

"But why are you here?" Lane asked. "Not that you aren't welcome," she added when he scowled at her. She missed the mischievous twinkle in his gray eyes but knew she couldn't ask for it back.

"I made you something." Reed unzipped his backpack and pulled out a long, rectangular mailbox carved all over with sunflowers and other wildflowers. It was stained a bright honey color and had mounts on the back so he could attach it to the siding beside her door.

"It's beautiful," Lane ran her fingers over the relief.

"I couldn't let you keep using that beat up hunk of junk."

"You didn't have to."

"I wanted to. Besides," he took the mailbox back, and headed up the porch steps, "It's a prototype. I'll sell them."

"When you said you'd make me one, I expected something simpler," Lane said. "All that carving must have taken you ages."

"Just means I can charge more." His voice was gruff, and Lane let him work. As he installed the new box and removed the old, Lane piddled about the yard, pulling weeds from her new flower beds. She'd planted pansies the week before. Having never had a garden before, she was afraid everything she did would kill them, but they looked nice.

When he finished tinkering, he pulled his big DSLR camera out of a saddlebag and photographed the mounted mailbox, positioning Lane so she blocked the sun.

"Did you hear about Celia and Andrew?" Lane asked.

"What about them?" Reed had only officially met Andrew once, and before he'd started helping her plan their web store, his interaction with Celia had been minimal, but now they spoke daily.

"They're running off to Vegas in a couple weeks to get married." They had told her at brunch that morning, even invited her along, but Lane had declined. The trip, she told them, should be about the two of them.

"They don't really strike me as the Vegas types." A hint of a smile curled at the corners of his mouth.

"I know. At first, I thought they were joking, but apparently, Celia will go to great lengths to avoid Andrew's mom."

That got a chuckle out of him, and Lane smiled. "You want something to drink?" Lane asked.

"Sure," he said. Lane retrieved them both glasses of water, then showed him around back to her ceramics studio, which he had never seen. They talked about the web store while Lane worked, carefully keeping their distance.

When Reed rose to leave a couple hours later, Lane was trimming mugs at her wheel. He placed a kiss on the top of her head, and said, "See you later, Benjamin. Don't work too late, okay?"

Chapter Thirty-Two

Before Celia and Andrew had left for the airport, Celia had told Lane that she expected her do something for herself over the weekend, and to not work herself to death. Lane thought she must be acting tired if both Reed *and* Celia were telling her to rest. When she looked in the mirror she still thought she looked cold and corpse like but no more or less tired than she had done for months. What Lane saw was a shadow of her former self.

But it seemed she was the only one who thought she looked awful. Just that week, she'd had a new counter guy show up. The owner of the new microbrewery down the street had told her twice how pretty she was. Whether he was angling for a date or for her to tap some of his beer, his flirting only made Lane cringe.

Physically, she was stronger, but she missed her old physique, the one that she associated with being happy and healthy. Her appetite never had returned. Lane still worked to get enough food each day. It had been easier when Reed was feeding her. Now, Lane made an effort to plan her meals instead of making herself too busy to eat. She had hoped she might gain some weight back but hadn't yet.

Having the weekend to herself left Lane restless. She'd enjoyed a quiet morning, reading with Pilot cuddled on her lap, but she wasn't used to sitting still for so long. She started a pot of soup, something easy for her to eat on all week long, and cleaned up around the house, trying to ignore the itch to head out to the garage and spend the rest of the day working.

It would be a simple and practical way to spend her day, but Lane wanted to do something for herself. The sun was out, and the wind that blew in from the south was hot and strong, sweeping up the salt and sand from the road and pelting it against the windows.

Lane wanted out in the sun. She'd considered running on the trails at Cedar Crest, a park around the Governor's mansion, but normally didn't give herself enough time in the mornings. Today, though, she had nowhere to be.

Grit bit into her skin on her ride out, but the trees shielded her from the sharp wind once she was inside their shelter. Lane ran for twenty minutes before circling a tree and finding a relatively flat, dry spot to do some crunches and a few push-ups before running down the way she had come. She stopped at an empty bench in a deserted part of the trail and stretched.

Lane let her headphones, music off, dangle around her neck and sat, her legs stretched out in front of her, her arms propped over the back, her head tilted up to watch the wind whip the new leaves on the canopy of oak and sycamore trees overhead.

The leaves whispered their secrets to one another and a dog howled nearby. Lane could hear feet crunching in last year's leaves as a group of people crested the hill to her left. She closed her eyes so she could ignore the passersby and focus on how good her body felt. Her lungs and muscles buzzed with vitality. Dirt clung to the exposed, sweaty skin. She hadn't shaved her legs since she'd stopped sleeping with Reed, and she didn't care who saw.

If she was going to be alone, this was the kind of solitude she wanted.

Lane was fantasizing about the baked potato she was going to have with her dinner, hot and starchy with butter and sour cream, when a familiar voice cut through the ambient noise of the woods. "See, I told you it was her moped."

Lane snapped from reclining to standing so quickly pain shot through her neck. "Gretchen!" she said too loudly. "When did you get a dog?"

Gretchen walked the large white and gray husky toward Lane. Though Lane didn't look at him, she knew Abe stood behind his daughter. A man who looked just like him, only older and clean shaven, stood next to Abe.

"Dad got him in February," Gretchen said. "Sit, Wolf." The dog sat. "You can pet him."

Lane knelt and held out her hand for the dog to sniff, then scratched him behind his ears as he happily panted in her face. "It's a hot one out today, isn't it boy?" She said to the dog. Then to Gretchen, "His name is Wolf?"

"Short for Wolfgang Amadeus Mozart."

"Of course," Lane smiled. "He looks like a Wolf." She could hear Abe and his father conversing in hushed Japanese, staying a few feet back. Lane glanced up again, and Abe was frowning at his father.

"That's grandpa," Gretchen said.

"I thought so," Lane said. "How's your shawl coming?"

"Slowly," she said. "Can I come by sometime this week with questions?" Gretchen's lessons had become less regular as she'd grown more comfortable with her craft, but they still met every couple of weeks.

"Sure," Lane smiled. "I'm always there."

"Great," Gretchen said and glanced back over her shoulder. Lane allowed herself to examine Abe's father. He was a touch shorter than his son. His hair was completely gray, but he had the same nose and cheekbones Abe shared with Gretchen.

"Do they do that a lot?" Lane asked, gesturing in Abe's direction.

"Talk so no one else can understand them?" Gretchen asked.

Lane nodded.

"All the time." Gretchen rolled her eyes. "They talk too fast for me. It's so annoying."

Abe's father noticed Lane motioning at them and took a few steps forward. "Introduce us to your friend, Gretchen." His voice had only the slightest hint of an accent.

"Dad knows her better than I do," Gretchen said, but the elder Fujikawa was already pushing his son forward to stand behind Gretchen and the dog. Lane stood and Wolf continued to nuzzle her hand.

"This is my grandpa," Gretchen said.

Lane held her hand out, conscious that in addition to being sweaty and dirty she was now covered in dog. "It's a pleasure to meet you, Dr. Fujikawa."

"Doctor?" He frowned at her. "Are you one of my students?"

"No, Sir."

"Just Fujikawa then."

"All right. It's nice to meet you Fujikawa. I'm Lane Benjamin."

"You are, aren't you." Lane hadn't known until then that he had any idea who she was. "Benjamin. Is that English or Hebrew?"

"English," Lane said.

"England is a beautiful country. Have you ever been?"

"No, Sir."

"Everyone should visit their homeland," he said.

Lane just smiled at him, busy fending off the dog who was begging for more of her attention and large enough to demand it if he wanted.

"Wolf," Abe said and made a clicking sound with his tongue. The dog backed up and sat at his master's feet. Gretchen handed her father the leash and sat down on the bench, giving Lane a significant look as she passed.

Lane was just getting ready to make her excuses and leave when Fujikawa asked. "How do you know my son?" The question caught her off guard.

"Gretchen told you, she owns a coffee shop in town," Abe said.

"That's how Gretchen knows her. I want to know how you know her."

Abe said something in Japanese, but his father spoke over him. "He reminds me that I know exactly how you know each other, and guards me against embarrassing myself," he translated for Lane. "But he doesn't listen to me when I tell him he should marry you."

"Dad, please," Abe said.

"I-" was all Lane could get out.

"But since you don't want her, maybe I'll marry her myself and have more sons instead of grandsons. I'm just as handsome as he is, don't you think?" The elder Fujikawa grinned and winked at her.

Lane could only blink. Was he teasing her?

"Dad let her get back to her run," Abe said.

Lane allowed herself to take in the sight of him at last. He held Wolf on a short leash and scowled at his father. He was dressed in jeans and white polo shirt left untucked. His hair was the same, though perhaps the steel gray streaks were more pronounced. His beard hadn't been trimmed, and there were more silver hairs by the corners of his mouth.

Lane hadn't expected desire to be what she felt upon seeing him for the first time in more than six months, but she longed to press her lips against his, to knot her fingers in his hair and find a spot just secluded enough.

"It's kay," Lane said, averting her gaze to the dog. "I don't mind."

"Of course it's okay," Fujikawa said. "It's good for old friends to meet." Then he switched to Japanese and Lane frowned. It was difficult enough to keep up when they were all speaking English.

"I'm sorry," Abe said. He had been studying her, taking in the differences in her appearance from October to May. "We came out for a walk. We didn't mean to bother you."

"I'm not bothered."

"Dad gets excited when Gretchen's around." Lane looked over her shoulder. She hadn't noticed Fujikawa sneak away, but now he was giving Gretchen a Japanese lesson on the bench. "She's staying with us all week, and he hasn't really seen her since last summer."

"How long is your dad staying?"

"We're leaving to visit some relatives in Tokyo next week, then I'll stay with him in Boston for a little while."

"Sounds like a great summer."

"I'll be telecommuting for most of it. I'm lucky to have time off at all, with session still going." Abe looked down at Wolf, who was straining at the leash. He clicked his tongue and the dog stilled. As a reward, Abe stroked Wolf's head. Lane fought the desire to play with Abe's new, longer beard. She wanted to slip her hand underneath his shirt and feel his athletic stomach, to feel him inside her. More than that, she wanted to be a part of this little family, to go home with them to dinner, to read the paper with them in the morning, to have Abe show her his favorite places in Japan.

"You look good," he said. "You always looked good," he qualified, "but you look like your new life agrees with you."

Lane reached out and pet the dog, placing her hand dangerously close to Abe's. "I work all the time," she said. "Gretchen comes in a lot."

"She tells me about your knitting lessons."

"She's a natural."

"I think she's dazzled by you," he said. "You're all she talks about these days."

"I'm not surprised," Lane said. "I'd suspect her of setting this up, if I hadn't decided to come here spur of the moment."

"You think she's trying to get us back together?"

"She's told me as much." Lane smiled down at Wolf. "I can't believe you got a dog." She wanted him to lift his hand from the dog's neck and close it around her waist. She wanted him to stop this stupid small talk and kiss her.

"We should get going," he said.

Her heart stopped it's frantic beating and dropping straight out of her chest. He hadn't forgiven her then, no matter how good he thought she looked.

"Sure. I've got work to do at home."

He nodded as if he expected nothing less.

That was it. She'd finally seen him, and despite her fantasies, there was no reconciliation. He didn't listen to her. He'd barely been able to look at her, she him. He was going about his life just like normal. Like she'd never been a part of it. And that was good. That was how it should be.

"It was nice to see you," she said, then couldn't help but add, "I like the longer beard."

"It's just because I'm on vacation." He gave her a sly smile anyway, a ghost of his grin.

"I think you could get away with it all the time."

She scratched behind Wolf's ears one last time and looked back up at Abe. She touched two fingers to his wrist, just to see if she had any effect on him at all and could feel his pulse racing. "I'll see you around maybe."

He swallowed and said, "Maybe," but didn't move to touch her in return. They stood close enough to kiss, if only one of them would incline their head just so. But he looked away instead.

Lane stepped out of range. She tucked the ear buds back in her ears and raced back down the trail to her moped.

Chapter Thirty-Three

Lane opened the shop like normal on Monday morning, even though it was Memorial Day and she knew it would be slow. She used the extra time catch up on other work and enjoyed leisurely chats with the few customers she had.

By the time Reed showed up at noon, the shop was empty again. He brought a sample of the maple he wanted to use for the spinning wheel he was going to build for her and confessed that Celia had called him that morning and asked him to check up on her.

"I'm a big girl," Lane said. "I don't need a babysitter." She had talked to Celia the night before, relaying the events in the park.

Reed furrowed his brow and pursed his lips. He sipped his coffee instead of telling her again that she didn't take very good care of herself. "Have you eaten today?" he asked instead. "I can bring you something." He ventured a stab at giving her a friendly smile, but it flickered out quickly when she didn't reciprocate.

"I had breakfast before I left the house," she said, wiping the counter with a damp towel.

"And now it's lunch time. What do you want to eat?"

Lane shrugged. "I'm not hungry."

Reed swiped the towel to the floor and grasped her hand between both of his. "If you're not going to let me do anything else, at least let me feed you."

It was the first time since they'd ended things that he'd given her any indication that he still had feelings for her. The tenderness he rarely showed to anyone lingered in his eyes, and Lane was overcome with how easy it would be to let Reed take care of her. He would rain down his love on her so hard she would be in danger of drowning in it. And it was tempting.

"What did you have in mind?" she asked.

"I slow roasted some pork this weekend," he said, the hint of a grin playing at the corners of his mouth. "And I have some ripe avocados and some salsa."

"Don't tell me. You made the salsa too."

"Just finished fermenting this morning."

Lane let a smile spread over her lips. "You are a freak, you know that right?"

"Says the woman with the spinning wheel behind her bar." Lane had brought it upstairs for the day. She so rarely had time to do it anymore.

"Fine." Lane said. "Bring me some of your freaky pork, but not a you size serving, a me size..." But something had caught Lane's eye out the front window and she felt herself go pale. A gray Mercedes had pulled right up to the front door.

Reed followed Lane's stare.

"Is that his car?" he asked, and Lane nodded, her mouth dry. "It makes him look like an asshole."

Lane was still holding Reed's hand. "He'd say the same thing about your motorcycle."

They watched as Gretchen got out of the driver's seat.

"Ah, it's just your knitting student."

"That's his daughter," Lane said.

Abe and his father followed Gretchen out of the car.

Reed gaped at her. "You never said anything"

"I can't believe you never put it together," Lane laughed, but Reed didn't look amused, so Lane said, "Teaching her to knit had nothing to do with you or him."

Reed nodded and turned his gaze back toward the front window. She took a deep breath and held Reed's hand tighter as Gretchen held the door for the two elder Fujikawas.

"You want me to get rid of them?" Reed asked, his gray eyes steady, his voice soft. Lane almost wished they hadn't been interrupted, but she could feel Abe's eyes concentrating on the hand that held Reed's. His frown obvious from across the shop.

Lane practiced smiling. "I always said he would be welcome if he wanted to come." She squeezed Reed's hand one last time before she took off her apron.

"Welcome, Fujikawas!" she pasted on her customer service smile. "See anything that strikes your fancy?"

Abe's dad was running his fingers over the weft of a black and gray striped scarf. "You sell scarves in this heat?"

"Not as many as in the winter, but the allure of wool and silk can be hard to pass up."

"Yes, but will my picky brother-in-law like it?" Fujikawa asked.

"I can't answer that," Lane said. "But it is unique, made by this here Kansas girl."

"You made all of this?" he asked.

"Most of the pottery and textiles. The jewelry and the candles were made by other locals. Reed did the soaps."

"Who's Reed?" Abe asked, speaking for the first time. He had maneuvered so he was standing next to Lane. Examining a bar of sandalwood soap had been his excuse.

"Reed's the big guy sitting at the counter," Lane said as Fujikawa moved off to peruse at the far end of the shelf. Gretchen was looking at a spinner rack of earrings, already ignoring them all.

Hearing his name, Reed turned on his stool. Lane smiled and motioned to him that he should stay where he was. Abe watched him nod and pull out his phone for a distraction.

"Is he your bodyguard or something?" He asked, still scrutinizing the other man.

"Kind of."

"Kind of?"

He took a step closer to Lane. She adjusted a silk scarf on its display, pretending not to notice he stood too close on purpose.

"Celia sent him over to check on me after yesterday. She was worried I might be upset."

Abe frowned, stepping closer to Lane and rested his elbow on a shelf. "Why didn't Celia come herself?"

"Because Celia's in Vegas getting married." Lane couldn't hide her happy smile.

"No kidding?" Dropping the jealous act, he grinned back at her. For the first time, she noticed he was wearing her favorite of his shirts, a rich dark blue Ralph Lauren. It was too hot for it, and he had the sleeves rolled up to his elbows. "Same guy as before?"

"Same guy," Lane nodded.

"Tell her I said congratulations." Abe sniffed a bar of beer soap, his eyes back on Reed. "He just makes your soap?"

"We work together," Lane said. "And we dated for a while."

Abe dropped the soap back onto the display like he'd just realized he'd been holding a roach. "Past tense?"

Lane knew he was thinking of Shawn, and how she had been holding Reed's hand when Abe arrived. "We dated, then we broke up, and now he works for me."

"That's it?"

"Why are you so curious?" she asked.

Abe shook his head and said nothing but didn't take his eyes off Lane's.

"Because he spent all night chopping wood," Fujikawa said.

Lane didn't understand and looked from Abe to his father for an explanation, but it was Gretchen who said, "Daddy chops firewood when he's upset."

"I was cleaning up that dead apple tree. It's needed to come down since last year."

"You've been finding a lot of dead trees lately," Gretchen said.

"I've never seen so much firewood stockpiled going into summer," Fujikawa said, and they all laughed, even Abe chuckled to himself.

"You two are no help," he said.

"You never would have come if Grandpa hadn't bugged you about it all morning," Gretchen said and winked at Lane through the mirror where she was trying on a necklace. Lane giggled as Abe smiled at her. There was a familiar light in his eyes, one that she recognized from before anything happened between them.

"Would you guys like some coffee?"

Lane took their orders and retreated to the bar, starting two cups of pour over and a mocha for Gretchen.

"Looks like things are going well," Reed said.

"They're civil. You want a refill?"

"Nah." Reed stood and cracked his knuckles. "I was gonna go grab lunch. You still want some?"

"I'll try to eat. But hurry back, just in case."

Lane turned around to grab a tray for the drinks to find Abe had sneaked up behind her, his eyebrows raised. "Just in case of what?"

Lane didn't say anything so Reed stepped forward and offered Abe his hand. "Reed Ross. I'm a friend of Benjamin's."

"Abraham Fujikawa," Abe said and gave Reed's hand a single shake. "Just in case of what?" he asked Lane again.

"In case we fight," Lane said, her voice barely above a whisper.

"I don't want to fight." Abe's voice was low and soft. "But I would like to speak with you in private."

Lane stared at him, afraid that any words he had for her would be devastating.

When Reed didn't budge, Abe said to him, "You can go. There's nothing to worry about."

"I just replaced her mailbox," Reed scratched the underside of his beard as he spoke. "It would be nice if you could leave without breaking anything else I'll have to fix." He turned to Lane. "I'll be right back."

Abe watched Reed start up his motorcycle and whispered to himself, "Of course that's his." Lane smiled to herself at his predictability.

Abe didn't waste any time taking the seat Reed vacated. "Does he know it's over?" Abe asked, "Because—

But Lane didn't let him finish, his words the spark that kindled the little flame of anger she'd carried around with her since their break up. "That's not the best way to start if you don't want to fight." Lane sat his coffee down in front of him with a thunk.

"You're right." He accepted the mug, pretending she hadn't sloshed half the coffee on the counter. "It's not every day you meet the guy you were traded in for."

"I didn't trade you in," Lane said. "You walked out on me, and I was heartbroken."

When Abe's response was to turn his skeptical frown to where Reed's bike had been parked, Lane slapped the counter. "No," she said, as Abe's eyes snapped back to her. "You don't get to do that. You don't get to judge me for trying to move on, even if I failed because I missed you too much."

Lane loaded the other coffees onto a tray and took off to deliver them so she didn't have to see Abe's response. He stopped her as she passed with a gentle hand on her forearm. "I'm sorry," he whispered, "I've missed you too." Then let go.

Fujikawa took his mug and sat at a nearby table to watch his granddaughter shop. Gretchen sipped at her latte as she inspected more of the jewelry.

"I'm sorry this the first time I'm trying your coffee," Abe said when she stood in front of him again, the bar between them. "It's really good."

"You should be sorry," she said.

"Lane," he said, offering his hand over the counter. "Don't."

"Don't what? Tell you you should have been here opening night and every morning since? Tell you that I wanted you to be here?" She ignored his hand, leaving it empty on the counter until he withdrew it.

"Lane," he said again. His voice was gentle, but firm, like he was scolding a very small child.

"Or maybe you don't want to hear that I think we should be the ones in Vegas getting married."

Abe set his jaw, acquiring something of the stern stature he had worn the night he'd left. "I know you didn't want me to leave that night, but I couldn't stay."

"You should have."

"I needed time."

"You could have let me explain."

"There was nothing left to explain," Abe looked over his shoulder to see if his family was bothered by their argument, but they were still absorbed in picking out gifts. "I knew everything I needed to know about you and that kid."

"I was thinking it would have been more a conversation about how we cared so much about each other that none of that other stuff mattered."

"But it did matter—it still does."

"Then why are you even here?" Lane crossed her arms over her chest and scowled.

"Because I wanted to see you."

"You've seen me. Now what?"

"You look so different," he said. "Last night, as I was outside chopping another tree, all I could think, over and over was, 'I did that to her. It's my fault she's half-starved herself.'"

"You were right," Lane said. "I haven't been able to eat since you left."

He scoffed. "How did I become the bad guy when you were the one sleeping with someone else?"

Lane had to bite her bottom lip to keep from cursing at him and spoke through clenched teeth. "Because I wasn't sleeping with anybody but you."

"That's not what it looked like."

"And I think you were taking your anger about what happened in your first marriage out on me twelve years later."

Abe's lips disappeared. "There were similarities."

"It wasn't the same."

"You lied to me." The quiet menace in his voice left no room for argument. But if he wasn't prepared to listen to her, why had he come?

"I was trying to leave Shawn behind and start something new with you, and if you would have stayed, I could have told you that."

"I couldn't stay."

"You could have let me take you to the ER."

He held up his right hand, which was long and lean and perfect except for a thin curved scar between his first two knuckles. "I didn't need an ER."

"You could have let me clean you up."

"How many times do I have to tell you I couldn't stay?" His voice was rising every time he spoke.

"Tell me again."

"It's better I left."

"You prefer things like this?" Lane motioned between herself and Abe.

"You don't understand how angry I was. I was furious. I was violent." He pounded the counter for emphasis.

"I don't believe for a second that you left so that you wouldn't hurt me, so try again."

Abe's shoulders slumped forward as the fight left him. "I would never hurt you. If that kid had come back, if he hadn't put his hands up and backed away, I could have killed him."

"You could have come back when you'd settled down." She too softened her tone, trying to meet him halfway.

"It took me a month to settle down." Abe looked up at her like he didn't like to admit it.

"You walked around that angry for a month?"

"Didn't you?"

"I wasn't so much angry as devastated."

"Don't say that." He dropped his gaze into his coffee cup, and when he looked back up, his expression was carefully neutral.

"I was in bed for a week," she said.

"No."

"I haven't been able to eat or sleep normally since."

"Don't say that," he said again.

"Why not?" Lane asked. "It's the truth."

"Because it doesn't help when you confirm my worst fears about us." He spoke into his coffee cup.

"Which are?"

"That you would have been better off had I never pursued you."

"Don't be self-deprecating," Lane wanted to call his bluff. "It's insincere."

"But you—"

"I only got all this," Lane motioned to the store, "because of you."

"I did nothing to help," he said.

"You told me I should."

"I wasn't the only one who said you could do this."

"You were the first one I believed."

Their eyes met for just a moment before Lane averted her to watch for Reed's return. If he'd gotten all the lights, he could be back any second, and then Lane wouldn't have to face the unyielding resolve in Abe's eyes.

"You look more like you today," his fingers landed gently on the back of the hand she had used to stabilize herself against the counter. He meant it as a compliment, she knew, but he hadn't broken character yet, and she knew worse was coming.

"Lane." He used his morning after voice now, raw and tender. Lane's stomach swan dived into her toes, and she flipped her hand over and held on to his fingers.

"Abe." She closed her eyes. "Whatever you're going to say, just don't." Lightning radiated throughout her body from where their hands met. His brown eyes were sweet and sad and full of regret, and even though Lane knew it was an act, it broke her heart all over again knowing what he was going to say.

"I have to," he said.

"No, you don't. Say what you mean instead."

He sighed and squeezed her hand. "You should forget about me and move on."

"I'm not going to forget about you," she said. "I love you."

Abe didn't stir, didn't breathe.

"You still with me?" Lane asked.

Abe hesitated, as if he had multiple replies all trying to get off his tongue at once. He and the character of himself were warring for dominance, but the character won. "Those words from your lips are the sweetest sounds in the world to me, but it doesn't change anything."

"It should change everything."

"Look at us," he said, wiping the single tear that had escaped down Lane's cheek with his free hand. "I'm not good for you."

"Being without you is torture." She leaned into to his touch, and he cupped her chin like he might kiss her.

"You should be with someone your own age."

"But you're the man I chose." He wiped away another tear with his thumb.

"You should be with someone like him." Abe nodded toward the window. The rumble of Reed's motorcycle announced his return. "Not someone people could mistake for your father."

Lane snorted. "I don't think anyone's going to mistake you for my father."

"You know what I mean." His hand fell away from her face.

"You are not old."

"I'm too old for you."

"That's bullshit and you know it."

"What are you going to do in thirty years when I am falling apart?"

"Be thankful for whatever time we have."

"I don't want to do that to you." The pain in his eyes was genuine.

"But we'd have thirty years."

"It's better this way. I'm not right for you."

"Yes," Lane said, grabbing him around the wrist. "You are. You're perfect for me." She reached across the counter with her other hand and finally ran her fingers through the thick black hairs of his untrimmed beard. He nuzzled her hand by reflex.

"Goddamit, Lane." He slipped from his script.

"Goddamit?" She smiled.

"That's not fair." He leaned further into her hand and buried his nose in her wrist.

"Why?"

"You know why." He brought her fingers to his lips.

"Do I?" Hope welled as her heart lightened. She almost had him.

He kissed her knuckles. Her palm. Her wrist. "You know I want you."

It was like someone had splashed her with icy water.

"What?"

"I want you," he said.

Lane pulled her hands back, and Abe's jaw fell open in shock.

"You *want* me?"

"Of course I do." He reached for her.

"Fuck. You. Abe."

The words rang out through the quiet shop.

Fujikawa and Gretchen left their coffees and passed Reed, going out as he came in.

"What about that was offensive?" Abe asked.

"Make up your mind. You either want me or you don't."

"I shouldn't want you."

"Fuck you," she said again, fighting the rage that was rising in her chest.

"But I do," Abe grasped for her over the counter, but she stayed just out of his reach.

"What would you do with me if you had me?" Lane asked. "Show me off to your important friends? Or just fuck me for fun?"

"You know I didn't mean it that way." His voice was ice, his stature frozen, fists clenched at his sides.

"How was I supposed to take it?"

"Like how you know I meant it."

"I asked how you meant it, and you didn't answer me."

"You know me better than that," he said through clenched teeth.

"I'm not sure I know you at all." Lane's voice rose again.

"How could you say that?" he asked.

"After you've been spouting bullshit at me like we're at the fucking statehouse?" Lane was so angry with him, she was screaming. "I don't know. How could you say *that* of all things?"

"You know that's not what I meant."

"So say what you fucking mean!"

"I want you!" he yelled. But what got to Lane was the steely defiance in his eyes as he ground out "I. Want. You." like Lane should be satisfied with what little he was prepared to give her and be happy with it.

She deserved more than that.

"You should go." Lane turned her back on him.

"Lane," he was back to the morning after voice. "Darling, we—"

Lane whirled and pointed to the door. "Go!"

Abe backed up two paces and clamped his jaw shut, panting through his nose.

Reed had made it to Abe's side without either of them noticing. He placed a large hand over Abe's shoulder and said calmly, "I think it's time to leave."

Abe swiped at Reed's arm, knocking Reed's hand away and stomped toward the door. The glass rattled in the frame as it slammed behind him.

Reed locked the door and flipped the sign from open to closed. "You're done for the day, I think," he said.

"I can't believe him." Lane's breath came hard.

"What did he say to piss you off?" Reed asked.

"It's more what he didn't say."

"What didn't he say then?" Reed mopped up some stray drops of coffee off the counter with a napkin.

"He wouldn't tell me that loved me."

"Isn't that what he meant, though, when he said he wanted you?"

Lane shook her head and covered her face with her hands. "Even when he's acting, Abe never says anything he doesn't mean."

"I don't follow," Reed said.

Lane rubbed her eyes, feeling numb all over. "It means he couldn't say that he loves me, which means he doesn't, so I'm done."

"No more Fujikawa?"

Lane took a deep breath. "No more."

"I'm sorry." Reed said.

"I'm okay with it this time." She squared her shoulder then asked Reed, "You bring food or what?"

"Sure. I'll go get it." He eyed her like he was waiting for her to break down. Lane wouldn't give it to him. She would eat, and she would clean the espresso machine, count down the cash register, and go downstairs to finish the knitting pattern Anita was waiting on, and she would be fine

Chapter Thirty-Four

Tokyo, Japan

Abe dripped water onto the floor as he shucked off his raincoat. He and his father tried to visit Tokyo in early June before the rains started, but almost never got the timing right. The weather had been sunny and mild for the first half of their trip, but that afternoon the skies had opened, and it showed no sign of stopping.

He attempted to straighten his hair in the Budweiser mirror in the entryway. It was impossible to keep it all back in this weather. With a sigh, he gave up trying to keep a lock in the front from falling in his eyes. Abe still hadn't trimmed his beard, so he looked even more like an unkempt American than he normally did, but it would have to do.

He was at the bar to meet his cousin, Ryousuke, whose rumpled suit and frizzy hair it wasn't difficult to outshine. Even though Abe was ashamed of himself for taking comfort in that, it was true. And Ryousuke could be an ass.

Abe had never been a baseball fan. That was Ryousuke's pastime, but if meeting him in the American style sports bar to watch the game meant getting him out of the hotel for the evening, Abe was happy to go.

The legislative session was still going on back home. Tensions were high, and every night when he turned on his computer, Abe found frantic emails from work. Could he call this senator? This client had questions. Would it be too much trouble to video conference with the representative at two tomorrow afternoon? Never mind that it was four in the morning for him. But it was his job to keep the retail liquor tax out of the budget negotiations as much as possible, and some of his clients were panicking.

He should have stayed. He took vacation at this time every year, because it was a month after session normally ended, and he'd wanted to stay. His bosses had insisted he not cancel his plans. Abe had reluctantly accepted, even as he suspected it was because his firm didn't want to get caught denying vacation to one of the only persons of color on the payroll.

Ryousuke was waiting, still in his suit, having come straight from work in the government district.

"You're late," he said. The table he'd chosen had the best view of the biggest screen, and the game was already in the second inning.

"I was shopping in Ginza and had to drop my bags off at the hotel."

"That's only a couple of train rides," Ryousuke said. "Or did the country boy get lost in the big city?"

Abe gave an exaggerated roll of his eyes even though he wasn't annoyed. This was their game. "I'm used to driving wherever I want to be in fifteen minutes or less."

Ryousuke sat back and sipped his whisky. He drank his neat and too quickly, which was why Abe always took his on the rocks. The ice slowed him down.

"Why do you buy clothes here? It's cheaper in the states."

"They fit better." It was a miracle, but he'd found shirts that fit through chest and shoulders as well as in the waist without needing altered. Most of his shirts had grown tight across his chest and pinched at his arms after he'd spent the last six months chopping wood.

"You're so peculiar about your clothes. Like a woman." Ryousuke flagged down a waitress. She was petite, shorter than Lane, and fine featured with long black hair that flowed in waves down her back. She wore a tight baseball tee with the bar's logo emblazoned across her chest and a short skirt that flared around her thighs as she walked.

When she returned with his bourbon and a basket of peanuts, she said with a wink, "So where you from, Slugger?"

Ryousuke laughed. He liked to tease Abe about his accent too. Though Abe always hoped that it was the beard that gave him away as American.

"I live in the States."

"You're American?" She switched to English. "You don't look American."

"Please," Abe said in Japanese. "This is the only time of year I get to speak Japanese."

Ryousuke laughed again, this time pulling the waitress's pretty eyes away from Abe. "He likes to pretend he's Japanese, but he's one hundred percent American."

Abe frowned at his cousin. Abe had never pretended to be anything other than what he was.

"You can be Japanese with me, Slugger." She switched back to Japanese and smiled. "I'm Mariko. It's nice to meet you."

"Seiji." Abe gave his middle name. No one every called him 'Abraham' in Japan, not even his father.

They both watched her walk away. Abe shook his head at his cousin. "I see now why you don't bring your wife to watch baseball with you."

"Ayame doesn't like baseball," he said.

"You're not paying much attention." Abe watched as his cousin followed one of the other waitresses across the dining hall with his eyes.

"It doesn't hurt to appreciate the ambiance," Ryousuke said, turning his attention back to the game.

Abe kept his eyes on the waitress until she traded of a tray with Mariko at the bar. Mariko flirted and laughed with her other tables. When she caught him staring, he winked at her and gave her his kindest smile, thinking that she reminded him of Lane when they first met.

His is stomach lurched. Thinking of Lane recalled his latest dream. In it, she'd sneaked under the covers with him. Her breath had been hot in his ear and she'd said his name. In bed, she'd always pronounced his name on the exhale, captured in the rhythm of her breathing.

"Abe, I need you," she'd said. Then she'd kissed him. "I need you now."

The Abe in his dream had been happy to comply, happy to penetrate her so fast that she'd gasped and scratched his chest. Dream Abe had been content not to wonder why she'd been there, while his rational mind screamed that something hadn't been right. The dream had won out, because that's where Lane had, and that was where he wanted to be. She had been cursing uncontrollably, his favorite sign of her imminent climax when his phone had started ringing.

He'd startled awake and reached for a Lane that wasn't there. He was alone in his dark hotel room about as far away as he could be from the woman he wanted so desperately, but who didn't want him—not anymore. Certainly not after the way they'd ended things two weeks ago.

It was moot to dwell on it now. He'd left her to the comfort of that behemoth with the red hair and tattoos. He couldn't help but picture them together. Abe didn't know how Reed didn't smother her new tiny figure with his massive body when they screwed.

Abe still had trouble reconciling his curvy, luscious Lane to the angular, athletic looking woman she'd become. She was still gorgeous. She could still take his breath away with a single smile. Her thinner cheeks and willowy frame suited her, but for months, he'd imagined her just as she had been. It was jarring to see how much she'd changed.

She wasn't the Lane he had known a year ago. If anything, he was more attracted to her. She was sharper, brighter, more confident than before she'd opened her store. Success had been good for her. For one fleeting moment, he'd thought she would share herself with him again, but he'd been wrong.

He was alone.

While Ryousuke was absorbed in the game, pounding the table sometimes, cheering in others, Abe vacillated between eavesdropping on the conversations around him and watching Mariko. He bought a burger and a beer so he could talk to her some more, just like he had bought coffee from Lane at first because she was nice to look at.

Part of his problem was that he'd always been too easily taken in by beauty. It was what had happened a hundred times since his divorce. A beautiful woman who knew how to bat her eyes and had even a glimmer of intelligence had him hook, line, and sinker.

Lane had been different from the start. When he'd taken her out that first night, she'd been completely unimpressed with him. Even so, he could feel her giving into her feelings for him. She'd wanted to kiss him. She'd invited him inside, and it took all his willpower to say no. Any other time he would have accepted, but he knew he needed to show her she wasn't like the women he used to tell her about.

In the end, it hadn't mattered. He'd lost her anyway. And he was still a sucker for a beautiful woman.

When Markio slipped him a note with his receipt asking him to meet her at the end of her shift, Abe folded it and put it in his pocket. A small smile played over his lips.

"How do you do that?" Ryousuke asked.

"Do what?" Abe feigned innocence.

"Pick up a woman by barely saying anything to her."

Abe shrugged. "Unfortunately, I have a lot of practice."

"I don't think there's anything unfortunate about it."

• • • •

ABE AND MARIKO DIDN'T talk much that first night. They didn't sleep much either.

The second night was supercharged by the success of the first, with Mariko only pausing long enough to confirm that he wasn't married.

"I am definitely not married," he said, and wasted no time stripping her out of her work uniform.

The third night, a Sunday, Mariko met him for a drink in the bar at his hotel. He found out then that she wasn't just a waitress, but also a thirty-one-year-old teacher who hated having roommates. Working at the bar paid for what teaching didn't, and it was a good place to meet men.

"All the men that know me as a teacher want me to marry them and then be nothing else. The men I meet at the bar usually just want sex, and that's easier right now."

Feeling guilty for being one of the latter, Abe asked. "What do you want?"

"A boyfriend," she said. "Someone to be myself with." She twirled her fancy pink drink with her straw. "What about you, Slugger?" she asked. "I find it hard to believe that you're not married."

Abe smiled and tilted his nearly empty glass so the ice cubes in the bottom raced each other from one side to the other. "I'd love to be married," he said. "I just haven't found a woman who wants to be my wife for the right reasons yet."

"What are those?"

"Any reason that doesn't involve my money." Then he explained that he had a little bit of family money and a job that paid well for the part of the country he lived in. After that, he told her about Kansas, and how beautiful he thought it was, and how much space there was. He told her about his house, standing on the tallgrass prairie and how his nearest neighbors were over six acres to the east. The others, a mile of pastureland to the west.

"I'd love to have all that space to myself," she said.

Knowing what it might sound like, he said, "It can get lonely."

She smiled and asked if was ready to go upstairs.

Abe did little else the rest of his vacation but sleep all day, meet his family for dinner, work until Mariko was done at the bar, then spend the rest of the night with her.

One night at dinner, Abe overheard his aunt, Ryousuke's mother, ask his father if he knew what Abe had been up to all week.

"Leave him be," his father said. "He's been having a hard time since he broke up with Lane."

"Lane?" his aunt asked. "Was that the almost trophy wife from last fall?"

Abe bristled, but didn't say anything, wondering if that's what his dad thought too.

"Is that what you all have been saying?" Fujikawa was shook his head. "She'll keep him on his toes if he can ever figure out how to keep a hold of her."

Abe excused himself then. His father told him often that he and Lane would figure things out, that she was fire and he was water, and it took time for a relationship like that to balance. Abe would have chosen to forget her if he could. It hurt too much to know that he would never see her again, never kiss her, never make love to her, never father her children. It was a deep ache that wrenched through his core like the great heaving sobs he'd given into two nights after their last fight.

• • • •

AS HE WAITED FOR MARIKO outside the bar that night, he figured out why he kept inviting her to his bed. There was no future to think about, and it was a relief. After all the turmoil he'd been through with Lane, even with the short, failed relationship with Olive, a woman who had Roxanne's wild red curls and Lane's tenacity, it felt good to loose himself in something temporary.

On Mariko's next night off, their seventh night together, Abe offered to take her to dinner. "Wherever you want to go," he said. "On me."

She took him to the conveyor belt sushi place near the station. "I can take you someplace nicer," Abe said, knowing this dinner would cost him less than fifty bucks.

"This place has the best sushi in town, which pretty much means it's the best sushi in the world."

He didn't argue and held her hand while they waited for a booth.

"Have you ever thought of moving back here to be with your family?" she asked, pulling a red plate from the belt. "In a couple of years, you wouldn't even have an accent."

He told her about how he'd lived there when he was younger. How he didn't fit in. How he felt claustrophobic and traveled to the country to hike when he should have been working.

"You should come back and try acting again. You're handsome enough to be in films."

Abe smiled and shook his head. He had zero desire to be in the spotlight again. He'd let that dream go somewhere on the trails at Enoshima. "I could never leave my daughter, and her mother would never in a million years let her move here with me."

"You have a daughter?"

Abe told Mariko about Gretchen. She in turn, told him about her students. She taught nine-year-olds who cared more about Pokemon than math.

"It's like that everywhere," he said.

"If I came to teach in the States, you think I'd have the same problem?"

Abe took his time choosing his next plate as a way to ignore the hints that she hoped he'd ask her to come back with him. "Maybe worse," he said, knowing it would be difficult for her to find a teaching job back home unless she wanted to teach Japanese.

He let her talk about school a little longer, waiting for only a short pause before he asked, "Do you want to get out of here?"

Back at the hotel, Abe opened the mini bar, reaching for a little bottle of whisky to dispel his fear that she was after more than a fling. With no ice, Abe drank too fast. Mariko matched him drink for drink.

· · · ·

ABE DIDN'T REMEMBER much of the night. He knew there had been sex, and that he had dreamed of Lane. She had moaned in his ear as he'd rubbed his chin over her shoulder then run his tongue up her neck. He'd thrust into her with long, slow, deep thrusts.

When he'd awoken, his head had still been spinning with the whisky. He'd reached out for the Lane from his dream like he'd always done, expecting to find cold sheets, but instead there had been warm body. His hand had landed on the feminine swell of a hip.

Good God.

It hadn't been a dream. Lane was there.

Her back was to him, and he pulled her against his chest, kissing her shoulder. Speaking softly into her ear, he said, "You're here." He placed more kisses on her shoulder. "Lane. Darling. You're here. Thank God you're here." He kissed her temple now. "I love you, Lane. I love you so much." Then he caught the smell of her hair and froze. This woman wasn't Lane. She smelled of citrus and alcohol, not coffee and lavender.

The woman in his arms rolled to face him. He took a deep breath, then opened his eyes to find Mariko scowling at him.

"Who's Lane?" she asked in English.

"Shit," Abe said. He rolled onto his back and covered his face as the last week came back to him in a rush like wind breaking through the fog over the bay.

"She's your wife, right?" Mariko sat up, taking the sheet with her.

Abe let out a string of curses in English.

Mariko kicked at him. "I knew it," she said in angry Japanese. "Men like you are always married."

"I'm not married," Abe said to the ceiling. She kicked at him again, trying to push him out of bed.

"Then who is she?"

"She's the woman I'd like to marry."

"Then you're not single. Not really."

Abe rubbed his eyes and sighed. "We're not speaking at the moment."

Mariko made a disapproving noise in the back of her throat and stood, wrapping the sheet around her like a dress as she searched for her clothes.

"I don't want to speak to you either." She pulled her shirt out of the pile at the foot of the bed, then threw his jeans at him. "If I had known you were pretending I was some American woman this whole time I—" Mariko bit her lip and turned away.

Abe pulled on his jeans. "I'm sorry. I dreamed of her last night. I was confused this morning, but I didn't pretend."

She hurled his shirt at his head and ran to the bathroom. "Don't be here when I get out!"

Abe could hear the tears in her voice.

"I'm sorry," he said again, and he was. He wished he could take it all back. He wished he would have had another drink with his cousin that first night instead of bringing Mariko back to his hotel room.

He hadn't meant to hurt her.

Abe grabbed his wallet and his phone and clumsily made his way to the street in search of coffee.

Waiting in line, Abe had never been so embarrassed in his life. He was sorry about Mariko, but for the first time, even as his head swam and the park around him swayed, he understood about Shawn. He had been Lane's Mariko. Shawn had been how she'd kept herself buoyed when her emotion and her intellect had threatened to capsize her. She had let it go on too long, just like he had, because she hadn't had anyone else until she'd let him in. Lane had known the difference right away, but Abe, who had been searching for partner for so long, hadn't seen it until now.

There was a postcard rack next to the register. Abe grabbed the first one he touched and scribbled an apology to Lane. When he arrived back at his room, Mariko was gone.

He collapsed into the armchair, staring at the wall as he sipped his coffee, waiting for the alcohol haze to clear. He stared out the window for a long time, mulling over the last year.

Abe didn't want to waste any more time.

Chapter Thirty-Five

Aside from the party Lane threw for Celia and Andrew upon their return from Las Vegas, Lane did nothing that summer other than work. Their wholesale coffee bean business picked up after they attended a trade show in June, and Lane was back to spending most of her time roasting to keep up—even after she'd trained Annie in the beginning of July.

Lane's days consisted of waking, roasting coffee, formatting old sketches into patterns, because she didn't have time to design anything new, and working in her ceramics studio until she fell asleep at her wheel. All weaving projects were on hold until fall, and she made nothing for herself anymore.

Lane told herself it was good that things were busy. It was a sign of success that each facet of their business was scaling up. They'd hired an assistant for Anita and were renovating the unoccupied space above B&C's, building offices for the knitters and their own photography studio. Once that was done at the end of August, they planned to build a wall between Lane's studio and the roaster. Annie was in the process of hiring new baristas so she could take over roasting once they were fully trained.

Celia was on Lane to hire an apprentice to help her with her pottery production, but since she mostly worked in the middle of the night, Lane couldn't see how it was practical. The standard response to Lane's resistance to change was a concerned frown, which Celia was wearing more and more lately.

"You're not on your own in this, you know," Celia said. But Lane felt more alone than ever. She was either in her studio at B&C's or in her garage at home. Celia, who was in the process of buying a house with Andrew, almost never came to chat in the evenings anymore. Reed still brought her coffee and sometimes food in the late afternoon, but even then, they usually talked about work.

Even Gretchen had ceased her knitting lessons and only occasionally visited with knitting questions. That was the main regret Lane had with how things had worked out with Abe in May. She saw so much less of Gretchen, who, she assumed, had decided Lane wasn't worth the energy. Lane missed her almost as much as she missed Abe.

There were days when Lane wondered if she had overreacted, if she should have accepted Abe's consolation. But then she remembered how he'd pushed her to be the one to let him off the hook or force his hand, and she knew she'd done the right thing.

She blamed the deep ache that still lingered in her chest on general loneliness. There was no one thing that hurt more than another anymore and carrying it all around was exhausting. And when she looked at her life, she wondered if she was any better off than she had been a year ago. Financially? Yes. Lane didn't worry about money. Mentally? Physically? Emotionally? Lane couldn't keep up with the pain anymore.

She was throwing a set of mugs for a wholesale order a couple of weeks after the altercation with Abe when she broke. She didn't cry. Didn't rage. She didn't say a word as she scrapped the mug she and started throwing a tea cup. She hadn't thrown any in months. She'd barely been able to meet her deadlines, but that night. Lane threw cup after cup, and little by little, she let the pain slip away.

When she received a postcard from Japan in late June, Lane was proud of her detachment. The front was a view of Mt. Fuji. The back read, "Sorry I was such an ass," and was signed in Japanese. The symbols were the same ones tattooed on the inside of Abe's right bicep. She tore it in half and dropped it in the compost bin by the espresso machine so it would get buried in wet coffee grounds.

When she came upstairs later that afternoon for a fresh cup of coffee, she found the postcard clean, taped back together and stuck to the milk cooler with two B&C magnets.

"How did this get here?" Lane asked Annie, who shrugged and said something about Celia thinking it was pretty.

"Did you read the back side?" The whole shop knew the story of Lane's recent shouting match with her ex-boyfriend.

"Not much of an apology, in my opinion," Annie said.

"That's why it was in the trash," Lane said.

"And what a generic postcard," Annie added. "Mt. Fuji from Japan. How original."

"He could have put more thought into it." Lane said. "He at least could have chosen one that has cherry blossoms superimposed over it so it doesn't look so barren." She plucked the post card from the refrigerator and slid it under

Celia's closed office door. If she wanted to look at the view of the mountain, she could do it in private.

Mid-July was always a difficult time for Lane. She marked the anniversary of Silas' birth and death with a long solitary walk down the wooded trail she'd traversed daily while pregnant. It was on this walk that she received the first of a series of phone calls from Abe. She watched her phone ring in her hand. Her heart thudded in her chest until her voicemail picked up. Though tempted to delete his message without listening, Lane's curiosity got the better of her.

"Lane, it's Abraham. I'm guessing you knew that already and didn't answer on purpose. I wanted you to know that I'm thinking of you today. I know it's Silas' sixth birthday and you're probably busy, but if you feel like talking, I'm here to listen. I'll try you again later."

Abe called her every day for a week. He left a voicemail each time, asking her to call him. Sometimes, he told a quick story about who he was meeting that day or how his latest tennis match had gone, talking to Lane through her voicemail as if they'd never stopped speaking. She listened to each one, then deleted it. Whatever he was doing, she didn't have time to deal with it.

On the seventh day, Lane was upstairs helping Annie get a catering order together when the shop phone rang. Lane cradled the handset between her shoulder and chin as she put pastry box together. "B&C's Roasterie. This is Lane Benjamin," she said.

"Lane," Abe said. "It's good to hear your voice."

Lane's heart skipped a beat, then she hung up and tossed the phone at Annie.

"Who was that?" Annie asked.

"Guess," Lane said.

"That man has no shame," Annie said. "You want me to screen your calls today?"

"Wholesale orders only," Lane said.

"You got it, boss," Annie saluted.

When the order was out the door and Lane was in the safety of her studio, she texted Abe and asked him to not call her anymore. He hadn't responded by the time Lane had gone to bed that night, and Lane had tucked herself in with a sigh of relief. She'd thrown a few extra tea cups before bed, and she'd felt like she'd finally been able to let Abe go.

Chapter Thirty-Six

With the excuse of having a grand new house to move into, Celia took the first two weeks of August off, leaving Lane in charge of everything. Lane barely slept that first week, and at the beginning of the second, Lane hid in her studio trying to spark the will to dig into the sales analysis Celia did every day. Instead, she scrolled through Instagram on her phone, not even bothering to pretend she was working when Reed clomped down the stairs.

"Bless you," she said as she took a steaming mug of coffee from him.

"You should take some time off too." Reed sat close to her on the sofa and placed one large hand over her knee.

"I wouldn't know what to do with myself."

"Sleep?" Reed suggested.

She scrunched her nose.

"You could travel," he tried again. "Go to Rome and eat your weight in pasta. Taste all of the Italian espressos."

"I do love pasta," she said, "but as much as I'd like to travel, I don't want to go by myself."

"Take someone with you."

Lane shook her head. "Unless you're offering, there's no one to take." The idea of running away with Reed was appealing, and for all the wrong reasons. They both knew that.

Reed squeezed Lane's knee. "I don't think Emory would like that very much."

Lane raised her eyebrows. "Emory?"

"The girl I've been seeing."

Lane hadn't known he'd been dating anyone.

"It's only been a couple weeks" Reed said. "But I like her."

"Good." She placed her hand over his. "I'm glad you found someone."

"I'd like to bring her here, if that's okay with you."

"Why wouldn't it be?"

Reed's lips twitched. "For a while, I thought, maybe after you got Fujikawa out of your system, there was a chance that we could try again."

"Ah," Lane said, part of her, a little sad that he'd moved on. "And now you've given up on me."

"More or less," he said, removing his hand from her knee.

"I think I'm destined to be married to my work." She looked around the studio. She didn't have time to think, to eat, to sleep. Just the idea of trying to meet someone and cultivate a relationship made Lane's head spin from exhaustion. Being alone was better. She even thought she was getting good at it. All she needed was her work and her tea cups, and cuddles with Pilot when he was willing.

"It took me awhile to figure that out, but I got there." Reed feigned a laugh. "For a few weeks, I was half hoping you might be pregnant."

She had been afraid of that. "It wouldn't have changed anything," she said.

"Even so. I think we'd have made good parents."

"I like how you can't go to Rome with me, but you can have a kid with me."

"Well not now," he said. "But we make a good team."

"We do," Lane said. "That's why you want to introduce her to me?"

"Yeah," he said. "Emory knows how much you mean to me, and she's excited to meet you."

"Then I want to meet Emory too." Lane inhaled the steam from her coffee. She was drinking it like water these days. "Tell me about her."

Reed had met Emory at a different coffee shop, where he hung out in the evening sometimes. The coffee was lousy, but it was quiet enough to work on his computer. Emory was a poet who had just moved back home after finishing her MFA in New York and trying to make it in the city for a couple of years. Now she worked in the leasing office at the new apartments in College Hill and organized poetry readings around town. She was cool, he assured Lane, very down to earth, very funny.

Lane nodded and when they had arranged a coffee date, she asked, "Will you take me to get a tattoo?"

Surprise spread over Reed's face. "What do you want to get?"

"My logo, right here," she touched the inside of her left forearm.

"The cattle brand?"

"That's the one. You know anyone who can do it?"

"I can make a few calls," he said. "When do you want to do it?"

"As soon as possible. I'm not very patient once I've made up my mind."

Reed laughed at her and promised he would get it done, placing his hand back on her knee.

• • • •

THE FIRST WEEK OF SEPTEMBER, they had the contractor out to find out how much it would cost to add a wall between Lane's studio and the roaster. If she was going to share her space, she wanted the option for privacy, even if it would put her temporarily behind. Annie was already training their new baristas and would take over roasting full-time as soon as the construction was finished. After that, Celia was going to train her on the day-to-day paperwork, so Celia could spend less time in her office, and more time courting buyers.

Lane was resting between batches, her feet up on the sofa when she heard footsteps on the stairs. Abe's work shoes squeaked against the wooden steps exactly as they did when he crossed her porch. She did not turn to greet him but let him explore her studio until he found her, tucked away in the corner.

Her heart hammered as she pretended to be so absorbed in the emails on her phone that she hadn't noticed his descent. Beneath the low constant rumble of noise from upstairs, she could hear him breathing, in and out through his nose. She could feel his eyes on the back of her neck. She began counting just to see how long it would take him to say something. She'd reached 157 before Abe said, "Lane, will you at least look at me?"

She turned her head. He wore his usual out-of-session garb, gray shirt and slacks with a blue tie that matched the streak in Lane's hair. A hint of a smile played on his lips as she stood to face him, but Lane only scowled. "What are you doing here?"

"I wanted to talk to you, and I knew you wouldn't answer if I called."

"There's a reason for that." Lane crossed her arms.

Abe donned an apologetic grin. He leaned forward so his hands rested on the back of the sofa, looking her in the eye. "I'm sorry for the way things ended in May."

"It's a bit late for an apology," Lane said.

"Didn't you get my postcard?"

Lane had forgotten about the postcard. And from the pained expression on his face, that wounded him. Good, because it wasn't enough. Not nearly enough.

"Yeah. It was kind of lame."

He sucked air in through his teeth and exhaled slowly through his nose as he clenched his jaw. "I was desperate at the time, I—" but he stopped himself, took another deep breath and tried again. "I would like to talk to you for a few minutes, if I may."

Lane rubbed her forehead, exposing the tattoo on her forearm. "I'm really busy,"

Lane watched him notice the tattoo and search for any other changes. His gaze lingered on her left hand, and she had to keep herself from rolling her eyes.

"I won't take long," he said.

Lane sighed. "I could use a cup of coffee. You?"

"Please" he said.

Upstairs, Lane dawdled as long as she could, giving tips to the trainees until Annie reminded her she had a visitor.

When Lane scowled, Annie launched into the story behind the handsome man in the basement.

"You've been spending too much time with Celia," Lane said. Annie sent her off with a flippant wave.

When she returned, Abe was holding the sketchbook she'd left open on the coffee table. His finger traced the silhouette of the dress she'd sketched out the day before. Lane sat beside him on the sofa, placing the tray in front of her on the table.

"What's this for?" He tapped the page.

"It's this year's symphony dress."

"You're going?"

"Celia talked me into it. Apparently, I made last year sound like so much fun, she couldn't miss it this year."

"I came here to offer you my extra ticket." A grin drew over his lips.

She crossed her legs beneath her and faced him. "I didn't think you ever had an extra ticket to anything."

"I haven't had much stomach for dating lately."

"But you came here to ask me to go with the symphony with you? That's a little bold, isn't it?"

"Not with me, exactly. I didn't want you to not go because of me."

"I don't actively avoid you," she said.

"I know." Abe shifted in his seat and cleared his throat. "I saw you at the symphony in February."

"I didn't see you."

"I was up on the balcony."

"You recognized me from that far away? Blue hair and weight loss and everything?"

He had the cognizance to appear contrite as he said, "I would know you anywhere."

"Then in May, when you said you hardly recognized me?"

"I said a lot of things I didn't mean that day." Abe scooted forward so his knees were touching Lane's. "I was feeling guilty and taking it out on you." He rubbed his palms over his trouser legs, like he was nervous. "I shouldn't have, because you have always been beautiful, and I am sorry."

She stared at him, gauging whether the show of anxiety was genuine or feigned. When she saw the sweat gathering along his hairline, she took pity on him.

"Did you know Gretchen has a boyfriend now? He's this tall blonde guy who skulks behind her while she asks me knitting questions."

Abe rolled his eyes. "All she talks about anymore is Zack and knitting. I almost miss the boy band phase."

Lane didn't try to hide her laugh. "Have you met him?"

"No, but I'm a little jealous that you have."

"She's probably worried you'd scare him off."

He rested his left hand on her thigh and relaxed into the conversation. "Or she doesn't want him to pick up any bad habits from me."

"And what bad habits are those?" Lane asked as she pointedly flicked at his fingers. He clamped down so as not to be dislodged.

"She teases me all the time that he's a better boyfriend to her than I ever was to you."

"It wasn't just you," Lane said, but Abe pretended not to hear her.

"Did you know she's spending all day with me on Sundays now?"

Lane shook her head.

"She spends the night, I make her breakfast, and I take her to school on Monday morning."

"You make breakfast?" Lane failed at not making herself sound incredulous.

"Only the best bacon and eggs in the state," he boasted.

Lane cracked a smile at the thought of him standing over his big gas stove top, cursing as he moved his frying pan off the heat so the bacon wouldn't burn, throwing his tie over his shoulder so it wouldn't catch fire in the still lit burner. "You've said that before, but you never had any food in your house when I was over."

"I'm sorry about that."

Lane switched her mug from her right to left hand and squeezed Abe's fingers. "I'm sorry too."

He squeezed back, rubbing his thumb over the bend of her knee She could see his pulse beating in his wrist. "I've been taking a little time off work lately to spend more time at home."

He was full of surprises, but Lane wasn't sure why he was telling her. "You cook and you're taking time off work?"

"I've cut back to forty hours a week when session's out."

"That's allowed?"

"Nobody's complained yet."

"I can't imagine you working a regular day."

"Eight to five, Monday through Friday."

"I don't know what I would do with myself if I did that."

"It's amazing what all I get done."

"Woodcutting? Something else?"

He swallowed, and Lane could almost see his anxiety manifesting itself on his skin. "Working on the house, finishing all of the little things that need to get done so I can sell it."

"Do what?" Lane nearly dropped her coffee in shock.

"I'm selling my house," he said.

"But you love your house."

"I don't need all that space," he said. "Not just for me and Gretchen and the dog."

"Where will you go?" Was he leaving for good? Was that why he was here? Was he moving back east with his dad? Or worse, out of the country, back to Tokyo?

He shrugged. "I've been looking all summer for a little house on a couple of acres, maybe on the north side of the city—a quick commute to downtown—but no luck."

She should have known he'd never leave Gretchen behind. Lane wanted to ask more questions, but she was too busy being gob smacked.

"Tell me what you've been up to." He gave her knee a small shake, and Lane blinked away her shock. "How's business?"

Lane told him about her plans to step back from the coffee shop and focus on the art business, and of Celia's idea of writing a book about how they made their business successful. And then developing an online coaching course after that. Lane didn't expect to be any less busy with the changes, but maybe she'd be more productive.

Abe kept his hand on her knee as he checked his watch, probably to keep his eyes from straying to her lips again. He wanted to kiss her, Lane recognized the signs, but she knew he wouldn't. They had been sitting together, holding hands for half an hour as they chatted, and everything was friendly. Just friendly.

"Why are you moving?" she asked. The idea of him leaving his house made her chest ache, but she wasn't sure why.

He stared into the depths of his empty coffee mug for a long while before he answered. "It's too big."

"But what about your big family?"

"I'm not holding out for that anymore. It's time to let that go."

"You'll find someone." As she said it, she identified the ache inside her. She didn't want him to be alone. And selling that house, admitting that it was too big, too empty. It was him giving up on his dream of filling it—filling his life—with a new family.

He shook his head almost imperceptibly, squeezed her hand, then said, "I should get back to work."

Lane groaned. "Me too."

He stood, leaving his mug on the coffee table. "It was really good to see you."

"It was nice to see you too." Lane joined him in standing. "You can come in for coffee whenever, you know."

He ran his hand through his hair, sweeping back a stray piece of gray that had fallen into his eyes, "You're coming to the symphony?"

"Yes."

Abe offered his hand and Lane shook it. He didn't shake hands with her like he did with his legislators, hearty and strong. This touch was more of a caress.

"Maybe I'll see you there?"

"Maybe." And because a handshake felt too cold, she stepped forward and kissed him on the cheek. The second her lips touched his beard she wanted to push him backward onto the sofa, slide his pants off and straddle his waist. She could be so swift, so fierce, they might be able to pretend it had never happened.

Abe's arm circled around her waist and he kissed the top of her head, leaning in to inhale the scent of her hair. "You still smell like flowers."

And he still smelled like pine and seawater.

"Abe." She pushed against his chest when he didn't let go.

"Sorry. Old habits." His smile told Lane he wasn't sorry in the slightest. "Good luck with the dress."

"I'm going to need it."

Lane let him disappear around the corner and out of sight, then listened as he climbed the stairs and let him fade from her life, like the sounding of his receding footsteps.

When Celia came downstairs a few minutes later and asked, "Was that Abe who just left?" Lane didn't look up from her sketch book but nodded.

Celia sat down next to her. "You okay, babe?"

"Yeah." Lane smiled for her friend. "I'm fine."

Chapter Thirty-Seven

L ane skipped brunch on Sunday to get a few extra batches of coffee roasted. Then Reed and Emory helped her transport her essential supplies from the studio to her house so she could work from home until the construction was done.

Emory was not what Lane expected. She was almost as tall as Reed, had bright fuchsia hair and wore a lip ring. The first thing she'd done upon their introduction was to turn to Reed and say, "God, have a type much?"

"Your house is so cool." Emory set down a plastic tub full of samples in the middle of the living room. "I would want to work from here all the time."

"I did for ages," Lane said. "But I like working where there's people."

"Right. That's how you and Reed got started isn't it? Two lonely artists working by yourselves too much." She didn't sound bothered by her boyfriend's past with Lane in the slightest.

"Exactly," Lane said. "Just have to remind myself that in a few weeks I'll be back in my studio with all my customers for company again."

Emory peeked out the window to make sure Reed was still moving boxes from the truck to the porch before she leaned down to whisper in Lane's ear. "Reed said that a certain prince charming came looking for you the other day. Are you afraid you'll miss him if he comes in again?"

Lane stepped back. "How do you know about Abe?"

"Reed told me all about you guys. He was stuck on you for a while, and sometimes I think it helps his ego to think you're still secretly in love with him. He got all annoyed when your old boyfriend showed up."

"That doesn't bother you?" Lane asked. "That he would be so upset by the idea of me and Abe together?"

"Why should it?" Emory shrugged as she opened the box with the samples in it. "He doesn't want to be with you anymore. And can you blame him? You didn't treat him very well when you had him."

"You're right. I didn't."

"Anyway, he doesn't trust this guy, so he was pissed, but I told him he should be happy for you." She pulled a new red shawl from the pile and draped it around her neck and caught her reflection in the hall mirror. "Oh, this is gorgeous! Is it for sale?"

Lane couldn't bear to tell her how much the scarf clashed with her hair, so she said, "Not yet. Maybe after the pattern is published."

"You should keep this one." Emory pulled a sapphire blue version of the same shawl out of the box and draped it over Lane's shoulders. "Do you always do two samples?"

"Yes," Lane said. "Different yarns appeal to different knitters."

"It looks stunning on you." Emory rearranged the scarf on Lane's shoulders like she was the knitwear expert. "You really hit the nail on the head with the whole blue thing. It is so your color."

"Thanks," Lane said.

"So." Emory stepped back to admire her handiwork, "Girl to girl, you gonna give your prince another go?"

"I hadn't thought about it," Lane said. Emory looked skeptical, and Lane admitted she was lying. "Okay, maybe I have, but only in a fantasy sort of way, where he comes downstairs and finds me asleep and on the sofa, he tries to wake me up and kisses me, but I think it's a dream until he sticks his hand up my shirt, and then it all goes to hell."

The stark whiteness of Emory's teeth struck Lane as Emory gave her a mischievous grin. Next to this woman, Lane felt dull and haggard. "Go for it Sleeping Beauty. I say get him naked first, figure everything else out later."

"Yeah," Lane said. "I don't think that's likely to happen either. I'll see him at the symphony, maybe a couple times a year if he brings someone in for coffee. That's all."

"Why did he come see you if he didn't want to start over?"

"The talk we had was all about closure." Lane sighed. "He's ready to move on. He's literally moving."

Emory said she hoped Lane was wrong, and Lane shrugged. She didn't hope for anything when it came to Abe anymore.

· · · ·

THE NEXT DAY, ANNIE came in to help train the new baristas after Lane had worked the morning shift. Reed was on the back sofa working on the web store when Lane got off duty. She collapsed next to him and allowed her head to fall on his shoulder.

"Do you mind if I just close my eyes for a minute?" she asked.

"How late were you up in the ceramics studio?" he asked.

"Two."

He sat back and wrapped his arm around her shoulders. "You need to sleep more."

"I could fall asleep right now."

"Go for it," he said.

"It's not professional to nap on your employees—or your exes."

"So, go home and nap."

"Can't. If I go home, I have to work."

"Then stop worrying about it."

Lane snuggled into his side. "Your girlfriend is exhausting."

"She's just trying to be friends."

"Is that it?" Lane's eyes were closed, her voice growing thick. "I can't tell if she likes me."

"She doesn't think you like her," he said.

"Sometimes she's difficult to keep up with."

Reed squeezed Lane's shoulders. "You'd do better if you slept."

"If I stay like this, you won't be able to work."

"I'm left handed." he held up his free hand. "I'll be fine. Go to sleep." But Lane was already dozing.

She didn't know how long she'd been asleep, but it wasn't long enough when Reed shook her awake. "Benjamin," he said. "Benjamin, wake up, your boyfriend's here."

"I don't have a boyfriend," Lane said.

"I'm serious," he said.

"Most people still think you're my boyfriend." Lane buried her face in his chest.

"Fujikawa is here," Reed said through gritted teeth.

"Stop teasing me. It's not funny."

"He's twenty feet away picking out bagged beans."

When Lane cracked her eyes, there was Abe's lean back, his wide shoulders, the two gray streaks in his black hair. "Holy shit. Did he see us?"

Reed nodded.

"Fuck." Lane smoothed her loose hair back into a ponytail, then stood to straighten her rumbled clothes, cursing to herself the entire time Abe paid for his coffee.

A smile curled over Reed's lips. "Are you panicking?"

Lane glared at Reed. "Don't make fun of me. God knows what he's thinking right now."

Reed reached out and tugged her onto the sofa. "Settle down," he said. "If he thinks it was anything more than it was, we'll set him straight." But as he spoke, Abe turned toward the front door.

"How am I supposed to do that if he's leaving?"

"Do you want to talk to him?"

Lane bit her lip but nodded. She hadn't expected to see Abe, especially not so soon, but if he was here, she wanted it to be for more than just coffee beans. She just hadn't known it until this moment.

"Fujikawa!" Reed yelled. Abe stilled and turned. He met Lane's eyes briefly, but when she tried to smile at him, she was overtaken by a yawn. He sat down anyway, shaking Reed's hand and nodding at her.

"Did you order coffee?" she asked.

He nodded, and she yawned again. "Obviously, I need some myself. Do you want anything?" she asked Reed.

"Nah, I need to get going."

Lane hurried back behind the bar and put together a French press. Abe and Reed were talking, but they were too far away to eavesdrop. With Abe's tendency toward jealousy and Reed's protective streak, she didn't want to leave them alone for long.

Sure enough, as she returned, she heard Abe say, "I'm not overly fond of you either."

To which Reed replied, "Good. That's something we can agree on."

"What are you agreeing on?" she asked as she sat down. "I hope it's on getting along for my sake."

"That's exactly what we agreed to just now," Reed said, standing. Somehow, Lane wasn't so sure. "But I've got to go." He stooped to kiss Lane on the forehead. "Stay strong, Benjamin. Don't take any of this guy's bullshit."

She smacked his arm, "Get out of here."

After Reed left, Abe took the seat next to Lane at the same time the new girl brought his coffee over.

"So, twice in one week, huh?" Lane poured her own coffee.

"Your coffee's good." He took a sip to emphasize his point.

"Of course it is." Lane put on a knowing smile. "Why are you really here?"

"I've missed you," Abe said.

Lane nodded. Telling him that she'd missed him too didn't even start to encompass the ache she felt deep inside, but she said it anyway. It made him smile.

"After our talk last week, I kept wondering if maybe we could be friends."

"Coffee friends?" Lane asked.

"Sure," Abe said, but he hesitated. "We can have coffee and talk about things."

"And that's all you want?" Lane asked. "My friendship?"

"Well, no." He took her hand, his fingers warmed by his coffee cup. "I still have feelings for you. Probably always will."

"Oh, Abe." She let his words wash over, feeling the sweetness of them for just a moment before the regret set in. If only they had come to this point sooner. "I can't do this again. I just—"

He squeezed her hand. "I know. It's fine. I didn't expect you to reciprocate." He let go of her hand and stood. "Will you be here Thursday afternoon, same time?"

"I'm here every day til five at least," she said.

"I'll see you Thursday then." He stooped and kissed the top of her head, just like Reed had done, and then he was gone.

• • • •

ABE CAME IN EVERY MONDAY and Thursday afternoon during September. Since Lane's studio wasn't going to be finished until October, every meeting, as short as they were, was in full public view. Their conversations had been light; Lane would tell him what sort of work he was interrupting, and he would tell her how he'd been undefeated on the tennis court lately, and then invite her to play.

"I didn't think women were allowed at your fancy club." She was making notes on a knitting pattern, the moss green sample spread out in her lap.

"Just because I don't play with any women..."

"So, you want me to come to your club and embarrass myself?"

"Of course not. I could give you a few pointers. We could play doubles against Jeff and Bryce."

"Bryce is?"

"My contractor friend. He's good, better at racquetball, but—"

"Wait, wait, wait." Lane held up he open palm. "You brag about beating these guys every week like it's a challenge, and you want me, who's played tennis three times in my life to play against them?"

"You'll never get better if you don't play," he said.

"You're assuming I want to get better."

"I'll give you lessons." His wolfish grin spread over his lips. "It'll be fun."

"I'm sure those lessons would be completely innocent, too."

Abe put his hands up. "I swear. We'll play at the public courts. They're all outside. It would keep me honest."

"I'm surprised you don't have your own court by now." Lane counted her stitches even though she didn't need to.

"That's a good idea, maybe I'll call my realtor and have her keep a lookout for a place with a court."

"I think tennis courts only come with giant houses like the one you're trying to get rid of."

"Maybe I'll retire, move to a townhouse and become a tennis trainer instead."

"You would be bored out of your mind."

"Yes, I would be." He checked his watch then kissed her on the cheek, lingering just a second too long before standing. "I'll see you Monday."

• • • •

ON THE LAST MONDAY before the symphony, Reed and Lane were creating marketing plans for their holiday lines when Abe arrived. Reed vacated his seat, saying he'd go fill Celia in.

"You know you're edging in on Reed's time," Lane said as Abe sat too close.

He held out a mug of fresh pour over for her, handle first. "He can have you the other five days of the week."

Lane nestled her coffee down between the cushions and focused her attention back on her laptop screen. She needed to finish her outline by five so she could get home and work on the pottery she needed for the upcoming First Friday.

"Do you actually take a break for Reed, or does he only get half your attention too?"

"Depends on what's coming up on deadline," Lane talked as she typed

Abe tapped on the top of her screen, just above the webcam. When she met his eyes and saw his soft smile, she lost her breath. He pushed the lid shut and snatched the computer out of her grasp before she could compose herself again.

He laughed and blushed as Lane stared at him.

"I was working on that," she said when she found her words again.

"It'll be there later."

"But I have things to do later."

"Darling," he smoothed her bangs out of her eyes and brushed his knuckles against her cheek. "Don't take this the wrong way, but you look exhausted."

"I am exhausted," she said.

"You should take a break," he said.

"I am taking a break—apparently." She pried her coffee loose and stared down into the steam.

"You should take a vacation."

"That's what I'm doing this weekend."

"The gala is only one night."

"That's way more time than I usually take."

"Let me take you out. Get you away from work, away from home."

Lane shook her head.

"The sushi chef at Shogun has been asking about you. We can drink sake and eat tuna rolls, while you flirt with Akihiro. I won't even tell him what a handful you can be."

"I'm not interested in your sushi chef." The idea of going back to Shogun with Abe made her want to cry.

"Even better." Abe grinned. "You can flirt with me instead."

Lane rolled her eyes. "Give me my computer back."

"Come out to dinner with me Friday."

She held out her hand, palm up. "I'm not trading you a date for something I already own."

"We can make a weekend of it," Abe continued, ignoring her. "I'll pick you up for breakfast Saturday morning. Then we can go for a hike around one of the lakes before the gala. The leaves out at Perry are changing already."

"Kudos on not assuming I'd stay over."

"It can be on the table if you're interested." Abe waggled his eyebrows.

Lane couldn't help the giggle that escaped as she remembered Emory's advice about getting him naked, but said, "No."

"No to staying the night? Or the whole proposal?"

"I'm busy Friday night."

"Working?"

"Reed and I are shooting the holiday line for the web store."

Abe rolled his eyes this time. "About the only thing that guy and I agree on is that you need to take some time off."

"I'm not blowing Reed off to go drinking with you."

Abe rested a hand on her knee. "We don't have to drink."

"Of course we don't." Lane lifted his arm by his wrist and dropped it back into his lap. "Because we're not going anywhere together. We're just coffee friends, remember?"

"I remember." Then Abe leaned forward and kissed her on the mouth in a short, sharp, smack. In any other situation, it would have been comical. "I'll see you Thursday."

"Bastard," Lane said loud enough for him to hear, but she wasn't really offended.

• • • •

THAT WHOLE WEEK, CELIA pestered Lane to go to the salon with her to get their hair and makeup done before the gala.

"I was going to do my own at home, like last year," Lane said.

"Please come with me?"

"They'll want to curl my hair, and you know the curls will fall out before dinner even starts. It'll be a waste of money."

"You could have them touch up your blue."

Lane shrugged, but after Celia bothered her for another ten minutes, she asked, "Why are you so set on this?"

"Because it's the only time I'll get to spend with you on Saturday."

"You're the one who's going to abandon me to dance with Andrew all night."

Celia glared. "Like you aren't going to ditch us the second Mr. Fujikawa shows up."

Lane blinked. "I won't ditch you. Why would I?"

"Come on." Celia leveled her with a knowing stare. "It's pretty obvious what's going on between you two."

"Not to me."

"I saw you kiss him the other day."

"He kissed me, and I'm bailing today before he gets here."

"Why?"

"Because the kiss crossed a line."

"That's such horse shit, Lane." The sound of Celia slamming her desk drawer clanged throughout the small room.

Lane jumped at the crash. "Hey,"

"You like the attention. Stop pretending you don't."

"Why are you getting upset?"

"Because I've been watching you make yourself miserable for a year, and I'm sick of it."

"I've had a great year," Lane said, but even she could hear the hollowness in her voice. "I'm doing everything I've ever wanted."

Celia sat in the armchair next to Lane's. "No, Honey," she took Lane's hand, "you're really not. You're finding excuses to work yourself to death—and at first, that was fine, but I'm not going to let you do it anymore. Tell me who we need to hire."

"Someone to help Annie bag and ship coffee orders might be useful."

"Sure." Celia nodded. "How about an assistant? Someone to wind your yarn and type your notes for Anita?"

"I don't need an assistant," Lane said.

"Honey." Celia grasped both of Lane's hands. "No one else here works more than forty hours a week, including me. You're clocking close to a hundred and forty. That's too much."

"I am really tired," Lane said.

"I know."

"I wouldn't mind working a little less. Maybe I can cut back in a few weeks."

Celia smiled. "You're taking the weekend off."

"I can't. We've got a big order to get out the door on Monday and Reed and I have to get the web store updated, and—"

"You're leaving tonight and you're not coming back until Tuesday," Celia said.

"I can't take four days off."

"You can and you will."

"What am I supposed to do for four days?"

Celia checked her watch. "You can start by having coffee with a gorgeous man who's desperately in love with you."

"Shit." Lane checked her phone. "I have to go."

But just then Annie arrived in the doorway to announce that Lane's boyfriend was waiting.

Celia's smile was positively feline. "You could spend your whole weekend with Mr. Fujikawa."

"You're not funny," Lane said, but she was already halfway out the door.

Lane plopped down next to Abe and sighed. He handed her a steaming mug and asked her what was wrong. When she explained about her forced vacation, he laughed at her.

"I'm surprised Celia didn't do it sooner."

Lane expected him to renew his invitation to take her out to dinner, and she might have taken him up on it, but he didn't ask. He didn't even kiss her on the forehead when he got up to leave, just turned around at the last second and said, "Save me a dance on Saturday."

Surprised, Lane said. "Sure."

Chapter Thirty-Eight

Lane double checked her reflection in the mirror as she waited for Celia and Andrew to pick her up for the symphony She wore a fitted black dress with long sleeves, a high neckline and an open back. The narrow skirt ended high above her knee with a slit up one side. Paired with her black hose and heeled boots, Lane looked just as scandalous as she'd planned.

At the salon, they'd refreshed her blue streak and pulled her hair back into a tight twist. She wore no jewelry but her nose ring and finished the outfit with the blue shawl Emory had liked on her.

When Andrew came to the door, he stared at her, open-mouthed.

Lane tugged on the too high hem of her dress, "What?"

He shook his head, blinked, and offered her his arm. In her boots, she was exactly as tall as he was. "This is the first time you've looked the way Celia described you when we first started dating."

"How's that?"

"Like you're hiding knives in your boots."

"What, like a spy?"

"Or an assassin." Andrew nodded. "This all for Fujikawa?"

"No," Lane said as he opened the car door for her. "It's for me."

• • • •

SEATED AT THEIR DINNER table, Lane scanned the room, looking for Abe's gray streaked black hair. Like the year before, the table was made up of couples, two sets in their fifties, Celia and Andrew, then Lane and empty chair next to her.

"Is he here?" Andrew asked.

Celia was already talking up their dresses to the two older women and stood to show off the drape of the pink gauze as it cascaded down her back to the floor.

"He should be," Lane said. "You see him?"

"I don't know what he looks like."

"Tall. Asian. Gorgeous," Lane said, craning her neck.

"Beard? Black hair going gray?" Andrew asked.

"That's him." Lane searched the crowded room, still not seeing him.

"Looks like he's alone," Andrew said, nodding over her shoulder.

A few seconds later a warm hand landed between her shoulder blades, but before she could react, the gentleman to her left stood to shake Abe's hand. The spot where his hand had been growing cold without his touch.

Abe made polite conversation with the couple calling them by name, Alan and Barbara. He had no more glanced at Lane than the other couple at the table caught his attention. Abe's smile never faltered as he moved around the table away from Lane, addressing this couple too, by their names, Anderson and Stephanie.

As he was helping Stephanie back into her chair, Celia stood and said, "Don't think you're going to get away without saying hello, Mr. Fujikawa."

Abe did her one better and twirled her in a circle so her gauzy dress caught the air, then kissed her on the cheek. "Celia, you look stunning. Did Lane make your dress?"

"As if I would wear anyone else."

"I'd expect nothing less." Abe looked to Andrew. "Is this your husband?"

While Celia was introducing them, Lane overheard the other two couples exchanging comments about how strange it was that he didn't have a date and couldn't help the self-satisfied smile that crossed her lips. Abe didn't have a date because of her.

Lane knew she was in for a treatment similar to Celia's and was prepared when Abe pulled her to her feet and led her into a turn as if they were already on the dance floor. His hands lingered on her waist as he whispered, "My God, you are radiant," in her ear. Then, he kissed her, not the short peck he'd given her a few days before, but a real kiss that she had time to react to, to participate in. It l lasted just long enough for a thrill of satisfaction to course down Lane's spine. But as soon as she leaned in to him, Abe stepped away and for everyone else's benefit said, "I've always liked you in black," leaving Celia to explain to the table that Lane always wore black before they let out a confused, subdued chuckle.

When he took the chair next to Lane, she asked, "You're sitting here?"

He held up the place card so she could see his name printed on it.

"How'd you manage that?" she asked.

"A phone call." He shrugged. "You mind?"

"Depends, on what you're planning,"

"Not taking my eyes off you to start." He ran eyes up and down her seated form again, lingering on the vast amount of exposed thigh, until Lane knocked him in the chest.

His eyes shone with mirth as she said, "You are so full of shit."

Abe only grinned wider and leaned in to whisper in her ear. "We could talk about how I'd like to finish the night instead."

Lane's lips brushed his ear as she whispered back, "Prove to me it's a good idea."

"I intend to." Their secret conversation having drawn the attention of the table, Abe said louder, "You've outdone yourself with this dress. It's pure scandal."

"What about you?" Lane said, straightening the new black bow tie she'd knocked sideways during their kiss. "Your new tux is very vintage Connery." He had traded in his old jacket with peaked lapels for one with a satin shawl collar and his old cummerbund for a sleek black satin waistcoat. Even his cuff links were new, silver-rimmed onyx with a small sapphire set in the center.

"Funny thing happens when chopping wood becomes your hobby." He draped an arm over the back of Lane's chair. "None of your clothes fit across the shoulders anymore."

"I thought something was different," Lane squeezed the ball of his shoulder through his jacket. "Impressive."

Alan interrupted and asked what Abe meant by chopping wood. While Abe explained, he ran his thumb over the exposed skin on Lane's back. Lane listened to them talk about fitness for a few minutes, but as the round man recorded the name of a trainer from Abe's racket club into his phone, Lane's attention turned to the conversation that Stephanie was having with Celia about B&C's.

"Celia's the reason we're so successful," Lane broke in after Celia explained that they didn't normally deal in ball gowns. "She's a genius."

"Don't be so modest," Abe interjected. "Without you there'd be no business."

"You could say the same for Celia," Lane said. "We're partners."

"I think he's right," Celia said. "All I really do is sell you."

"Now that is too modest," Andrew said.

"Maybe," Celia said, "But I sell way more of Lane's work than I ever did pills or houses."

"That's because it's quality work," Abe agreed. "Gretchen gave me one of her sake sets for my birthday. The server keeps the sake warm for hours."

Lane raised an eyebrow at him.

"You think I didn't recognize it?"

"I figured you might have mentioned it before now." All the eyes around the table were on her and Abe as silence fell between them. Lane diverted her attention to her wine glass to avoid the sizzle of fire she felt stirring in the air between where she ended and Abe began.

"Abraham," his friend said, "How do you know these young ladies?"

Abe only said, "Lane makes the best coffee in town."

To help fill in the blanks, Celia told everyone that Abe and Lane had come to gala together the year before.

"Aren't you together this year?" Barbara asked. Lane could see the rest of the table were confused by the discrepancy between their affection for one another, and their words.

"We're just friends," Lane said. Celia snorted.

"We didn't come with anyone else," Abe said to her.

"You could have invited someone. You have your extra ticket."

"I donated that to someone who didn't get one in time. Besides," he cradled her cheek in his palm, "I only wanted to come with you."

Lane could feel the rest of the table holding their breath for her response. She covered his hand with her own and replaced it in his lap. "Let's not talk about this now."

"But we'll talk about it. Tonight."

"Tonight," Lane agreed. "After the concert."

Abe gave her a wide grin and squeezed her hand under the table.

After dinner, Abe acted as host, introducing Lane and Celia to anyone he thought she should know as he circulated the mezzanine. Lane kept close his side and introduced him to some customers of hers that he didn't know.

When the crowded mezzanine began to clear, Abe checked his watch, then said to Celia, "I'm afraid it's almost time to switch partners."

Celia cringed.

"What?" Lane looked from her best friend to the man on her arm.

"Andrew took my extra ticket," Abe said. "So unless you consent to sitting with me, we'll have to split up the newlyweds."

It took a few seconds for the implication of Abe's words to sink in. But of course they had planned this whole night. Together. In advance.

Lane glared at Celia. "I should make you endure my company as punishment." Abe chuckled over her shoulder. She whirled on him, shaking a finger. "And don't even get me started on you."

"You can sit with Celia if you like. It'll give Andrew and I a chance to get to know one another."

Celia shook her head behind Abe's back. Leaving Andrew, who had never like the idea of Abe, alone with him tonight would not be a good way to start their relationship.

Lane sighed. "You two would get into a fist fight over politics after two seconds."

Abe wrapped an arm around her waist, whispering, "You're a saint."

She pushed him off. "Don't be affectionate with me. I'm annoyed at you right now. And you." She poked Celia's arm. "You owe me."

"You can name your first born after me," Celia quipped and dragged Andrew toward the stairs.

"You aren't really annoyed with me, are you?"

"Yes, I am. You've obviously been planning this for weeks."

He led her to the balcony by the hand, and the only reason she didn't pull away was that she couldn't remember where his seats were.

"Months, actually."

They filed down a row in the middle of the balcony. When Abe covered her knee with his hand, she shoved it into the armrest. He tried running his fingers over the exposed skin on her back, she hiked the shawl up over her shoulders.

"You are annoyed." He folded his hands in his lap.

"You should have asked me to be your date if that's what you wanted."

"But you would have said no."

"So it's better to disregard my feelings and trick me into it instead?"

"I wasn't thinking about it like that."

"Of course not. You were thinking, 'Lane. Mine. Gimme.'"

"I wasn't," Abe said softly. "I was hoping if I could show you a good time in the place we fell in love last year, maybe you would give me another chance."

Lane crossed her arms over her chest, pulling her shawl in tight. "Don't count on it."

"I don't expect anything from you," he said as the house lights flickered, "but don't expect me to give up."

Lane shook her head and ignored him as the lights faded. Abe kept his hands to himself, and Lane did her best to forget who sat beside her and focus on the music.

It turned out to be the longest concert ever. Shame mixed with equal parts fear and elation at what she would have to face when the lights came up. She hated that she'd been excited for this night, and it had turned out to be one big manipulation. At the same time, Abe's words, *the place where we fell in love last year,* echoed through her mind in time with the music.

He had never told her that he loved her, had never said those exact words. At first, Lane thought he didn't need too, but after their breakup, after May when he couldn't say it, she had been able to convince herself that he never had been in love with her. He had been in love with the idea of what she could give him: children and a warm, willing body.

But he had just said he fell in love with her last year. Here. Not when he went home with her after, not in the weeks following the symphony, but here, where she had seen so much of who he really was that she couldn't help but fall in love with him too.

During the final piece, Lane allowed herself to look at him as his attention was on the orchestra. She could see the tension in his shoulders, held rigid instead of his usual easy slouch. Every minute or so a muscle in his jaw twitched, as if he were clenching his teeth. None of his thick, wild hair escaped his styling tonight, swept back perfectly and held in place with three expensive balms, where his seawater scent originated.

She counted six white hairs by the corner of his mouth, just on her side, and wondered if in a few years, he'd have silver stripes in his beard to match the ones in hair.

As he noticed her staring, he gave her a warm, confident grin. When he caught up her hand, Lane knew she wanted to be around to see the silver lines settle in and squeezed his fingers until the song ended. The idea of missing that left a gaping, aching hole were her stomach usually was.

Abe dropped her hand as they rose to applaud, then escorted Lane down the stairs on his arm. Lane was at peace with the situation until they exited the building just in time to see Celia and Andrew driving away. Lane's temper returned in full force as fear and panic slammed into her, and she shoved Abe away. "They just left me! Didn't even wait for me."

"That's because they know you're safe with me."

Lane scowled at him. Abe had walked away from her last year. Had devastated her utterly, and Celia trusted him enough to leave without even checking in? As she stalked away from the valet station and into the parking lot she wished she really did have knives in her boots, if only so she could slash all of their tires.

It had been a long time since Lane had called a cab, but she was pulling her phone out of her clutch to do just that when Abe caught up with her.

"Lane." His hand closed on her elbow, but she wrenched it free and kept typing her search. "Lane, stop. Let me drive you to the gala."

She turned to glare at him as she dialed the cab company. "I'm not going to the gala. I'm going home." She kept walking away from the concert hall and toward a parking lot at the edge of campus. The tap of Abe's shoes against the pavement fell away, leaving the click of Lane's heels and the ringer in her ear.

"Megan don't go home. Not yet."

Lane ended the call, reared around, stomped up to him and pushed him. "Don't ever fucking call me that. My name is Lane."

Abe didn't budge. "Your middle name is. Your dad told me your first name."

Lane froze, hands raised to push him again. "You've been talking to my dad?"

"Just the once."

"Oh, for fuck's sake. Why? How?"

Abe stepped right up to her raised hands and wrapped his fingers around her wrists. He pulled her close enough that she was surrounded with the scent of him. "I thought he might have some insight into how to get you to talk to me again."

"Calling me a name that I hate isn't the best way."

Abe chuckled. "Your dad said the same thing, but here you are."

Lane wanted to smack his smug grin right off his face, but his gentle but firm grip still restrained her. "You are such a bastard."

"Let me take you to the gala," he said. "Please."

"As your date? Or as your friend?"

"Whatever you want to go as."

"If I want to go as your friend, would you respect that?"

His thumbs skimmed across the sensitive insides of both her wrists, sending a thrill over her shoulders. "I will never stop loving you, but if you need to move on, I will try to understand."

Tears stung the corners of her eyes. "I can handle flirting and showing off." She stepped into him, extending her fingers. When her nails reached his beard, he dropped his hands to her hips, and she cupped his jaw with both hands. "I could even handle taking you home and showing you how much I've missed you." Abe's hands tightened and he pulled her against him like he might kiss her, but Lane slid a hand down his chest, because she needed space to get these words out. "But if I have to watch you walk away from me again, it might kill me."

With a hiss, Abe let out the breath he'd been holding, and rested his forehead against hers. "I'm sorry. I will do anything to make it up to you."

"Even let me go?"

"If that's what you need." He placed a soft kiss to her forehead. Her nose. Her lips. "But I'd like a chance to earn your trust first."

Lane closed her eyes, unable to withstand the intensity in his eyes. A tear leaked out, and Abe wiped it away and kissed her forehead.

"I love you," he said.

Three more tears and one deep breath later, Lane grasped the hands Abe had cupped over her cheeks to catch her tears and tugged him back toward the valet. "Come on. Let's go to the gala."

• • • •

"WOULD YOU LIKE A MARTINI?" He asked as they entered the ballroom, "Or maybe club soda?"

"Definitely a martini."

"Coming right up."

While he waited at the bar, Lane hunted out Celia's pink dress only to find she and Andrew already out on the dance floor. The traffic forced her against a wall, and she was about to join Abe at the bar when the booming voice of Brian Benton called to her from halfway across the ballroom.

"Ms. Benjamin!" he hollered a second time. He was waving and repeating her name with delight. Trailing behind him was a short, stout woman with red hair and a peacock blue sequined dress the same color as her eyes. Over her shoulders, she wore the dove gray shawl that Lane had knitted while in bed last fall. Abe had told Lane that she was radiant, but she didn't hold a candle to this woman.

"Representative Benton." Lane smiled and offered her hand, "Congratulations on winning re-election last year."

"Thank you, love, but I'm already full steam ahead into the next campaign." He shook her hand so hard Lane was almost rocked off her heels. "The election will be here before we know it."

The woman behind him cleared her throat and he ushered her forward. "This is my wife, Cecily. We were hoping we might run into you tonight."

"It's nice to meet you." Lane offered her hand, but Cecily kissed both cheeks instead, the smell of vodka heavy on her breath.

"Oh, I am delighted!" she said, her voice had a hint of an accent. French, perhaps? "I can't tell you how much use I get out of your shawl. I tell everyone who will listen where to find you."

"We do a fair business in commissions," Lane said. "I'm sure I have you to thank for that."

Cecily beamed. "I've decided I need another. Something that makes an impact like that stripe of blue in your hair."

"How dramatic would you like to go?" Lane asked. "A bright teal would match your eyes, but a true red would really bring out your complexion."

"Oh, red!" Cecily's eyes lit up. "I hadn't thought of that."

"I'm thinking a bold geometric pattern in the lace." Lane pulled out a business card out of her handbag. "Call me next week, and I'll have some sketches ready."

Cecily squealed in delight as Abe joined them. Brian shook Abe's hand, sending Abe's whiskey sloshing over his fingers.

"Abraham, Abraham, Abraham, I was beginning to wonder if Ms. Benjamin was on her own this year, but here you are, together again."

Abe shook off the whiskey and opened his mouth to reply, but Brian cut him off.

"You should have seen what a grump this man was all last session," Brian said. "Could hardly get a grin out of him, and you know how easily he normally smiles."

Abe closed an arm around Lane's waist. "Be fair, Brian. It was a lousy session."

"But we all know it wasn't politics that had you down, old boy." Brian laughed. "I'm so glad that you two have reconciled. You will invite us to the wedding, won't you?" He and his wife tittered together as he led her off.

"Did you hear that?" Abe pulled Lane flush against his side. "We've reconciled."

"Not so fast, handsome." Lane squirmed out of his embrace.

Abe caught her hand as she stalked away from him, just as she hoped he would. "Aren't we?"

"No." Lane took a long sip of her drink as she held just tight enough to his hand so he would know not to let go.

"Would dancing change your mind?"

"No," she said again, and guided his hand to her waist, then wrapped her free arm around his neck and stepped up on her toes to reach his lips. She brushed them at first, barely touching once, then twice. Then she pressed her whole self into him, running a languid tongue over his bottom lip, before replacing her heels to the floor and standing back, her heart hammering.

He tasted like his whiskey and his longer mustache tickled her nose. That lazy, wolfish grin of his was back.

"What was that for?" he whispered in her ear.

"For saying you love me," she whispered back. "And because I love you, too."

Lane didn't have a chance to think before Abe's lips were on hers. His kiss was slow and seductive. The angry tongue of flame that had been living in her center for the last year flickered and went out, replaced by a slow burning desire.

"Please tell me we're reconciled now," he said when they finally separated.

She shook her head. "Nope."

"Anything I can do to change that?"

"Give me some time."

"Time apart? Because I think we've done too much of that recently."

"Just time to think."

"What do you want to do right now?"

"Right now," she flattened his lapels, "there's a party going on."

Abe looked over his shoulder at the crowded dance floor then back at Lane. "Dance with me."

Keeping up with him was easier than last year. No matter the tempo, she was next to him, laughing as he led her into turn after superfluous turn. Like the year before, they didn't stop until the band did. While Abe fetched fresh drinks, Lane excused herself to the ladies room.

Returning, she found Abe standing at a table with Celia and Andrew. He gave her a bottle of water, then put an arm around her waist. She leaned her head into his chest, and he rested his chin in her hair.

"Oh my God, you guys are so cute," Celia said.

Lane blushed as other couples around them turned to stare. "We're still figuring this out and aren't exactly ready to broadcast it."

Andrew snorted. Abe ran his chin over Lane's ear and Celia said, "Then you probably shouldn't have been making out in the corner earlier."

"We weren't making out," Lane said, but just then Abe nipped the shell of her ear, and she squeaked.

Celia gave her a knowing smile and grabbed her husband's hand. "Come on, babe. Let's leave these two to *figure things out*." Andrew nodded and shot Lane a concerned look, like he was worried she'd been bewitched, as his wife dragged him back onto the dance floor.

Abe nipped her ear again.

"What are you doing?" she asked.

"Trying to get up the guts to ask you if you want to get out of here."

"You have to work up courage for that?"

"You could ask me to take you home. Which isn't exactly what I have in mind."

Lane exposed her neck to him as he kissed his way down her chin. "Abraham."

"Yes?"

"Don't you dare take me home."

Chapter Thirty-Nine

A be lost no time in retrieving his car.

"I want you to know," he said when they were on the road, "this wasn't my intent for tonight."

"I don't know." Lane reached over to flick a stray lock of hair out of his face. "You were trying pretty hard in there."

"That's because you are irresistible, and I am only human." He grabbed her hand and kissed her fingers, before quickly returning his hand to the gear shift.

"I might have intended it a little bit." Lane kept her eyes on the street lights passing her window. She could hear him smiling as he asked her if she was serious.

"I've been thinking about it since that first day you showed up in my studio."

"I wanted to kiss you, but I thought I'd scare you off. "

"You probably would have, but I still wanted to take your pants off and straddle you on the sofa."

"We should try that."

"If you're lucky."

"At Cedar Crest, it was all I could do not to take you up against a tree."

"That's what you were thinking," Lane pinched his thigh. "You were so inscrutable that day."

"If it had just been you and me, I might have."

"I wonder if that would have changed anything," Lane said. "If your family hadn't been there, I mean."

Abe said, "Probably not. We haven't been ready."

"Speak for yourself," Lane said.

"Then I wasn't ready."

"What changed?"

"What do you mean?"

"Between Memorial Day and when you mailed me that awful postcard, what happened to change your mind?"

"It's a long story," he said.

"We've got all night."

Abe wrung his hands around the steering wheel. "It's not a nice story. It makes me look like a heartless ass, and that's the last thing I want you thinking of me right now."

"I've seen you at your worst."

"You haven't seen this side of me."

"Don't hide from me. Not now."

Another sigh and then, "I met someone in Tokyo. I guess you could say we had a fling. It was right after we'd fought, and I was so angry with you. I thought I'd just offered you everything you wanted, and you'd rejected me so violently. I thought I'd left you to find comfort in someone else."

"Who?"

Abe shot her a quick scowl, before returning his attention to the road.

"Reed?" He nodded, and Lane snickered. "No. Not since April."

"I missed you so much. Seeing you again brought everything back, and I thought I'd lost you for good—again. And I knew it was my own damn fault, so I invited this woman back to my hotel room every night for a week. I thought it meant nothing, but now I think maybe I was leading her on a little bit."

"You can be reckless," Lane said. "Is that all?"

"No, but I really don't want to tell you this story."

"Best get it over with then." He was nearing the curve on the access road that led to his driveway, and Lane wanted the tale out of the way before they arrived.

Abe told her how they'd gotten drunk and he'd woken confused, how he'd call this other woman by Lane's name.

They passed the edge of his property, where it switched from alfalfa fields to wild tallgrass. A large for sale sign stood next to road. The tube for holding pamphlets was empty.

"She accused me of lying to her about being married and kicked me out of my own hotel room. I went for coffee while she got dressed. I was desperate. I was panicked. I had to do something right then to try to make things right with you, but it was late in the States and there was a postcard rack in the coffee line."

Lane imagined him, standing in line at a Starbucks, in jeans and a wrinkled shirt, balling his fists and glaring.

"I'm sorry I called your postcard lame." Lane watched the reddening maple trees slide by. She wondered what had happened to this girl, how much Abe had led her on, if she'd fallen in love with him. It was an easy thing to do.

"I'm sorry it took something like that to make me realize how much you mean to me." He pulled into the garage and cut the engine. "You still want to go through with this?"

Land didn't even have to consider. "I've seen that side of you. It's what got us here in the first place."

"You're not angry?"

"You can't get in trouble for something that happened while we were apart."

He nodded, but his shoulders were slumped, and he didn't meet her eyes as he came around to let her out of the car.

"I do feel sorry for that poor woman though." Lane reached for his hand and was relieved when he squeezed her fingers in return. "Do you know what happened to her?"

Abe shook his head. "I thought it best I leave her alone."

"I hope she found something that made her happy."

Wolf howled in the distance, almost drowning out Lane's words.

"Damn dog. Always howling in the middle of the night."

Wolf met them at the back door, panting excited circles around them as Abe removed his shoes and his jacket. He filled Wolf's dishes while Lane worked her way out of her boots and reacquainted herself with the dog. The cool wood felt therapeutic beneath her sore feet, and she wiggled her toes in her stockings to work some life back into them.

Abe took her hands in his and drew her to him. "Hey."

"Hi yourself." Lane stood up on her toes, so much shorter than him without her boots, and kissed him. She was gentle, apprehensive at first, but his firm hands on her hips and his breath on her lips soon extinguished her nerves. Lane worked her fingers under his collar, scratching softly. He grabbed her waist and hoisted her up onto the counter top.

She arched her back so she pressed into his chest. He took advantage of the deep slit in her skirt to push it back up over her hips, freeing her legs to wrap around him while he searched for the waistband of her black hose, then pulled them off. Lane tugged on his tie, and it melted into a pile of silk on the floor.

The heat from his urgent kisses spread and Lane broke into a sweat beneath her silk dress. She needed out of her clothes, but even more than that, she needed him free of his. She kissed her way down his neck and unfastened the studs in his shirt, piling them on the counter behind her.

She snapped off his cufflinks and pulled open his waistcoat, then slid his shirt to the floor. His shoulders and chest were broader, the muscles more defined. She ran her hands up and down the new lines, kissing her way up his neck to his mouth.

He clutched her hips, pulling her down to the edge of the counter so they were center to center. Abe ground into her and said, "Let's make a baby," against her lips.

Lane pulled back, her hand still resting on his waistband. "Are you insane?"

He stood straight, still holding her suggestively against him. "I've never been more serious,"

"We have a lot to talk about."

"We do," he agreed, then ran a finger up her side then along her neckline and down her back where he searched for her zipper. "I thought you wanted kids."

"Only if I'm married," Lane said, even as she tugged his belt open.

Abe found what he was looking for and unzipped her, kissing her neck as he said, "I'll have to run upstairs for a condom then."

"There's one in my handbag."

. . . .

IT WAS AFTER TWO BY the time they made it upstairs, where it was apparent that if Abe hadn't planned on her coming home with him, he had certainly prepared for it. The green plaid shirt she'd always slept in was draped over the armchair on her side of the bed. In the bathroom, there was a new toothbrush on the counter next to the body oil and lavender perfume she'd left behind. Her spare hairbrush, the one she'd been looking for for months lay next to Abe's comb and beard trimmers, as if she should have thought to look for it there in the first place.

When Lane left the bathroom, she found Abe reading in bed, nothing on but a pair of black-framed reading glasses. Her dress hung on the back of his closet door, and her handbag and a glass of water were on the bedside table next to a spare phone charger. He set the novel and the glasses aside to join Lane under the covers, where they lay with arms and legs entwined.

As Lane started to drift, he asked, "What changed you mind?"

"Nothing. I never stopped wanting to be with you."

"But the last few months? Not answering my calls?"

Lane snuggled against his side. "I was protecting myself."

"Why?"

"Because I couldn't hurt anymore. It was too exhausting to always be in pain."

"Because of me?"

"Not just you," Lane said. "But letting you go made everything else easier too."

"If I could bring your mother back, I would," he said. "If I could have somehow saved your son . . ."

Lane squeezed him tight. "The only thing you can do is give me yourself."

"I do think we should have children. The sooner the better."

She peeked at him through one eye. "Negotiating already?"

"I want to give you the family you deserve."

"Only if we give them my last name." Lane yawned.

"No deal. It's Fujikawa or nothing."

"Too bad." Lane was unable to suppress her sleepy giggle. "Guess I'll have to find someone else to father my children."

"Don't you dare." Abe clamped his arm down around her shoulders as if she might try to escape.

"Don't worry," Lane said, patting his chest. "I came to terms with your patriarchal ways a long time ago."

He kissed the top of her head. "It's more about heritage than ownership."

"I know."

• • • •

TOO SOON, DAYLIGHT peeked through the windows and Lane felt a hand running over her bare hip, snaking over her waist and up her shirt. "Already?" she asked.

"Do you know how hard it is sleep with you in my bed?"

"I slept great." She arched into his touch as she stretched. "I feel like I could sleep all day."

He rolled on top of her, undoing her buttons. "I'd be tempted to let you if I didn't know you'd disappear the second I have to leave."

"Maybe I'd just sleep."

He kissed down her sternum as he parted the fabric over her chest. "You'd run away, and I'd have to convince you take me back all over again."

"I'm not running, but we do need to talk."

"Let's pretend we don't, just for a while longer." He ran his tongue between her ribs.

"What are you afraid of?" she asked as he settled between her legs.

"That this is as close as we'll ever get."

His kisses were slow and reverent. Last night had been a flurry of impatience and intensity that neither one of them had given into for hours. This morning, Lane's residual soreness added to the pleasure of Abe's delectably languorous strokes. Lane couldn't stop kissing him. She wanted his lips against hers, their mouths mimicking their hips as his breath filled her nostrils.

Lane surrendered to the relief that was the pressure of his body over hers. The weight of her worry and her grief fell away and Lane just was. She was her body, her pleasure, her pain all at once.

Abe's tongue caressed hers at the same time one hand closed over her breast. She arched up into his touch and urged Abe to up his pace with a rock of her hips. She inhaled, long and slow, savoring Abe's answering groan. Lane allowed pleasure to wash over her on the exhale.

Chapter Forty

Lane luxuriated in bed while Abe pulled fresh clothes from his closet. While he'd been in the shower, she'd sneaked into his dresser and examined the ring Gretchen had found.

It was just as Gretchen described it, a silver band set with a diamond, flanked by two blue sapphires. There was even a card in the box that certified the diamond as conflict free. That he had put that much thought into the ring, sent a surge of warmth through her. Then she'd heard the water go off and scrambled back into bed, hoping she hadn't left any clues to her snooping. But all he said was, "Do you want something to eat?"

"When do you pick Gretchen up?"

"Not for a couple of hours."

"Don't you two normally go out for breakfast?"

"It wouldn't be the first time I only ordered coffee." Abe poked his head out of the closet. "Do you want to come? That would make her day."

He wore only a pair of worn jeans and a white t-shirt that showed off his new physique.

"I think I had better not this week," Lane said. "You guys enjoy your time together."

Abe sat next to her on the bed to slip on a pair of white sport socks. "Does that mean you'll join us next week?"

"We can talk about it then," she said.

"What are you going to do today?" he asked.

"Meet Celia and Andrew for brunch and move as little as possible. I'm sore in places I've never felt."

"You're welcome." Abe tickled her knee as Lane batted at his hands. He stood and kissed her forehead. "I'm going to start the coffee. Come down when you're ready."

Lane showered but decided Abe's old shirt was more comfortable than her dress. She descended the front stairs so she could wander through the living and dining rooms to see if he'd changed anything. Everything was more or less the same, but each room was more complete, more polished. There were no more missing outlet covers. All the nicks and scuffs in the paint had been covered up. There was a new ceiling fan in the dining room, new curtains in the kitchen. There was evidence everywhere that he was letting go of this house. She had thought at first that it meant he was letting go of her too, but now she had no idea what he was up to.

Abe stood over the stove top flipping eggs, the bacon already cooked and set on a plate to cool. Wolf sat at his feet, waiting for Abe to drop him a morsel. A mournful Miles Davis played over the stereo. There was a stack of newspapers next to a mug of coffee on the counter. Lane helped herself to some coffee and stole the arts section while Abe cooked.

"Will you always walk around without pants when we're home?" he asked as he set a plate of bacon, eggs and toast down in front of her.

"Only if you always do the cooking."

"Does takeout count as cooking?"

"Not even a little bit."

"Damn." He sat down next to her.

They read the newspaper as they ate, and before Lane knew it, she had cleared her plate.

"There's plenty more if you're still hungry."

"More coffee?"

Abe refilled her mug, then led her out onto the front porch, pausing to grab the throw off the back of the sofa. It was a chilly, gray morning. A light drizzle fell, and Lane could hear the cattle from the ranch next door lowing in the distance. He tossed the throw over their laps as they snuggled together on the porch swing. She rested her head on his shoulder, looking out past the street to the south to where two low, rolling hills covered in golden grass met with fog lingering between them.

"It's beautiful out here, isn't it?" he asked.

She nodded against his chest.

"So peaceful and quiet." He paused and the only sounds were the soft patter of rain, the creak of the porch swing, and the livestock. "I've been spending a lot of time out here lately, just sitting. Saying goodbye."

"I still don't understand why you're moving," Lane said. "You love this place."

He took a deep breath. "I love you more."

"I never—" Lane started.

"I know." Abe kissed her forehead. "It wasn't an easy decision. It was the only thing I could think of to do that day in Tokyo. Then I wrestled with it all summer. Even while I finished up all the little things I've left undone for years, the molding in the pantry, sealing the floor in the basement, replacing the vanity in the upstairs bathroom. I told myself that I was finishing the house for me. I didn't have to sell it when it came down to it, not if I didn't want to, but I knew if I wanted to be with you, I had to."

"But this house is you. It's your whole life."

Lane could feel his heartbeat tick up in his chest. "I had just come from the realtor's office when I came to visit you that first time. I thought I might be going insane, but then I saw you, and I saw how much your studio looks like your house, and I knew I was doing the right thing."

"But why? Why is it the right thing?"

"So that you know that there's nothing I wouldn't do for you."

"I don't need grand gestures, I just need you to stick around."

Abe tipped her chin up with his fingertips so that her eyes met his. "I am in this completely. The only reason I'm gone is if you tell me to leave."

"I want this to work," she said, "But I'm afraid. And you selling your house terrifies me."

"I've hidden behind this house for years, building it into a sort of sacred space for the life I wanted, but when I brought you here that first time, I realized that despite all the space, I had no room for the life you wanted. "

Lane allowed his words to sink in, and wandered, not for the first time, where her ceramics studio might go. "Have you had any offers?"

"I accepted one Friday night."

"Where will you live?"

"The couple who's buying it aren't moving here until January, so I have some time to look. I was hoping you might help me."

"You want me to help you look for a new place to live?"

"For us to live. Together."

"You want me to move in with you?"

"I want you to marry me, but I'm afraid you'll slug me if I propose right now."

"Smart man." Lane snuggled back into his side. It would be like him to want to jump right back into where they had been before they broke up. She was so comfortable with him, she was tempted to do the same, but there was so much for them to discuss. She couldn't do it. Not yet. Even so, she asked, "Can I see the ring?" just to see what he would say.

He pulled a blue suede pouch from his back pocket and poured the ring into her hand. She glanced at the initials on the inside and raised an eyebrow at him. He didn't even blush.

"I can't believe you didn't cancel the order."

"How'd you know I had it?"

"Gretchen found it in March."

"Snoop," he said, but he didn't sound upset. "The artist called and told me it was done before I ever got up the nerve to cancel."

"I didn't realize you had it on you, though."

"Just in case."

Lane slid the ring onto her finger and admired the sparkle in the gems.

"Do you like it?"

"Very much."

"You should keep wearing it."

Lane smiled up at him but slid the ring off her finger. "Not yet."

She held it back out to him in her open palm, but he closed her fingers around it. "You keep it. The offer it represents doesn't expire. When you decide what you want to do with it, let me know."

Lane dropped the ring in the bag and snuggled back into Abe's side. His fingers played in her hair and Lane felt the last of the pain that had been dragging at her for a year fall away. Not because she was back with Abe, though that helped, but because she was finally being honest enough with herself that this place, with this man in her life, was where she wanted to be.

Epilog

Three Days After Thanksgiving

For the first time in a long time, Lane was completely alone. Abe had gone to Massachusetts to visit his dad and was due back any minute. Celia and Andrew were in Arizona with her parents. Reed and Emory had gone camping somewhere it was too cold to camp this time of year. Her brother and his family dropped her off on their way back to Colorado. After her sister-in-law, who was pregnant again asked to use the restroom, she'd taken the whole troop inside and showed them around even though she hadn't tidied before she'd left. Her bed was unmade. Her work clothes from the week before were in a pile in the corner. The tie Abe had been wearing the night before he'd left for the airport was still draped over the back of her sofa. Her cereal bowl was in the sink, and Pilot had scratched a hole in his kibble so it was spread across the kitchen floor.

They'd stayed two hours, the kids each taking a turn on her pottery wheel, making formless blobs, then watching in awe as she made them each a little cup that she promised to send to them with their names inscribed on them when they were finished.

Pete hugged her when they left, reminding her to let him know as soon as she and Abe decided on a date, so he could schedule time off work. Her sister-in-law said she hoped they'd get a chance to meet Abe and Gretchen at Christmas.

"His dad will be here too," Lane said.

After a few weeks of speaking to Abe every day. After a few weeks of nightly dinners, of sharing a bed and waking up together, seeing him every day stopped feeling like a dream, and Lane settled into her new reality.

Abe wasn't going anywhere.

Though she hadn't agreed to marry him that first day, each conversation from then on had been a negotiation on their future. A few weeks after their reunion, they'd stayed up all night arguing about how they would split expenses. Abe complained that keeping separate accounts was tantamount to her not trusting him. Lane maintained that she wanted nothing to do with his money, and anything they did together should be within her means too. They followed this path until they had argued out what each other's expectation in marriage was, how it should work, and what their hard lines were. By morning they'd come to an agreement about contributing to a joint account for monthly expenses in proportion to their income and spent the rest of the day in bed recovering.

Two days later, Lane slipped Abe's ring onto her finger while she dressed to meet Abe and Gretchen for Sunday brunch. Gretchen had just turned sixteen and was chattering so much about the joint birthday party she'd had with a friend, she hadn't noticed Lane's finger until halfway through breakfast. She broke off her sentence and turned to her father, "Holy shit, Dad. Were you going to tell me you were engaged?"

"We didn't want to overshadow your birthday, Sweetie," he'd said, as if they'd talked about it beforehand, instead of just noticing that Lane had decided to marry him after all.

He hadn't been able to stop grinning but had been able to hide his ardor until after Gretchen had gone to bed.

Reactions to their engagement had been mixed. Celia was ecstatic. When Lane told her during their Monday morning meeting, she pulled a folder out of her desk drawer full of magazine clippings and printed pictures from blogs, chock full of wedding ideas. "And I have a Pinterest board," she said as she handed over the file.

"How long have you had this?"

"I started it the day I walked in on him speaking to you in Japanese at Cristo's."

Andrew was skeptical, but grudgingly admitted that Abe and Lane suited one another.

Reed was helping Lane set up a photo shoot later that same day when he saw the ring. She was modeling her latest shawl, her arms spread wide, holding it across her back to show off its wingspan, and he was leveling her arms when she felt him still.

"What's this?" He tapped her finger.

"My new ring."

"Looks like an engagement ring."

"It is."

"Fujikawa's not wasting any time, is he?"

"We've already lost a year."

"Were you gonna tell me?"

Lane dropped her arms and tossed the shawl on the stool behind her. "I was trying to figure out how to ask you out to lunch without making you suspicious."

"You have never taken me to lunch."

"I know," Lane said. "But it's not every day you have to tell your best friend that you're marrying a guy he doesn't like."

Reed stared at the jewels as they caught the light from his lamps for so long, Lane began to fidget. She couldn't tell what he was thinking any better than she ever could. "It's not that I don't like him," Reed said. "Dude's the most gregarious man on the planet. But I'm still not sure why you trust him."

Lane smiled. "That's easy. He's the most honest person I've ever met."

"I'll have to take your word for it," Reed said, and posed her again.

Half an hour of photos later, he switched off the lamps and said, "Best friend, huh?"

Lane punched him playfully on the shoulder. "Sure thing, dude"

Reed punched her back, then grabbed her hand to steady her. "Does that mean I get to be a bridesmaid or are you gonna make me stand up on his side?" he asked as he fiddled with her ring.

Lane couldn't help laughing at the idea of Reed dressed up in the tea-length blue dress with the poofy tulle skirt she'd sketched out a few days before, meant for Gretchen and Celia. It would be a good color on him, but he'd look better in a suit.

Maybe Reed could stand on her side and Gretchen on Abe's. Gretchen would like that idea, a lot, probably. So would Abe.

"You'd do that?" she asked.

"Benjamin, I'd be offended if you didn't ask."

• • • •

WHEN   LANE   HAD   TOLD   her   family   during
Thanksgiving dinner, they'd all looked at her like she was
crazy.

"This is the man from last year?" her dad had asked.

"The one you were crying about at Christmas?"
Meredith had asked.

When   Lane   said   yes,   she'd   been   hammered   with
questions. How long have you been back together? Isn't that
fast? Why don't you date for a while? Are you pregnant?
When are you getting married? When do we get to meet
him? Are you sure this is what you want? How can you be
sure he won't bail?

All of which she'd done her best to answer, but there
seemed no good way to explain why to the people who, yes,
loved her, but had barely seen her in the last year.

Eventually, they'd moved on, but her dad kept asking if
she was sure when he thought no one else was listening. To
which Lane had faithfully answered, "Yes, Daddy. I am."

She and Abe still hadn't found a place to live. After two
months of looking with no luck, Abe had widened his search
and   sent   Lane   links   to   properties   in   other   counties   he
thought were a reasonable drive. Once he emailed her a link
to a beautiful farm in Connecticut that had been a sheep
ranch. "You always wanted sheep, right?" he'd texted after
he sent the link. The property was gorgeous, the pictures
professionally taken with the sunlight peeking through the
trees and shining behind the immaculate red barn.

"You'd never last in Connecticut politics," Lane told him later.

Abe had taken her to look at ten different properties over the last two months, but none had been quite right. The neighbors were too close, the houses too big or too small or too new. Out of frustration, Abe had started sending her empty acreages, trying to convince her to let him build them a house. She always responded that she'd like to move in before she was fifty.

The day after Thanksgiving, Abe had forwarded her an email from their realtor about a property that was about to go on the market. Did they want to see it first thing Monday? His caption read, "This is it."

The property was south of town. It had twelve acres with pastureland and woods. The house was a modest three-bedroom cottage that hadn't been redecorated since the 1970s. The barn was in good condition and there was an extra outbuilding that would make Lane a good studio with a little work. There was a swimming hole and the entire property was enclosed by a black four-board fence.

She'd told him to set it up. Though he'd only responded with the time, and the offer to pick her up from B&C's, she could feel his excitement from halfway across the country. She liked how enthusiastic he was about the prospect of a new project, but she was anxious for him to come home. They hadn't been apart since their reconciliation and Lane ached for Abe's company.

Lane wasn't supposed to be working. She had promised to take the whole holiday weekend off, but she didn't want to leave things a mess in the garage overnight. She cleaned up the clay her niece and nephew had played in, then unloaded the kiln that had been sitting idle of almost a week. She loaded it with greenware before sitting down at her wheel to throw just for herself.

She finally felt like she was getting the hang of *yunomi*. It wasn't that they appeared any more or less precise than the ones she'd been making since she was in school, but she had finally learned how to throw them without adding any of her emotion into them. Over the months of being alone, she figured out to be quiet with the process, how to exert just the right amount of influence for the cup to take shape, but not so much that she overpowered the clay.

Her tea cups had become so popular in the store and online that, with a little help from Celia, the collection she was building tonight would be going not to a boutique, but to an art gallery in New York.

Something about the unending solitude she felt when she had been in her garage had clicked into place when she had been so tired and so desolate over the summer, and people were taking notice. When she was at her wheel, throwing for herself, she'd learned how to detach herself from the loneliness. Extending that feeling of calm to work, to sleep, to the everyday was something she had still been working on when Abe returned.

After the gala, she'd had to work to maintain that same sort of calm for the opposite reason. Her bliss had threatened to overwhelm her. Her satisfaction had the tendency to lull her into a torpor where she would lie idle in the presence of the man she loved. Practicing her *yunomi* had helped her to stay on an even keel. It had helped her dismiss the misgivings of others and to deny the temptation to spend every waking moment in Abe's presence—and the non-waking ones in his bed. Most importantly, it had helped her to feel at peace with the question she got from absolutely everyone. What would she do if it didn't work out this time either? What if this marriage failed?

Behind her, she heard the soft squeak of Abe's shoes on the concrete, and the creak of the door frame as he leaned against it, watching her.

Lane already knew the answer. She had known it before she and Abe had reconciled, because she had been learning how to do it even then. Lane would go on without him, and she could be satisfied in knowing that if it didn't work, it wasn't because they hadn't given it everything they had. Secure in that conviction, Lane was able to let everything fall away until there was nothing but the motion of her wheel and the slip of the clay beneath her fingers.

Keep Reading for Chapter One of Marla Holt's second
novel:
Ethan & Juliet
A Second Chance Romance
Coming December 2018

Ethan & Juliet

Chapter One

Juliet slapped her palm against the steering wheel as traffic closed in around her. She should have known better than to get on the highway at eight o'clock in the morning even if it was the fastest way to get from Overland Park to Midtown. And she needed to be in Midtown ten minutes ago.

Fifteen minutes ago, Juliet had stepped out the front door of the birth center into the brittle warmth of the spring morning with no other plans than to go home and nap. She'd squinted past the newly leafed trees and into the sunlight. Juliet had basked in the afterglow of assisting in the uneventful birth of a healthy baby girl. The high of witnessing new life never got old, but the adrenaline of it had already worn off. Exhaustion had pressed down on her shoulders like she'd been carrying both her physiology book and her pharmaceuticals book in her bag at the same time again. She'd wanted to go home and sleep and sleep and sleep.

Juliet had taken one deep, cleansing breath in through her nose and out through her mouth and had just turned toward her heap of a twenty-year-old Toyota when her phone had buzzed in her pocket.

The screen had flashed Gina's name, and Juliet's heart had ticked up a notch when she'd heard panting over the line instead of words.

"Gina? Gina are you OK?" she'd asked.

A whimper had been her answer.

"Gina are you in labor?"

Juliet had heard her friend draw in a deep breath, then in a shaky voice, she'd said, "Regular contractions, getting strong fast. And they hurt more than last time. A lot more."

Juliet had done a mental sun salutation since she hadn't had time for a real one, then she'd pivoted on her heel and walked right back into the birthing center. On her way, she'd asked if Gina was experiencing pain between contractions and if she'd noticed any spotting. A yes to both.

"And Colin is still . . . out of town . . . and it's too early." Gina's voice had been a sharp whine interrupted by hard pants.

Gina wasn't due for three more weeks, but that hadn't been what had Juliet worried. Not by a long shot. "It's not too early. Call Rich to stay with Noah, and I'll be there in a flash."

Gina had groaned as another contraction came on.

"Scratch that, I'll call Rich. You hang tight."

Juliet had snagged Charlie, the midwife she'd worked with the night before and filled her in.

"She needs to get to the hospital," Charlie said.

Juliet nodded in agreement. "She's only a few blocks from KU Med. I can have her there in thirty minutes."

Charlie had offered to take care of the official transfer and meet them there. Then Juliet had been off, only to wind up stuck in traffic ten minutes into a twenty-minute drive. The wait was long enough for every awful thing that could be wrong with Gina to pass through Juliet's mind. When she felt panic crushing her diaphragm, she focused instead on how good it had felt for Gina to adopt her when she'd first moved to Kansas City. How all the nights drinking wine and dancing had forged a sisterly relationship that withstood Juliet's split from Gina's brother.

Juliet's pulse slowed as she remembered and breathed. They were both strong women. Gina would survive this. Juliet would get her to the hospital. The University of Kansas Medical Center was the best hospital in the area, with the best doctors. Gina would be fine, and Juliet could do this. She was a nurse, almost a full-fledged midwife, she was trained to stay calm in these situations, so she would, even when it was one of her best friends in danger.

Juliet practiced breathing in through her nose, out through her mouth, and it did almost as much as a good round of yoga.

Then she remembered she'd offered to call Rich and cursed.

Juliet fumbled her phone out of her satchel, and scrolled through her contacts, keeping one eye on the road in case the car in front of her moved.

"*Durand.*" He answered, with a perfect French accent.

"Are you going by your last name now?" Juliet asked.

A pause, and Juliet imagined a sexy, confident smile sliding onto his face. "Oh, Juliet. It has been too long."

Juliet snorted. "Whatever. Have you talked to your sister lately?"

"I'm on call for the baby."

"Yeah, well, the baby's coming now."

All the flirtation fell from his voice as he said, "Is everything okay?"

"I'm on my way over so I can take her to the Med Center. Colin's still out of town, so I need you to get over there now. Stay with her until I can get there, and I need you to take care of Noah and let Colin know what's going on. If she starts bleeding or can't handle the pain, call an ambulance and don't wait for me, got it?"

From the scraping and scuffling noises in the background, Juliet guessed Rich was gathering papers off his desk. "I'll be there in fifteen minutes." Then he hung up.

It might have been the least amount of flirting Rich had ever pulled off in one conversation. At least he understood the situation. Rich had always respected her professionally, even if he hadn't been good for her in any other way.

When Juliet arrived, Rich was making Noah eggs, but paused to help Juliet get Gina into the car. Juliet's hope that Rich had somehow been horribly scarred in the last two years were dashed the second she laid eyes on him. His thick, wavy dark hair fell in his earnest brown eyes. His olive skin glowed in the morning sun as he gripped Juliet's hand and thanked her for being there for his sister. Looking up at him, Juliet was reminded of the first time they'd met. He was just as gorgeous at thirty as he'd been at eighteen. Possibly more so.

Juliet snatched her hand back and only just resisted wiping it clean on her scrubs. "I'll call with news as soon as I can." Then she joined a groaning Gina in the car.

The drive to KU Med took less than ten minutes, and Charlie met them at the emergency room doors along with a nurse who got them checked in and into an ultrasound. Then they were admitted to the high-risk wing of the Labor and Delivery ward. Juliet helped Gina through contractions while Charlie coordinated with the hospital staff.

After what Juliet considered far too long, the door opened and a man in a white coat entered the room.

Juliet's heart might have stopped beating when he snapped the file he'd been reading shut, revealing his rugged face and bright blue eyes.

It was him.

Juliet knew she would run into him eventually. To have made it four years without meeting him when they worked in the same field was almost a miracle.

What wasn't surprising was the near scowl he wore as he took them all in one at a time. He'd always hated midwives, and here were two, along with a patient in distress. That would make him cranky. And if his greasy hair and thick stubble were any indication, it was well past the end of his shift. Oh yeah, he would be in a great mood.

Gina squeezed Juliet's hand, and Juliet tried to give her friend a reassuring smile, but that was when the doctor spoke.

"I'm Dr. Harvey," he said, pulling the last empty chair in front of Gina's bed. "I'll be performing your cesarean today."

"Cesarean?" Gina blinked.

Juliet and Charlie had explained to Gina that they thought she had a partial placental abruption, but the hospital staff hadn't said a word. When asked, the nurse had said they were waiting for the doctor to get out of surgery to confirm the results. The doctor they had been waiting on was now exchanging glares with Juliet's boss.

"She doesn't know?" he asked

"Your staff hasn't exactly been forthcoming," Charlie said. "We warned her it was a possibility."

"It's the only way to deliver safely at this point," he said, angling his head back toward Gina.

"Is the baby okay?" Gina asked, her voice quavering in panic.

"The baby is fine," Juliet said, nodding toward the fetal monitor. "Dr. Harvey means that a vaginal delivery is too risky for you right now."

"And for the baby," Dr. Harvey said. "Stillbirth would be the most likely outcome."

Gina let out a little sob of shock and her heart rate monitor beeped a little faster.

"Ethan!" Juliet sent him a silencing glare as she felt Gina go rigid beneath her palm, then said to Gina in a soothing voice, "C-section is the best way to make sure you don't bleed too much if the placenta detaches, but the baby is okay."

Gina looked to Dr. Harvey who said, "The risk of hemorrhage is high."

After grimacing through another contraction, dulled by the pain medication they'd given her, Gina asked Juliet, "You'd do it?"

She was pretty sure she heard Dr. Harvey's teeth grind.

Juliet made sure she smiled as she said, "In a heartbeat."

Gina nodded, looking determined. "Alright then. Let's do it."

Dr. Harvey explained the surgery and recovery as if his life depended on him doing so in fifty words or less. Then he swept himself from the room with a dark look in Juliet's direction. She didn't flinch. It wasn't her fault his bedside manner was so atrocious that she'd had to translate for him.

"That's it?" Gina panted through a contraction.

Charlie said, "He's abrupt, but if you have to have a c-section, he's who you want."

Juliet nodded and squeezed Gina's hand back, and said, "He's the best," trying not to let anything else show on her face. In her mind, Juliet was poking Gina in the shoulder, saying "Oh my God, oh my God," over and over, and maybe throwing a "He's the one!" in there.

Juliet hadn't seen him since she'd finished nursing school. Her life was completely different now, but Ethan hadn't changed at all.

He was still broad and sturdy like a rugby player, only three or four inches taller than she was. His shaggy, dark hair still escaped from beneath the surgical cap that matched his blue eyes. He still couldn't take the time to talk to his patients and was apparently working so much he couldn't even be bothered to shave. The Dr. Harvey she remembered had always been miraculously clean shaven, even at the end of a twenty-four-hour shift. He looked more ruffled this morning than he used to get, but Juliet had to admit she liked the beard. It matched him somehow.

Gina huffed, her face still contorted in pain. "I hope he's better at surgery than he is at conversation."

A nurse with a consent form arrived then, and Juliet focused again on Gina, and not on the way Dr. Harvey's eyes had looked at her in annoyance. Not that she wanted him to look at her at all, she wanted him to focus on Gina. Juliet did not want to talk to him, or about him. She'd avoided all reference to him for four years. All she had to do was to make it through this surgery, and she could go back to forgetting he existed.

Only once the surgery started, Juliet had trouble not watching him. She was positioned by Gina's head, so she couldn't see his hands, but the poise of his shoulders, the stillness of his body as he worked, the soft whisper of his voice, efficient with his words as he directed the staff. Juliet noticed every breath he took. He was impressive, and despite herself, Juliet felt a pull in her belly to be near him as he worked.

She wasn't the only one. When she'd been in nursing school, Dr. Harvey had been the young, handsome doctor who notoriously never dated nurses. Which meant each of Juliet's classmates had wanted to be the exception to the rule and flirted shamelessly whenever he was near.

Despite her attraction, Juliet hadn't bothered. She'd had Rich back then, and they'd been talking about getting married. While she'd noticed Dr. Harvey's sparkling blue eyes and unshakable confidence, she'd also noticed they came with an air of entitlement and a healthy dose of arrogance. He didn't just not date the nurses, he spoke to them over breakfast with half-teasing condescension, and sometimes even a hint of derision. Even among his fellow obstetricians Ethan incited controversy and lead discussions with a tone that implied anyone who disagreed with him was an idiot.

Rich's soft charm and poise had been magnetic by comparison. Rich's passion had been so intoxicating that even when Juliet had met him at fourteen, she hadn't been able to imagine loving another man. Most days she still couldn't, but she was no longer as naive as she had been four years ago when she thought she and Rich would get married, have babies, and live happily ever after.

In that moment of regret, Dr. Harvey raised his eyes to hers and held. It lasted only a moment before his eyes were back on his work. She wondered how he remembered that night, and if he despised her for being there with a birthing center patient.

"Birth," she remembered him saying about at a group breakfast one morning, "could go from normal to dangerous in a split second. Why would anyone endanger themselves and their child by choosing not to have every modern option available?" It had maybe been those words, more than anything else that had kept Juliet from seeking him out again, not when she'd been angling for the job at the birthing center near the end of her nursing degree, and not after she'd started her midwifery program two years ago.

A cry broke through the quiet stillness of the operating room, and Juliet left her memories to share a tearful smile with Gina as Dr. Harvey said, "It's a boy." He handed the baby off to a nurse and returned his attention to Gina.

Juliet stayed with Gina until the surgery was over since Gina's husband had arrived just in time to accompany his new son to the nursery.

When they wheeled Gina to recovery, Juliet escaped back to the room and collapsed into the nearest plastic chair.

She let relief wash over her. Abruption could be so, so bad, but they'd gotten here in time.

Every muscle protested in exhaustion as she checked her watch. It was after eleven. She'd only slept four hours in the last two days. Juliet couldn't remember the last time she'd eaten, and she'd have to be here another couple of hours at least.

The door opened, and Juliet sat up, expecting to see a nurse wheeling Gina in. Instead, Dr. Harvey leaned against the door frame.

"She's doing great," he said. "She lost a lot of blood, and she'll be here a few days, but she will be alright."

"Thanks," Juliet said. It wasn't information a doctor confided in a colleague, but family. She sat up straighter. "Your bedside manner is still abominable."

"A compliment so soon?" he chuckled, then sobered, his eyes narrowing in on her. "You were smart to bring her straight here."

Juliet sat up straighter and squared her shoulders, looking down her narrow nose at him. "I'm not exactly new to all this."

The corners of his mouth twitched, as if he were trying to smile at her, but couldn't bring himself to follow through. "You're wasted at that freestanding place."

Juliet thought, that considering the circumstances, she was just what they needed, but said, "Are you offering me a job?"

"How about breakfast? Dino's?" It was the diner across the street, the usual gathering place.

The allure of eggs and hot coffee was too good to pass up. "I sometimes dream about Dino's breakfast."

A real smile lit up his face this time. "Great. I've got paperwork to finish up, then I'm done. Meet you downstairs in an hour?"

Juliet nodded, knowing her confusion showed on her face, but he smiled like maybe he didn't despise her after all.

About the Author

Marla Holt grew up wishing the heroines in the fairy tales she loved had more to choose from than marrying the prince or utter devastation, so now she writes modern day fairy tales with a feminist flare. She's living her own dream come true, writing and knitting in Topeka, Kansas with her husband and three boys.

Read more at tinydinostudios.com.

Printed in Great Britain
by Amazon